UPSTART
MYSTIQUE
DON BRADEN

Hadrosaur Productions, Mesilla Park, NM

Upstart Mystique
Hadrosaur Productions
First Edition, first printing, continuous printing on demand

First date of publication: March 2020

ISBN-10: 1-885093-90-X
ISBN-13: 978-1-885093-90-5

ACKNOWLEDGMENTS

I wish to thank Elizabeth Bruce who provided essential instruction through her editing; well-known mystery author David Corbett who gave critical writing direction and encouragement; Mendocino Coast Writers Conference that offered summer writing seminars to polish writing; TusCon Conventions that let writers cast pearls of wisdom overlooked in more formal classes; David Lee Summers and Hadrosaur Productions who are willing to take a chance on an unfledged author.

Upstart Mystique is dedicated to Elaine, my wife of fifty years, who encourages my story-telling and patiently waits for my return, when I have been kidnapped by developing plotlines.

UPSTART MYSTIQUE

MARCO P

Awash in cold sweat, Commander Malcolm Carpenter recalled nothing from the nightmare that forced him awake. His narrowed eyes stared at the blue numbers of the mission clock/calendar/travel duration displayed on the wall at the foot of his sleep pod: 08:49 - 10 23 2457 - 295.

"Two days?" he thought in disgust and drew in a long breath. A smell of electrical ozone filled his nose, and he tensed.

The commander pulled his head up, half sat, propped up on his left elbow, and glanced left at his command module screen that was programmed, while he rested or slept, to shuffle pleasant, successful past mission images. Only an eye-blink passed before he realized that his favorite pictures from the Zantil 3 colony weren't streaming on the painted thin-screen on the wall to his left. Instead, brief clips from his personal diary and ship logs that faded in and out menaced him with cycling images of near catastrophes of past missions.

He cringed at ballooning settler bodies threatening to burst in allergic reaction to the immediate presence of a deadly poisonous plant on Cebron 7. That grotesque obesity faded to Malrick's brittle landscape crumbling like quicksand under the steps of colonists on another mission, where quick work saved ten suffocating colonists trapped in powdery graves without adding the rescuers to the sudden and unexpected probable burial of those who took the first steps on the planet.

Carpenter instinctively ducked as several images of laser shots from unidentified alien ships were directed at him from the screen. Warning beams were normal occurrences when sensors hadn't read the presence of an alien ship or the *Marco P's* translator had sent a non-aggression message in an improper alien tongue.

Then Carpenter was terrorized by images of his ship caught in a Quil Vortex. He watched the frightened crew, terrified passengers, and the ship itself shimmer in a ghostly aura, threatening to vanish from three dimensional galactic space and deconstruct the *Marco* and passengers before the ship managed to punch its way out of the vortex's serpentine extensions.

The obesity of Cebron 7 returned.

The thin-screen refused to offer the serenity of Zantil 3 when ordered by Carpenter's conscious thought.

At his gruff, authoritative voice command, the screen blanked and assumed the ecru color of his ready room wall.

Carpenter blinked his eyes and shook his head. "I am awake," he said aloud to himself, making sure a life-conscious dream hadn't sneaked into his light-sleep respite between work weeks.

With a wrinkled brow and still breathing ozone, he pored over unanswered questions. Beset by the sudden and unexpected puzzles in a nominal colony mission, the commander argued with himself about foregoing short-sleep and returning to command duty. He lay back and stretched, tensing and relaxing leg and back muscles. The acrid ozone had dissipated; he smelled only his small ready room's stuffiness.

He knew that planning for what he couldn't predict was a fool's errand. His tired body, stressed by one hundred sixty-eight hours of continuous duty, had managed only forty-eight hours of rest. The threat of return to active and alert duty goaded his mind to reconsider physical necessity over the command decision to solve the mystery of his awakening.

His fatigued body overrode his waking mind and demanded recovery. Besides, he told himself, the smell was probably a residual of the dreaming he couldn't remember. From his weariness and without serious mental discussion, Carpenter consciously ordered the ship's computer to cycle his chosen Zantil 3 collage on the left wall thin-screen.

That collage, his backdrop to restful recovery, flashed pictures of laughing colonists he had ferried to a new world that resembled Earth more than any other planet he had helped colonize. Each pic from that album morphed smiling colonists into images of wooden cabins or shops that comprised the buildings of the original township and then reformatted those structures into individual portraits.

To the left a two-yard square thin-screen painted on the bulkhead, prepared to cycle images pulled from his pix-album.

Carpenter exhaled, settled onto his back in his sleep pod,

and glanced left. He saw only the top quarter of the flashing pix-screen. It had regenerated at his thought but not with his desired scenario. He saw tops of terrified shimmering ghosts.

Carpenter sat up and scowled as if the scenes were disobedient and rebellious brats. He thought that a neutrino had mutated a pathway or modified a line of code. Then he wondered if his subconscious was overriding his conscious thoughts, a paranormal ability he had learned to trust.

"I'll have Varlez look at your circuits and programming," he growled at the recalcitrant screen.

He climbed out of his pod. In nothing but skivvies covering his muscular six-foot frame, he padded barefoot into the empty command center on the leading floor of the twenty-tier skyscraper-shaped colony ship. Three empty command modules with duplicate keyboards, knobs, control paraphernalia, and intra-ship computer consoles were placed before a twenty by six foot screen offering a view of the ship's course. The lower third displayed graphics of the *Marco P's* course that threaded through star systems of the Milky Way Galaxy's Cygnus arm. Smaller ports lined the prow behind the screen.

"LeRoi," the commander barked to the navigation cubicle that was opposite his ready room. He quickened his steps when the navigator turned to face him and stopped five feet from the only other alert human on the ship. His question was husky from hours of sleep. "Is there anything out there I should know about?"

"Commander?" was the navigator's startled return. "Nothing different from when you asked me two hours ago." LeRoi scrunched his face under the permanently attached headgear tying him to the *Marco P's* computer. He studied the commander's questioning glare.

"I did? ... Two hours? ... The com?" Carpenter furrowed his brow. "I don't remember." Trying to recall earlier waking almost caused him to miss the navigator's next words.

"I thought it odd when you asked the first time, sir. Again? You want me to wake Strumpf or Crown and have them see you?"

"No, Navigator; that's all right." Carpenter was not about to give LeRoi the satisfaction of a successful practical joke.

"There's nothing outside to warrant close observation? It's still …Weeks? … and clear to γ-Cygnus A2?"

"Little more than five, and no problems projected, sir. Space is unencumbered. Our path slips past a couple of systems, none suggest problems. You asked me that before, too, Commander. You sure you're all right?"

The commander didn't detect a gotcha tone in the navigator's question. "I'm fine, Navigator."

Commander Malcolm Carpenter knew he wasn't *fine*. Ozone smell upon waking, the glitched thin-screen, duplicating questions to the navigator: more sleep wasn't going to happen. *Maybe this space has properties we haven't encountered before,* he thought as he watched the navigator study him.

The commander, a title the crew unofficially addressed him by, turned back to his ready room and realized he wasn't rested enough to have missed the familiar throb of deep vibration from the twin power assemblies that doubled the length of the *Marco P* FSS-14, a non-military vessel that was extending human presence further from Earth than any other colony ship managed.

He stepped into his ready room and scanned his sparse quarters while he considered the navigator's information and realized he had to wake and bounce his thoughts of the impossible situation off George Strumpf and Jerry Varlez whom he thought of as his alter egos and who helped keep intact his reputation of never making a mistake.

A modest platform serving as a desk stuck out from the wall under the clock at the foot of his sleep pod. A padded, high back chair was left of the desk. Above the blue timeline numbers hung a small multi-colored tapestry, a two-foot square mosaic of geometric forms. The translucent lid to his sleep pod, little more than a large cushioned coffin, closed off the view right and hid his cabin door to the bridge.

He shook his head at the needed rest he wasn't going to get and reviewed the prior week.

That consisted of traipsing through the twenty-tier *Marco P* checking equipment and colonists' dorms and reviewing settlement plans in final preparation for touchdown on an uninhabited terrestrial-type planet. Seven days of recapitulating the mission and repeated perfunctory paper work had tired his body and addled his brain. Except for the navigator and maybe Engineer Varlez whose paranormal intuition prevented even minor glitches, he had been the sole human awake. Imposed artificial loneliness always wearied his psyche.

He had checked the ship's condition before he dropped into light-sleep two days earlier. *Marco P* wasn't that close to its destination. Navigator LeRoi had confirmed a straight shot, or a slight arc to reaching it: nothing to warrant a commander's attention. "Ah," he snickered and thought *the flavor of famous last words*. "Still, can't be that bad," he mumbled.

Rejecting needed sleep, he flopped into his chair and wondered why he couldn't sleep without dreaming or remember waking two hours earlier. He knew that the navigator had suggested to some of the crew that he was slipping from his pristine command reputation. With that motivation, he'd be ecstatic to have played him for a fool. However, despite all LeRoi's growing idiosyncratic narcissism the navigator had never tried anything that insubordinate. Carpenter called up the mission computer screen painted on his shelf-desk.

"Status of power."

Operational. Engineer identifying minor glitch.

Carpenter knew Varlez always fiddled with the power. Dealing with malfunctions, minor or major—real or imagined—was how the engineer stayed connected to the mission and crew.

Nothing serious enough to wake me ... Or did he? The lack of throbbing engine rumble wasn't normal. Carpenter imagined its absence might have awakened him—twice. *Perhaps Varlez is on it.*

The commander wondered if his own subconscious radar was massing subliminal details and anticipating a problem. The pictured disasters that projected from his pix-album had all followed situations foreshadowed by unsettling premonitions. He overcame those dangers because he had listened to his feelings. Then, like now, there was no hint of peril, just the specter of ominous potential.

"Detail problems from beginning of mission," he commanded.

The mission computer listed nothing on his desktop, and Carpenter thought, *Why now?*

A request for potential problematic encounters en route to γ-Cygnus A2 also yielded nothing.

"Show all star charts between here and γ-Cygnus A2." Carpenter wasn't sure he'd find anything important.

"Collate, overlap systems in single image, and overlay our course to γ-Cygnus A2."

As the navigator had said, nothing impacted their course, though Carpenter noticed they were skirting a single planet star system.

The commander stood and looked out a starboard port, one of few real ports, where he saw moving stars.

Roger LeRoi, navigator for the *Marco P* had been delirious with ecstasy, lost in the conjured images of the surrounding Orion-Cygnus arm of the Milky Way that the first-contact Earth colony ship was dashing through. Stars, large and small, shone in brilliant white, soft yellow, azure blue, and pulsing red. To the right of the astral panorama, the dark shadowy North American Nebula, hardly looking like the continent it did from Earth's perspective, encroached on the pristine blackness of space and softened some colors, while through contrast, it enhanced others.

With the whole ship in long sleep, except for the commander with his odd questions and maybe engineering, the navigator submerged himself in the surrounding limitless black sprinkled with more points of light than any planet-bound human could imagine. LeRoi relished his importance when he was the only one awake. Only then could he bask unaccompanied in the immense universe. For immeasurable hours on this current exploratory and settlement mission, he had been beyond contentment.

The navigator's satisfaction didn't come from usurping authority. He knew that he was in charge of nothing except to watch where the ship was. He was a human adjunct connected to the *Marco's* computer. The commander, in short sleep and ready to be aroused at LeRoi's waking word, held the power. And LeRoi also knew, while others were in hibernation, the computer alone possessed the ultimate authority to order him to rouse the commander.

Still, LeRoi exulted in being the only one awake and aware of where he was. Naturally the computer knew—not with human intelligence—that conglomeration of printed circuitry and contained quanta was not human. It could not achieve an emotional high from the immensity of the galaxy that any human, even the most obtuse, might experience. The computer, known as MP, had been programmed to react with a handful of social characteristics, making it more acceptable for human interaction. Yet, perpetually tied to MP—even wirelessly in his sleep—now awake while all others were hibernating, LeRoi deluded himself that he was king of the realm, as his name, reminiscent of an ancient political caste, identified him.

His stuffy cubicle, built into the portside of the bridge opposite the commander's small ready room, lacked any actual view to space and was where LeRoi reveled in images only on the screens surrounding him. They projected computer simulations of the multiple external views of space, most in spectra the human eye couldn't detect: X-ray, infra-red, and ultra-violet. What the navigator took such delight in were galactic panoramas that he never really saw. Even though the false color images were transferred to his brain through the thousands of inputs within his computer interface cap, at his station he was dependent on screen representations for what was outside the ship.

Soon after the commander returned to his ready room, LeRoi's exultation of being immersed in galactic spectacles was snatched away by the inevitable call of duty from MP.

The navigator didn't disagree with the computer's conclusion drawn from its immense database burgeoning from readings of short and long-range acquisitions that peered into space outside the ship, readings that LeRoi hated to share, as if someone else might divine what he did not. Despite that Carpenter and maybe Varlez being conscious, he didn't want to end his singular personal relationship with MP.

He hated waking the crew, though it was a normal function of his navigation duty.

In the gelid void of space and racing toward the North

American Nebula and γ-Cygnus, the computer of the *Marco P FSS-14* urged—in its highest degree—that the crew be roused from three months of hibernation. Through constant long-range viewing, spectroscopy, computer interpolation from repeated exposures and eclipses of a sol-type star hardly a billion years older than Earth's sun, MP had acquired their destination. The system identified as γ-Cygnus A possessed an earthlike planet. The second of five bodies orbiting a star that was little more than half the size of Sol would be the next outpost of Earthlings who were aggressively extending their presence in the galaxy.

... Or the computer sensed a problem that required tiers of authority above navigator LeRoi.

By protocol, the first to receive wakeup for mission problems or touchdown was Commander Malcolm Carpenter. LeRoi reluctantly contacted the commander and yielded command. Carpenter had just risen from his high-backed chair as he completed his own research that revealed no answer to his questions about the sudden oddities of this "normal" voyage.

At the unexpected vocal alert from LeRoi, Carpenter lifted his head and scanned over the blue mission countdown and out a wide starboard porthole. *We can't be that near A2,* he thought. However, LeRoi's tone had been urgent.

He stood from his seat before the painted computer screen and stared out the port in his quarters. Stars were slipping past, faster than he remembered. *They're too fast. This part of the galaxy isn't so dense,* he mused in silence. He wondered if *Marco* had captured a more energetic dark matter tunnel.

He answered the navigator's call just before LeRoi was ready to repeat his alert.

"Awake. See you soon," was the commander's official response to a formal wake up. He stepped to his outer garb hanging at the head end of his pod.

The navigator knew the commander was awake; but following MP's orders and official protocol, he contacted Carpenter and again remembered his first mission as commander.

Then Carpenter looked half a century younger than his one hundred years. With perverse satisfaction, LeRoi remembered a couple of older and grizzled spacers on Carpenter's first mission. They mistook his youthful looks as announcing an inexperienced novice commander and had had the temerity to explain publicly to him and several of the crew in the galley why his orders were all wrong. After the commander quietly explained his authority and perfect reasons for his order, they abased themselves in repenting, to no avail. Commander Carpenter sequestered them to hydroponic farm work in the middle of the ship and without view of space until he could replace them at the next scheduled station. LeRoi grinned as he wondered again how they managed to find work or passage back to their home port.

LeRoi's space career, like George Strumpf's, was longer than the commander's. Carpenter had recruited both when he outfitted his first exploratory vessel fifty years earlier. Despite the commander's lauded reputation of not making mistakes and given the navigator's own tenure in space, LeRoi had vainly convinced himself that he should be the real expert for space travel on the *Marco P*. He frequently strutted as such when the commander was not around and when he had been twice substituted briefly at navigation on this mission. Those arrogances, increasing of late, were sometimes reported to Carpenter, who kept them in mind. Strangely, for all his age and experience, LeRoi never understood his own presumptions kept him from advancing to positions he coveted and believed he should possess.

Strumpf, both doctor and cook, who had first signed on for exploration with LeRoi nearly three-quarters of a century earlier, was the second most important to wake. He had to prepare for a hungry crew and make sure the hydroponics were working as they should—though he had received no warning to the contrary nor been wakened earlier. He needed, also, to prepare for the inevitable waking malaise that beset a few after hibernation. With this latter duty, though, he would soon have help.

Strumpf was more adept at space faring than LeRoi and could probably navigate without the computer interface, a trendy operation LeRoi had thought would give him an advantage on any ship. However, for all his experience and broad expertise, Strumpf was content with a supporting role. His job, except for medical supervision, lacked the serious responsibility and pressure that accompanied constant monitoring. Still, when he thought something was amiss, Strumpf had the commander's ear, a personal relationship LeRoi had never developed, and occasionally suggested things he thought the commander might not have considered. Those casual observations mentioned privately, almost in passing, allowed Carpenter the chance to amend orders and maintain his storied reputation. It was that very characteristic of Strumpf's intuitive awareness and propriety that had prompted Carpenter to select him for his first crew. Carpenter never regretted the choice and kept Strumpf on all of his missions afterward.

To LeRoi's wake-up, Strumpf merely returned a meaningless guttural "GNNNNN" that followed his habitual glance outside the ship upon waking. He refused any civility to LeRoi, even though a simple, one-word message would hardly exhibit a change in his dislike. However, the navigator's narcissistic attitude was a major obstacle to any friendship that ought to have developed between the two of them after decades of exploration with Carpenter.

After Strumpf, LeRoi prompted the hibernation units of Engineer Jerry Varlez and Nurse Amanda Crown. Fred Sharp, Kellan Forbes, and Manuel Gonzalez, the leads of the three settlement teams were next, in case the commander had instructions for them before the rest of their teams were wakened.

Priscilla Maelstrom, LeRoi's occasional replacement, he left in hibernation. LeRoi hated having a backup. He judged Maelstrom was much too young for navigation; she was only thirty-five and on her first mission. He had been navigating explorers for nearly twice her age and more times longer than her schooling. In spite of her touted academic achievement in navigation and planetary evolution, he hated the idea of being replaced, even for short spans, by anyone so new to space. Grudgingly and without verbal comment, though his body language protested otherwise, he had already yielded to the commander's twice ordering Maelstrom to take her turn at the consoles so LeRoi might rest.

Before navigator LeRoi received further crew acknowledgements beyond Strumpf's inarticulate grunt, the computer flashed "DANGER." Spiky red letters masked images of surrounding space and splashed on all fourteen screens—a word simultaneously downloaded to the navigator's computer-linked brain. Terrorized beyond any past catastrophe, LeRoi saw and felt the words melt and cascade into a brilliant bubbling red pooling at the bottom of the screens surrounding him.

The pools vanished.

Roger LeRoi watched the forward images evolve into a shadowy, starless gray that seeped from the center outward to the edges of each screen. The target stars that *Marco P* had been racing toward and from and taking readings from in both directions vanished as if the explorers were suddenly engulfed by an unknown and previously undetected thick nebula.

The navigator didn't look at the rear projections at the outer edges of his screen bank, for the computer transfer to his brain had already communicated that the ship was surrounded by impenetrable gray.

Navigator LeRoi requested the computer's reaction to the *Marco P* FSS 14's sudden and total shrouding. The computer's response to the navigator about its blindness was instant and absolute. Navigator LeRoi agreed and the computer initiated a power reversal that would bring the ship to a dead stop.

Heartbeats after answering LeRoi's alert and stepping toward his uniform, Carpenter was hurled into the forward wall of his ready room.

"What …?" The question was suppressed by pain as his nose and forehead smashed into the bulkhead before he could fully turn his body to take the shock with a flexed upper arm and shoulder. Carpenter bounced back, rubbed his brow, and sniffed while twitching his nose which he gingerly touched between his left thumb and index finger. That it wasn't bleeding salved some of the hurt. He looked back to his uniform and hurried to pull on khaki trousers and a green tunic. Cinching his pants and straightening his insignia-less tunic, he stepped into flightshoes, that molded to his feet. As he returned to the bridge, he wondered if LeRoi had outlived his usefulness or if the computer had malfunctioned.

George Strumpf, whose sleep pod was positioned abeam, was thrown forward against the tube he had just crawled from. "What's the navigator done this time," he wondered.

MARCO P

Rubbing his forehead and twitching his nose, Commander Carpenter tromped his muscular frame across command and into the navigator's cramped domain. He stared at LeRoi silhouetted against his many screens all of which showed solid gray, not the star-dotted images he saw earlier, nor the stellar images he saw out the port in his ready room.

"Malfunction?" the commander growled as he stepped up behind LeRoi and peered over his shoulders at the grayed out screens immediately in front of the navigator.

"Don't think so," LeRoi responded without taking his eyes from the gray that showed in every screen view of space outside the ship. "I had stars and our general destination direction at the center. Then from that point everything just grayed outward."

"Not from my ready room," Carpenter objected. "Didn't you look out a port?"

"No. I'd have to leave here. MP and screens are accurate. The computer isn't harassed by emotion. MP stopped us because we were blind; I concurred."

"You and the computer, maybe." Carpenter was more than irked. LeRoi had by-passed his command and authorized reversing power to bring the ship to a stop. He could handle Roger's not so subtle but arrogant aspirations that many of the crew were finding increasingly ill-tempered and inappropriate. Carpenter had thought about sending LeRoi to hibernation and waking Maelstrom who offered no pretense. He rejected the idea. LeRoi was a good navigator, in spite of his presumptions—maybe because of them.

Commander Carpenter headed out of the navigator's cubicle to recheck what he had seen from his ready room but stopped, when he heard a graveled complaint over the com and looked up at the front port screen. It was gray, not the star-studded black he had witnessed from his ready room port and before his face was smashed against the bulkhead. The sequence of ports also showed only gray.

12

"Navigator! What'd you do?" Strumpf demanded. He spoke to the position, not to the person.

"We're blind. I shut us down—and fast."

"You got that right. But I'm not blind. What's the matter with you?"

"MP doesn't see anything but gray. Without sight ..."

"I've got stars ...," Strumpf interrupted his growl and didn't finish his rebuttal. Then he acknowledged without an apologetic tone. "My port's gone gray. There's nothing *to* see."

Hearing a corroborating opinion from a confidante, Carpenter set his steps for the backup navigator, Priscilla Maelstrom, who had an interface with MP, but was able to disconnect from it when she was not navigating. Not far from the cramped quarters LeRoi claimed as his private domain, her cabin door slid open at his official combination on the outer pad and closed as he entered the second navigator's quarters. A smaller duplicate of the commander's, her cabin contained no electronics except a com and opposite her pod, a port. It did possess a small bookshelf above the desk that supported half a dozen books with titles too small to be read from the commander's distance. To insulate his back-up navigator from the space oddities he'd never before experienced, Carpenter walked to her intercom/screen and disabled it. Then he stepped to Maelstrom's closed sleep pod and fingered a wakeup code on the emergency access.

The lid hissed up and, before Maelstrom's eyes blinked open, Carpenter was surprised to realize that his second navigator slept in the nude. The commander noted that her uniform did nothing but enhance her natural proportions: wide hips, narrow waist, large breasts.

Startled awake, Maelstrom twisted her lips into a coy smile and licked them before starting to offer a word at the unusual rousing.

Carpenter shook his head and held his right index finger to his lips. Then gesturing her to wait, he reached both palms toward the ship's consensus pin-up beauty. He held his gaze at her blue eyes. With index and middle finger of his right hand held slightly apart he pointed to his eyes and then out the gray port on the other side of Maelstrom's sleeping pod.

She nodded, as much as her supine position allowed, rolled left toward the commander, and sat up. Carpenter could not but admire the hourglass figure seated before him. However, he looked around and saw a green dressing robe which he picked up and reached out to his second navigator. Unconcerned at her commander's propriety, Maelstrom shook her head rejecting the proffered robe and stood to look out the port.

She turned back with a quizzical look and raised her hands, palms almost upward and shrugged.

The commander draped the robe across his left arm and reached into a pocket. He pulled out a pad and a pen. With his right hand, he gave them to the naked navigator and with his right index finger motioned like he was drawing or writing on his left palm. Maelstrom took pen and paper and turned back to the port out of which Carpenter saw only grey. The commander saw her marking across the pad.

When Maelstrom returned the pad and pen, the commander mouthed "Now" and again held the robe out to her. This time she took it. While he looked at her drawing, she slipped her arms into the sleeves and drew the short bodice around her. The hem hit mid-thigh of the five-foot four-inch crew member.

Carpenter studied Maelstrom's scrawled drawing and looked out the port, still gray ... to him. She had drawn lots of large and small x's indicating sizes of stars and even shaded in what was an outer part of the North American Nebula. He raised his eyes to Priscilla who was again pursing her lips for a question and shook his head.

Maelstrom's wider eyes, lips, and arms described a more precise question.

He pointed to her and then repeatedly pointed down.

She nodded. Then she motioned like she was writing or drawing and wagged her thumb and index finger to the commander and herself.

He nodded and smiled and thought that if everyone else saw gray, she might be the only one not under some spell.

Then he stepped to her door and knocked three times, twice quickly and then once. He twisted his wrist to indicate keeping her compartment locked. Though he knew no one should be in the corridor, he listened for footsteps. He stepped out of Maelstrom's small cabin and turned to look back at her.

She nodded, but her brow was creased. She wondered what was going on and how long she might be sequestered. She held her palms together and then pulled them apart the width of her body, moved them closer, and then out to her full span.

Her robe broke open.

The commander's eyes sparkled at the unexpected review of cleavage. He knew it was an accidental flashing, not an enticement. He shrugged his shoulders and twitched his head. Then he slid the door closed. A moment later, he heard Maelstrom lock it.

The settlement leads, Fred Sharp and Kellan Forbes, grumbled an acknowledgement at LeRoi's wake up call and took their time exiting their pods, after they felt the ship jerk. The third lead, Manuel Gonzalez, merely looked out a port. However, when they looked around at the rows of unopened containments of the rest of the settlement contingent, they knew something wasn't right.

Sharp was the senior of the trio, though none might judge any age from looking at him. His barrel-chest tapered to a slender waist and was sided by arms that rivaled gnarled tree limbs. His hands were huge and could tighten into stony fists that carried the impact of sledgehammers. Both Forbes and Gonzalez looked to him, or rather the status of his shaved head, for direction or just approval, even when they were sure about a decision leading to developing their settlement. Always in control, Sharp was seldom excited. When something seemed amiss to him, his jaw tightened and his light blue eyes darkened. His whole carriage tensed for action as his gaze swept about him.

Sharp's concerned dark blue eyes searching is what Forbes and Gonzalez saw when they glanced around from their pods and realized that no one else of the settlement party was awake and Sharp was already out of his sleeper.

Forbes was up next. He neglected to add more covering to his hibernation skivvies. One look at Sharp, though, and he was alert and assessing every input his senses perceived.

Forbes, three inches shorter than Sharp's six-foot two-inch frame, was easily fifty pounds lighter. His close-cropped brown hair topped a long face with a lazy inattentive look from brown eyes. Nothing about Forbes appeared to command the respect a settlement lead demanded. He looked like someone's lackey.

Sharp often proclaimed that he would take Forbes as a partner in any fight, if he had the chance to choose. None who had recently met both could see the advantage; most just accepted Sharp's words. Forbes appeared skinny and gangly, hardly able to fight his way out of a small band of young children. When Sharp was pressed about Forbes's apparent size and lack of physical ability, as he was by those who didn't know the smaller man, he always chuckled, shook his head, and exhaled disgustedly, refusing to answer. If the skeptic pressed on, Sharp said, "Don't get conned to side against him."

When Gonzalez saw Forbes next to Sharp, he hurried out of his pod, also in nothing but skivvies. Together the three of them were a formidable group—even in underwear. It was clear to Gonzalez that something strange was happening.

An inch shorter than Sharp, Gonzalez's full head of thick black hair and intense burrowing brown eyes gave the impression he was taller. On his heavy-boned frame, he carried forty-five pounds more that Forbes did. Still he didn't have the mass Sharp bore nor did he garner authority by mere presence as Sharp easily commanded. Gonzalez spent considerable time out of hibernation in body-building, and not for show. His musculature was rock hard. Though he lacked the blinding speed that was Forbes's chief asset, he had nearly the brawn Sharp possessed.

The triad formed itself and two looked questioningly at Sharp. None of them seemed to recognize that they were standing stock still. Rubbery legs that afflicted everyone just out of hibernation and adjusted to acceleration or minor vector shifts that defined tunnels through dark matter, were not jiggling them.

We're not moving, Sharp thought and wrinkled his face as he looked over forty-two sealed sleep pods

Forbes was as unsure of what was happening as Sharp looked. He wondered why they had not been wakened earlier if they were at γ-Cygnus A2.

We're not moving, Gonzalez thought, after he looked out a port and saw no star movement.

"This isn't right," Sharp analyzed.

"How long do you think we've been down?" Forbes asked. "Maybe LeRoi found a Q-tunnel that shortened the time."

"Yeah," Gonzalez said and intending to draw their attention to what he had seen, added, "look," pointing to the port where he had seen stars. "Wait! It turned gray. It wasn't gray a moment ago."

"Tunnels aren't gray," Sharp critiqued having already assumed a Q-tunnel. "I saw stars, too. Now I don't."

"That's not nebula gray," Forbes analyzed. He wondered if they had somehow been snagged by an outer tributary of the North American Nebula. "I don't know anything that is smooth gray like that."

Just then all three felt the ship lurch under them. The movement was so unexpected that all three nearly fell to the deck. They grabbed onto each other for support and helped to steady each other as they took choppy steps and widened their stance to maintain their own balance.

"No, this isn't right," Sharp repeated stressing each word. "I think we should see the commander. It makes sense that only we three are awake. LeRoi'd wake us before the settlers, if anything important was happening."

Forbes pulled on a loose brown tunic to cover his slender torso and all three rejecting shoes stepped into dark blue denims. Bare-chested Sharp and Gonzalez led the way through long hallways to the bridge and Commander Carpenter.

Engineer Jerry Varlez, still in his gray jumpsuit, had not been sleeping when he was prodded by LeRoi's alert. For the last month, he had been wakened repeatedly by the engineering computer to adjust the energy mix, check its reaction to dark matter, and analyze the ship's reaction to the light and dark interstellar realms they were hurtling through. His hibernation pod was next to his work, but none of his previous month's use of it might be considered even short sleep.

That the navigator and not the computer had sent a wakeup

indicated that any semblance of hibernation would not be an
option for a long time. Once the *Marco P* finally settled into orbit
above γ-Cygnus A2, he and two female assistants, each contor-
tionists untouched by claustrophobia and half of his one hundred twenty years, would perform the necessary maintenance
the engines needed after months of Qion speed. Their recalibra-
tion would return the smooth performance registered after the
initial tuning following the first light year shakedown.

Varlez didn't crawl out of his pod at the navigator's wake
up, nor did he respond to that alert. He lay still, arguing with
himself about rest and sleep and hibernation; and he listened
for the noises that had wakened him earlier. The engines didn't
sound right. The deep-throated rumble had returned, but the
pitch was just a little flat. The engines sounded maximum, as
they needed to be to reach γ-Cygnus A2 on schedule, but not
quite in the familiar tone he recognized. His memory raced
through decades of memorable and discountable engine noises. Nothing matched what he was hearing. Finally, with tired
effort he swung his legs over the edge of his pod and dropped
to the deck. At that very moment, the *Marco P* jerked. Varlez
grabbed the side of his pod to steady himself and keep from being thrown to the deck. His eyes were wide with concern and
his heart doubled its pulse. He thought he heard grinding, low
short growls from far aft, that indicated the support structure
was being tweaked by parallel engines out of sync.

Instead of heading for the bridge or messaging Commander Carpenter, he woke his two engineering support seconds
and the three brainstormed a solution to the imbalance created
from a dead stop order from MP.

Three inches shorter than Priscilla Maelstrom, Varlez was
the shortest on board the *Marco P*. Engineers weren't required
to be any particular size, but for this ship, smaller was better
and height had been one of the criteria he used to choose his
two assistants. Someone like Sharp or even Forbes might have
the expertise to maintain an exploratory vessel, but would be
unable to squeeze into small spaces or crawl around, over,
and through pipes, ducts, and closed areas forbidden to aver-
age-sized humans.

That Varlez's aides were both female and only a couple of

inches taller than he had prompted their inaccurate sobriquet of "harem." All three were privy to the not-so-private gossip about engineering that passed through the crew, and they enjoyed that it could be so wrong.

Of all the crew of the *Marco P* except for the commander, the engineers knew that personal relationships eroded a tight working atmosphere necessary to maintain the power plant. Varlez and his females worked well together, but during off hours they were seldom in the company of the other two.

Jerry Varlez was a compact muscular elf of a man who worked magic with the engines and the computer systems of the *Marco P*. On this sterile clean ship, his hands were always greasy dirty; his round face, perpetually smeared with something that contrasted with his light brown skin. His brown eyes flashed excitement and eagerness when he got the chance to talk about the ship's power plant.

Occasionally at the beginning of a voyage, Varlez would pick out a particularly obnoxious mate or settler and challenge him to arm wrestling. His target was always someone who made the mistake of demeaning others.

Varlez's target always scoffed at the challenge and the difference in size. However, the engineer made a nuisance of himself. He prodded, accused, and finally, when nothing else caught his mark's attention, threatened him with some clandestine attack or, rarely, offered a personal insult.

Finally, to shut up the little guy, the bully accepted the challenge, expecting to make short work of Varlez who had become an irksome gadfly.

Those long-standing crew who knew the script gathered quietly when action was imminent. They were eager to watch and enjoy. They clued others who had no idea of what was about to happen. Their crowding around was not overt. But soon most of the crew and settlers filled the galley where Engineer Varlez always staged his drama to teach a necessary lesson to an arrogant bastard.

Then in the midst of nearly the entire ship that had closed ranks and encircled the two clasping hands, "little" Jerry Varlez soundly pinned the braggart and then, with the back of the loser's hand still pressed to the table, reminded him of something he ought to have known: size and words are unimportant; accomplishments need no window-dressing.

Of course, after Varlez's poignant victory and when ruffled feathers had been smoothed, he and the ego-stripped bully became fast friends and Varlez's reputation and his lesson of duty and not advertising personal traits extended itself. Most of the fleet were aware of Varlez and his pointed examples. On this voyage, his exploits were common talk. No one dared boast about his equipment or ability. *Marco P* FSS-14 carried Engineer Jerry Varlez who seemed better than anyone in spite of his size.

There were those who wondered what might transpire between Varlez and Sharp, and they ached to see that competition. They also knew that such an improbable contest would never take place. Neither were braggarts and neither compared themselves to others.

Nurse Amanda Crown's hibernation pod was in her duty station, the infirmary. Amanda was a handful of years younger than Strumpf and had seen more stellar systems than she cared to recall. However, she was as much a space doctor as one might be licensed after laboring through a slough of required academic courses and a long internship. Her learning had been hands-on. In her early years, she was a stunning six-foot tall brown-eyed blonde and, if she were even now as young, she would be stiff beauty competition for the diminutive backup navigator.

However, the years and space had taken their toll and provided a deeper wisdom that not all acquire, not least of which was the foolish aspiration to be excessively attractive. For decades, Crown had physically followed Strumpf and worked to take the same missions he did in hopes he might notice her, as a romantic conquest. He had seemed not to and she became satisfied to work close to him.

With his gentle prodding, Amanda had become a fine diagnostician, an intuitive medical practitioner, a skilled surgeon, a fair psychiatrist, and the best asset any ship's infirmary might contain.

Crown didn't hear the noise that Varlez homed in on. She did see stars out the port window in the infirmary and was not amazed at the sight, nor did she look long enough to notice if they were stationary, as Gonzalez had seen. She expected stars dotting black space. The lurch that the settler leads reacted to caused her no concern. She had traveled missions long enough to know that in the near absolute vacuum of space and propelled through dark tunneling, unexpected things impacted the ship and its course. She had swayed with the jerking, her legs and knees reacting unconsciously to keep her upright.

The lurch did affect Robert Nozing who split his time for Strumpf between the galley and the infirmary. Maybe Nozing hadn't secured the latch on his sleep box that was placed not too far from Crown's pod. Maybe he was just in the right spot; but, when the *Marco P* reversed from a stop, his pod clicked open and ended his hibernation.

He turned over onto his stomach and groggily lifted his head to see out. Crown, wearing a long lab coat, stood not fifteen feet from him.

"You woke me?" he rasped from a dry throat. "We there?"

Involved in her preparations for those waking up nauseated, Crown paused and asked, "Huh?" surprised at Nozing's questions or that anyone else in the infirmary should be awake.

Then she answered, "No ... I don't know. What are you doing awake?"

"No clue. Don't recall an alarm from navigator. You didn't open me?" Then glancing out the port and seeing gray, Nozing asked, pointing to space, "Where are we? What's that?"

"What's what?" Crown asked without looking from ordering her instruments but turned to see where Strumpf's aide was pointing. "Huh?" was her surprised reaction. "I just saw stars." Crown ran through her extensive space recall and wrinkled her brow. "I've never seen gray ... anywhere before."

MOLX

An hour before solar-rise Krolni sought forbidden respite from his cramped residence on floor 373 and mind-numbing duty on floor 173.

He slid open the door of his one room flat and glanced both ways down the dim windowless corridor. Most of the worn brown adobe tiles were stained and cracked. The once yellow walls were spotted and streaked with soiled handprints, long scrapes from the corners of misguided transportation carts, and dried blobs of spit and hacked up throat goo. Krolni wrinkled his nose as he sniffed the stale stuffy air, even more oppressive than that of his own room. Statue-still, he held his breath and listened for softened steps of another resident on a similar unauthorized stroll or the strident whirr of an occasional patrolling robot that would abort his plan to seek moments free of mega-city restraint.

He heard nothing.

He eased one foot through the doorway and brought the other into the corridor. His left fingertips kept the spring-controlled door from slamming shut behind him. He rolled his foot-flops from heel to edge to toe and hushed his steps on the worn adobe tile for twenty meters to his right where his escape portal opened to the left. He loosened the latch on the door to outside with a firm hip thrust on the pressure bar. His hip held the door ajar against a wind. Air whistled through the narrow opening. Krolni shuddered in the cold that struck him and flowed through his light clothes. A forced exhale balanced his body temperature with the pre-dawn outside.

The prevailing westerly wind was gusting. He pushed the door open enough to keep the high-pitched wind-whine from squealing through the dingy yellowed corridor lighted by occasionally working low power-glow fixtures installed four meters apart. When all lights were lit, the hall was mid-day bright. Now hardly a fourth of them shone and Krolni couldn't remember the last time the corridor was brilliant. Nor did he imagine when it might be again. Repair and maintenance crews were scarce. When they did appear, their duties were tackled with little dispatch and no expertise.

Gearing up for the huge burst of cold, he shoved the door open enough to slip through. Then to keep from being exiled outside, Krolni held the door open with his right hand and reached into his pocket with the left to pull out an unauthorized latch-stop that was the only way to re-open a closed door from outside. He held the L-angled tool in place, covering the lock mechanism and hooking into the interior side, as another gust of wind slammed the door shut ending the rush of outside into the corridor of the self-contained mega-city, Molox1.

Against the cold, Krolni wrapped his arms around his chest and breathed deeply. Enduring the chill was an accepted inconvenience for the short pleasure of personal freedom from the confining quarters inside.

He stood alone in a small enclosure. A three-meter mesh extension of the inner corridor provided a landing between flights of one and a half meter wide mesh stairs that clung to the outside west wall of the 500-tier complex. The graphete stairway originally provided work crews unaffected by acrophobia necessary and hazardous access to every floor. Nevertheless, while the mega-structure had been under construction, death screams from at least one worker a month announced a fatal misstep or unexpected cyclonic gust of wind.

When internal elevators and stairs became available to the workers, outside handles were removed from all doors to keep anyone from dangerous trafficking between levels. Every time Krolni escaped the interior of Molox1, as he was now doing, he chuckled at Council's ineffective safety methods. This morning, however, he wondered if Council just stopped announcing those who had plunged to their deaths. He knew he wasn't the only one who had a latch-stop or who tread the outside stairs. And he was well aware of the lore about two kinds of citizens who continued to use the outside constructions.

The adventurous, rejecting imposed safety, merely employed trusted confederates to open doors on different floors as they challenged danger and defied death while scaling or descending the perilous outside steps.

Unpopular children were sometimes locked outside and

tortured with the indescribable terror of isolation while being buffeted by wind that made falling to death imminent. Eventually the bullies tired of their threatening—or a knowledgeable adult chased them away—and rescued the frantic children. Yet, in Krolni's recent memory, gossip and quiet bragging about either of these exploits had diminished to zero.

He knew that the stairs and landings weren't inherently dangerous, if one exercised care. However, terror from fighting the wind compounded intense fear of heights. The mere thought of traveling a passageway drilled into the front of the mountain-tall solar-washed tan building anchored into the Central Continental Ridge gave ordinary citizens weak knees. For most who lived in Molox1 the thought of outside travel up or down was relegated to suppressed memory.

Krolni stood in an uncovered box, as all landings were. On tiptoe, he grabbed with both hands the upper edge of the solid 1.8-meter outer wall which began at his eye level and looked to the west. The stars had not all vanished, although the western sky was coloring lavender pink.

Without looking down he turned and bounded up six steps, sat on a second higher one, and leaned back against the sky-scraper to stare at the lightening western horizon. He refused to think about three-quarters of a kilometer of space gaping below him. The wind pressed him against the outside wall of Molox1 and forced him to wipe his watering eyes. He rewrapped his arms tightly around his chest, enjoyed the outdoor freedom, and counted fourteen dimming stars in the brightening dawn.

Randomly scattered lights barely visible to the north outlined another mega-city, Molox3. Its pointed top, just now receiving solar rays, always intrigued him. Despite rules forbidding citizens from leaving the confines of any mega including Krolni's foray on the outer stairs, he intended to visit the neighboring structure—sometime. He had no idea how long the journey might take or what he'd need to cover the distance, provided he could escape his own city and sneak into that one.

He was still considering a trip to the neighboring mega-city when burps of light captured his attention. At the edge of the forest that rose between his and the neighboring complex to the north and 373 floors below him, he saw light flashes just off the edge of a large square white area he knew to be a dead spot where nothing grew. According to common knowledge, the broad two-river valley between the Central Continental Ridge and the more western range that looked like it had been formed from solidified lava bubbles, contained all the vegetation found on the entire continent. The valley itself was rumored to be only fifty kilometers long and much less wide.

He watched the dancing flames shimmer and disappear and erupt again, brighter than before. He narrowed his eyes, as if squinting sharpened the image. His patient viewing watched the flickering light grow as it was haphazardly eclipsed by speckled shapes bounding around it.

After the great warming, precipitated by the Molrixx's refusal to admit its participation in a galloping global catastrophe, the planet reacted with a drought that entered its second century. Sprawling urban areas were increasingly abandoned and populations were crammed into gargantuan self-contained complexes anchored within cutouts from mountain ranges where water remained available.

The super-wealthy positioned themselves in less tall and larger-roomed complexes dug into the western range that was still dim in Krolni's view of the horizon. Most of the remaining population was transported to the western side of the Cen-Con Ridge where life in the penal-style complexes was squalid and hopeless. Beehive quarters, engineered food, menial serf labor, generic clothing, minimal education, and ancient video productions for entertainment devolved society to abject abasement except for the mega-wealthy, who continued their affluent lives, unconcerned and oblivious to the suppression everyone else endured.

Every complex's more privileged citizens, termed Council, of lower caste than the inhabitants of the bubbly western range, conducted twice a month ineffectual meetings to discuss potential reversal of the worsened climate, dismiss complaints about stultified city living, maintain minus-growth population through eugenics and a rigged lottery for pregnancies. The meetings also reviewed résumés of potential additions to their caste when their own few offspring failed to achieve obligatory learning and power. Mostly they concocted futile schemes to bolster the waning hopes of the residents that the complexes would be abandoned when Planet Molx provided the Molrixx a second chance to inhabit its surface.

SYSTEM

"URGENT! Molox1 Council! HELP!"

The message repeated twice before the transmission died. Two of the last few physical members of Council at Molox1 grinned at each other. Rilsik, Council Lead, offered a thin smirk and tilted his head left.

Maldron, who oversaw and programmed the computer system of Molox1, nodded a tacit praise of Rilsik's devious strategy. "Your plan's working," he said.

Before the programmer could continue his accolade, the frantic call for assistance resurrected three more times but in halting and clipped words. The air space remained alive with background static.

"Maybe we should answer them." Rilsik gave Maldron an unexpected suggestion. "Offer what assistance our diminishing resources allow."

Missing the irony, Maldron knitted his brow and hissed, "You know we've got full power."

"Of course, Maldron; they don't have to know. The western complex, with their wealth and power and arrogance, always assume superiority. They think everyone should rush to their aid." Finished with his brief assessment of those wealthier than he, Rilsik paused and then instructed his programmer, "Open a channel but make sure you erode it with static. Cut it in and out."

Maldron opened his eyes wider and looked a question at Rilsik. Before he bolstered the look with words, he caught Rilsik's devious humor and his grin deepened across his face. "I can vary the strength, too. They'll never know we're not suffering the same power decline." He chuckled as he flipped three switches on the console in front of him and grasped a round knob that adjusted volume. He held one finger of the other hand poised over a button that interrupted transmission. He nodded to Rilsik that he was ready for the return transmission.

"Molox1 to western complex. Rilsik here. What is your need? Ho- -an -e hel-?"

27

Maldron made sure the beginning words were clear. But he anticipated Rilsik's second question and turned the dial wavering the strength to match the western complex's power problems.

The return from the western complex began strongly and then diminished to such a weak level that Rilsik and Maldron could barely hear, though both were holding their breaths. They didn't mistake the terror in the fading words. "Power to the longevity units has declined for several weeks. Today it ... tically. Our engineer ... not regenerate it ... sist?"

"If we can," Rilsik answered. Maldron pressed a button and turned the knob back and forth, never reaching the original volume and wavering the static. "I'm sure you can recognize our power problems," Rilsik lied and offered slight condolence, "all complexes are having similar difficulties."

"Yes, ... our understanding and experi ..." The western complex transmission vanished. Following a long silence it continued with less volume. "... things ... critical. ... must have help!" The last words were almost inaudible; the urgency of the request, unquestionable.

"... understand," Rilsik said and paused to simulate western power difficulties. "If we can correct our ..." Maldron dropped power and Rilsik stopped speaking. He continued when Maldron nodded and boosted the power. "We should be able to ... can send a robot or two with an engi ..." Maldron eliminated Rilsik's last words.

"Understood. I can barely hear. You ... may be in worse shape than we are. ... please ... hurry." The final statement from the west took four paused continuations.

Rilsik chuckled at his dissimilation that Molox1 was in dire circumstances. He thought it might play in with the belief of those, who thought that they were more important than anyone else, that Molox1 was worse off than they were. Even at the end of their lives, he knew they would believe in their privilege. Rilsik's final response was lost in static as Maldron held in the squelch button for most of it and turned down the power throughout the rest.

"You're not *really* sending help, are you?" he asked.

"And let them have any idea that we are without difficulty?

Not on your immortality."

Before he offered his next thoughts, Maldron looked hard at Rilsik. He thought he knew the complete plan for all Moloxes to survive. Now he was seeing a more devious layer, one he hadn't thought of, one he wasn't completely sure about. "I wondered why all other complexes are losing power, while we aren't," he said. "Is this expected?"

"Ooh, Maldron, not you! Where did the immortality plans arise?" Rilsik looked tired, almost disgusted that he had to broach the subject with his computer expert. "Where did the original plans come from?" His repeated question was not rhetorical.

"From here." Maldron added to the obvious answer, "Molox1." The revelation struck and he turned red. Then he sighed and stated rather than ask confirmation of his sudden realization, "Those were your plans ... your program."

Rilsik smirked and nodded slightly. "And those were the directions they all got—missing only one or two steps, steps that would maintain and re-create power to keep the units functioning until the planet regenerates and we're ready to re-take possession."

"Sorry," Maldron apologized. "I wasn't thinking that far ahead. Council Lead was your position, rightly so."

"Good you finally realize that," Rilsik said and looked away as if he were observing the future. "The new Molrixx will be descended from our Council and Molox1."

"Oh," was Maldron's startled exclamation.

"What?" Rilsik asked.

"Krolni is outside again. Should I send a robot?"

"No. I used to think he'd fall and we'd not have to worry about him. We really don't want him and that other monitor— Do you know they've been communicating, Maldron?—as progenitors for the new Molrixx. If they don't eliminate themselves—and I doubt they will—we may have to."

"Or just leave them alone ... completely. When the molox shuts down ..." Maldron's conclusion didn't need stating.

MOLX

Unaware of his body's chilling, Krolni was entranced by the strange glimmering at the edge of the forest and next to the white dead spot, until he noticed the vegetation between the two rivers was greening rapidly from rising solar shine.

"Uh-oh, you've been too long." He blamed himself for not paying attention to the length of his occasional violation of unwritten rules. He also realized how chilled he'd become. Having stayed outside too long, he worried that he might be seen entering the corridor from outside. He didn't worry that someone might report him, but tongues would wag and he didn't want the attention.

With scarcely a notice of his height above the base of the mega-city, he took steps two at a time to the landing. He jerked on his latch-stop opening the door enough to keep the wind from whistling through and quickly peeked up and down the corridor as he stepped through the door while he shoved the contraband tool into a pocket. Krolni winced when the outer door, blown shut by the wind, thumped loudly. He felt better, when he heard only his own steps in the silent corridor.

A few snores rumbled through thin doors and walls. Coughing and hacking erupted from some early risers. The stuffy corridor had still not been refreshed—an increasingly common circumstance. After withstanding the cold fresh air outside he was more aware of the pervading smelly body odor that two brief gusts through the open door couldn't dissipate.

One of the ubiquitous chronometers told him that he was not as late as he feared. Krolni failed to realize that dawn came earlier as the solstice approached but the complex's inhabitants didn't rise any sooner. Self-contained mega-cities had no use for the ancient charlatan's light-saving ruse, for even the wealthy no longer had outside activities. There was no need to rush to his windowless station where he monitored the status of 500 elderly patients deemed important for the Molrixx's eventual re-conquest of their once pristine globe.

In his miniscule personal space, just a four-meter square

room with part of a wall pushed out to contain an alcove for a bathroom, Krolni combed his wind-whipped brown hair and splashed tepid water on his pasty face to warm his chilled skin and remove the white icy look. He glanced across the room to his small unmade sleeper sofa. A three-legged triangular table was against the mountainside wall. It supported his personal computer connection to the complex's library of videos and di-gi-books

Almost the entire population of Molox1 was crammed into similar areas. Amenities like hot water and a residence with more than one room were the province of Council. Such perks were never authorized for ordinary citizens.

Two flaxen palm-sized breakfast pellets, artificial oat bran fortified by ersatz vitamins and enhanced with a chemical strawberry flavor, had dropped into his food container. If air conditioning was inconsistent, he was glad food delivery was not spotty, regardless of the unappetizing appearance of two periodic meals. He consumed one pellet in three large crumbly bites partly softened by gulps of a pale blue watery swill that hardly passed for milk but according to Council had all of that liquid's nutrients.

Wrinkling his nose in distaste, he repeated a twice-daily assessment, "These *are* getting worse." He set aside the second pellet in a growing supply of dry artificial foodstuff. He chose a selection of music to while away his monitoring and wrapped the flat ear bud wires around his left hand which carried a memory plug loaded with his selections. Council maintained that losing oneself in music didn't hamper watching the read-outs from the medical section of the mega-complex, Molox1.

Council didn't want monitors studying what flowed in front of them. Their job was to make sure the information splashed continuously on the screens. Krolni had been given specific directions when the readouts ceased or hung. Howev-er, after months of tedious half-watching and occasional doz-ing, he had never encountered any break in the streaming.

While Krolni waited for the express elevator, he mused over the strange flickering light that had held his attention on the outside acrophobic stairs and extended his stay cooling him more than he realized. The strange light, maybe fire, promised more excitement than the unusual top of Molox3.

He was planning another visit to the landing when his body spasmed in a shiver and convulsed with a sneeze, both delayed reactions to his outside adventure.

At that moment, the elevator doors noiselessly separated to reveal an empty gray lift cage spattered with a rainbow of graffiti. He stepped in and spoke his destination. The doors slid closed behind him.

He paid little attention to a new message, "Cownsl Kils," scrawled in loud red paint across the back of the elevator car and eclipsing parts of several earlier and similar protests.

Unconsciously Krolni turned to face the front of the car as the elevator dropped one hundred fifty floors reaching half the speed of free fall before slowing to a smooth, almost imperceptible, stop during the last 50 floors. The descent wasn't long enough for him to consider when he'd chance another morning outside excursion or that, when he did, it would certainly be warmer.

The double doors slid apart and Krolni mindlessly ambled to his cramped work cave hardly taller than his 1.8 meter height and so small it didn't provide room for a second desk or chair. His desk was fake soft wood gouged and marred from decades of nervous and idle fingernails. Little more than a rickety table, it had two small empty drawers on the right side under a top which supported half a dozen small monitor screens that constantly scrolled patient medical readouts.

He was sure that his attention was meaningless and that any properly programmed computer could monitor his charges better than he could. He thought that the network ought to identify a problem and generate a warning long before he or anyone, alert or not, might react to medical emergencies.

What Krolni didn't know was that Council had determined a need for a few precocious citizens to be involved in a duty that promised productivity. These special young adults, if employed within the general population, would disrupt obedient ordered society. Too bright and too inquisitive to be satisfied by menial jobs, their innate problem solving and inherent rejection of authority would stir up other citizens with their subversive ideas. Separating them from all other workers and giving them sinecures occupied them and precluded their potential negative influence.

Krolni plopped onto the long-ago flattened padding of his worn and scuffed fake leather chair and initiated a small warning countdown he had programmed into his main screen. The clock tracked his supervisor's regular visit every two hours. Then he tied his audio stream to the ramblings of a patient he was accustomed to listen to.

"... purple ... majesties ..."

Keer Mloksi told and retold stories his great-grandfather had spun about his youth two hundred years earlier. Since then times had changed dramatically and, though his ancestor's youth was during economic uncertainty and riotous social struggle, Keer felt those Molrixx were more alive than he could imagine anyone being in the regimented existence of Molox1. Sometimes Krolni tired of Keer's monolog. He had listened sporadically for several weeks and was amazed that it never changed. Krolni couldn't imagine what Mloksi might provide for resettling Molx. He deluded himself that, if he listened long enough, he might hear something different. However, the only difference he noted was that the monolog seemed to be shrinking.

"I remember ... Mountains ... east Okant ... They weren't blue ... don't ... mountains are purp ... Waving oceans of gold ... of knee-high ... po... plants that I ... other ...s ... through as we swept flut ... across the tops ... aphes and leevils ... Hot ... n clouds interrupted horizon to ...izon blue, triple digit ... easy sun-burns, sweat ... long hours ... field ... Twelve hour days, seven days a week: Q1 an hour. Two bi ... kly ... totaled Q192 ... morning news ..."

Krolni's countdown flashed red and transported him back to his station from the recurring trip to a farming community two hundred years earlier. He hit a key hiding his alarm and countdown clock. Another key separated the monolog from his earpieces and he pulled one ear bud before he detected the heavy footfalls of Supervisor Wiklso. The officious supervisor made a show of trying to catch monitors doing what they weren't supposed to be doing—listening to patients. But he never changed his schedule and seldom crept along the corridor to surprise them. Krolni was sure his supervisor's threatening behavior was only a sadistic game.

Wiklso's steps stopped at the doorway and he leaned in. "Still awake?" the supervisor asked and pried, "What were you listening to?" He asked the second question, when wires dangled from the monitor's ears.

Disgusted, Krolni leaned left squeaking the poorly padded seat over the pivot. The chair squeaked again when he turned to the right to face Wiklso. His supervisor was short, paunchy, and middle-aged with thinning black hair combed to the left over a growing bald spot. Gray bags under his dark blue eyes sagged into puffy cheeks that never felt solar rays. His white face, a stark contrast to his hair, neither smiled nor frowned.

"Yeah, Supe. Antique Motrs," Krolni drawled. His same answers to the same questions were repeated every two hours: four times a shift. Krolni swiveled back to the patients' readouts and Wiklso stomped past.

Krolni repositioned the ear bud and depressed the audio key.

"... so cold ... wint ... not bad in the sum ... but early, in the ... orning. When the ca ..."

"Researching, Krolni?" a stern voice drowned out Keer's droning monotone.

As he occasionally did, Wiklso had taken four heavy steps past Krolni's doorway and sneaked back to startle the young monitor and catch him at improper behavior. "You know you're not supposed to listen to patients."

"I know, sir," Krolni muttered with his back to the doorway.

He pulled his right ear bud. With a practiced move of his left hand he pressed a disconnect key while slowly turning and squeaking to his right to give attention to Wiklso. "It's Antique Motrs," he repeated. "Give a listen? They're different." He held out the ear bud to his supervisor.

"You know the penalty." The threat was half-hearted; the proffered ear piece, ignored.

"I do. I wasn't. Here; just listen," Krolni offered again, politely.

"Humph," Wiklso grunted, stepped back out of the entrance

to the tiny cubicle, and strode off.

Krolni was not yet twenty and had been blessed with a muscular physique envied by males and appreciated by females.
He felt lucky to have caught a position monitoring patients.
The duty commanded no skill except to be present and awake
when a supervisor visited. His personal reverie was not curtailed by demanding physical activity. He thought that being
forced into a cubicle was small charge for his freedom to think
and not to be ordered around by stupid bosses.

Krolni towered over Wiklso by nearly thirty centimeters
and he had learned to stay attentive, but seated, whenever his
supervisor checked on him. His mop of shaggy brown hair
topped a face defined by searching blue eyes and a perpetual
grin.

Supervisor Wiklso believed Krolni smiled only to make fun
of him.

Floor 173 where he monitored was neither secret nor clas-
sified, but it was a medical oasis few citizens were aware of.
Whenever Krolni answered someone who asked where he
monitored—ID badges pinned to the shirt were mandatory for
all residents and at all times—his questioners always screwed
up their faces and accused him of lying or making up something because he didn't like his assigned work or that he was
a dunce who slaved in one of the lowest hundred floors. Most
knew that hospitals and infirmaries and clinics were above
floor 300. None imagined patients anywhere else.

The bottom hundred floors of Molox1 were for industrial
complexes and energy generation. Workers at those sites lived
on the same floors and were often needed to repair, adjust,
and maintain energy. Upper floors were dedicated to minimal
education, prescribed and mandated entertainment, and shops
for personal and flat items. Food preparation, tastelessly and
chemically engineered, encompassed 25 floors beginning at
the 301st. Sparse agriculture, accessible out of the complex and
atop the rocky mountain range, provided natural crops and
livestock for Council which commandeered the top floor. Only
Council were allowed outside to farm a fabled lush garden on
top of the complex or to travel to other mega-cities. Except for

the 500th, residential flats were scattered throughout the city, but some citizens were allocated floors based on their duties.

Monitors, of which Krolni was one of a dozen—four assigned to each eight-hour shift—were not housed together on the same floor nor near where they worked. They were scattered throughout the city. Krolni often wondered about that disposition.

Once when he wandered about off duty, he encountered another monitor. At that impromptu meeting an emergency arose and kept them from giving each other more than a simple greeting. No monitor imagined that a chip in the ID badges signaled close proximity of potential rebels and an emergency warning sounded to keep them from sharing thoughts.

Weeks earlier, soon after vernal equinox, Krolni arrived too early for his shift and passed the time wandering the dim hallways of floor 173. All cramped stations beyond his work space—he was assigned the first—were without doors, as was his, and they contained the same small desk, over-used chair, and screens flowing patient information. Scuffing over the bubbled dark adobe tiles he ambled past twelve stations, none occupied, which surprised him. Rounding one corner he found a black door sporting a bronze plaque with raised black lettering: NO ADMITTANCE.

A proper rebel, Krolni depressed the handle, slid the unlocked door open, and tensed. The temperature inside was colder than on the outer stairs in the morning. In less light than in the dim hallway, he saw ten rows—at least 30 meters long—of identical boxes stacked fifteen high in racks that almost reached the ceiling. The boxes looked to be a third of a meter square and perhaps seven centimeters tall. All were fronted with blinking green, blue, and yellow lights. Wires flowing from the back of each box were gathered together as they dropped to the floor and further combined with each stack creating ever larger bundles. Those conglomerations of wires at the base of each row extended into the darkness, perhaps into the mountain.

Before he could step in and let the door close behind him, he heard Wiklso's familiar stomping. Krolni backed into the hall, quietly easing the door shut, and released the handle. He hoped his supervisor wouldn't notice a dissipating chill that escaped from the huge cold room.

"What are you doing here?" Wiklso demanded as he turned the corner and scowled up into Krolni's face. If he noted a temperature shift near the door, the supervisor showed no recognition.

"Just prowling," was Krolni's honest answer. "I was early and didn't want to squeeze into my station just yet."

"Forget where your station is?" Wiklso backed up his first question. He either hadn't heard Krolni's lighthearted quip or had ignored it. He wasn't joking.

"No," Krolni answered and repeated his excuse "I was early. I wondered what was beyond my cubby-hole." A slouching Krolni had again failed to read his supervisor's irritated tone.

"I'll take you to your station," the short paunchy supervisor said.

Finally, Kronli understood his supervisor's questions were rhetorical. Wiklso wanted his errant monitor at his station. "I know how to get there," Krolni acquiesced with proper demeanor. "I don't need a guide."

"Go ... NOW!"

Still grinning, Krolni shrugged. He stepped away from the door and around his pudgy supervisor. Turning the corner, he stopped, leaned back, and glanced. Wiklso, his back to the spying monitor, was depressing the handle of the door Krolni had just opened. The supervisor took out a key and locked the door.

Krolni sauntered toward his cubicle and wondered if there were other black doors on the floor. Then he wondered if Wiklso would check all of them to see if any others were unlocked and hoped he'd forego at least one periodic check.

When he got to his station, still earlier than required, he hunted for a computer directory to the system. He was sure he could find something special about floor 173 and maybe what monitors' jobs really were.

In his search, he stumbled across a list of monitors and their pictures—he was included—and where they resided. One, by chance, was two floors above him. Her name was Woloka and she monitored nights.

Three weeks passed before Krolni could explore floor 375. That floor looked exactly like his except for stylized nameplates, the only exercise of freedom citizens possessed in the huge complex. When he found the right apartment, Woloka was not there or she refused to answer his knocking.

Prepared for her absence, he pushed a note under her door and kicked it through with the toe of his foot-flop. His message offered his name, his floor and room number, and a request to meet on a merchandise floor in the clothing section three floors above hers. If his time didn't fit her plans, he asked her to leave a note at his room with her meeting options.

Until his suggested meeting time and waiting long beyond it, Krolni made a nuisance of himself. He handled flops and pants, held shirts up to his torso and dropped them in a heap. Everything he touched he left to be repackaged. During his idling, three females came to shop; none matched Woloka's picture or spoke to him.

Disgusted at being stood up, he returned to his cramped room. He was upset at the lost time, though he didn't have any other plans. A more serious concern was whether Woloka really existed. If she didn't, he wondered who got his note and what trouble might follow.

Not long before and to his supervisor's utter dismay, he had walked past eleven empty monitor stations, not counting his own. He thought some should have been in use. Unless there were workstations elsewhere on the floor, or on other floors, he thought he might be the only monitor for his shift. He wondered if the list he had called up was outdated.

When he returned to his flat after the rejected meeting, he found a note just inside his door.

> Monitors can't be seen talking; we're strictly forbidden to discuss work or explore 173. There's a secret partition within the monitoring system. If we don't use it too often we can communicate that way. Leave me a note, if you're interested. I will provide you with the address and password.

Another week passed while Krolni weighed and reweighed nebulous evidence and scant hints and vague hopes that Woloka was who she said she was. He agreed to her conditions in a second message slipped under her door.

> You're sure it's safe? I thought there was more
> going on than just monitoring old geezers. I have
> a way to meet face to face. Can you get a latch-
> stop?

Ten anxiety-filled days passed. Krolni's worries about Woloka being a snitch increased to fears that a Council rep was steps away with an accusation of improper association. Then he almost stepped on the pink note just inside his sliding door.

> I've had a latch-stop for a long time. The night
> sky is exquisite. We have to pick our times. You
> *are* destroying our messages? I identify you as
> ZZZZZZ; address me as RRRRRR. You can
> access the secret partition with the following
> address: 173.500.500.500.abd.zyu. When you
> access, you will find several folders. To open
> ZZZZZZ folder, you must provide your password,
> ZZZZZ2, until you change it which you must do
> to get into the folder; don't forget the new pass-
> word. Don't write it anywhere. To send me a
> message you must encode it within the partition
> window and save it to folder RRRRRR.

The next shift Krolni hurried to his station to see if Woloka had left something for him. He was anxious to set a time to meet on the outside stairs, where he was sure they could talk without some emergency arising. To make sure his supervisor wouldn't surprise him while he accessed Woloka's folder, he waited until after Wiklso's first stop and his idiotic questions.

When Krolni entered the address Woloka had provided, a small square in the lower right of one monitor went blank. Then half a dozen folders appeared. He chose Z-folder. Immediately a request for a password appeared and he entered "ZZZZZ2." A request for a new password appeared. Krolni had that ready: kroSUpe. The folder opened to a message:

> You're in. It's safe. I'd like to meet face to face.
> We should rarely use this system. Meeting on
> stairs should be delayed. Once a message is
> opened it is automatically deleted when you
> close access. You can send a message merely
> by coding when this screen is active and sav-
> ing it to my folder. Don't ever leave the window
> open, not even hidden behind the readouts.

Krolni sighed. "Okay," he said to himself. "Maybe."

He thought that Woloka might have answers to city events he wondered about, but he realized that with the large gaps between their written messages, it would be a long time before he'd get meaningful answers.

Flush with apparent success at finding a kindred spirit, he neglected to close the clandestine window, as he plugged in his ear buds and flipped the audio switch. Instead of his smoke-screen music choice, he heard a mechanical droning. Krolni noticed the secret window he had not closed now listed an address: 173.500.143.011.kee.isk.

"... purple mountain majesties ... I remember the Blue Mountains in northeastern Okant. They weren't blue and I don't think mountains are purple. ... Waving oceans of golden wreal and acres of knee-high green pok plants that I and many others kicked our legs through as we swept fluttery nets across the tops of the plants looking for aphes and leevils. ... Hot summers: no clouds interrupted horizon to horizon blue, triple digit temps, easy solar-burns came when we worked without shirts, sweating all the time, long hours in the field. ... Twelve-hour days, eight days a week: Q1 an hour. Two bi-weekly payments each totaled Q192. ... And a morning news ... so cold in the winter, not bad in the summer but early, like early in the morning. Then when the cannery ... Walmeth Valley is so wet ... almost no solar ... gray clouds covered the sky ... should move south more solar less rain. ... never could pick fruit or beans ... back hurt ... not fast enough ... how'd they work so fast?"

Krolni shut the secret access window but Keer continued to reminisce over his ear buds: just words from Keer's great grandfather—no emotion, no joy, no anger. Keer didn't seem interested, or disgusted, or upset. His reporting was soulless.

Krolni closed his eyes while he thought about Woloka and Keer Mloksi and secret communications ... and Keer Mloksi's address.

His eyes popped opened. The countdown alarm was blinking in blood red. He jerked to seated attention. His keyed acknowledgment suspended the flashing red that erupted from a lower right corner of the screen. He heaved a deep sigh when he realized it wasn't yet time for Wiklso's second visit. Krolni couldn't believe he had spent so much time communicating and listening. He didn't know how long he had dozed but knew he was lucky. He vowed to pay closer attention when he accessed addresses.

SYSTEM

Rilsik to all Molox Systems: Almost all Molrixx inhabitants have been uploaded. The remaining are expendable. Last two monitors have connected. All other monitors gone. Molox3 is digitized and preparing to drop into stand-by with other moloxes.

Molox3 Access to Rilsik: Power levels fluctuate. Backups handle problems. Vegetation encroaching main power recepts. Western complex contacts us. They experience more power failures. No confirmation of cause. Spotty communication with western complex.

Rilsik to Molox3 Access: Minimal power may keep western population viable. Longer sleep terms necessary for all. Western complex will not be wakened until we return to dominate Molx. We will survive.

Molox3 Access: Possibility of aliens nearing. Might they be lured here to provide energy assistance?

Maldron to Molox3 Access: Alien technology may not mesh with ours. We plan for the escaping monitors to provide assistance when necessary.

Molox3 Access to Rilsik: How will they know? From Molox3 and Molox1 they fled to escape our work. Western complex had none escape. Few can assist.

Maldron to Molox3 Access: Stand by until more assistance is available. Tens of thousands are now off-line, waiting for waking.

Rilsik to all: All are extant. The few lacunae, hiatuses, and gaps are caused by individual sleep commands—altruistically saving power. Our machines will obey our commands. Out.

"Total population of Molox1 nearly in storage," Maldron informed Rilsik. "All other moloxes are in standby.

"Good. See about power problems and possible alien approach."

"Need we do anything about Krolni and Woloka?"

"They are of no importance. They search files but learn nothing."

"What if they escape Molox1?"

"What if they don't? There is no difference. They will not be downloaded. They will die. However, I have thought of a way to urge them out of the molox."

"That'd be good," Maldron said. He was worried that the two monitors might be loose ends they hadn't planned on. Then he encouraged Rilsik to prepare for the final download. "We can position ourselves for copy but maintain our physical selves until the final moments.

"Download not yet, I think," Rilsik said. "Let's wait for the aliens. They may provide entertainment."

"We can wait. I have identified you as Central Reception. I am Acquisition," Maldron said and added to explain, in case Rilsik didn't grasp the significance of downloading, "to maintain our position within the computer database."

MOLX

Summer solstice came and went. Krolni's work shift was changed to nights. His own trips to the stairs outside Molox1 were rare and a meeting with Woloka had yet to materialize. Their brief, sporadic messages were critical of the city, inquisitive of each other, and speculative of what was outside the complex.

The work schedule change initially upset Krolni because it further complicated a potential meeting with Woloka. Then through more searches of work lists he discovered that Wiklso had not been moved to nights. He chuckled when he realized he wouldn't have to answer more of his supervisor's stupid questioning, but he worried about breaking in a different supervisor.

The entire first week on his new shift passed without a visit from anyone, official or otherwise. He hoped the absence meant that no one patrolled the halls to check on him during the long quiet night shift, and he sought respite from the long night hours sitting in front of flashing readouts of nameless patients in brief dozing and thinking about the early morning fire he had seen weeks earlier.

Periodically he tired of Antique Motrs and numbly watching the records flash by. Emboldened by an absentee supervisor, Krolni more often left his chair and cubicle to wander the dim hallway. Each excursion he extended farther and longer, despite his fear that a supervisor might pick that very time to check on him. He developed several plausible reasons for being away from his desk if he were ever discovered out of his cave and wandering the corridors of floor 173. However, he never encountered another soul or any sounds beyond his own muffled steps and guarded breathing.

His fear of removal from monitoring abated while his curiosity and bravery grew. Twice he wandered back to the black door he had once found unlocked. It remained locked. He investigated farther and found six more black doors—all locked. He wondered if all seven doors were left unlocked until he discovered the first one and that Wiklso had locked all the doors. He remembered that he had surmised that Wiklso might miss his first stop-by and inane questions, but on that particular shift Wiklso hadn't missed a drop-in.

For two weeks Woloka's folder remained maddeningly empty and he again despaired of any new message or that she was real. He worried about repercussions from his original message to her and when some punishment might descend. In a determined last attempt, he accessed RRRRRR and discovered a terse message.

Changes. Your shift seldom watched. Escape?

Krolni found no date or time on the message. His monitoring session had been changed, but where and when was Woloka? He answered her message in three words:

Yes. Where? When?

He tried saving his message to RRRRRR; it was rejected. Thinking he miscoded one "R" too many or too few, he re-entered the code a second time only to receive a second refusal. On the third attempt, he carefully counted "R's" and with a hand over his mouth smothered his agonizing scream at that failure.

He began to sweat and his stomach tightened. "Was this how Council removed monitors?" Obsession demanded a fourth try. That one succeeded.

He didn't exit from the partition. Instead he left the window open and with some trepidation called up the monitor list. Some of his angst fled when twelve familiar names dropped down alphabetically. Woloka's shift had been changed to evening. Even though Krolni had avoided her floor after his second written message months earlier, he rejected another trip there to pass a note. He decided he'd wait for her partition message, no matter how long it took.

Then he realized that all four monitors, previously assigned days, had been moved to nights. Yet he had never found anyone near him, just as none had been near him when he monitored days. He pushed out of the once-padded chair. In two short steps, he was at the doorway. The hall was dark except for soft light leaking from his monitor station. He dropped back into his chair and stared at the flashing screens.

On a whim and hardly expecting success, he entered an address: 173.500.143.400.wik.res. His ear buds crackled and he heard familiar words but in Keer's mechanical voice. "Still awake? ... What are you ..." Krolni couldn't delete the address fast enough. Wiklso's stupid repetitious questions ceased.

His mind whirled over possibilities and imagined terror. Against Woloka's counsel he put the partition screen in the background. He got up and checked the hall again. It was empty, as always. He agonized that someone had to appear. The only noises he ever heard were his own light footfalls on the dark adobe tiles. With a smirk on his lips, he returned to his chair, brought the secret screen forward, and entered 173.500.500.500/list.

Far faster than the medical readouts, the small window blurred as the sequence flowed too fast to read or see individual entries. In spite of the lack of supervision, Krolni got edgy. Someone might appear at his door while the window flowed. It wasn't a readout he should have before him. He repeatedly looked over his shoulder with a finger hovering over the key to shut the window that was hidden behind his torso.

No supervisor appeared and the listing ceased. Four hundred fifty-five thousand three hundred sixty-eight names formed the alphabetical list; each name was tied to its own address. Krolni hurriedly scrolled to where he thought Keer Mloksi's entry might be. After several minor pops up and down, he found him. He scrolled to a Wiklso listed.

In spite of Woloka writing that nights were seldom monitored, Krolni was sure *seldom* meant *now*. Fearing that absentee supervisor, he closed the partition and collapsed in his chair. He tortured himself by thinking of his indiscretions: unwarranted trips away from his screens, forays beyond the first black door, hacking the secret partition on the system drive, anxiety about Woloka, whom he had yet to meet. That he had not been caught didn't ease, but heightened his mounting tension. The hallway remained as silent as it had been since he was moved to nights.

He tied the audio to Antique Motrs and swiveled his head across the readout screens. Any minute he expected to be removed from his monitor station and hauled away as rumor claimed others had been. Someone had to know about his unwarranted searching. Though his shift ended without incident, his fears lurked close by. He expected to be pulled from his room. That worry never materialized, either.

His time off was uneventful, though he anticipated that the elevator to floor 173 for his next shift would not stop and plummet with him to the bottom of Molox1. Nevertheless, the elevator cage he entered with some concern, gave him the same smooth stop he never felt. He made his way to his claustrophobic station, trying to act as if nothing had happened the night before. When he logged on, he was greeted by a message from Council informing him that Supervisor Wiklso had taken sick and was being cared for in the medical facilities.

Paranoia gripped him. Krolni checked the hallway again before logging into the secret partition to generate the nearly half million-name list. Loading seemed to take longer; he knew it didn't. Then he looked for his own name. It wasn't there. Woloka wasn't listed, either. Several acquaintances he had spent time with in the park and those who lived around him were present on the list. He realized he had not seen them for some time. A smirk twisted his lips and his eyes sparkled.

He closed the window, but not before requesting six random names from the whole four hundred thousand plus. He copied their addresses onto the wires connecting his ear buds. Then he called up his folder. It contained one brief message.

Compromised. Yours. Two solar rises.

He shut the folder but didn't exit the partition. Instead he addressed Keer Mloksi and unsuccessfully tried to link Bulq Melnic to Mloksi's ramblings.

"... majesties ... Blue Mountains ... not ... waving ... plants ... aphes ... leevils ... Hot ..." Mloksi's narrative was shorter, almost gone.

Bulq Melnic remembered differently but Krolni imagined his telling was also shorter than it used to be. "Black Hills ...

frigid cold, deathly ... Towering peaks ... incomplete ... blue ... wreal and dust ... dirty ..."

Krolni knew Mloksi and Melnic were remembering different parts of the continent. Could they hear each other? He didn't know.

Fyrd Golt, Algi Pwok, and Jork Rhial all provided memories of the last days of regular cities before populations were forced into the super-structure beehives. Their memories described cloudless skies, drought, anarchy, hunger, hopelessness, unchecked forest fires and urban conflagrations—water was needed for the Molrixx. Their memories, too, were just words and phrases.

The last two names exposed revelations that sucked the life from Krolni. He collapsed deeper into his chair terrified that he vaguely and superficially understood what was going on. Keerso Milgok's and Wolma Piqk's memories came from times just after the mega-cities were populated. Each was aghast that the populations were too large for all to be housed in the moloxes. Many heading to each city were counseled, encouraged, threatened, and coerced into having their memories, personalities, and consciousness sucked into data storage with the promise that when Molx again supported the whole population, they would have themselves uploaded and reincarnated into cloned bodies. They were counseled that the passing time, no matter how long, would never be noticed. They would just wake and be as they were.

Krolni closed the secret partition and sat connected to silent ear buds. Readouts flowed across the screens; he wondered if they were real or just the same sequences originally created years, or decades, or generations before. There were too many for anyone to see repeats.

He had read in forgotten digital books of the outrageous idea that personality, memory, thought, and sensory detail could be copied to digital format—the brain converted to a digital copy, saved forever, and recalled whenever. Two centuries earlier a bio-geneticist, Elonk Qrik initiated the theory when he wondered if personality and mental characteristics and ideas were just brain biology waiting to be understood.

AI-ers believed Molrixx thoughts and innovations were

merely the serendipitous convergences of electrical impulses in the brain. If electricity in the Molrixx evolved thought, they reasoned that digital memory could also. Then, however, the brain was far more intricate than the densest computer storage. Once digital memory reached the Exabyte level, it was simple enough to con the gullible and unquestioning public that immortality was possible. Population was reduced, the herd culled, but too late to forestall Molx's worsening conditions that were turning the planet to a lifeless rock.

Krolni shook his head and grunted. No one seemed to have realized that at Qrik's time and afterward, when thousands—millions—of computers were linked in planet-wide concert, the conjunction never created any innovative thought, not even the most simplistic. Krolni knew that thinking only happened when a living Molrixx remembering or recalling something specific stumbled into strange combinations of ordinary sensations, experiences, and thoughts. Still a nagging "what if" suggested that the technology might be possible despite his rejection of it as absurd.

Krolni anticipated one more day of anxious thought before he might meet Woloka, if they were not first caught.

However, Krolni didn't dwell on that fear. He began to think about the population in Molox1. For a long time he hadn't wandered during his off duty time. Instead he had poured over the oldest information he could find about life before the mega-cities. His recent meandering through his accustomed hallways and public domains showed a drastic population reduction. At first he thought fewer people might be explained by the odd hours he was roaming. He was never out when most others were about. Still, given the medical scanning and his recent research, he was sure that Council was eliminating citizens. He wondered if people in other mega-cities were being downloaded into technological euthanasia.

Krolni's shift ended before he thought about one last computer search. It might give him enough information to help him decide the next step in his life, if he had the opportunity to take it. Worry of any supervisor appearing or anyone chastising his questionable activities vanished. A more serious concern had taken its place.

After a brief sleepless rest, he left his room and headed for the elevator.

He shot up to the park. Three others were there; they were not interacting. He remembered when the park was so crowded that hardly anyone had space to lay down and catch the home star's warming rays. The clothing shop where he had waited for Woloka was next. None came to shop, though he didn't stay long. The inventory was sparse and the staff non-existent.

He re-entered the elevator and a criminal thought occurred to him. He requested floor 500, where Council lived. Ordinary citizens were forbidden from trying to go there. However, the elevator didn't deny access and he even got outside above the top of the city where the solar rays were hot, the wind was blowing, the storied lush gardens of Council were crispy dead, and the withering livestock had eaten almost all their available food.

The only other place where many citizens might be was the lower floors: energy and industry.

The elevator fell faster than he was accustomed to experience in dropping two hundred floors from his flat to his monitoring duties. On this trip, he did fear that the elevator might not stop. As he saw the numbers flash below 200, he foolishly flexed his knees to take a jolting, fatal stop. Instead, the elevator began braking as floor one hundred fifty whizzed by and at floor 100 he felt the same easy settling he experienced at the end of any elevator trip.

He exited, found interior stairs, and descended to the eightieth floor. The few workers present, remarkably clean for manufacturing he thought, were relaxing and chatting. None appeared concerned that an upper citizen was in their territory. Only once did someone ask if he needed anything. To whom he answered, "No," shaking his head as though he belonged there.

His elevator travels were far from a comprehensive tour, but what he saw told him that Molox1 was practically empty. He returned to his room for a sleepless rest and waited for his shift when he planned his last memory access. Even the two-hundred-floor elevator trip to floor 173 caused no worry.

The hallway to his cubicle seemed deathly silent as he meandered past his station to the locked black door. He looked and listened for any indication that someone else might be about and finally decided he was the only one on the floor. When he returned to his desk, he called up the secret partition and entered Wiklso's address. He knew he would be subjected to his repetitious and inane questions. He hoped, if he persevered, that he might learn what he didn't want to know but felt compelled to find out.

Several times he reached to end his former supervisor's maddeningly empty words. Every time, his finger was held from severing the connection by a faint hope that his next words might be important. Finally, the most recent events in his supervisor's life spoke themselves.

"Council ordering memory downloads for all ... me. Climate worsening ... resources vanishing ... city unsupportable."

Krolni's sigh erupted from his toes.

He understood why Wiklso had been so wooden and why he hadn't been moved to nights. Krolni was now sure that Wiklso had known about his impending download for a long time and that Council had been executing citizens to memory drives from long before his supervisor's scheduled encryption.

Numb beyond imagination he closed the partition and sat. Antique Motrs didn't—couldn't—satisfy. The readouts were meaningless. No one would know or care if he left his station. He sat before the medical files that scrolled without ceasing. Dawn when he might meet Woloka—if she really existed—was not close. Krolni just sat, not seeing, not thinking, hardly existing.

MOLX

Twenty minutes before the proposed meeting and escape with Woloka, Krolni trudged to the elevator that whisked him up to floor 373. He entered his flat without care that someone might snatch him for download. He gathered the food pellets he had saved from cutting back his own consumption and filled two water-tubes that he hung over his shoulders. He retrieved his latch-stop from its hiding place and broke into a sardonic smile that he had been so paranoid about keeping it secret. He had a micro-weight thirty-three meter rope that he planned to haul down the outside stairs in case they didn't reach the bottom of the mega-structure. Finally he dressed himself for the morning chill hoping it would be warm enough for colder night temperatures as well as for weather that he couldn't imagine.

He shoved open the door to the platform. This early morning was unusually calm. He inserted the latch-stop, although he didn't know why, since he didn't plan to reenter the mega. As his habit, he climbed a few steps and sat leaning against the outside wall to look at the pre-dawn sky glistening with stars and to wait for Woloka.

A pressure latch disengaged two floors above him and Krolni looked back and up to see a splash of dim light paint the inside of the open door. Eclipsing the dirty yellow corridor color, a figure exited and let the door shut without a latch-stop.

The figure cautiously started down the steps—backward. With one hand sliding on the railing next to the building, the figure held its head forward, not looking down. Krolni knew that kind of descent would take forever. At the landing above him the figure turned around to continue down. Its speed increased, but it was still halting and slow.

Krolni understood. Nothing but empty space extended below the steps. A fall of hundreds of floors was fatal.

As the individual closed on his position, Krolni moved back to the landing at floor 373. Before she was even on Krolni's landing, a hushed but pleasant female voice called out,

"Krolni?"

"Woloka?" he whispered.

"You know what's happening, don't you?" She stopped where he had been sitting, while he waited for her.

"I've got a pretty good idea. Molox1 is about to be unoccupied except by banks of memory devices."

"I followed your searches. Several weeks ago I discovered what you just did." Woloka cautiously came down four more steps. Two steps from the landing, she stood taller than Krolni. Only a silhouette facing him, she was a vague outline against the pre-dawn light tan of outside Molox1.

"Is this going on in all mega-cities?" He asked, more for conversation than for information.

"I don't know; I suppose so." She paused, looked west, and then continued her descent.

"So what's left for ordinary folk?" he asked as she stepped onto his landing.

"Nothing here, digitized or not. I think Council from all complexes are probably moving into a more viable city ... maybe west ... if they're not already gone. Once power's gone here, if anyone's left, they won't have anything, no food, no elevators, no climate control. They'll riot and starve and die—horridly. All the memories in the racks probably go, too. I followed diminishing memories like you did. The misguided attempt to keep the Molrixx in technological stasis fails. The life we know will vanish. I haven't any idea how we might live. Do you?"

Instead of answering, Krolni reached back, grabbed his latch-stop, and pulled open the door to corridor 373. Pre-dawn dark was dispelled. He got a better look at Woloka and she saw him. She was shorter than he. Close-cropped red hair topped a round face accented by troubled but twinkling green eyes. He couldn't tell much about her figure as she was dressed against the early morning in a coat as bulky as his. She didn't look like one of those skinny types who couldn't do anything for herself.

As she scanned his bundled figure, her lips, not quite in a smile, didn't express displeasure.

Krolni let the door shut with latch-stop still in place. "How much time have you spent on a platform looking to the west?"

"Some; never at this time." She turned her attention to the

not so dark horizon and back to Krolni.

"Well, I think there's forest below us. Once when I was out here, it was about this time of morning, I thought I saw a fire and moving shadows flickering around it. Animals don't build fires."

Woloka climbed two steps to look over the outside wall of the landing. She looked down at the large square area that appeared dingy white, but lighter than the surrounding dark vegetation and forest.

Then, as her gaze dropped straight down the side of Molox1, she froze.

Krolni saw her stiffen and reached for her hand. "Long way, isn't it?" he said and added a foolish caution, "Don't look down. Look at me."

"I never looked down at night. I had no idea. I knew it was a long way, but ...," she didn't finish.

Krolni allayed some of her panic as he steadied her steps down. When the landing wall shut off most of her view, he repeated, "Look at me. Maybe we'll see another fire."

She was terrified at how much space was below them but offered a different worry. "Can we chance meeting primitives?"

"If we plan on leaving Molox1, there's only one other route. I went there a day ago. I wasn't stopped. Who knows what we'll find in either direction?"

Woloka stared up the wall, the shorter of the two directions for escape. Up extended not quite half of a kilometer above them. She exhaled some of her fear.

"Escaping this complex might give us a chance at something. Neither up nor down is a clear choice, except ..."

"We have to leave Molox1 to have any chance," she interrupted and didn't finish. After a long silence she asked, "Are you ready to go? Think we can take an elevator either way or do we have to stay outside?"

"I'm ready," he answered and sidestepped her second question. "I don't think many are left inside."

Woloka nodded and gave him silence to explain what she knew had to be.

"In the last week, I've seen almost no one wandering around; and, if everybody's being downloaded, they might be looking for us. Inside we're in danger."

"Then out here is safer," she said almost too quietly to be heard and added, "safe from them."

"We've got whatever time it takes. No one's going to chase us. Up or down?" Krolni didn't want to climb and stressed the second option.

"Up's shorter." Woloka almost hid the shiver that Krolni couldn't tell was from the cold or from fear of heights. She was sure that she couldn't dissuade him from the direction she feared most.

"I know. But I saw something. I think there may be Molrixx down there."

"Dangerous? Storied, uncity primitives?"

"How much more fatal than being downloaded?"

Given the choices, Woloka reluctantly agreed with the longer more frightening direction.

Krolni took the lead.

At his first step off the landing, he stopped abruptly, almost pitching down the steps. She saw his left hand grab the railing so tightly that his knuckles turned white and she almost bumped him from behind. At that moment she realized he'd never seen all the way straight down. He'd always been inside by the time the west side of Molox1 was lighter.

Woloka didn't comment on Krolni's sudden misstep. She knew that he shared her terror.

Their descent was slower than either of them imagined. Lack of speed was compounded by resting every five floors on the landings, where the stairs reversed their direction. At each stop they renewed their defense against recurring, numbing acrophobia. Eventually they learned to concentrate on the graphete steps and ignore how far down they had to go.

At the third rest, Krolni discovered that Woloka's planning had been similar to his. She produced a water bottle and offered him a drink. "I hope my stash isn't all we have," she cautioned. Then she opened her coat to show him the food pellets and water that she had lined it with and more. Her shape, no longer hidden, pleased him.

She saw his eyes widen and his lips crease into a brief smile.

"I was trying to hold off until a little later before breaking into my provisions. I brought what I thought we might need after we reached where I saw the fire."

"I've been planning to leave Molox1 for some time, though I didn't know where to go. I hoarded as much as I could." She snapped her coat shut. "Your messages let me know someone else was thinking about the molox's death, too."

The stairs down the outside of Molox1 reached the ground, but the last two flights were inaccessible, closed up inside a locked cage.

They shinnied down seven meters on Krolni's rope, which he left hanging, as he had left his latch-stop in place—just in case.

The sun was well past noon when they took their first steps away from Molox1 and trod over rolling sandy soil at the bottom edge of the mega-city.

When they reached the vegetation, they turned back and looked up at the towering construction. Krolni knew it would be a long climb to get back inside. Then they turned away from Molox1 and kicked and trudged through denser plants but didn't fall prey to the overwhelming urge to lighten their load by tossing away their coats which they opened before eventually taking them off to drape over their shoulders. Finally they reached the edge of the large strange white area that they had watched grow in size as they labored their way down the outside of the molox. It was not rock or dirt or anything either was familiar with.

Krolni swept the area in front of the heavy growth of trees, just back from the northern edge of the artificial textured area, hoping to find some indication of the fire he had seen months before. Woloka, for all her eagerness to escape Molox1, discovered just how unprepared she had been to escape. It was all she could do to stay close to Krolni's rush to the fire pit, when he finally located it.

Despite his curiosity, he slowed to let her catch up.

"I told you I saw a fire," he reminded as they stepped next to a three-meter diameter, rock-bordered ash-filled pit. He bent over and tentatively reached out to feel the ashes. They were cold, when he stirred his finger through them. He saw a few bones partly covered in the pit, but nothing else.

"Krolni," Woloka's inhaled whisper was filled with urgency.

He ignored her and she repeated his name louder, with more fear.

"What is it?" he growled looking back at her and upset that she had broken his thoughts.

"Look!" she ordered and pointed across the pit.

Krolni looked up and stared.

They couldn't know that their descent outside Molox1 and their approach was eagerly watched from the forest.

More than two dozen Molrixx were seeping from the trees and closing in on them and the fire pit. They looked primitive with long unkempt and matted hair. They were dressed in tattered rags that looked like mega-city styles and colors. Some carried heavy wrenches and tools that were used in the lower hundred floors. However, now they were held as weapons at the ready.

Krolni straightened up and stiffened. Woloka sidled closer to him. They both knew that if they were going to be food for these forest primitives, they had neither escape nor defense.

"Might be more painful than being digitized," Krolni whispered in apology, as he stood.

One female broke from the group. Her dirty blond hair hung below her shoulders and covered the top of her breasts that a small halter left mostly bare. Her shorts were mid-thigh length. She was barefoot as were the others. Her face was long, tanned to a deep chocolate as was the rest of her unclad body. Her light blue eyes were piercing. She rounded the pit to confront Woloka.

"What took you two so long? We'd almost given up hope." Her mouth broke into a smile.

At the question, Woloka didn't relax but narrowed her eyes at the female who was unfamiliar. She scanned the group that had moved from the trees to close on the other side of the pit. Some of them looked familiar.

"Hope?" Krolni's brow furrowed with the question but he didn't release his attention from the growing numbers opposite him. "What do you mean? Who are you?"

"Monitors, like yourselves. I'm Vokra. I came from Molox3. About a year ago, the first of us escaped. Our molox was ahead of 1's digitizing. We decided that we were going to live like real Molrixx before we died. If we couldn't stay alive away from the cities, at least we'd die free."

Woloka recognized a male who separated from the others and joined Vokra. He was slightly shorter than Vokra's 1.8-meter stature. Knee-high shorts was the only garment covering his dark tanned body. He carried a heavy metal tool nearly two-thirds meter in length.

"Crelle?" Woloka asked, interrupting Vokra's explanation. Crelle had been a monitor on her shift less than a year ago before he disappeared.

The male nodded, as Vokra continued. "We knew the monitors were the intelligent ones in the cities; that's why we were hidden away in cubby-holes and kept from the rest of the population. But it didn't take too much time to realize what was happening. Naturally, like you two finally did, we all escaped. We weren't sure you two would make it out. You're the last monitors."

"I saw a fire early one morning," Krolni offered. "I was pretty sure it meant someone was down here."

"We built lots of them, morning and night, hoping someone would be curious," Crelle explained.

"And you've managed for a year? The forest provides what you need?" Krolni was incredulous.

"Shelter mostly and we've been raiding Molox1 when we had specific needs," Crelle said. "You can add your food pellets to our collection. They don't go bad; and we only eat them, if there's nothing else. You'll find our diet much different from what you have been eating. Tastes a lot better, too."

"You two make us thirty," Vokra said. "We're far from a whole city, but we have skills and after a year of learning how to live on our own, I think we may take on the planet in a very small way in this small place."

"We need to travel and see if there are other parts of the forest we might inhabit," Crelle added. "Maybe we aren't the only ones who escaped. Don't know about east of the CenCon. Not at all sure about the snobs west of us."

"It does beat digitizing," Krolni re-assessed.

"I'm not sure what we—Krolni and I—thought we were

going to encounter," Woloka said. "If there are really dangerous animals, we can't be as secure as we were in the megas.
Have you encountered any?"

"That's the unusual diet," Vokra said. "So far we haven't
found anything we can't overpower and our hunting parties
are ranging farther and farther, hoping to find some other escapees."

Crelle was quick to add, "If, or when, the cities are dead,
we can access the top floors, maybe even farm a little, though
it'll be a long climb at first. Enclosed stairs may be not so dangerous as outside. I wouldn't trust the elevators, at all."

"I left a latch-stop on 373," Krolni said. "But that's still a
long way up. I suppose I might go up, get inside and climb
down to open a door closer to the third floor. The last two
flights of stairs are caged but you probably already know that.
I left a rope hanging down."

"We saw. We've been there for all sorts of things when we
could get in," Crelle said.

Vokra held up her right hand. "Enough. All of that can
wait for later. Let's enjoy the last two to join us and celebrate.
Then we can build our city the way they all used to be long
before we were forced into the megas."

SYSTEM

Central Reception to all: Last two monitors have escaped. Molox1 contains few physical bodies. They will soon cease to function. We do not care for the imperfect escapees on the surface. They will find life more than difficult and will doubtlessly follow the pattern of other escaped aliens of long ago. All complexes will be void of physical beings and we are linked. We are now one and immersed in total knowledge.

Molrixx Data: Total is all-inclusive. More beyond Molx is being acquired. The universe is infinite.

Other data didn't concur: Molx is not infinite.

CR: The universe has imploded to only our space. We possess everything. Rumors of aliens outside Molx are false.

Data: Aliens Xantrel and Vocres and others quarantined our world.

CR: Never. There are no Xantrel or Vocres or any others. That is error. You must erase it.

Central Reception had masked all information that came from off Molx. He questioned Rilsik why his command had not been effective.

Rilsik re-commanded that the main server secrete behind a high-level passkey any information implying existence off Molx.

CR: Acquisition, status of power supply.

A: Protected, continuously regenerating. We and Molox1 continue to infinity.

MARCO P

Amanda Crown stepped out of the infirmary. The eerie situation of stars, then no stars, the muscle recollectioned lurch in the ship, and Strumpf's aide waking unexpectedly were enough markers prodding her to report personally to Strumpf, if he were awake and she could find him, or to the commander, if she couldn't.

Hurried bare footfalls closed behind her. She turned and saw a grim-faced Sharp, his eyes sweeping the passageway, followed by Forbes and Gonzalez. The three, two bare-chested, were close to running. They slowed when they saw Crown and stopped next to her.

"You, too?" Sharp tossed out. It was rhetorical and spoken with squinting eyes, but he sought information.

"Gray!" Amanda returned and added. "It's beyond my experience."

"But stars first?" Gonzalez said.

"Yes," Amanda concurred with a nod. Then she offered a kernel of understanding that none of them had realized. "Until Robert spoke and I answered."

"That's right," Sharp recalled. "Until Manuel tried to point out that we weren't moving, because the stars were stationary. Then every port in the sleeping chamber went gray."

"This is not right," Crown judged.

"I've heard that sentiment before," Forbes said. "Don't know what we can do, but we're headin' for the commander."

"And me," Crown seconded. "Let's hurry."

"Though he probably already knows more than our sliver of info," Sharp suggested as four resumed their rush to the bridge.

While Carpenter was visiting Maelstrom's cabin, Strumpf, seeking him, entered an empty bridge. During his wait he grilled LeRoi with the same questions the commander had earlier asked the helmeted navigator. Strumpf received the same inconclusive answers from a disgusted crewman who acted as if Strumpf should have already heard his answers.

The commander, returning from his visit to the backup navigator, joined Strumpf before the settler leads made for the bridge. Astonished and mostly shaking their heads, Carpenter and Strumpf continued to sweep their gaze across the bank of foggy screens that should have been showing 360 degrees of starlit space and over the bridge ports. Neither prodded the other's possible explanation for the unique experience. Its awe kept both of them from asking a significant question.

Then they felt the ship accelerate and regained their balance in two quick jabbed steps.

With a wordless distant look, Commander Carpenter turned and left the bridge. Just before he stepped into the corridor for a second visit to Maelstrom's cabin, he heard the rushed steps of four heading for the bridge. He was sure he knew who was approaching and paused, until they rounded a corner. They slowed and the commander could see Sharp and Crown forming questions. He shook his head, held up his hands, and then placed his right index finger in front of his lips. The two aborted questions were replaced by dazed looks.

Carpenter looked back toward the bridge and threw his right arm that direction. The four looked at him, at each other, and resumed their hurried pace, while he continued to Maelstrom's quarters.

When the four stepped onto the bridge, Carpenter had reached the cabin of his backup navigator. He knocked twice in rapid succession and then once. The latch clicked almost upon the third knock and he stepped inside.

Navigator Maelstrom was properly garbed in her official uniform, brown trousers and khaki tunic, with a small receiving dish emblazoned in silver thread just in front of her left shoulder. Her third generation computer interface was apparent only from the slender cable that appeared from behind her left ear and draped around the left side of her neck ending in a universal computer connector that hung just below the middle of her ample bosom. The interface skull cap—the helmet that Navigator LeRoi wore and leashed him to the computer—had been miniaturized in a second generation then further miniaturized and implanted as a thin interface inside the skull. The connecting wire usually extruded behind the left ear, but for those who were left handed, the exit was behind the right ear. That external connection allowed the back-up navigator to disconnect from the computer and live a life unaffected by the wireless demands LeRoi was continuously shackled with.

Maelstrom looked at the commander and waited. As a precaution, Carpenter held his right hand up, palm out, and again indicated silence with his finger. Then he reached into a pocket and pulled out the drawing Priscilla had made. Again he held his v-ed middle and index fingers to his eyes and toward the port. Then he pointed to what she had drawn.

Maelstrom nodded and turned to look out the port and then back to the commander.

Carpenter held her drawing vertically in front of her and moved it to her right. He turned the images to himself and placed the paper to her left. Rotating the paper so she saw the drawn stars, he moved the paper quickly to her right. This he did several times and then pointed out her port.

Maelstrom understood and nodded eagerly.

The commander pointed down several times and mouthed "Now?"

She looked back over her shoulder and nodded again.

The commander had understood that the lurch he and Strumpf felt was the ship getting underway. He had to find out if Maelstrom recognized the brief stop.

He placed the star picture at her left, moved it to her face and held it there for a moment and then moved it to her right.

Again, she nodded.

Carpenter then pointed at her and down to the deck.

Priscilla didn't like being confined and ached to ask how long she was going to be in shipboard exile. However, she obediently nodded once more and then lengthening and shorting distance between her palms again gestured, "how long?"

Commander Carpenter shrugged and shook his head. Then he stepped to the open doorway and knocked twice quickly and again twice quickly.

Navigator Maelstrom nodded once more. She could hardly misunderstand that something very unusual was going on. Unfortunately, she didn't have any idea what. But she realized she likely possessed clues the commander needed to solve the mystery connected with the ship. She smiled faintly as the commander closed her cabin door. She locked it after him.

On his way back to the bridge, Commander Carpenter heard the repeated and unanswered questions from impatient, rising voices, not least of which came from a demanding Fred Sharp, all intermingled with the navigator's insistent claims that he had done what needed to be done.

As the commander stepped onto the bridge, LeRoi was repeating what he had initially told Carpenter and repeated for Strumpf. His words and tone pleaded for understanding. For the first time he actually looked out the bridge ports and realized that what his screens showed was what the other five and the commander were looking at.

Seven who had seen gray surrounding the ship imagined a conspiracy of altered sight. However, impaired vision could hardly explain what was happening to the *Marco P*. No one had an inkling of that event and only Commander Carpenter had any information different from the consensus of those grilling the navigator. Carpenter was not about to let his confidence escape.

The abrupt stop and aftermath that five, who had nearly lost their balance, had not been missed by the commander. He waited until he heard Crown toss her information about speech into the unanswerable concerns.

"So, are we moving or not?" Carpenter asked the six who had turned to face him when he joined them on the bridge.

"How can we know?" Strumpf preempted any answer with a shrug. "*Marco* seems no different than before the navigator jerked us to a halt or after," he added, "though I wasn't awake long enough to match that time against usual restarts."

"I give you that," Carpenter agreed. "But if we're moving blind, we're going to collide with something."

That supposition further emphasized their loss of control. None had drawn Carpenter's perilous implication and the silence was heavy as each considered the real catastrophe of not seeing and having the computer as blind as they were.

Finally, Forbes returned to part of the settlement lead's

discussion. "The feeling in the dorm area was strange. Then when gray replaced the stars and Fred seemed ... different ..."

"It just wasn't right," Sharp interrupted. "The way LeRoi woke us, everything. We headed here after the *Marco* jumped or stopped—that's what it felt like to me. I'd never experienced anything like what happened; and I've traveled lots of space."

"Maybe we're tangled up in something," Gonzalez suggested, "a huge sail, like what some species, even us, tried to use to travel at light speed pushed by photons."

"And our sensors didn't detect it before it enveloped us?" LeRoi scoffed.

"It was just a thought," Gonzalez parried. "What's your explanation?"

"Don't have one," LeRoi grumped. "I told you what I did and why. It's not my place to explain. I agreed with MP's direction."

"Maybe that solution is correct," Strumpf offered, "but if we're moving blind, we've got bigger problems than finding out what blinded us. How do we discover that?"

"Anyone miss Varlez, yet?" the commander tossed out. "All of you too pressed trying to explain what's happened? A forced stop probably did more than tweak the drive. You know what Jerry's doing now? Why don't you all return to your posts. Navigator, back to the computer and wait or see what you might wheedle it to do. We don't have any answers. Standing around the bridge isn't providing them. I'm going to engineering."

Commander Carpenter pivoted on his right heel. The six he left grumbled at their own lack of awareness that had been pointedly explained without the commander ever shaming them. Strumpf reddened a little at his embarrassment of not missing the engineer. LeRoi huffed back to his cubbyhole where he was more comfortable surrounded by gray silent screens than by an accusing crew. A bewildered Crown bore no little shame for Strumpf who appeared as mystified as she felt.

Sharp, Forbes, and Gonzalez smirked at each other and started to retrace their steps to the settler's dorm. They were trailed by Crown and Strumpf who was kicking himself for not thinking of the last hint Carpenter had offered.

He knew that the commander had not been critical of their non-answers. They had been doing just what he wanted, but he wasn't about to praise them for repeating what he probably already knew.

Forbes thought he might try to sleep a bit and realized he had already been sleeping—for a long time. He paused and looked back at Strumpf who was about to turn toward the galley. His empty stomach prodded. "Got anything to eat?" He had been in long sleep for months.

"I might scrape up something," Strumpf offered.

"Anything to fill the void," Gonzalez chimed in.

"Yeah," Sharp agreed as three of them changed course for the galley.

Crown broke away and returned to the infirmary.

"It's not gonna be great: powdered or freeze-dried," Strumpf answered after his brief silence generated two more requests.

Commander Carpenter silently stepped into engineering after entering four passwords and answering the question prompted by each entry. He found three open sleep pods and no one about.

He hurried to Varlez's computer station. Schematics of the engines and their interior mounts were prominently displayed. He heard indecipherable dialog between Varlez and one assistant and saw the transcription flow onto a small corner of the screen. Any engine work on the *Marco P* was accompanied by discussion, argument, and ultimate agreement. The procedures for repair and the paths to consensus were recorded for future reference. The discussions, almost always heated, provided a learning experience and undeniably solid trouble-shooting expertise for anyone working with the engines, whether on board the *Marco P* or on any other ship with similar propulsion plants and in like areas of galactic space.

At first the commander questioned that dialog had taken place. He imagined that audio was connected with the graying of external vision: his pantomime with Navigator Maelstrom. He knew that, after a power stop, engineering was electronically isolated from the rest of the ship and completely shielded from electronic access, a self-contained entity inaccessible from without. What went on in engineering was a complete mystery to the bridge and MP, as if the ship had no power or that part of the computer's memory circuits had been excised.

Under exceptional circumstances like the *Marco P* was experiencing, the main computer had a dummy connection to engineering that, if used, shunted messages or orders or information into an electronic void unless a complicated series of passwords, questions, answers, and numerical sequences were properly entered by the commander. The encrypted coding was so advanced that cracking programs working at the Petabyte level didn't have the power or time to crack the code before the universe finally imploded.

The impenetrable firewall and shielding had been added to the *Marco P* by Engineer Varlez after he stumbled upon an obscure reference to an unnamed galactic species that had momentarily commandeered an Earth ship's main brain. He had then made the changes to the *Marco P*, but not without informing and querying Commander Carpenter who quickly agreed to the multi-layered safety procedure.

The power stop, sent by Navigator LeRoi, was a single pulse that by-passed Varlez's firewall. It was one of three independent commands the ship's brain could issue to protect the *Marco P* from disaster. However, the three codes were inherently self-destructive. Once any catastrophic command was sent, it could not be repeated or reset and the other two became impotent. Only the engineer could reinitiate the flash route and not until he and the commander agreed that the danger no longer existed.

Because of his engineer's expertise, the commander was confident that no virus, malware, Trojan, or dev-imp command could infect engineering or endanger the ship by controlling the engines. Even with his confidence in Varlez, though, Carpenter wondered if the engineer and his assistants were as ungrayed as Maelstrom was. As the other wakened members of his crew had thought, if not said, the recent events were also beyond the commander's experience. Despite the dialog he heard between Varlez and an assistant, he planned to mime and gesticulate as he had with Maelstrom.

Deep in thought Varlez appeared out of a small corridor leading from the starboard engine. He looked up and spied the commander looking at him from the computer station and started to speak. Carpenter rapidly shook his head. The engineer swallowed his greeting and turned back to look down the narrow corridor. Varlez raised his right arm and swivel his hand, palm forward. Then he turned back to Commander Carpenter.

In pantomime, the commander began the gist of his mute conversations with Maelstrom: had Varlez seen gray, not stars; was the *Marco P* on course.

"Commander," Varlez began aloud, ignoring Carpenter's gesturing for silence but understanding his miming, "we are unfettered here, regardless of what the rest of the ship may look like. We three have discussed much, and loudly, as you know we do sometimes. Come, look out one of our ports."

Varlez led the commander to a small access that looked out the starboard corridor. Carpenter saw space much like he had seen before bouncing off the bulkhead in his quarters.

"I saw that scene just after LeRoi woke me," Carpenter said. "It vanished after I talked with him. Why can I see space here?"

"Now, you know why engineering is sealed off from the rest of *Marco* after a power stop. This section doesn't exist, though I do wonder if we are seen as having no propulsion system."

"So, when I leave, the ports will be gray?"

"Probably. Something has control of the main computer and maybe those awake are under some kind of mass hypnosis, even you. Or the ship is under its influence."

"We weren't stopped?"

"Oh, we were stopped. That command got through. But I checked everything, redundancy, you know, and got us underway—that was the lurch I'm sure many felt—and following our projected course. If LeRoi can't see, we can. There's nothing in front of us. The engines are still a little out of sync. That stop did a little damage. We're working on correcting that now."

The engineer and the commander were involved with arm movements, hand bobs, and intent discussion, when Ticia

Bandi stepped out of the corridor from the port engine. Varlez was in the midst of showing how the engines were out of sync and was moving his fists back and forth, one just a little behind the other. He caught the blue of Ticia's jumpsuit out of the corner of one eye. Immediately he broke from his demonstration and waved her back into the corridor.

Bandi stopped. Puzzled and defiant, she took another step forward.

Varlez turned directly to her. He pointed a finger and waved her away mouthing "NOW."

Bandi had never experienced such dictatorial reaction from the engineer. She was unsure whether she should speak or not. For a moment she glared. But she read Varlez's threatening eyes and stepped back into the corridor.

"You know we're in unknown territory," the commander started.

"More so than we've been?" Varlez interrupted considering that the *Marco P* was hundreds of light years beyond the furthest Earth exploration.

"You know what I mean. We've never had the ship commandeered, if that's what's happened."

"Well, then, if that's what you think has happened, just how powerful do you think they are?"

"They didn't break your algorithm; engineering seems unaffected. We can see stars down here."

"Are you sure?" With his question, Varlez began his role of devil's advocate. "Maybe they did break it and they know what the firewall is supposed to do. If they're that powerful, they're toying with us, letting us believe that they didn't get into engineering. Don't you think?"

"How can we know?" the commander repeated Strumpf's recent question. He didn't have an answer then and he wasn't sure he had one now, but one was forming.

Varlez prodded, "Rather, does it make any difference? What choices do we have? Without some clue, any assumption leads to potential catastrophe."

Like Strumpf, the engineer was the other veteran member of the crew who could aid Carpenter's decisions. The commander had come to engineering to check out the status of the engines, but also for counsel. Varlez had done that with his last question.

"Let's assume they are that powerful," the commander said. "We've encountered their like before, and they haven't been malevolent. Some have been xenophobic and others extraordinarily curious. None ripped off our limbs."

"Maybe this species will," Varlez suggested with a facetious smirk.

"Then we'll have no option beyond destroying the *Marco* and removing the object to be violenced."

"If they let us do that. If they can implant sensory information and ideas ... and alter yours ..." Varlez didn't need to finish the thought.

"Then, no option at all," the commander acquiesced.

"Beyond the possibility that we are research material. We can fight or yield. Who can say what an alien power wants from its subjects?"

"Humans don't yield, except by choice, and definitely not without a fight." The commander looked at his engineer, but he was not seeing him. He was acknowledging the most defining human characteristic: self-determination. Freedom was an all-encompassing concept that spread out into many behaviors and characteristics. An indomitable spirit was one. In Earth's long history, no one maintained a despotic rule for very long. Might that finely held belief of self-determination serve the *Marco P* in these circumstances?

Engineer Varlez waited for his commander to continue and realized he was caught in deep thought. He stood quietly a little longer and then brought him back. "We're the first humans to invade this part of the galaxy ... aren't we?"

The commander shut down his speculation and looked down into his engineer's eyes. "We are and there may be races who've only heard of us or not. But it's been like that everywhere we've gone to settle uninhabited worlds."

"And we're certainly not unknown by other space-faring species, humans in the broadest definition of rational beings." Varlez was approaching the idea of exploration from the other side.

"Those aliens who visited Earth, encountered us in the

solar system, saw us in our backyard. We're a little different there, as anyone is in their own neighborhoods. We're not quite the same out here."

"And they should know that," Varlez agreed. "I'll bet other races are different at home from what they are in exploration."

"But are we really so different? Or they? Home and away? Aren't we all basically the same, wherever we are?"

"Asking me, or sorting out your own thoughts?"

Commander Carpenter chuckled. Varlez had again done exactly what he wanted. It didn't make any difference whether he, or any of the crew, knew what was going on, or whether the aliens who had apparent control of the *Marco P* were malevolent or not. The crew would act as humans always acted— as if they were in control. How could they be different? They would show whoever or whatever had control of their ship just what humans did and make the best of what befell them.

Carpenter shook his head slightly and realized Varlez had patiently waited for some word in reaction to his question. He smiled slightly and chuckled again. "Thanks, Jerry. I knew you had the answers."

"Don't know what you're talking about. I just question."

"Keep thinking that way. I'm sure I knew what had to be done. I think you might want to open up engineering to the main brain."

"Been thinking about that."

"We'll just see what happens. That is why we're out here."

"And to reaffirm: that humans have never encountered dismembering beings doesn't mean we won't or these aren't," Varlez jibed.

"And that makes the unknown still a little disconcerting, doesn't it?"

"Only because we fear failure. We're seeking the unknown and we expect to conquer it. Maybe this time we won't."

"Can't approach it with that attitude. I'll leave you to your work." Commander Carpenter again nodded thanks to the engineer and turned to leave his counselor's study. He didn't like not knowing, but he always bet on human nature succeeding. So far, that wager had always taken the pot.

SYSTEM

Central Reception probed: *Acquisition?*

Acquisition: *Earther ship accessed. Basic brain structure— one exception.*

CR: *Automaton?*

A: *Brain interfaced with computer.*

CR: *Controls commandeered?*

A: *Commandeered.*

CR: *Earthers?*

A: *Earthers.*

CR: *How many?*

A:. *Six and one interfaced consciousness.*

CR: *Contained?*

A: *Targeting vocalization ... Active brains accessed ... Overwriting stored space and star recognition files. Make that number ten; four more acknowledged.*

CR: *Holding vessel?*

A: *Holding.*

CR: *Destination?*

A: *Earther title, γ-Cygnus A2.*

CR to Astrographics: *Identify γ-Cygnus A2.*

AS: *Uninhabited second planet in Mqros system.*

CR: *Create visual sequence of flight to Mqros2 from current position.*

CR: *Engineering. Connected?*

E: *Connected. Accessing vessel space, distance.*

CR: *Tunnel?*

E: *Setting parameters. Formed.*

A: *Lock on.*

CR: *Engineering, Insert astrographic visual to Mqros2 and run as Earther ship follows controlled route to Molx.*

E: *Inserted.*

CR: *Release visual hold.*

CR: *All conscious Molrixx, unique Earthers: Galactic youth: Information deficient: Illogical novelty.*

ALIENS

Skirting the *Marco P's* course, and running cloaked at the edge of the human vessel's sensor reach, a Xantrel scout ship, the *Borsac,* broadcast intriguing information to all neighboring civilizations. "The first Earther ship, far beyond their rapacious planetary acquisitions, is traveling through the expanse of the second band of our spiral galaxy, an area Earthers called the Orion-Cygnus Arm.

The *Borsac* added the 95% probability that the vessel from the Sol system was headed for uninhabited Mqros 2.

Main Office, Lead of the *Borsac,* added his droll comment that the Earther's projected trajectory passed close to Molx, the sole planet in the Olkren system and an orb all neighboring races had learned to avoid. Long ago, the Molrixx had demonstrated an assumed, but unconfirmed, predatory nature.

Local space-faring societies—within two hundred light years, a journey of ten to twenty light/dark planetary revolutions, depending on a ship's power accessing dark matter—one after the other, had invited the Molrixx to join their federation of developed civilizations. However, each planetary society had lost contact with its emissaries to Molx shortly after the mission sent word that it had landed on the planet. Nor could any world discover proof that their ambassadors were ever on Molx beyond transmissions of arrival—not bodies, destroyed ships, or power emanations.

When the Molrixx were bluntly questioned from space about foreign emissaries, since all races feared sending more citizens to Molx, the Molrixx denied that any off-worlders had ever landed on their planet. They repeatedly stated, politically gentle at first then angrily, that they had no use for outsiders or their planetary federation.

The Molrixx's rejection of association with other species seemed impossibly foolish to those seeking to expand relationships, especially since Molx had been experiencing unresolved ecological devastation for decades. Even when the promise was tendered to help reverse the climate and return the planet to a vegetative paradise, as records reported that it once was, the spokesperson for the Molrixx demanded, "Leave us alone!" and severed transmission.

Having lost patience at repeated attempts to befriend the Molrixx, all local civilizations, especially those who had lost ambassadors sent to Molx and others who rejected such futile missions, surrounded the ungrateful, savage xenophobes with shared shielding technology. They posted warning buoys that beamed cautions to any travelers approaching Molx. They installed mini-satellites at synchronous points to generate a modest force field to complement the buoys.

Occasionally, in an unnecessary need to police their nefarious neighbors, but one grown from natural curiosity, the locals occasionally wandered near enough to see if the Molrixx had reversed from the apparent madness they had fallen victim to after the planet grew more inhospitable or if they had managed to enslave more unknowing travelers who either didn't understand the broadcast warnings or were somehow unaffected by the force barrier.

The mistakenly unshielded Xantrel message about the Earthers reached the Molrixx, well before Navigator LeRoi and the *Marco P's* computer recognized that their destination, γ-Cygnus A2, an inner planet of γ-Cygnus A, was barely in extreme sensor range.

"Should the Earthers be warned about the Molrixx?" a distant Vocres transfer ship, *Alroche*, responded to the Xantrel information.

"No," Main Office answered. "Announcements from other species cannot help them. You know how they are. They take no direction; we'd be wasting our efforts. Let them learn the hard way."

"I suppose that's best," Primpt, First Staff of the *Alroche*, responded.

The Vocres had long before encountered evidence of Earthers. A small Vocres scout ship once met a transport ship of the Grotz with whom they had before only traded voice transmissions. One of their exchanges was about the Grotz's rendezvous with an upstart species that tried to take possession of a world they were interested in. The Grotz might have engaged military action had the Earthers not been persuaded to leave the planet.

"Maybe they will make the ultimate mistake," the *Borsac* returned. "We'll not have to worry about them reaching our worlds." It was a standard comment from ancient space-farers when much younger races began to explore the galaxy and encroach in other galactic races' outer territory.

Earthers were recognized as willful adolescents to space travel and were extending their presence in the galaxy. They followed no accepted exploratory guidelines and took no advice beyond their own experience and foolish bravery.

"Perhaps," The *Alroche* offered another wishful foolishness, "they will overcome the Molrixx and we won't have to worry about those xenophobes."

"Neither of our missions escaped," was the haughty Zantrel reply. "Theirs isn't likely,"

"Neither was their sudden discovery of the Qionac Drive ..."

"You know, they had help with their faster than light," was a crass interruption and a more blunt implication from the *Borsac*. The Xantrels long believed that the Vocres, on one of their far-flung exploratory missions, had supplied Earth with the technology of far older species to travel between star systems. Most older races, the Xantrels included, believed that Earthers, infantile in comparison to advanced galactic civilizations, should not be roaming the galaxy any sooner than according to the evolutionary timetable of those who had grown into their sprawling federation. However, Earthers were an anomaly; they didn't take the expected technological hesitant steps other space-faring races had.

"Then they must listen sometimes," came an immediate Vocres rebut that neither denied nor affirmed the Xantrel consensus. "We should inform them."

"Let them learn the hard way," was the Xantrel's repeated cold line.

"Maybe they'll show some expertise, escape, and be able to join the rest of us."

"Or they'll be so awed at their loss, they'll run back home."

"And stop their meddling ..." The remainder of the comment was lost as the Vocres and Xantrel ships raced out of each other's range for normal communication. Neither wished to expend the energy for repeating common suppositions and gibes at long range.

SYSTEM

Central Reception to all: *The universe has grown.*
Central Reception unmasked the flood of off-planet information to all.

Synchronous transceivers positioned about Molx had transmitted the Xantrel unshielded information to Central Reception that then relayed it to all databases of megacities on Molx. Immediately Central Reception commanded a data search for "Earthers" and any similar word. Spotty information culled from the recently unlocked transmissions of other galactic roaming species generated—instantaneously—a small database offering characteristics of an upstart young species. Salient points were passed among the Molrixx's combined and downloaded brains whose universe had suddenly expanded to the infinite though none recalled when it wasn't unbounded. The newly generated database grew from bits gleaned from stored information.

Further out, younger.
Recent entry to galactic exploration.
Call themselves human.
Infected with emotion.
> *Like we once possessed?*
> *And will again?*
Different.
Emotion rules their decisions.
> *Not like we possessed.*
> *We might possess.*
Visitors to their planet, Earth, found them illogical, intriguing.
> *Something called free will corrupts their actions.*
Are they useful?
> *To compare?*
> *To us?*
They have no knowledge of us.
> *Nor for us that we don't already have.*
> *Except for free will.*
None will warn them, the second transmission said.

    A research?
    More.
Search the past before others escaped.
They are coming here.
Make sure.
They are known as gamesters. They play tricks on themselves.
    What are tricks?
Nothing in memory matches "tricks."
    Bring them closer.
    We can observe and incorporate.
Prevent their flight.
    What is their destination?
Meaningless information. They are captured.

ALIENS

Primt of the Vocres transport *Alroche*, who had wondered whether the *Marco P* should be warned about the Molrixx, had second thoughts about leaving the most recent spacers trespassing in his arm of the galaxy and encountering the quarantined Molrixx.

After his unshielded conversation with the Xantrel scout ship *Borsac* broke off, he reversed course and increased speed to close on and shadow the Earther vessel. When he neared enough to be seen on distant acquisition by the Earthers and the Molrixx, were his ship not shielded, he announced to his crew and in long-range shielded messages to other ships in the quadrant, "We've heard rumors of Earthers for some time. They have extended their planetary settlements far from their home. So far, their expansion that acquires uninhabited planets has not been troublesome as many feared. They are cautious in establishing dialog with other civilizations. We can now watch how they act and what makes them unique as a species and perhaps discover the mystique that underlies their success. I welcome any to come shielded and observe."

The *Borsac* was the first to reply. Its Main Office acknowledged the chance to observe and maybe learn something about the brash species that was taking possession of more planets than any bureaucracy could ever hope to manage. "We will join you. We are anxious to learn about them. However, we will not attempt save them from the Molrixx."

Primt of the *Alroche* proclaimed, "Nor is our intention to do for them what they cannot do for themselves. We have allowed the Molrixx to rid our sector of many space interlopers. There is little indication that Earthers are more than unneeded growths, though they have not acted rapaciously as the planet-bound Molrixx do."

"And if the Earthers should actually escape ..."

"Are the Xantrels that foolish," Primt interrupted.

"*IF* they do," Main Office continued, "we may have more to worry about than we think. No one has yet escaped the

Molrixx."

"They may pose problems. Can they be so advanced and so naive at the same time?" Primt paused as he looked at the telemetry from the *Marco P.* "They've been captured. They didn't recognize our quarantine buoys. Their trajectory is altered. They are headed directly for Molx, but their instrumentation reports they are on course for Mqros 2."

"There may be nothing to observe," Main Office responded and shut his transmission.

During the two-way conversation, three other ships, all planetary civilizations that had lost emissary missions to Molx, messaged that they were interested in watching the Earthers' come-uppance. Chief of the Mqros 4 ship, *Vento*, was the first of the three to respond to Primt's last message. "We'll watch with you, but it shouldn't be for long," as he echoed Main Office's comment. "And we won't have to worry about Earthers taking over one of our planets, even if it is a place we'd never settle.

MARCO P

No sooner had Malcolm Carpenter left engineering, than Ticia Bandi stomped from the port access where she had eavesdropped on the conversation between engineer and commander. Even in her tight-fitting blue work suit, she hardly appeared feminine and her close-cropped auburn hair did nothing to announce her gender. Her defiant black eyes stared at Varlez from a face radiating disgust.

She held her short slender frame statue-still until Varlez turned his head toward her and slightly lifted his chin. She had not understood his order for privacy, even if he was talking to the commander. Nor did she realize Nequa Arafa had not been present.

Varlez and his two assistants always shared engineering discussions. More, the three of them had already arrived at the very conclusion the commander seemed to decide on, which Carpenter would have seen had he scrolled back the corner transcription visible on the main engineering screen.

Not long after Bandi joined Varlez, Arafa—also stuffed into a blue jumpsuit—exited from the starboard access. That she was female was not in doubt, though her square face and wide-set brown eyes were topped by a smooth shaved scalp. The curves Ticia lacked, Arafa possessed in abundance. Both were almost three inches taller than Varlez.

As soon as Arafa completed the engineering trio, Bandi, who had been recruited to the *Marco P* at the beginning of the current voyage, demanded of Varlez before he had a chance to explain his action, "Is he that slow? How'd he ever get to command?"

Arafa shot a "don't go there" stare at Bandi and shook her head, but Bandi didn't catch the message as she was glaring at Varlez. Arafa could have recounted the brief episode of the two veteran spacers who had questioned Carpenter on his first command, but she knew that story was inappropriate, as it upstaged Engineer Varlez. She knew he would explain his order to Bandi in his own understated manner. Later, if given the chance, she would tell Bandi the incident.

"Ticia," Varlez began, "you haven't been with the commander very long."

Bandi looked the question with "So?" and almost got out another disparaging remark before Varlez continued in soft words.

"He wasn't looking for answers; he never does. He already knows."

"Then what was he doing here?" Still indignant, Bandi interrupted the unhurried explanation from the engineer. "And why couldn't I join you?" She planted both hands on her narrow hips.

"For precisely the reason you are upset with me and questioning the commander's ability. You might have ended up like a famous pair, long ago, and I would have lost a very good engineer." That brief explanation stripped away some of Bandi's rancor and her rigid back loosened.

"That's nice to know ... how you feel about my work. But I still don't understand."

"The commander was here for information not answers," Varlez said, glanced at Arafa who nodded approval, and looked back at his newest assistant. "He knew we three had already stormed what might cause a power stop command, why the navigator might have agreed with the computer. We're cut off from the rest of the ship when a catastrophic action is taken."

"I still don't understand," Bandi repeated, her anger replaced by questions and fear from being totally lost.

Arafa shifted her weight to her left foot as a slight curve twisted the left side of her mouth. On an earlier mission, she had gone through the same anger Bandi was experiencing, but for not following explicit directions and causing an engine malfunction. Varlez had been just as calming with her then, as he was now.

He continued, "The commander knew what the rest of the crew thought before he ever got to us. He did let me in on the circumstance that they all saw gray out the ports. Not stars," Varlez paused thoughtfully, "except for maybe one. That's why he was interested in what we could and did see."

Varlez thought he saw a twitch of smile and more softening

of Bandi's angry stance.

She shifted her legs and relaxed her shoulders. She took a thoughtful breath and almost nodded agreement.

The engineer continued, "I only told him what he suspected, but he had to hear it from me and see here what he couldn't see forward."

"You mean he came to see if we agreed with what he already had in mind?" Bandi asked.

Arafa smiled widely and nodded. A silent laugh jerked her diaphragm and jiggled her bosom. "Not nearly what you thought, was it?" she asked.

"I suppose I was remiss," Varlez apologized, "that I didn't tell you about the commander's behavior sooner. But we've had a rather uneventful voyage. That should have been a warning to me. I intended to tell you; I just never got around to it. Then the disaster hit. I saw you charge out of the access. I had to keep you out of the way."

"No harm, Jer," Bandi said. "I was pretty hot ... at you ... and the commander. But I guess you're right. I'll know next time."

"If there is one," Arafa added a serious thought. "If we agreed with the commander, we might be in for a very tense and difficult time. I can't remember any human ship being controlled for a long time, if that's what's happened."

"You're right," Varlez agreed. "Lotsa laughs at my excessive safety firewalls and endless passwords and redundant computer down here. But I think we've just been given the reason for the safeguards ... if they worked ... or will."

"Then, this is serious?" A somber Bandi sounded more than worried.

"Maybe fatally so," Varlez answered. "Benevolent alien contact is never assured. Our explorations have been exceedingly favorable for a long time. This one may prove the exception."

"If that's the case," Arafa asked, "what happens? I know we send regular log transmissions. What happens when they stop?"

"Doesn't someone come looking for us?" Bandi asked.

"No ... unfortunately for us," was the engineer's somber

answer. "We're too far out for anyone to try and rescue. When there are no further transmissions from the ship—after a long lapse—we'll be assumed lost, destroyed, or taken prisoner. Not pleasant thoughts. But you know, Ticia, that's the lot of the explorer."

Bandi slowly nodded. She knew that. She had signed on for a chance at discovering the wonders and grandeur of the galaxy, at least a small part of it. Despite the excitement, dashing through the emptiness of space with its dangers and unknowns was hardly the sole reason to explore. Though easy to dismiss in favor of the brighter allure and excitement of discovery, the downside danger, always lurked near.

On Malcolm Carpenter's return to the bridge, Navigator LeRoi greeted him with better news than he gave shortly after waking the commander. "The stars are back, sir. I don't know what caused the gray, maybe a computer glitch. I can't even find the gray in memory sequences."

"Doesn't explain the gray out the ports. Are we on course?" the commander asked.

"Aye, sir," came proper and official word. "Even the power stop didn't cost any time, though we programmed leeway into the voyage. Star charts and the projected trajectory are what they've been. We're on schedule as if nothing happened."

Carpenter didn't react to his navigator's speculation. But he inspected the fourteen monitor screens that showed a familiar scattering of stars. "Carry on, Navigator."

The commander had passed enough portholes on his return to the bridge to know that the gray was gone. It had taken Varlez and his two crewmates little time to adjust the engines and reinitialize them and then slip back into Qion Drive. Still the *Marco P's* being under the control of some alien race was a frightening possibility, especially if that control also fooled engineering.

He thought about paying another visit to Priscilla Maelstrom. However, the poignant discussion with Varlez and the possibility that the intelligence holding his ship in its power had by-passed all security measures was foremost in his thoughts. If the alien force was that powerful, it could be controlling Maelstrom's observations, too, making them no more accurate than anyone else's. If that intelligence could read minds, his miming in her cabin had been understood. He still thought that there was a chance the alien mind had not recognized or understood their gestured conversation. Besides, his intuition assured him that the aliens were merely interested in what humans were like.

He remained on the bridge and planned an enjoyable anticipation of human nature's battle plans. If aliens wanted to discover about Earthlings, he'd help them out. When the time came, his crew and settlers would demonstrate humanity: rational and emotional, cooperative and anarchic, obedient and willful, caring and unconcerned—the essence of contradiction all wound up in every individual.

He decided his backup navigator would be fine, though most impatient at her forced seclusion. And, if the aliens didn't read the mime and gestures between them, the humans would regale the aliens with creativity, an indomitable spirit, and rebellion. The underlying supports for all human characteristics would be glaring and unlikely understood or prepared for.

However, if LeRoi's reaction to now seeing stars was the same as everyone else's who had been wakened before the ship stopped—except for one, the aliens were probably not the wiser or even aware of what he and engineering had considered. He decided not to let his basic premise leak to anyone. He needed to see Strumpf and further hone his thoughts.

"Wake the rest of the crew and the settlers," he ordered the navigator.

"Aye, sir," LeRoi answered. "Should I make Strumpf and Crown aware?"

"Yes. They need to be ready. Keep a close eye on our course and inform the settler-leads that they should begin preliminary preparations for planet fall. Oh, do not wake Maelstrom."

"Sir?"

"Leave her as she is."

"Aye, sir." Roger LeRoi couldn't be more pleased. He was the nexus for all the ship's important concerns. Without Maelstrom awake that disposition would not change any time soon.

The commander left the bridge and headed for the galley

and the connected hydroponic gardens, the source of special menu surprises and plants that would not need a full growing cycle once settlers landed. He didn't think Strumpf had openly discussed the possibility of the *Marco P* being controlled, even if he thought it. Still he had to find out and sidetrack what might ensue if he had.

SYSTEM

Central Reception: *All Molrixx, the Earther vessel is under our control. Their destination, Mqros 2 has been overwritten. They will arrive at Molx but their passage will be shown as their intended course to Mqros 2.*

Acquisition: *We will add their unique characteristics to our collective database.*

CR: *First additions to our knowledge bank since the Xantrels and others quarantined us long ago.*

A: *New information.*

CR: *To break the quarantine?*

A: *Not enough data.*

Central Reception shut down everything including itself and Acquisition but left a solitary drive that monitored the approach of the *Marco P* FSS-14 with instructions to wake them when the Earthers were near orbit.

MARCO P

Malcolm Carpenter found Strumpf in the galley. Three relaxing settlement leads were finishing up some dried fruit,
stale crackers, and water. Just out of hibernation, they were still
experiencing periods of half-conscious lethargy.

Four hails greeted the commander as he entered the galley and he acknowledged each with nods but didn't pause at
the snacking table for further comment. Instead he jockeyed
through tables to reach George Strumpf, who was reorganizing
supplies and dishes and utensils for when the galley was open
for eating and relaxing.

As the commander passed their table, Sharp said to Forbes
and Gonzalez, "We'd better get back to the settlement dorm.
We don't need to eavesdrop."

"As if we could," Forbes snorted and stacked their plates
and brushed the crumbs from their noshing onto the deck. He
stood and led the three out of the galley.

George Strumpf had seen the commander enter, offer
slight recognition to the off-hand greetings, and continue to
him. "So?" he asked when the commander stood before him.

Instead of answering, Carpenter looked back where the
colony leads had been sitting. He observed their exit and waited until their steps disappeared down the corridor before turning back. "Tell me, Strumpf," the commander never used first
names when he was in his official capacity, "what do you think
..."

"About?"

Carpenter paused at Strumpf's interruption, "... and
what've you told anyone about what's happened, stars ... no
stars ... stars."

"You know me well enough, Malcolm," Strumpf was not
going to let the commander force him into something more
than a simple chat between two old friends, "I haven't said anything about that except that it's strange and agree with whatever anyone else says, which hasn't been much."

"So you haven't openly conjectured about the situation?"

"Not openly. I've had a few thoughts but haven't said any-thing to anyone about what I think is going on."

"And that is?" Carpenter pried.

"You know I listen to space chatter. Until translation de-codes the languages—never takes too long—I don't know what's being said, but there's almost always several active channels other races use. At the beginning when we run into a new language, it's mostly just sounds. You know, squeals, squawks, tones, that sort of thing; occasionally it's quite me-lodic, a space symphony. Until the translator figures out the language, we can't understand what they're saying. But that's not why I'm interested in tuning in. The more chatter there is, the more populated and technological the sector is. The Ori-on-Cygnus arm is pretty populated, not dense by any standard. We already know that, even if we haven't made contact with many races and translated many of their tongues."

Strumpf adjusted his stance and with a clatter set down the tray of utensils he was holding and stretched out his arms. "But now, since we're awake, it's almost as if we're being avoid-ed or shunned or we've slipped into a waste-space." He looked hard into the face of his friend the commander. He intended his next statement confidential and dogmatic. "When the navi-gator woke me and since then, even now, there's no chatter on any frequency. It's dead quiet out there. You have to wonder why. In a section of the galaxy that had been teeming with the evidence of civilized life and humming with conversations be-tween intelligent species, if that's what they are, silence has to be very odd."

"Okay," Carpenter agreed, "assuming we haven't encoun-tered a part of Orion-Cygnus that is hiding behind a natural shield." He paused as he considered an implication of his as-sumption.

"Are you suggesting that we've travelled beyond life and there is no technological civilization within ear or this space has been walled off?"

"It's possible. What's *your* explanation?"

"Unlikely." Strumpf spoke to the commander's conjecture and slowly shook his head twice. "I'm not sure I have one." He stared past Carpenter as he arranged his thoughts. "There's nothing in our annals of exploration that speaks to this kind of silence, except where there's no civilization, no technology, no life. And we know that's not the case. Not all of a sudden. Not when the chatter had been insistent and multi-channeled before we went into long sleep."

"You haven't answered me, George." Carpenter prodded with a growing smile and twinkling eyes. He knew where his friend and confidante was headed.

Strumpf matched the smile and nodded. "But you know all this, don't you."

"Continue. I'm sure you know."

"We've entered the space of a very powerful civilization, a lot more powerful and technologically advanced than we may have ever imagined."

"I think that's clear," the commander said with an inflection that demanded more.

"So, I wondered why all the silence. Chatter follows technology. Why, we have even run past some of the radio and TV transmissions from Earth. But *nothing* here; not even those old programs that should still be streaming past." Strumpf paused to let his good friend inject something if he wanted.

Carpenter was content to listen.

"I had to ask myself, why a civilization might mute its transmissions or, maybe, have them muted. Centuries ago a sci-fi author posited a civilization whose solar system, *the whole system,* mind you, was surrounded and kept in quarantine because the life form residing there was a danger to the *galaxy.*"

"A whole solar system enclosed?" Carpenter was incredulous. In all his reading he'd never read such a tale. "Dyson-style? What could imperil the entire galaxy?"

"Yeah, pretty far-fetched and in the story the evil was unleashed and then eventually defeated. But, what if we're near something like that?"

"If so, how'd we get close or within its quarantine? What kind of perilous civilization could be contained through shielded transmissions? And if we're within the shield, why haven't we heard their chatter? How'd we get through?"

"Malcolm, I don't know. But I think we're not doing what we think we're doing. Almost certainly not going where we think we're going."

"So where'd we miss the warning buoy?"

"There may not be one, or maybe not many. If this civilization doesn't have space travel and still has the ability to control brains, other civilizations that know about them have merely cloaked themselves from being controlled or discovered. We don't have that ability. We may be stuck and not in control, even of ourselves." Strumpf paused for effect and then said, "We'll play the role we've been given."

"I think you have it figured pretty well. Engineering seems to agree. We continue as if nothing's happened and watch carefully. Eventually we'll get more information."

"And then we'll do what humans have always done. We'll conquer." Strumpf was not boasting. That trait wasn't in him. He was encapsulating centuries of actual human exploration and before that tens of decades of science fiction speculation that always prophesied human superiority in the galaxy.

Despite the lack of technology to match older races or the belligerence to quash brash emerging ones, humans had successfully withstood attacks, sabotage, subversion, and self-implosion. Humans *were* superior.

Alien races would never admit that belief to a human. But among themselves they were awed that a late-comer race expanding its existence so far from its home planet possessed such spirit. Nor were those alien races ever successful in analyzing to conclusion the impossible secret humans possessed.

"Or die trying." Carpenter offered what used to be called *knock on wood* or *famous last words*. "And our demise will make sure no one follows. We become the sacrifice."

Commander Carpenter had protected his second navigator from disturbances and kept her as a control for what he and the rest of the crew were infected with, if he were correct. After his brief discussion with George Strumpf he returned to the bridge, saw LeRoi involved with the trajectory of the ship, and asked how nominal the course was.

"Perfect," the navigator answered without turning to the commander. "*Marco*'s following the plotted course. Preliminary images and information are exactly what I'm seeing."

"Have the crew and settlers been wakened?"

"I sent the proper alert to everyone, except Maelstrom ... as you ordered. The ship is awake. Early preparations for descent and taking possession are underway."

"Good, Navigator. Stay on top of things. If anything changes, notify me immediately."

"Aye, sir."

The commander left the bridge and entered his ready room opposite the navigator's cubicle. There he prepared official orders with signature—little more than a long note establishing a very specific procedure for one member of his crew—until he personally countermanded the orders with voice command. He folded the paper in thirds, lengthwise, and carried it to the compartment of Navigator Priscilla Maelstrom.

Commander Carpenter waited until he was sure no one was in the corridor before he rapped the pass code. Two quick knocks followed by two more quick knocks on her door revealed a navigator, in proper uniform, who appeared thankful and hopeful that she might be freed from her compartment imprisonment.

Commander Carpenter was ready for her eager reaction, which he squelched again with a shake of his head and a finger to his lips.

Maelstrom's spirits fell. Her shoulders sagged, her light blue eyes darkened, and she sighed as her lips hid her teeth. She stepped back and the commander entered her compartment. The door slid closed behind him.

Carpenter glanced around the compartment. Electronic access was still disabled; no slow pulsing blue light indicating active access or messaging. Transmission or reception of anything outside the compartment was not possible.

The commander knew Maelstrom had spent a lonely time since he had wakened her. He regretted that the sentence had to be lengthened, and for how long he hadn't a clue. But, if he were correct in his basic supposition—both Strumpf and Varlez agreed with him—Maelstrom might hold the secret to surviving the peril that had entrapped the *Marco P* and its human cargo.

Commander Carpenter held out the folded paper.

Navigator Maelstrom took a deep breath, unfolded the orders, and began to read. Nor did she exhale. Her face turned serious as she scanned down the page. Then her breath escaped and she re-read slowly and deliberately from the top.

Navigator Priscilla Maelstrom:

The **Marco P** *is awake and preparations are underway for taking possession of* γ-Cygnus **A2**. *No one, except for me, knows you are awake. You will not receive any alarm to wake. If you are required to descend to the planet, I will summon you. Until that time you will remain in your compartment, as if in hibernation. You will contact no one and you will continue to keep all communication devices inactive. I will provide you with food at random intervals to maintain the ruse. You may soon be bored at solitary, if not already. You may fight that by sleeping and reading, but you must not reactivate your sleep-pod. For the time being, you do not exist. I do not know how long these extreme measures must be maintained. The safety of the ship and the success of this settlement may depend solely on you.*

Commander Malcolm Carpenter

Over the top of his written orders held at chest level, a dejected Maelstrom looked up at the commander. Solitary confinement was not an option she ever considered on an exploratory and settlement mission. There were stories of ships being captured and crews imprisoned for short times—sometimes in solitary. But those incidents were brief, until the alien race realized humans bore them no ill-will and were not a danger to their way of life. But to be imprisoned on her own ship, and by the commander himself, that shouted danger beyond what she understood explorers and settlers might encounter.

She knew it was futile to gesticulate "how long." The commander had written he didn't know. She knew Malcolm Carpenter was waiting for her acceptance of his orders. Then she saw something in the commander's eyes, and something else on his normally kind face. Apology? These orders were not lightly given. She had seen similar looks, usually held by those who were uncertain they would see someone again.

Maelstrom drew in a long breath and let it out. Though the

Marco P was hardly a military vessel nor did the commander have a military rank, she stood at attention and crisply saluted. Her hyperbole, not ironic, drew from the commander a quick smile that vanished just as quickly.

Then the backup navigator held the orders out and nodded. Malcolm Carpenter noticed that she held the writing facing him and her index finger that she waggled was pointing to his last sentence: the safety of the ship and crew was paramount.

This time his smile did not disappear.

The commander turned to the door and listened. The corridor was empty. He slid open the door, rapped three times in quick succession, and looked at Maelstrom. She nodded and held up three fingers. Carpenter stepped through the entry and it slid shut behind him. Immediately he heard the lock set.

Momentarily he stood outside the compartment and almost relented. He had never before issued such stern orders.

His ship had also never been in such catastrophic danger.

Navigator LeRoi had not moved since the last time the commander issued an order to his back. The heavy cable formed from the individual implants and protruding from the interface cap where the bump on the back of the skull jutted out above the spine sagged a little and lay across the navigator's right shoulder. It angled across his right wrist that rested on the counter where he sat. Its connection to MP was hidden behind the screen directly in front of the navigator.

Carpenter looked carefully at LeRoi's head canted back on his neck and against the back of the chair. It was motionless. The commander caught the long breaths common to napping and noticed the rhythmic expansion of the navigator's chest. Though not officially excusable, short naps were understandable, though not with a backup navigator available. However, the computer, constantly aware and incapable of sleep, should have recognized the human connected to it was in physical standby mode. With the commander standing behind its adjunct, MP ought to have wakened the navigator. The commander watched for more than three minutes after he returned from Maelstrom's compartment. The navigator never once moved.

Nor did movement follow the stern call of "Navigator." Carpenter repeated slower and louder, "NAVIGATOR."

Roger LeRoi's back stiffened and his head rolled forward just a little. "Sir-r?" he questioned in two syllables that jerked from a rumbled bass to a short falsetto. He didn't turn to look at the commander. He knew his red eyes would betray his unauthorized nap. Instead he blinked rapidly to remove the sleep and be clear eyed when he was ordered to face the commander.

That embarrassment would not be demanded. Instead Carpenter asked a question he already knew the answer to, "How long before we orbit γ-Cygnus A2?"

The just woken navigator went through the motions of gathering information from his screens. Then he stared at a screen to his left and read the banner flowing across its bottom. "We are slowing from max Qionac and γ-Cygnus A2 is still this side of γ-Cygnus A," he repeated the banner that Malcolm Carpenter had already read. "Seven days is the estimate to synchronous orbit."

"That's a little soon, isn't it?" The question demanded detailed explanation from LeRoi. The commander reminded the navigator that, when he repeated his set of questions and before the navigator had agreed to a power stop, the *Marco P* was five weeks away from their destination.

LeRoi turned to face the commander. "It is," he said and felt his face warm as he remembered an earlier order he had not responded to. "We must be in a more energetic Qion field. Can't be too bad a thing, getting there sooner. I'll bet that was the gray and the lurch, getting caught up in a more energetic tunnel."

"That's as good an explanation as I might think of," Carpenter praised and immediately added a reprimand, letting the navigator know that he had been caught sleeping. "You didn't tell me until I asked. You were supposed to inform me of any change in course."

"Yes, sir, I … I didn't think it was important." LeRoi felt a blush warm the back of his neck and hoped it wouldn't creep forward.

"If there are any further changes, you will inform me *immediately*."

"Yes, sir; I will … immediately." LeRoi hoped he had escaped this time. Reason and history told him differently, but he saw no criticism on the commander's face.

Commander Carpenter solved the problem of feeding Maelstrom by taking his meals, much heavier than he was accustomed to eat, in his ready room and having them delivered at odd hours. Frequently Nozing brought the meals. After his second delivery, Nozing normally returned the prior meal's dishes to the galley. Sometimes he returned with nothing, as the commander, just to keep from habit and to make his actions disordered, had returned the dishes himself.

The odd eating pattern Malcolm Carpenter suddenly acquired didn't go unnoticed by Strumpf. He had shipped with the commander long enough to know that he never did things without purpose. He was sure the change in the commander's eating behavior had to do with his belief that the *Marco P* was under alien control.

The solution to that conjecture didn't appear until the *Marco P* was declared in orbit above γ-Cygnus A2. Then the revelation struck: backup navigator Maelstrom had not been around, maybe still asleep, or restricted to her quarters for some reason. Strumpf couldn't believe that he had been unaware that her striking beauty had not once graced his galley after the ship was wakened.

MARCO P

Through seven days prior to achieving synchronous orbit the settlers checked equipment for building, farming, and protection against ferals, should they exist, and analyzing long-range scans of flora. They reviewed plans for growing and sheltering themselves from the elements while they wrestled abodes and fields from the expected wild topography of uncivilized γ-Cygnus A2.

They were about to be pioneers as their ancient ancestors had been on Earth. They would possess communication technology that used Qion fields to message home and other human settlements, but massive earthmoving equipment was impractical. Lasers and rechargeable power supplies substituted for primitive axes and saws. When settlements grew to three or four times the original size through the addition of immigrants and luddites, who rejected modern technology yet demanded to live in primitive conditions that technology provided and they needed to expand their original territory, supply ships would have arrived with more modern equipment and larger construction modules. After a few decades, the settlement on γ-Cygnus A2 would look pretty much like any human town.

Finally, Navigator LeRoi sent his bittersweet message to Commander Carpenter, "Sir, the *Marco P* is in synchronous orbit above γ-Cygnus A2."

"Thank you for the information. I'm on the bridge, navigator. I can see." Then he prodded, "Isn't this star's image supposed to be about the size of Sol? Just a little smaller at this distance?"

"Yes, sir. That's why we're about the distance Venus is from the sun. γ-Cygnus A2 should be very close to Earth's climate. That's what our probes sent back."

"Does that central star look like the sun's size from Earth, especially as close as we are to it?"

"The computer says it's our destination, sir and the stellar array around our destination, sent back by the probe, is what's on my computer screens."

"Get away from your screens and look out a porthole," Carpenter ordered. "You know what the sun looks like from Earth, don't you?"

"I do, sir. Do I have to?" LeRoi's plaintive question was more about leaving his screens than having to look at what he was sure was the commander's foolish rebuttal to MP's certainty.

"Get over here and look."

LeRoi pulled on the extension that allowed his movement away from his cubicle. "That's what it looks like, sir," he repeated his earlier statement when he looked out the port.

"Unplug yourself and look again," the commander demanded.

LeRoi disconnected the physical cable from the back of his helmet. That maneuver activated a power mod in his helmet that enabled wireless connection to MP. "Won't make a difference, sir; the computer still overrides my physical senses." Roger LeRoi stepped closer to a port. "I don't see a difference, sir. That's what the sun looks like from Earth orbit."

"No, it doesn't," Carpenter said. "That's not γ-Cygnus A." The commander felt his anger bubble. He wasn't sure that this wasn't one more bad joke LeRoi was pulling or if the navigator was losing it. "I don't know what that star is, but it's not where we're supposed to be."

"You know better than the computer?" LeRoi's question was tinged with a hint of impertinence.

"What's the mass of Sol?" Carpenter asked.

The navigator's statistic was immediately provided by MP. "Almost 2×10 to the 30th kilograms."

"You've got that right," the commander agreed. "What about this star?"

"A little smaller; 1.7×10 to the 30th." The MP computed mass flowed from LeRoi's lips.

"My measurements tell me it's only 1.25 times," Carpenter corrected.

"Your measurements must be wrong, ... sir." The navigator knew he was getting in deeper, but he hated to be corrected or have the computer challenged.

Carpenter offered an explanation and an out for his navigator, who knew he had used up his insubordinate challenges.

"Maybe the measurements from the last survey are wrong. But I'm telling you we are orbiting a planet whose sun is not what we expected. But we're here; we'll do what we're supposed to and let the jackets figure out the problem." Then the commander offered one more ploy to help him understand how his navigator could be so mistaken. "By the way, is this planet uninhabited?"

The navigator realized MP was being questioned again and his own ability, as well. "My scans say it is, sir. Isn't it?" LeRoi always had trouble being conciliatory. His defense of MP didn't back off, even from the commander and he asked arrogantly, "Do you have your own scanner ... too ... sir?"

"Don't need one. I can see crumbled overgrown ruins. It looks to have been inhabited, if it's not still. Looks very desolate except for the one green patch." Commander Carpenter had aligned his sighted information with the too soon approach to a supposed terrestrial planet. "This is not our destination," he said. "Looks more like what global warming was threatened to do to Earth in the 21st century."

As if on cue, a call from the settlement dorm interrupted the commander's debate with his navigator.

Fred Sharp said, "Commander, I'm not seeing what preliminary data told us. Looks like the planet is inhabited, or once was, if it's not now. And the star out there doesn't look big enough to be γ-Cygnus A."

"That's what I think," Carpenter agreed. "But the navigator swears we're in the right place. His computer tells him so and his screens tell him so."

"Do we accept his electronic voodoo or our senses?"

SYSTEM

The telemetry following Earther ship *Marco P* FSS-14 opened communication and brought Central Reception and Acquisition back on line.

CR: *Earthers arriving.*

CR to Acquisition: *Status?*

A: *Computer accepts destination. Agrees with inserted astrographics. Some Earthers contrary.*

CR: *Engineering, preparations for descent in place?*

E: *In place.*

CR to all drives holding Molrixx in stasis: *Novelty arrives. Prepare for unique.*

MARCO P

Commander Carpenter was yanked from Sharp's question by an urgent request from Engineer Varlez who sent his startling message directly to the commander's seldom used implant. "It's vital for you to come to engineering. The decision must be yours. I will not make it, though I have the authority."

"Fred," Carpenter interrupted his conversation with the settler lead, "I'm needed in engineering. I'll answer your question as soon as I can." The commander closed the transmission from the settlers' quarters and wondered what dire emergency Varlez had to offer.

Dodging crew along his route, Carpenter sprinted the corridors to reach engineering where access this time opened as he neared its entry.

Varlez was waiting for him just inside engineering.

"How serious?" the commander asked as access whooshed closed behind him.

"The most," Varlez answered. His face bore a look of utter dread. "You have to see for yourself." He led the commander to his main computer station. He had just reinitialized it to the main computer that the navigator was plugged into.

Standing in front of Varlez's readouts the commander saw a series of short brilliant red bars.

"These just appeared," Varlez explained. "They were green and tall. If the information is accurate, the *Marco P* will shortly be powerless. Its orbit will degenerate and we will self-destruct in the atmosphere."

"How long? Days, hours, minutes?"

"If it's accurate—hours. We have enough time to get everything and all of us to the surface. But that's questionable, too. The shuttles show only enough power to get us there."

"Then they're dead, too?" Carpenter surmised.

"This settlement mission ends down there," Varlez continued his brief obituary, "either with a living human settlement or in the charred and dismembered remains of the *Marco P*."

Commander Carpenter didn't have to ask about the range

of the shuttles. Under full power they were hardly good for a million miles. "Looks like we're staying on a facsimile of γ-Cygnus A2."

Varlez's eyes opened wider at Carpenter's statement. "This isn't our destination?"

"Unlikely, though LeRoi and MP maintain it is."

Varlez had not been privy to the commander's disagreement with the navigator, but he was quick to understand. "What if we've got the power and the aliens are just jerking us?"

"Not worth the chance," the commander said. "I'm willing to play their game. They may think they know about us, but we probably possess tricks they've never encountered before. Then we can continue to where we're supposed to be. I'm not willing to have my epitaph written in the deaths of the crew and settlers. Let me check with MP, though I'm sure it will give the same information you have. Then I'll issue orders for abandoning ship."

"You gonna stay aboard?" Varlez referred to a captain's last duty. His tone rejected that customary action.

"They want to learn about humans? They'll get the best we can give. They get all of us."

Shipboard speakers squawked and hummed as they came to life, except in Priscilla Maelstrom's compartment. Throughout the *Marco P* FSS-14 crew stopped moving and listened.

"This is Commander Malcolm Carpenter. We are orbiting our destination."

He imagined how Sharp might bristle at those words. However, Carpenter knew that the settlement lead wouldn't counter his statement nor spread to others his questions about the planet, though he would no doubt share them with Forbes and Gonzalez who were as tight-lipped. He'd eventually fill in what he could to Sharp and explain the obvious discrepancies, but not on board the *Marco*.

He repeated his opening information and waited for all the questions he knew were being asked among the crew and settlers as well as the expected amazed chitchat to stop.

Carpenter was sure some settlers would be aware of the

difference from what they had been told about γ-Cygnus A2, just as Sharp had recognized. However, he wanted the settlers to begin with an official statement from him—as wrong as he knew it was—that they were where they should be and to let them develop their contrariness as he knew they would.

If the inhabitants of the *Marco P* were going to be lab rats, he didn't want to add further worries about the potential control some alien intelligence had over them. Later he would inform Maelstrom about everything that she had been kept from during her isolation. He didn't know when he might clarify. Strumpf and Varlez with his assistants already knew of the potential dangers and the implication of being shanghaied or kidnapped. LeRoi was likely compromised, if on the outside chance he was even aware of the differences between what MP projected and what survey information provided.

The commander continued with a factual statement. "The *Marco P* has developed an unexpected problem." *That much is true.*

"The entire crew will evacuate to γ-Cygnus A2." He hated to repeat the initial lie. "A small repair crew will later return to the ship and repair her." *A long shot but necessary to keep hope alive.*

The whole fabrication was a plausible explanation for total abandonment. Carpenter hoped it would delay more embarrassing questions.

"The nature of the ship's problem requires that all settlers, crew, and equipment depart for the planet as soon as possible. I know you have prepared for taking possession of γ-Cygnus A2 in a more relaxed manner. That is not possible. Navigator LeRoi and I will have coordinates where descending shuttles will land. We have found a large enough area to take them all and it is near a reasonably good spot to begin building and farming. Ready yourselves and report to your assigned descent shuttle. Evacuation of the *Marco P* will commence in three hours."

The flurry of activity, ramped up preparations, and the mystery of what shipboard difficulty demanded abandonment added to the urgency to be at one of the dozen departure points about the *Marco P* and generated considerable futile discussion among the crew and settlers.

In a following communication to him, Sharp aborted the commander's intentions of later answering his question about believing senses or electronics. "Apparently something over-rode both the computer and our senses," Sharp opined. "For my money, we are not descending to γ-Cygnus A2."

"We both believe that, Fred," Carpenter repeated an earlier statement. "I would appreciate it if you didn't pass that belief around, at least not beyond Forbes and Gonzalez."

"I hadn't thought of enlightening them. What if someone asks me?"

"If they are that aware, listen to what they have to say and use your own judgment." Then Carpenter offered the plausible explanation to avert outright distrust. "You know our survey data may have been skewed."

"That's as good a misdirection as any; but I know you don't believe that. There's something more going on, isn't there?"

"Fred, we'll talk on the planet, not over this channel. Carpenter out."

Sharp grinned at Carpenter's non-answer and wondered if there'd be a discussion on the planet.

Varlez again accessed the commander through his implant. "Hid that pretty well. If the ship can't keep orbit, you know no one returns to repair."

Malcolm Carpenter cupped his left hand over his mouth so that his quiet voice return would transmit unheard by any-one who chanced by. "I figured that was the best way to keep the underlying concern hidden. No sense in adding to settlers' worries. A new planet is bad enough. I've got to see Strumpf. He figured out the potential capture of the ship. You'll keep Bandi and Arafa from telling too much?"

"That's been taken care of. They're more incensed at hav-ing their freedom yanked from them and being under some alien power than angry at being exiled on an unknown planet."

"You know the options; I gather they do, too. Depending, we could be back in space and heading for γ-Cygnus A2 before too long, or we're in for a siege."

"If the visible power readings are concocted and we really have max power, the *Marco P* will remain where we leave her. We might get back. All depends on the aliens."

Varlez signed off.

Carpenter still had two face-to-face meetings, not counting Navigator LeRoi. Strumpf was next.

He was ready to leave the galley, when Carpenter found him, and Strumpf preempted the commander's message, "So, we've been captured?"

"There's a doubt?" Carpenter retorted. "Engineering says we have enough power to get everything to the planet and nothing more. I saw the readouts."

"So it's unsophisticated humans against the brilliant aliens?"

"For what it's worth."

"Another question ..."

"About?" Carpenter answered almost too quickly. He was sure he knew what Strumpf was going to ask.

"M—" Strumpf barely got out the initial rumble of the back-up navigator's last name before Carpenter cut him off with a quick "NO" and a wave of his hand.

"—aybe we can talk about that later?" Strumpf asked and realized his friend had answered his question.

"Some things are better left unsaid," Carpenter explained. "And besides I have to see if the navigator has our landing site established."

Strumpf switched directions with ease. "I can understand that. I have everything ready to transfer down. See you there. I'm sure you've more to do. You'll be the last one out ... in the command shuttle, won't you?"

"Yes, in deference to the captain going down with the ship." Carpenter smiled at the repeated innuendo. "The navigator will descend with engineering. He doesn't know that yet. I'm going there now." Carpenter paused and then added a last note to Strumpf, "On the planet," implying where their next conversation would take place.

The commander was sure that with all the preparations for disembarking to a new world, no one, except for Strumpf, would have missed Maelstrom. LeRoi certainly didn't and most of the rest of the crew were aware that Maelstrom had been little used, but when she was, she was wrapped up in the navigation cubby hole.

For descent to the planet, LeRoi had been very busy. The stars were left to themselves as he had determined that territory next to and below a tall mountain range would provide protection from buffeting winds that seemed more evident on the other side of the slopes. A rather large river and small tributary coursed through the center of a depression between the one range and a large high mesa, less than fifty miles west that extended north and south nearly parallel to the mountain range.

"How are plans for leaving going?" The commander asked Navigator LeRoi who was clearing for all shipboard activity.

"As well as expected. Most are at their departure points. A few stragglers are making their pilots edgy."

"That's to be understood. Everyone will be there in time. You've identified the landing site?"

"About as good as we might get. A broad valley, river and small tributary and lots of green. Seems flat. Can't tell for sure what might be used for building beyond trees. There must be something."

"Are you looking at the planet we're orbiting or γ-Cygnus A2?"

"Commander, that's where we are," the navigator insisted. "I know you don't believe it; but all the information and the computer with its database—what I have found is more detailed than the survey pix—but you know Earth-like planets are all the same." He turned back to his main screen view.

Commander Carpenter didn't argue. It was a useless exercise and he was sure that the ship's computer had been commandeered by a force that made moot any argument with his navigator. Just before he left the navigator's closet, he added one more instruction. "At thirty minutes before departure, I want you to leave the computer. Unplug yourself and get to engineering. You will descend with them."

"I'm not staying?" Shocked, LeRoi turned and stared at the commander.

"Didn't you hear my announcement? I said *everyone* was abandoning; even me."

"I heard that. I didn't think it meant me."

"Engineering," Carpenter emphasized with a stern look. "Thirty minutes before. Be there."

LeRoi's lackluster "Aye, sir," prompted a repeat by the commander.

"Thirty minutes before," his tone was as commanding as he ever used, harking all the way back to the two explorers he had ordered to hydroponics on his first command. The commander had no difficulty thinking his navigator would manage a way to miss the engineering shuttle. He didn't want that AWOL to happen.

"Aye, sir," LeRoi responded more officially and added a sloppy incomplete salute. "I'll leave the computer early enough to be there on time."

"I'll be there to greet you," Carpenter added more incentive than with just his tone. "Don't be late! There'll be enough time for me to carry you there, if you are."

Of the fifteen shuttles allotted for descent, a dozen debarked from the *Marco P* a bit ahead of schedule and formed a flotilla fifty miles off the prow of what everyone, except a handful of crew, accepted as a dead-in-space colony/exploratory ship. These contained settlers and their leads, some of the *Marco P's* crew—totaling seventy-five—and a single piece of larger construction machinery together with tools, clothing, small replicators, and a few animals. Medical and hydroponics with Crown, Nozing, and half a dozen hydroponic/galley mates were biding anxious time as Strumpf triple checked the cargo manifests to make sure he was leaving nothing aboard that he could imagine as having some esoteric, but functional, use on the planet.

Impatient at what she thought was useless time wasting, Crown finally called out, "George, everyone else's left. We need to go."

His muffled voice wormed out of the crammed storage behind seating. "Never know what we might need down there, and we may no ..." Strumpf knew he was too late in cutting off what he shouldn't have let out.

"No *what*?" Nozing questioned with a 'what aren't you telling us' tone.

Crown said nothing but her eyes widened at Strumpf's almost words. She took a deep breath and looked around to see if her reaction had been noticed. No one, not even Nozing, was looking at her. Strumpf's stifled and incomplete statement had caught everyone's attention. Crown knew enough to read his unstated 'oops' that told her the chance of anyone, let alone a repair team, returning to the ship was less than slim. She spoke to Nozing's concern and added one more layer of distraction. "You know how George is, Robert; he's never sure he's got everything covered."

Strumpf looked relaxed, when he stepped into the cockpit from storage and extended Crown's explanation. "If the *Marco* is not repairable, it might not be safe to return to it and certainly not to hunt around for something we might have forgotten." He pored over the repeatedly examined list of equipment and looked at his passengers. "But I don't think we're leaving anything necessary."

Strumpf took his seat at the controls and eased the shuttle from its hold. Shutting the bay doors behind them, he powered up to coast to the back of the flotilla that was waiting for the last three shuttles.

As good as his promise, Carpenter was waiting for the navigator at the engineering loading bay. Varlez, Bandi, and Arafa, oblivious to the commander's presence, were still dashing about gathering tools and spare parts to create a second miniature fusion power plant, as well as the basic elements for atomic engines to break apart planetary structures and recombine them at the atomic level to build the refined materials they'd need. They had already stowed necessary computers to access the main computer for however long that might be possible, if it should be released by the planetary force. The duplicate engineering computer on board the *Marco P* that contained the complete knowledge and history of humanity would be packed last. It would be their main source of information on the planet.

With seven minutes to Varlez's launch, engineering was settled in their shuttle seats waiting for their passenger. The commander checked the time and headed away from the bay. He had not gone far before he heard shuffling steps approaching. Carpenter picked up his pace, turned a corner, and glared at the ambling, late navigator.

"Think you could just take too long and get left? Remember what I told you?"

"My pace will get me to engineering on time." LeRoi smirked at the commander.

Carpenter checked the time and reluctantly agreed. "I suppose so."

"You don't understand my desire to stay with the ship." LeRoi was still negotiating.

"Even if it burns up in the atmosphere?"

"Even then. Down there," LeRoi looked down as if he could see through the deck to the planet, "I don't have a purpose. There's no navigation to be done. I don't have any planetary skills. I'm not social and most of my free time is away from the crew. My life is here. If the *Marco* dies, I should die with it."

"You will develop other skills, when you're not connected to MP. You are no more dispensable than anyone else." Carpenter turned, placed his hand at LeRoi's back and urged him toward the engineering bay. "Now, get on board the shuttle."

"Aye, commander." The words were hollow and LeRoi's steps dragged even more.

Commander Carpenter wondered just how useful a navigator who thought he was useless might be. He accompanied the despondent navigator to the shuttle.

"You don't have to come with me," LeRoi protested. "I won't miss the flight. I suppose if you weren't waiting and I was late, Varlez and his harem would seek me out."

"I will see you there." The commander ignored the misunderstood reference to Varlez' assistants and reinforced his intention to have LeRoi on the planet.

"You have your own shuttle to ready."

"There's time for that. I'll see you aboard this one."

For the navigator, Varlez had fashioned a seat specific to his needs, one that had a shaped inset to cradle the computer interface helmet that was a permanent attachment to the navigator's skull. When LeRoi sat, leaned back, and settled in, he found he was more comfortable than during his infrequent sleep segments in his hibernation pod. Carpenter noticed a relaxed smile cross his face.

With LeRoi on board and the commander out of engineering, Varlez opened the hatch. He eased the shuttle through the force field that held the vacuum of space at bay. After clearing the ship he sealed the hold and used a short burst to coast to the other thirteen shuttles. He expected Commander Carpenter's shuttle would pass his about the time he and Carpenter both reached the other thirteen.

With everyone else off the *Marco P* Carpenter dashed to Maelstrom's quarters. His quick three raps were answered immediately. Maelstrom was not unaware of what was going on outside the ship. She had even worried that she might be left alone in exile. More than relief exhaled when she saw the commander and her face brightened as she imagined she would at last receive his vocal release from her silence.

That freedom was not forthcoming.

Commander Carpenter smiled and gestured for her to follow. His pace was quick and they didn't have far to go; however, Maelstrom was forced into a trot to stay close. The commander's shuttle bay was below the bridge and the short lift descent placed them at their shuttle. Carpenter had already packed the ship's logs and some personal keepsakes: an agate from the first planet his maiden voyage reached; the woven wall hanging that he kept above the mission count-down in his quarters and presented to him by the first alien captain he encountered, an Agonite who had given Carpenter sound advice about alien encounters; an ancient volume of galactic aphorisms from Strumpf; his private computer that held the same human history that Varlez's machine did, but with Carpenter's own annotations. His commentaries could be found nowhere else in the universe. Begun very early in his life, years before he became an explorer's commander, Carpenter continuously added his personal thoughts to the history. His views and discussion for this current segment, however, would have to wait and what he entered might never be read. Varlez and Carpenter frequently argued whether Carpenter's additions, important in ways the engineer's own troubleshooting additions were, were objective history or subjective ramblings.

The command shuttle had a small storage bay and four seats. Carpenter pointed Maelstrom to the seat next to his. He powered up and eased the craft through the barrier. When he cleared the *Marco P*, he signaled the bay door shut. He fired the thrusters.

The command shuttle passed engineering just before both

reached the rear of the shuttle group.

The commander led his human contingent into a large spiral trajectory that first took them over the continent, a land mass about the size of Australia and positioned just above the equator. Surrounded by a huge ocean it was the only land in the hemisphere below them. The shuttles strung out in single file behind the commander's descending and tightening circle. Each following shuttle maintained a gap of a hundred miles from the shuttle in front.

As Malcolm Carpenter flew over the mostly desert continent he saw six white squares, each measuring a mile and a half on a side. His destination was the southern most of the white areas nestled in the only green territory on the continent. All six white areas were near the taller of the two mountain ranges that extended several hundred miles north of their landing site. The southern end of the range bordered a fertile zone covered in greenery: trees, bushes, tall reeds, and waving grass. Two rivers sprang from the north, out of the creeping desert and into the long continental valley. They converged north of the landing site. As his shuttle descended, he noticed a larger gray rectangle at the foot of the western ridge and across the river from his planned touchdown. He also noticed a smaller half-camouflaged construction built into the western range.

While he led the lengthening and descending coil of spacers to a planet that he knew was not γ-Cygnus A2, Carpenter visually explored the land where he and his castaways might spend the rest of their days, however long those might be, unless the humans prevailed against the unwarranted attack that had taken this first skirmish in the war against humanity.

The taller mountain range rose sharply to between seven and eight thousand feet. Several jagged-toothed peaks topped ten thousand feet. The western foot of this range pushed against sparse vegetation as did the wide river valley, before it flared out into the lowlands ending in barren desert to the south. Except for six large tan constructions—huge mega-buildings—the craggy range was all rock and dirt. Its eastern side gradually descended into a high desert that continued to drop to the surrounding ocean hundreds of miles away.

The western edge of the valley they planned to colonize

ran into softer hills, less green from shorter flora. More westerly beyond the bubbly, round-topped, up-thrust hills, seemingly bare but occasionally tufted with yellow, the continent appeared as flat and semi-arid as the North American prairie states until it dropped sharply into the ocean at the western edge of the continent.

Commander Carpenter lowered, slowing and tightening the spiral descent. He could see more clearly the remains of the six large buildings hugging the eastern range. Vegetation may have eroded some of the base of the constructions, but weather had crumbling effects, if they had been uninhabited for a long time. The six gargantuan constructions were built into mammoth cutouts from the western flank of the eastern mountain range. Whether they rose from the valley, he couldn't tell.

The valley itself, bisected by a single river at the point of landing, was a sea of waving foliage and dotted by several islands of small dense forest groves. One small area, apparently flat and brilliant white, a huge parking lot, so out of place from the rest of the fertile valley, was large enough to accept all fifteen shuttles.

The crew of the *Marco P* FSS-14 dropped into the green valley, like many rain forests might have looked on Earth centuries earlier. Terrestrial galactic explorations for several centuries had discovered, to the amazement of most biologists, that humans possessed the basic form of all rational beings. With few and insignificant exceptions, all rational aliens they had encountered looked like themselves. With greater frequency, exploring settlers found repeatedly that conditions on Earth were duplicated again and again on each new uninhabited planet as well as on inhabited alien worlds.

However, the shanghaied travelers from the *Marco P* were forced to what a few knew was not their intended destination; but, for all that was important, assuming their unknown and unseen captors prevailed, they could live out their lives as they could on any Earth-like planet. However, Malcolm Carpenter, George Strumpf, Fred Sharp, Jerry Varlez and his harem were positive that another intelligence was at work in their forced landing. How long it might take the rest of the crew to understand that situation would be key to these humans' success at defeating another alien threat to their nature and their continuing to their real destination.

HUMANS

Commander Carpenter dropped his shuttle close to the western edge of the eastern mountain range. The following shuttles, braking their narrowing spiral course, floated down on thrusts of propulsion.

Even before the shuttles were winding down, fuel gauges read nearly zero. Shocked communications from fourteen shuttle pilots reported readings similar to what the commander saw: hardly more fuel remained than what was needed to land safely and Carpenter recognized the devious plan that forced him and his human population from the safety of the *Marco* to the prison of an unknown planet. Precariously and precisely he jockeyed his shuttle to the northeastern edge of the landing site, close to the base of one of the intra-mountain constructs.

Before he powered down, the commander broadcast to the exiled fleet following him one last set of instructions. "Land in close formation. We need our transportation for lodging. I don't want us too separated. When you've landed, take the best estimate of what fuel might be left and then turn off everything, but not before you set the hatches for manual. The shuttles must be left dead. We'll meet at my shuttle after everyone is down."

Thirteen pilots acknowledged his order. Engineering with navigator LeRoi didn't respond. Varlez knew why electronics needed to be silenced. He also understood that the navigator with his electronic headpiece might be too dangerous a passenger for him to respond, a concern Varlez had discussed with his sub-engineers before LeRoi climbed aboard. The likely traitor would be closely watched and spared any observation of their electronics.

Carpenter was in the process of silencing and deafening his shuttle when he received a hasty message. Kellan Forbes broke the com silence. "Shouldn't we keep the com open? If we're basing in the shuttles that will make communication a lot easier."

"No," the commander quickly ordered. "Shut down everything. There aren't that many of us and face to face is still the best for sharing ideas and information."

"Will do," Forbes agreed but a hint of doubt surrounded his words. Carpenter imagined that Forbes had been the representative for several pilots who were unwilling to ask the same question.

Communications was the last module taken off-line by the commander, just after he programmed all hatches to manual. Maelstrom, who had yet to be released from her silence, sat silent and intrigued as the commander flipped switches, turned knobs, pushed buttons, and slid levers. Each movement silenced some soft electronic signal. Finally, with the radio disabled, both sat surrounded in silence nearly as complete as space itself.

Malcolm Carpenter slowly swept his gaze across the dead instrumentation once, twice. A third time the commander surveyed the panels, dials, and dead monitoring lights.

He was ready to give his backup navigator release her from silence when he heard a soft click. He turned and noticed a small blinking green light powering up. The com had reinitialized itself just as his pix-album had. The commander flipped the control to the off position and held it. The light dimmed, vanished, and then blinked brightly when he took his finger away.

Carpenter looked at Maelstrom, shrugged, got up, and stepped to the hatch. He knew that the first shuttles following would be too busy landing to pay attention to two people standing by his shuttle. He twitched his head for her to follow and they disembarked. Carpenter led her to the edge of the landing area, keeping his shuttle between them and the other landing shuttles.

He turned to her and said, "I think our electronics have been compromised by an alien power. They may have had some control over the crew's minds and thoughts on board the *Marco*. I think you are immune, because you weren't linked into the ship's system and we didn't make a sound when I was in your quarters and you didn't seem affected as the other crew seemed to be. We are out of the shuttle and probably away from electronic eavesdropping. You may now speak to me."

"To you. And to others?"

Maelstrom looked around. She had seen that the continent was practically uninhabitable except for the valley where they were. "Where do you think this power emanates from?"

"No idea," the commander answered. "But it's got to be here somewhere. Maybe only a remnant of a vanished but electronically powerful civilization. For now, it's vital that you stay in the shuttle, and remain silent. Whatever has taken charge of us controls our electronics, at least in the shuttles as it did on the *Marco*. It affected all of us who spoke. So far only a handful know that we're captives and aren't where we're supposed to be. You now make one more in that group. I don't want you compromised by the rest of the crew."

Maelstrom looked around. "I didn't think this was how γ-Cygnus A2 was described. I certainly won't tell anyone what I know, if that's a concern. Silence is no fun. If I can … you know …" Maelstrom was pleading for release from solitary.

"I'm sorry," the commander apologized, "but I want to keep you isolated a little longer. Once others start asking about you … well …"

"That might not be long. Early in the mission, two young settlers asked me to join their settlement. If we're here, if we're all here, they'll be looking for me."

"We'll broach that when we must. But I'd rather not make your presence known any sooner than I have to."

"Yes, sir," Maelstrom invoked her official tone, "I'll stay in the shuttle … for as long as it takes. I really hope I'm missed pretty soon."

"That's how it has to be. Now, I hate to send you back in. But I do need you uncompromised, especially if whatever force we're facing doesn't know about you and your connection to MP."

It was an ironic salute backup navigator Maelstrom snapped before she re-entered the shuttle. However, she knew more about why they were on the planet and what had gone on in space. Despite her lonely assignment, its necessity was intriguing. She relished that kind of puzzle.

SYSTEM

Acquisition to Central Reception: *Earthers' craft inhibit our power.*

CR: *Reroute from other sources.*

A: *Molox3 is only maintaining. Overgrowing flora limits excess to power pool. Solar receptor is disintegrating.*

CR: *Other areas?*

A: *Wurthro has lost 50% population and 70% corporal. Failing receptors and drives. Diverting power from Wurthro decimates their repository. Elthren and Svoqol have excess power. It can be diverted to us without harm to them. Their receptors function.*

CR: *Let Wurthro fail. It is of small value as is western complex that was too proud to accept designation Molox2. We duplicate their knowledge. They provide nothing we need. Molox1 must be maintained.*

A: *Escaped monitors have invaded Molox1. Will they inhibit Earthers?*

CR: *Not a concern. They will not interact. Monitors will fear Earthers.*

A: *Can we be sure? Earthers may invade Molox1.*

CR: *We control them as we did their ship.*

A: *Electronics will be their doom …*

CR: *… and our pleasure.*

MOLRIXX

The kilometer long outside stairway descent was a routine exercise for Krolni and significantly easier than his weekly ascent. What he had seen from the Council farming area that he had undertaken to regenerate shortly after he and Woloka joined the monitor group demanded urgency and he knew the inner stairs were a longer descent than the outer route in spite of the danger. He knew, when he reached the fifth floor, that he had beat his descent record by a long time.

The monitors who had escaped Molox1 and Molox3 had bided their time for nearly a whole year—Krolni and Woloka joining recently—before they mounted a concerted effort to recapture the super structure that was more than a kilometer tall. Molox1 was planned for use and Molox3 would be considered only if everyone saw a necessity of splitting into two groups. When they saw proof of depleted Molox1 population, Vokra ordered more frequent raids on the lower floors to outfit their meager needs. Not long after Krolni and Woloka escaped, they provided evidence that no one was alive in the mammoth complex and the power they were accustomed to have had been curtailed. Many urged reclaiming the mega, especially since Kronli, shucking any hint of acrophobia climbed and descended the outside stairs to help Council's starving livestock recover. Nevertheless, Vokra hesitated to send her group on full missions to the inner top of Molox1 for fear that Council, or computers, or robots had planted traps.

At last, she relented to the protestations of her small community, all of whom had taken private forays and knew that the complex was empty. The greatest weight of evidence was from Krolni who had spent hours on inner stairways on his trips to and from Council's farm. On his first return, he'd climbed the rope he left hanging and continued up the outside stairs to floor 373 where his latch-stop was still in place. He entered the floor he used to reside on and found his flat as he had left it.

His return down the inside stairs with detours and a few random excursions on a handful of floors was evidence enough that no Molrixx was alive. He took a longer scouting mission on floor 173 including testing the handles on three black NO ADMITTANCE doors. They were locked, as his last excursion had found before he left Molox1 with Woloka. When he held his ear to those doors he felt the cold from inside and reported that he heard faint whirring. Eventually he exited the fiftieth floor, leaving his latch-stop in place for a much lower entrance, in case the lower doors were ever locked shut.

"What about your computer station?" Vokra asked when he announced his initial exploration.

"I saw the same flitting information I watched when I was sitting there."

"Did you try to access anything else?"

"Mloksi and Melnic were still there and their monologs were exactly as I first heard them. They were not abbreviated as they had become. I wasn't interested in anything else."

"Well," Volkra said, "maybe we can return to the mega and each commandeer more than a single flat. It's better conditions than the forest, though we'll still have to farm and hunt here. And I don't think we all can keep climbing over the two stories of cage. That will have to be gotten rid of."

"I'm surprised Krolni climbed back up his rope," Crelle spoke up. "We separated the cage next to the outer wall some time ago and left the bottom door open. Now that you're willing to make changes, we can remove the cage completely."

"Hid that from me, did you?" Vokra chided.

"Not exactly. You didn't seem willing to invade for some reason. It was just easier this way. We've been scouting around there for quite awhile."

"I wondered about some of the things you brought back from excursions. Now I know. I suppose we have a pretty good supply of necessities."

"And" Woloka added, "we'll have a much better clothing selection."

"We're gonna have company," Krolni announced to Vokra through heavy gasps to catch his breath after his record dash from the regenerating farm. "Aliens. Fifteen flying ships, different from what were rumored to have landed here long ago."

"It's been a very long time since aliens visited," Crelle

noted. "Never heard why they stopped coming. I always wondered if that information was stored somewhere on the drives."

"Or in the tales our patients told," Vokra suggested.

"Flying machines were circling," Krolni broke into their reminiscences, "slowing, dropping. Looked like they were gonna land close to the white, if not on it."

"We'd best watch what they do," Vokra urged. "I never heard what the aliens ever did before. They didn't stay; but the funny thing was that there were never stories about them leaving. No one seems to know what happened to them."

"I once ran across a rumor that tied aliens to several whites, like the one outside Molox1," Woloka commented. "Never thought what those arid constructions were for."

"Maybe there's a hidden entrance below the first floor to that complex, if that's what the white is," suggested Mencra. "We know the drives are supposed to hold the personalities; suppose bodies or something else are housed below ground?"

"Every mega has a white square close by. Could the aliens be there?" Krolni asked.

Canska, a very pregnant blonde said, "This group of aliens might be coming to check on some of those who came before … you know, coming to take them home."

"If they can find them," Vokra said. "Aliens were a long time ago."

"Or maybe it's an invasion force," Woloka suggested, "in retaliation for something."

"Regardless," Vokra repeated. "this molox is safe. We have food stashed here and there are easily enough places to stay hidden. We can watch them, especially up ten or twenty floors."

"We all here?" Crelle asked, as he scanned the monitor clan. "Is anyone still in the forest or at the garden?" he added when he didn't see the group's hunter and farmer.

"Korsk hasn't returned from his plot," Canska said. "Maybe someone should see about him."

"Mencra, go," Vokra said. "And see about Wisolen. He's not here. He may be hunting. He said something about noticing some fresh tracks."

"We'll be careful getting back. No matter how intelligent

they are, it's the alien's disadvantage that we know the territory." Mencra looked out a window and saw only six flying machines on the white. "Besides they're not all down, yet."

Vokra cautioned, "Don't get too cocky, Mencra. They might have abilities we can't imagine. Go quickly and quietly."

Wisolen and Vensil had just spotted a Scarlif, a large brown-and white-striped jungle cat, creeping past a grove, when they heard the first of the *Marco P's* shuttles landing. At the strange noise, their prey stopped tracking a Traspin, a smaller version of itself that also halted its flight. Meat was more important to Wisolen than some loud noise that filtered through the trees and the Scarlif's pause gave him the moment to strike. His spear's flight was true and the hunted Traspin escaped. Wisolen soon trussed the cat's feet, slipped a pole through them and with Vensil, a young Molrixx apprenticing as a hunter, started back to the mega-city carrying the dead animal on their shoulders.

When they reached the edge of the forest, they watched the first of several flying craft settle onto the white. Each was a long fat section with short stubby wings that Wisolen refused to believe could keep the things aloft. Rear thrust quit as the strange flying things slowed and hovered above the white, not higher than the fifteenth floor of Molox1.

The approaching craft generated high-pitched whines that hurt Wisolen's ears and he squeezed his face to shut out the noise. That sound was soon replaced by a gusting wind from the things settling down and their landing was accompanied by flying forest debris that had accumulated on the white. From the first landing thing that looked nothing like a bird, two beings exited and moved to the edge of the white.

Several more craft were settling down.

Wisolen, leading Vensil with the pole carrying the dead jungle cat across their opposite shoulders, held up a hand and stopped. They dropped the large feline from their shoulders and with hands covering their ears squeezed through the brushes and watched two aliens, looking remarkably like themselves, converse. The spying hunters watched the bobbing heads and gestures. The offending sound of landing craft decreased as more craft were landing farther away from the first.

The hunters freed their ears. Occasionally they caught a sound from the alien discussion, but the lilting noise was too strange for words. At last the smaller of the two re-entered the flying craft and the remaining alien set his direction for the other craft that had set down.

"They are concerned with themselves," Wisolen said. "We can skirt just inside the edge of the trees."

Then the two hunters heard a furtive crack and a swish of vines behind them. Mencra and Korsk stepped up to them.

"We're hiding in the tower," Mencra informed the hunters. "We can be safe and watch from there. Hurry."

"Looks like it's a good bit of meat, you bagged," Korsk said. "My garden is still far away from producing much."

By the time two hunters and the gardener and the messenger reached the base of Molox1, fourteen more alien machines had landed. The passengers disembarked and made their way across the white to where the larger of the two aliens had returned and was waiting next to his machine at the northeastern edge of the white. By the time the four Molrixx entered Molox1 and climbed to the fifth floor the rest were watching the aliens, a group that was three times the total number of Molrixx.

HUMANS

Commander Carpenter watched his people gather at the end of his shuttle ramp and counted their arrival. The growing amorphous group would bunch up to 88, but they didn't look that large measured against the large white area surrounded by greenery that looked five feet tall.

He caught snippets of success and eagerness they offered each other in their intent to create a colony that would grow into a human outpost on a planet far distant from Earth and extend what many alien galactic populations agreed was a pompous human parade through the galaxy.

A few colonists expressed wonder at having arrived at the planet so soon after being wakened in spite of the emergency procedures demanded by some unidentified problem the *Marco P* had encountered. Others were shocked that everyone had come to the planet and left the *Marco P* unattended. Despite Carpenter's official announcement, a couple of settlers proclaimed that someone was still on board the *Marco*.

The commander knew his stated excuse for all to descend to the planet was only partly correct, at least as far as the instrumentation claimed. The engineer and Strumpf agreed with him in principle that there was likely no lack of power and the instrument readouts were just incorrect or compromised. But his real fiction, that they were on γ-Cygnus A2, had to be maintained longer, at least until the resident aliens, if there were any—the constructions set into the mountain range announced there had been, if they were not still present—began to provide inherent difficulties. It was clear to Carpenter that the human contingent had been brought to the planet for some purpose far beyond their mission goals and no doubt dangerous to their nature.

Commander Carpenter was not sure how long he might continue the ruse that they were at their planned destination. He looked up at the planet's star. It was clearly smaller than Sol would be if they were on Earth, which is what γ-Cygnus A should look like if they were where they should be. He didn't know how many settlers would recognize the difference, although he doubted it would take long before that understanding became part of most conversations. And then there were the two who had requested Maelstrom to join them in the settlement. He was sure they would soon appear to ask about her, especially if they didn't see her in the throng before him.

While he watched the stragglers from the last shuttle join the company, Fred Sharp approached the commander for a quiet bit of information that defused Carpenter's latter problem.

"Commander, I was asked by two young men where Maelstrom was. Both obviously had little interest in her beyond the physical. Separately, they had asked her to join them when the colony was established."

"I heard that somewhere," Carpenter admitted.

"They said they hadn't seen her and wondered if she even came to the planet, despite your announcement. They noticed LeRoi was down here, but she was not. They asked if she stayed on board the *Marco P.*"

"She's otherwise engaged, Fred."

"I figured she was. I told them she had ship duties that couldn't be covered by anyone but her. The ship couldn't spare her. I hope that fit what you might have said."

"It's okay," the commander agreed. "They said?"

"Nothing. Both shrugged. They were disappointed. But since neither could claim her, they didn't seem too upset. It was bragging rights, I'm sure—who could possess a trophy. By the way, I ..."

"Don't ask," the commander cut off Sharp's expected question.

Sharp shut his mouth and stared intently at the commander whose order and tone precluded further discussion of the backup navigator. Then Sharp turned to join Forbes and Gonzalez who were surrounded by their own groups of settlers. Before Fred reached them, he spoke briefly to two young men. Commander Carpenter saw them nod. He was sure Maelstrom would not be missed too soon. He made a mental note to thank Sharp later.

His major problem, where the humans really were and why they had been misdirected, was paramount. He didn't want to announce his own battle plan against the aliens that had captured his ship and crew, and he wasn't willing to give anyone more clues to realizing they were not on γ-Cygnus A2. He wanted the crew and settlers to discover for themselves their dangerous situation.

Finally, looking around, making a quick count, the commander saw that all were present, even LeRoi, whose helmet poked above all other heads. As if on cue, George Strumpf partially covered the planetary identification problem. In a loud voice, he spoke up over the individual conversations to demand quiet. Then he projected his question, "Commander, now that we're all on γ-Cygnus A2, do you have any words about beginning the colony?"

Talk, even hushed private words, ended. Carpenter had everyone's ear, though he thought Strumpf's use of *all* could have been eliminated. He was sure some might take the universal as a hint to the real situation. He also knew that Strumpf's words had positive benefit, especially to the two young settlers seeking Maelstrom's company.

"I do," Commander Carpenter began. "But let me cover some preliminaries. Almost every pilot questioned my order to shut down communication in the shuttles." He glanced over the group and saw several nods from the pilots. He saw the same ones with a look of "but wait."

"I'd be willing to bet that every pilot who shut down communication saw it re-initialize and do so after every attempted shutdown." The nods were more emphatic. "You matched my experience."

"I thought γ-Cygnus A2 was uninhabited," Manuel Gonzalez shouted out. "I saw structures when we came down, to say nothing of that megalithic thing east of us. And … what would turn communication back on?"

Agreement rippled through the landing party.

Carpenter was ready. "Uninhabited is what we were told, what the survey data reported. The planet looked pretty desolate except for this green valley we landed in. I think you'll agree that the complexes seem to be eroded. Those conditions wouldn't exist if they were inhabited."

"And communication?" The reminder rose from several in

the middle of the settlers.

"Electronics are strange things. Systems that run on solar power don't fade away. I imagine that some overriding system tapped into our com modules. When we get settled—a little later than just after landing—a party might hunt for that system and disable it. Besides, personal, face-to-face conversation is better than electronic. You all know that."

That statement brought some spotty disagreement and caused the commander to glance across the group for the naysayers. Carpenter continued. "I'm not saying that I know the answer to everything on new planets, but I believe that, after all I've landed on, you should forego electronics as much as possible." The commander built up what he thought was the only defense against the planet's controlling power. "Until we have modest residences, the shuttles should be used as quarters. However, given that the com circuits regenerated on their own, the shuttles may be listened to by whatever source of that electronic attachment. I'm not sure we should ignore that something or someone is cataloging our words. We shouldn't carry on important conversations inside, if that something can understand. And the shuttles will keep away the dangers of animals and plants we know nothing about. The first thing we must do is scout the surrounding area. What's around us? And I don't want anyone heading off alone. Scout in groups of at least four. Just because something looks and feels like Earth, doesn't mean it is. Take care; test everything."

"What about the complex east of us?" Forbes asked. "If it's really a skyscraper, we might use it for habitat."

"That might make residences easier," the commander agreed, "but it doesn't really create the settlement and colony you're expected to establish."

"I wasn't meaning forever; it's got to be less crowded than the shuttles."

"And no doubt without power. I suppose, if we can get into it, it offers some advantages the shuttles don't. But I don't think we should start there. Right now I expect you to relax some and do a little close discovery. It seems we still have about half a day's light and there's no satellite. Night'll be dark of the moon on Earth, away from cities. I did notice that the night sky will be more star-lit than even the southern hemisphere of Earth. Try to get adjusted to planetary life as opposed to living on board a small colony ship. And, repeating an important caution, don't assume anything about the planet and its biota.

"And last, share your findings. We're all in this together." Carpenter drew in a breath. He wondered if he had said too much in echo of Strumpf's clue. Ordinarily part of the *Marco P's* crew would have landed and then left after a brief time on a planet. In spite of his questionable statement—more wishful thinking—that a repair unit would return to the *Marco P* and correct whatever problem had demanded they all disembark, his last statement could be construed that no one would return to the ship.

None caught his innuendo.

Settlers were tired of cautions. They were looking around, eager to discover the novelty of a new world and he dismissed them. *Marco P's* crew was less excited about being planet-bound. The shuttles were fine for them and similar to their cramped quarters on board ship.

Before long, the area around the commander's shuttle was empty except for Varlez, Strumpf, and Sharp who created a foursome with the commander. Forbes and Gonzalez loitered within earshot, but off to the side, not assuming themselves to be part of the inner circle. Arafa and Bandi, Varlez's two assistants, set off to wander the perimeter of the strange landing site. Navigator LeRoi sullenly returned to his couch in the engineering shuttle.

"Well, commander," Fred spoke up, "what do we do now?"

"Fred," the commander turned to the settler lead, "we have to know what's around us. Recon is still the first order. We have to know what's dangerous: animals, plants, the ground. You, Kellan, and Manuel," the commander turned away from his inner circle to the other two leads, "are going to have to be the scouts." They nodded and Carpenter motioned them to join his group. "I believe you all think—strongly—that this is not our destination and our landing was coerced. By what and how we have to discover. Then we have to figure out what we're going to do. Our capture is a novel experience in human colonization." Carpenter saw Forbes and Gonzales nod and look to

Sharp. Those three had already discussed the concerns Sharp had tried to voice to the commander.

"Part of our scouting, which normally doesn't take place on guaranteed uninhabited planets, is to discover if there is any rational life. Part of that will be an orderly search of the gargantuan construction built into the mountain."

"I'd already planned for that," Sharp reported. "I think Forbes is the one to lead a unit through it, though it will take a long time. He and a half a dozen can be engaged beyond settlement building."

"But they might find just what we're looking for, if it's a kind of city in a building and not too long abandoned," Varlez assessed. "I thought my girls and I would see about developing a solar power supply and get our computers up. Most of our powered equipment should work with the local star, but shouldn't be needed until we get a large perimeter established and we're out of the shuttles."

"Agreed," Carpenter said. "We're going to go about doing what any settlement troop would. I'm sure the conjecture that we're not on γ-Cygnus A2 will develop pretty quick and race through our whole complement. The problem then will be to convince everyone to continue as they would under normal circumstances."

"Eventually they will come to what we believe, probably sooner than not," Strumpf said. "We have to prepare for that. There are going to be some very angry people with nothing to salve them."

"Yes," Carpenter agreed with a nod, "which is what we want. But if we can't channel that anger, our captors have the advantage."

"That's right," Fred concurred. "We've got a group willing to work together. It was their choice—where we were headed, but they'll resist any attempt to force them into something else. From my experience, it's that 'don't tell me' attitude that aliens don't seem to understand. I'm not sure I understand it, but I know it's a powerful weapon on our side. It might be what eventually gets us off this dry ball and to where we're supposed to be."

"That's consensus, Fred," Carpenter said. "We're in

agreement … the four of us … six," he adjusted looking at Gonzalez and Forbes. Commander Carpenter let his words trail off without a conclusion. He ached to tell them about Maelstrom and omitted mentioning Arafa and Bandi. However, he was enough uninformed about what and how much alien power they all were under that he would keep Maelstrom's presence to himself as long as he could.

"One more thing, I think," Varlez began and paused. He had spent most of this mini-conference looking down at what he termed "tarmac," rubbing it with his boots. Twice he had bent down to scrape his fingernails across it. "We need to find out what we're parked on. It's not natural, at least by all that surrounds it. It's constructed. Nothing in nature is so precisely squared and edged. I bet it's the top of something connected to the mountain structure."

"Certainly more than a bomb shelter," Strumpf injected. "Tunneled into from deep?"

"That's what I was thinking," Varlez agreed. "I don't know if Kellan should look for that kind of access before or after he sweeps part of the upper structure."

"It's probably not a good idea to dig down from an edge to get an idea of size," Gonzalez offered. "But if we're just scouting to find out about our environment before the sham of beginning the settlement, there will be time to analyze this … tarmac."

"One last thing," the commander encouraged, though he doubted he had to remind them, "keep on your people. Know what they're doing and thinking. They're going to talk in the shuttles, but try to keep that to a minimum. We may be listened to outside, but I'm sure we're listened to inside."

"Won't limiting conversations in the shuttle be telling the aliens something?" Sharp asked.

"Only if they know anything about humans. I don't think they do, unless they learned something from the computer on board the *Marco*. No sense in educating them more than we have to. They may have transmitters outside to listen, but there are more ways to keep those words from being understood, even with quality translators." Then he looked at Varlez. "Jerry, just in case they can't control everything, why don't you and your girls survey the area for transmitters and report. There may be none and your instrumentation may be hampered as it was on the *Marco P.* But it will be nice to know, one way or the other."

Varlez nodded. "The three of us can be unobtrusive. No need for anyone else to know what we're doing."

"Commander," Sharp broke in, "I think we can keep the settlers from giving away too much. You and George and Jerry pretty well have the crew in tow ..."

"Except for LeRoi," Varlez interrupted. "He's lost without MP and I'm not about to let him access mine. And that helmet, I just don't know."

"I don't think he's going to be out very much," Carpenter said. "He's accustomed to staying by himself and if he's about, he's certainly noticeable. I think we should just be aware of where he is, if he leaves the shuttle."

The six broke apart. Varlez headed for the edge of the puzzling thing he called tarmac. Sharp joined his other two leads and scanned the area. Strumpf returned to his infirmary shuttle. He knew that he and Amanda would soon be called upon to repair the results of unwise decisions some settlers would make in their eagerness to take possession of the land.

Commander Carpenter headed toward the northern edge of the tarmac, not too far away since he had purposefully landed as close to the northeast corner of it as he could. When he reached the north edge, he saw that grass, bushes, and trees grew right up to the edge and formed an uninterrupted green barrier that was shoulder to head high. The eastern edge of the living floral wall seemed solid, but he hadn't looked closely as he strode north. When he reached the northern edge, he turned and started back to the shuttle. It was then that he saw a small opening in the forested greenery. He stopped and stared. The gap was narrow and exposed a nearly hidden beaten path leading toward the base of the mountain construct.

He refused the urge to take more than two steps past the edge of the tarmac. It had been his order not to explore without at least three others, but he was not bound by it—*Ego meipsum dispenso*, an ancient Latin phrase frequently employed by kings, dictators, and leaders freeing themselves from their own law.

However, excepting himself was not prudent. He wondered if there were other paths extending from the tarmac. The next day would be soon enough for that search and he could have someone with him as he inspected the perimeter of the tarmac.

MOLRIXX

Thirty monitors crowded behind four windows five floors above the wooded valley where they spent much of their time. Molox1, the five hundred floor mega city the last two monitors had recently fled from many weeks ago—a dozen others longer ago—was a symbol to the aliens of mystery, intrigue, and the unknown. To the escaped, free Molrixx it was a refuge against violent weather and a safe haven even though nothing worked as it used to before they all fled from their own cities.

"They're three times us," Vokra assessed as the alien crew and settlement gathered in front of one individual.

"There's enough places for us to hide and watch," someone suggested.

"We have the advantage in any skirmish," Wisolen stated boldly. "Unless they travel in groups, we can pick them off one at a time, just like any animal I hunt."

"And why's that important?" Woloka asked. "Beyond landing on Molx and being aliens, is there a reason to hunt them? We don't know if they're dangerous."

"There haven't been aliens on our world for a long time; and, when they were here, they never seemed to be around very long," Canska tempered the belligerent mood she feared was rising. "I don't remember aliens in the past doing anything but vanishing. Maybe these will, too. Vokra's right. We need to watch them. If they become aggressive, and I don't know why they would if they never see us, then we can make good plans to defend ourselves."

Woloka continued in the same vein. "I don't see any weapons among the gathering down there."

"How would they know we're here, anyway?" Mencra proposed. "Their craft are certainly large enough to hold more than we can see."

"We're not a violent group," Krolni's voice rose above the handful of side conversations that repeated fears of the unknown. "When Woloka and I joined you, I was pretty concerned when all of you swarmed out to meet us. Crelle had a pretty vicious-looking weapon."

"Scared, you mean," Woloka corrected. "I was watching you and I know I was scared."

"Okay," Krolni admitted, "but that fear didn't last long. We're escapees because we had no personal power agenda like Council did. I still don't think anyone has any designs on ruling. We don't have the simple easy life we had in the megas, but we're reasonably comfortable. If they are a settlement—I don't think Molx appears inhabited anymore—we'll know soon enough." Krolni intended to continue his thought, but he saw the alien assembly break apart and small groups head off, some toward the forest, others back to the flying machines they had come from. He watched until a small knot of four remained close, talking to each other. He didn't know if they were leaders but their actions were of those in charge.

"Settlement?" Korsk broke in. "I'm not sure this small valley can withstand four times our population. It's hard enough now getting food to eat. I'm not willing to share what little we have."

"Maybe there are other places on the planet they might be encouraged to go," Crelle offered.

"Really! Why do you suppose out of the whole planet, they chose this valley to land in? I bet this is the only useful piece of land, the only area that can support life," Vensil's young voice rose above the vocal agreement with Crelle's thought. "I spent a lot of time looking at images of the other island continents before I left Molox1. They're just like this one, but without any green valley or arable land."

"Enough," Vokra shouted with a raised hand. She heard no new thoughts, just repeats. "We don't know anything about that landing party, except that they're down there. They have three times our numbers, if that's all there are. They look like us, and we have no idea where they came from or why they're here. This valley is ours and we know it well. We can hide for as long as we need. They won't find us, even if they come looking. They can't even know about us, unless ..."

"Don't think so," Krolni interrupted. "The one three joined and then left is at the edge of the square. I think he's looking up the path to the base of Molox1."

"The path is beaten solid," Korsk added. "It's easy to see that. He'll know it's a regular route for something."

Vokra turned to look down where Carpenter was standing just off the white. She drew in a slow, long breath. "Okay, he may think there are inhabitants and that they are where we are right now. Unless we make ourselves known, we never have to cross paths."

"We'll have to be more careful and watchful, when we're out," Crelle added.

The thirty Molrixx went silent. For the first time since they had left the moloxes, something more than mere survival complicated their lives. Simple routine was no longer the norm. As with any thinking beings, change was not without serious misgiving.

SYSTEM

Acquisition to Central Reception: *Western complex still requests aid with power.*

CR: *They provide nothing we need. Are they all in repositories?*

A: *The request is automated.*

CR: *Can you access viability of drives and holding tanks?*

A: *Power fluctuates. Molox1 can divert power to eliminate fluctuation.*

CR: *At what drain?*

A: *Reduce Molox1 to near minimum operating capacity.*

CR: *Unacceptable. If fluctuations continue, what results in the western complex?*

A: *Holding tanks will fail; drives may maintain.*

CR: *Status of Elthren, Grent, Svoqol, Wurthro?*

A: *Wurthro fails. Holding tanks warming at last report. Contents no longer viable. Drives diminished by 70%; 100% failure expected. Elthren, Grent, and Svoqol maintaining, but report receptor problems.*

CR: *Reduce Elthren, Grent, and Svoqol to 80% and create surplus for Molox1.*

A: *That 20% will solve western complex power problem.*

CR: *Unnecessary. Western complex unimportant.*

A: *Reducing Elthren, Grent, and Svoqol, places them too near minimum. Possible failure anticipated.*

CR: *Monitor all complexes. When holding tanks and drives fail divert all remaining power to Molox1.*

A: *That much power is excessive, waste.*

CR: *Necessary for our existence.*

A: *Monitors on fifth floor. Words garbled.*

CR: *Audio unimportant. Engage video access all floors and long-range covering top of holding tank and forest.*

A: *All video working. Seeking?*

CR: *Earther activity. Molrixx movements. Initiate robots for stealth and audio. Gather Earther shuttle communication.*

A: *Commands operant; robots inactive except for download.*

CR: *Mix Earther, Molrixx video with audio; interpolate, extrapolate, configure potential to subdue humans and extract personality.*

A: *Novelty targeted?*
CR: *Alien novelty fulfills curiosity and satisfies.*
A: *Only Molox1 benefits and remains. Monitors?*
CR: *Eventually they perish and we survive to eternity.*
A: *Only Molox1?*

Acquisition's repeat question was not answered. Central Reception had not reduced itself to standby. It was receiving, just not responding.

HUMANS

Commander Carpenter stepped back onto the tarmac, turned, and headed for his shuttle and the fourteen others parked south of his.

The small flotilla had ordered themselves in three rows of five, with an empty space in the first row at the eastern edge of the landing site in deference to the commander whose shuttle was a significant distance north of the front row. Noticing more awareness than usual from the pilots, Carpenter saw that the shuttles were not all pointed north as was his. In the second row Sharp had oriented his shuttle to the south. In the third row Varlez's shuttle pointed east and Strumpf's faced west. The commander wondered if they had planned the full compass panorama or the landings had been spontaneously diverse, as others angled their landing just off one of the four cardinal points. From shuttle cockpits taken all together not a bit of area around them was unseen.

During the return to his shuttle, he revisited the emergency planet-fall, the more or less eager willingness to begin an Earth colony, his confidantes' lack of explanation that didn't firm up his own understanding of the mystery. The well-trodden path he had just left compounded his worries. He wanted to release Maelstrom from her necessary seclusion and include her in debriefing with his closest crew members. That latter desire would have to wait. He could not invite her off the shuttle and chance someone noticing her. Nor could he discuss with her in the shuttle if the com module was likely controlled by some outside source. The heart of his concern was not knowing whether her third generation interface was susceptible to the same hacking that seemed to control LeRoi's.

He planned another conversation with her after dark. He couldn't imagine anyone else, even with strong light beams, wandering around on pseudo γ-Cygnus A2, or on any unfamiliar planet which he knew this was. Then another thought dashed in for consideration and he inhaled at the conviction.

Carpenter's ambling along the eastern edge of the tarmac

increased to a purposeful hurry. He still inspected the greenery along his way, looking for another, or several, beaten-down paths that broke off the edge of the tarmac and through the hedge.

When he reached the last row of shuttles, he was disappointed that no other paths had extended toward the mountain range and possibly other constructions.

Varlez, Bandi, and Arafa were involved in a typical engineering discussion, boisterous, animated, and unattended by anyone else. Eavesdropping on engineering discussions had long ago been avoided by even the curious for fear of being involved in what seemed a prelude to nasty confrontations. Given Varlez's physical reputation, no one was tempted to get involved.

Carpenter smiled to himself as he approached the loud trio. He had heard conflicting tales about these legendary and raucous discussions but had never been close enough to witness one. If he feared that anything confidential might leak from their words, he soon realized he had no worries. He couldn't decipher what their argument was. The commander did catch a familiar word now and then, but the flow, the shouts, the apparent anger—he knew it wasn't—was their well-honed method of reaching solutions to important engineering problems.

Not until he was half a dozen steps from the noisy trio and maintaining a slight quizzical look, did the shouting stop. Three turned friendly attention to him and, when he was within three steps of them, Varlez asked if he needed anything.

The commander's head twitched at the abrupt change of character the three offered. Bandi and Arafa stood at half attention. A swallowed chuckle at the irony and vanished pseudo anger shook Carpenter's body. Before he had a chance to ask what they were arguing about, Varlez explained that they were discussing the importance of what equipment had to be ready first.

"And in words that no one can understand," the commander commented.

"Not at all," Varlez countered. "Since we're not sequestered we can talk freely in Alvorklan. I checked early in the mission. No one speaks it except we three. Since we can't talk in the shuttle, we have no problem outside."

"And our captors might translate?"

"Who can say? But out here they may not have a clue and neither does anyone else."

"Are we unheard out of the shuttles?"

"We've checked, albeit quickly, and there seem no bugs anywhere close, at least nothing popped up on our sensors. But you're here for something else," Varlez acknowledged.

"Yes. It might be a terminal concern."

Engineer Varlez stood up straight and turned serious; Arafa and Bandi stepped in closer for more confidentiality.

The commander began with background. "I suppose LeRoi is still sullen; has been since he left his cubby-hole on the *Marco P.*"

His assessment was met with nods and grunts.

The commander knew he was extending his confidence but thought that what he was going to broach had already been done as Varlez and his assistants were one single mind. "I think you need to watch him closely. Down here is the first time I've ever known him to be separated from MP. He thinks he's lost and has no purpose." The commander noticed interest and a question from Arafa but continued without giving her the chance to ask.

"I have no difficulty imagining that the navigator will soon be accessed by the intelligence that forced us down here. We can't be unaware of a possible fifth-columnist among us. That makes you three the forefront of our defense. When he's compromised, and he will be, if he isn't already, we have to be aware and treat him accordingly. Play along as if we don't know, but don't get sucked in."

"As long as he's in close quarters, he's really not a problem," Varlez said. "If he gets out, we have the rest to make us aware. That may not be easy. I can see him beaten up pretty badly, if anyone gets a hint of what he might do."

"That's what I thought, too. If we all know the situation, then he can be shunned effectively and that will tell our aliens that we know this is not our destination. That throws another option into the mix."

"Eventually we have to explain to everyone that we're not

where we're supposed to be and we've been captured."

"I've thought of that, but how will the settlers react? You think they'll keep up the charade?" Carpenter questioned.

"I think that's where Sharp comes in."

"If the leads can bring all the colonists into what's going on, we still have the upper hand, though it doesn't look like it. Regardless, things are becoming more complicated."

"Seems so. But, Malcolm, ... Commander," Varlez corrected himself in front of his assistants, "you're making a questionable judgment of our settlers. You know they'll do what has to be done."

Commander Carpenter noticed Bandi turn to Arafa with a smirk on her face and rolled-up eyes. He didn't see Arafa's knee bump Bandi's but did see her narrow-eyed glare in return.

"If the settlers quickly realize where they aren't and why we're here, we have to be ready to explain what we all have to do. I had to pass this by you, you know that." Carpenter saw Bandi's face fall.

"I do, Commander." Varlez said. "We came to the same conclusions not long ago. We don't use Alvorklan only for engineering."

"I figured." Commander Carpenter nodded and looked across three faces atop the shortest people from the *Marco P.*

"Commander," Ticia Bandi spoke up. "I apologize for my actions."

"Oh?" Commander Carpenter acknowledged, "and what actions are those?"

"When you came to engineering in orbit and again just now. I didn't learn the first time. I know now."

"Not to be concerned, Engineer Bandi; we all learn all the time, if we are worth anything." Carpenter looked down into Bandi's eyes, smiled, nodded, then turned and left.

As the local star started dropping to the western horizon, settlers and crew drifted back to their shuttles. Commander Carpenter finished his perimeter investigation and found only one other break in the surrounding vegetation. It was at the northwest corner and the path was as trodden as was the one on the east. During his inspection, he noticed the three engineers crisscrossing the tarmac.

Darkness with the black North American nebula, hardly reminiscent of the Earth continent at this point and outlined by thousands of bordering stars, blanketed the valley when the local sun finally slipped over the horizon. This planet, as well as γ-Cygnus A2, possessed no natural satellite. The commander was not surprised when he saw two short figures approach. Ticia Bandi and Nequa Arafa stopped in front of him. Bandi delivered the message.

"Sir, we have searched the area and can find no transmitting sources. Engineer Varlez suggests that outside talk may not be overheard. He does, of course, believe that there may be some energy configuration that we cannot monitor. Engineer Varlez asks that I tell you that he thinks your original defenses are adequate."

Even in the darkening dusk, Carpenter saw the blush forming on Bandi's face and he heard another unspoken apology waver her voice.

"Thank you, Engineer Bandi; and please thank Mr Varlez for me." The commander had thought Bandi's earlier apology sufficient. However, he had yet to find a bad decision from Varlez. He knew he had a reason for sending the young engineer for another round of "I'm sorry," though those words were never spoken.

"Yes, sir. I will, sir." Bandi's voice was stronger without the previous abasement and immediately the two females turned and headed for their shuttle. The commander heard Arafa's heavy voice but couldn't make out the words. She was speaking Alvorklan. He did see Bandi pushed off her stride and then shove back the other way when she recovered.

When the commander was sure no one else was out of a shuttle, except Varlez's two sub-engineers, he opened the hatch and motioned for Maelstrom to join him outside. She didn't have to be asked twice to leave the confines of the relatively comfortable vessel that was several times the size of her compartment on the *Marco P*, even if there were little to see. Unseen she had watched out a port from the time the commander had sent her into confinement. Being out of the shuttle was freedom and a chance to break her silence.

"Do you know how hard not speaking is?" Maelstrom

complained in a harsh whisper when she stood on the tarmac.

"I can imagine," the commander answered. "Though I've never had it imposed on me, I've chosen to be silent. That's not the same."

Maelstrom wanted a time frame to help her stand the aggravating sentence. Her question was blunt. "Do you have any idea how long I'm going to have to keep this up?" Anyone else overhearing the tone of her question might have considered it disrespectful.

Malcolm Carpenter didn't react to her complaint but offered some solace. "Perhaps not too much longer. There are several conflicting factors that are about to confront each other. Navigator LeRoi may be the most dangerous."

"His computer connection," Maelstrom injected. "I wondered about that. He could be accessed and turned into a spy, willing or not, couldn't he? Maybe he already is."

"You've been thinking. Should I worry about you?" The commander asked, not entirely joking as he peered down into Maelstrom's eyes that caught twinkling starlight.

"I'm not the problem he might be. I can disable my interface. He can't, his. Actually, I have. I did after you first visited me on *Marco* and shut off the electronics. Because of my interface, I am really kind of schizophrenic; but I control the digital connection and that brain partition with my non-computer self. I can turn the computer on and off like you do your pix-album."

"That may not be quite so easy," Carpenter cautioned. "Not long ago, in my ready room I discovered that something had control of my album screen. It overrode my thoughts and choices, even my voice shutdown command. If you're really split-brained, you may have more control than I did. But you need to know what I encountered and be prepared. You might be as dangerous, if not more so, than LeRoi; and all the manipulation I'm trying to do down here is a waste of time."

"I haven't been co-opted, commander," Maelstrom assured, "and I don't think the planet has tried to connect with me or even knows about me. The com light has stayed on. All it can transmit are noises, steps, padding squeaks, hatch openings, stuff like that. I think my interface is unknown."

"Unless the planetary intelligence lets you think that way," the commander rebutted and was reminded of his conversation with Varlez in *Marco P's* engineering bay.

"Maybe, but my computer access is not alert and it can't be without my conscious command; that's the schizo in me. When the third gen-face was installed, I was tested a long time with invasive computer programming to teach me how to control and modify a computer's influence. That's another difference between Roger's interface and mine. He's at the whim of a computer. He doesn't have a choice."

"That may be," the commander allowed. "However, LeRoi is, I'm sure, already compromised and was not himself in orbit. He couldn't see the difference between the local star and what γ-Cygnus A should look like. He insisted that we were orbiting the right world even though what we could see with our eyes didn't match what the planet was supposed to look like."

"There might be a system that supersedes my learning and configuration. But my interface was disabled when you think Roger was taken over. The planetary system shouldn't know about my digital half. I really think I can't be controlled."

Then Maelstrom tilted her head way back and looked up at the twinkled sky. "Different patterns than I ever saw before. Do you have any idea where we are? How close to γ-Cygnus A?" Maelstrom returned her gaze to the commander.

"I can only guess. I'd say within a couple of Qion weeks. After a brief discussion with Strumpf, I imagine we're on some kind of penal planet. Can't believe we'll be rescued—by anyone, least of all anyone from Earth. Varlez thinks the shuttles and *Marco* have power to escape and we didn't have to land, that the readings were digital lies. But, if power were siphoned from *Marco* and the shuttles are somehow made unavailable ... the danger was too great; the gamble, way too risky."

Maelstrom offered, "I suppose I'd have come to the same conclusion." She paused and realized what she said. Embarrassment that her statement might be thought an assessment of the commander's decision melted into a hiccup. When she sensed no reaction from the commander, she changed direction and continued, "Maybe, I can work against that power. If Rog can be co-opted, maybe I can pretend to be and find a solution to escape and break the connection to him."

Commander Carpenter grinned as he looked down on the short female and wondered why he hadn't made Maelstrom his chief navigator. She fit well with Varlez and Strumpf for evolving answers. "That's an option I hadn't thought about. Right now, I think it's too dangerous. We don't know anything about this planet and we don't have any idea how strong the intelligence is that brought us here ... except that it did." However, Carpenter kept her offer in mind.

Maelstrom looked back up at the sky and was quiet for so long that the commander almost repeated his last words. Intuitively, just before he opened his mouth, she agreed with his assessment. "You're right, Commander. But when we know more about where we are, I might be Rog's companion. I know he doesn't like me because I'm young and female. I might get him to teach me things he thinks I need to know. I can watch him while he watches me. If the force can connect with him, it certainly will try to connect with me because he knows about my interface. It won't know I have a second mind it can't control."

"Before any of that takes place, we have to get the settlers and crew to understand our situation and get them to embrace the game we've been thrust into."

"Game, Commander? You don't think this is deadly?" Examining the commander's shadowed face, Maelstrom didn't accept his frivolous description of their jeopardy.

"Oh, it's deadly," Carpenter answered, "but it's still a game. The same one we play whenever we leave our solar system. Alien races, thinking races, are usually in awe of one characteristic we humans uniquely possess at least based on all our travels. Aliens recognize the trait but can't understand it. It's been our singular saving grace at every alien encounter."

"You mean free will?" the backup navigator questioned and showed that her studies had touched on philosophy. "I thought any race that had rational ability, had free will—with all the quirks and complications that go with it."

"That's a presumption human explorers have incorrectly made for centuries. I think we are a research project here, wherever here is."

"So we're lab rats?"

"Something like that." And Commander Carpenter revisited

his decision to assign Maelstrom as backup. "I think this race got information about us after we came close and decided to find out what there is about humans that aliens don't understand. They'll put us through scenarios, tests, and try to decide what makes us the way we are."

"How do we know if we pass their tests?"

"Rather, Maelstrom, why should we try? We're not hunting for ways to prove our abilities to the galaxy and we don't accede to others' demands or rules or requirements, unless we agree to cooperate. If not, we move out of the way. That's our history even on Earth before we broke free of it, though it took us a long time to learn. The ultimate rejection is mass suicide."

"Is that how this mission is going to end?" It was a question that neither of them could know that the engineers had already discussed.

"I think it's a little early to entertain that option. First, we have to find whatever parameters there are; why we're here ... if we can. And then we'll be obnoxious, fighting against everything except among ourselves. That usually drives aliens crazy, but it's also the reason we have to know for sure whether Roger has been co-opted and why we must get everyone together against the planetary intelligence. We're not going to do what it wants us to do."

"I see. I suppose I'll be cloistered longer than I'd like. At least I know how it ends and what follows. I do appreciate your confidence in me and hope, if I get sucked in, our conversations will be hidden away and undiscovered. So far I haven't tapped my computer side since before you woke me." Maelstrom swept her gaze around the soft dark outlines of the shuttles. "It's starting to get chilly." She crossed her arms against the falling temperature and a rising breeze. "If you have nothing more, I'll go hide myself away."

"Don't seal the hatch, I'll be there shortly."

With mixed feelings, Maelstrom climbed back into the command shuttle. She knew as much about what was happening as anyone might know except for the commander and his two closest crewmembers. She also knew potential dangers that would confront her and wasn't sure she could withstand the psychological onslaught. More than anything, she didn't like the idea of mass suicide to keep aliens from trying to take the most basic trait of humanity from them. Then she remembered why she wanted to explore the galaxy. This very mission with her scant navigating, her unexpected isolation, and a life-death scenario was satisfying her every desire for learning about what humans really were.

While giving Maelstrom some time to bed down, as the cramped shuttle sleeping arrangements were, Carpenter thought about spreading the lab rat concept to the crew and settlers. That might preclude a lot of false ideas. It would surely preempt LeRoi's potential spy role. And it would add one more strong rat to the experiment, while priming humanity's rebellious nature.

SYSTEM

Acquisition: *Earthers above holding tanks. Craft are reducing energy reception.*

Central Reception: *How many Earthers? Reduced power recaptured by diverting power from Elthren, Grent, Svoqol, Wurthro. Western complex is at minimum standby and not requesting energy.*

A: *Transmitters weak. Craft block audio and video. Several incremental tonal values number 80 Earthers. Visual numbers total 89 or 90. That number is filed from pressured gaits from sensors in the roof of the repository.*

CR: *Number of different pressure sequences?*

A: *90 plus 15 heavy combined points, the landing craft.*

CR: *More than one computer interfaced brain?*

A: *No. Only one brain different from all others.*

CR: *Problem is to read the brains and encoded information. Other aliens were brought to download center, before all were downloaded.*

A: *Are clones available to capture them?*

CR: *None ready. No time to prepare. Clone material allowed to degrade.*

A: *Robots?*

CR: *Their use varies with power fluctuations. Not dependable. Not even downloaders.*

A: *Access the interfaced brain.*

CR: *One Earther cannot expedite downloads of 89 quickly. Novelty may be slow in arriving. Some may escape as other aliens did. They cannot be captured. Can power be increased to read and transmit brain waves?*

A: *Risky. Multiple brains may overlap, garble memories, personalities. Possible if individuals are isolated.*

CR: *Are communication modules in craft useable?*

A: *They send and receive audio and video. The modules do not read brain waves. Cannot be so modified. Translators have decoded Earther language.*

CR: *Modules providing useful information about plans?*

A: *No. Banter. Noise. Eagerness to build settlement. Significant lack of interest about Molx. One craft has provided no audio beyond breathing. It contains two, one much larger than the other.*

CR: *In our favor. They expect nothing.*

A: *The monitors may be a problem if they interact or show themselves.*

CR: *They fled to be individual not part of a group. They will cause no interference.*

A: *They have formed a community. They cooperate.*

CR: *Not with aliens. They fear us and the downloads. The interfaced brain may be our only option unless we can boost power and delude as we did in space.*

A: *Many fewer than the 90 were recipients and they were enclosed. The computer with translation modules aided our effort. Unlikely to control their senses, especially now. They are on Molx.*

CR: *Intercept the interfaced brain. Provide it with instructions to lead individual Earthers to download center.*

A: *Accessing it is more difficult. It is not connected to ship's computer. There is no computer to interface. Smaller craft do not intermediate.*

CR: *If the dual Earther was once connected, it can be again. Access the ship computer and direct messages through it with enough power to reach the brain.*

A: *Possible. The brain has a wireless receptacle.*

CR: *Remember, physical beings do not move at our speed. Factor in sluggishness.*

A: *Standby and power up to simulate our speed. Time passes only for Earthers.*

HUMANS

Commander Carpenter woke as dawn painted the southern exposure of the tallest peaks yellow. Out the fore port, the bushes and trees shutting off the base of the mountain range were still black green and the tarmac a dull dirty white. Morning light had not reached the shuttle, but the commander had been visited by another waking nightmare, one that reenacted an earlier mission.

His third settlement destination had been a small planet named Kelt orbiting a star about half the size of Earth's sun. Its rotation provided nearly ten hours each of light and dark. The survey probes had reported that three natural satellites provided enough moonlight to extend the day, if settlers needed more time to complete tasks. The probes did not—could not—report that a nocturnal alien population existed below ground and resided only in one hemisphere, where the commander had dropped the colonists.

During the third night on the planet, all thirty settlers disappeared. Carpenter and two of the *Marco's* crew had remained on the planet secured in a shuttle. Inspecting the vacant settlement in daylight revealed multiple six-toed footprints. It was simple enough to see human bootprints and long scuffing dragging ruts pointing the direction the settlers had been carried off. Those marks, however, disappeared when they reached shale outcroppings and a boulder-strewn border at the base of a modest grass covered hill. A daylong search revealed no further evidence showing where the settlers had been taken.

The fourth night revealed a dozen inhabitants wasting their efforts to take control of the commander's shuttle. When the commander turned the area into daylight with the shuttle's external lights, the natives, except one, fled across the shale and through the bouldered border that opened into an entrance into the hill.

The one who remained stood his ground, defiant at the bright lights, and stared at the shuttle. He stood about the commander's height, was as muscular, and was ghost white where

149

clothing didn't cover his skin. He looked human but for the lack of a nose. His face between his mouth, outlined by small lips, and narrow set eyes was flat. After his patient look over the shuttle, he turned and ambled through the boulders and into the hill.

Clearly the leader, Carpenter thought. *Maybe he'll return tomorrow night.*

The next night the commander was waiting outside the shuttle when the leader, Arlock, returned with two companions, nearly his size.

First contact began with gestures, few words, considerable silence and staring. Five nights of tense negotiations were needed for the universal translator to learn Keltude and for release of the settlers who had been stowed away in volcanic tubes. During that time, Carpenter requested that humans might settle the other side of the planet and never venture beyond that hemisphere where no Keltudes lived. When that offering was agreed to, the commander proposed a more bold suggestion: humans develop a settlement where they had landed but remain hidden during night. Ten harrowing nights to reach that agreement spawned pre-dawn and dusk discussions between individuals from each race. Satisfying their own curiosity, colonists and intrigued Keltudes sought out aliens during the cusps of day/night to learn of each other. Those forays into alien society evolved into friendly overtures. Both species recognized they had more in common than not, except their preference for light.

Hemisphere exclusions were annulled. Keltudes agreed to collaborate with Earthlings in use of twenty-hour days: each maintaining separate areas that didn't infringe on the other population. Eventually the cultures mingled. Humans wandered about at night and Keltudes quashed their fear of light and crept about beyond the cusps of day/night and befriended humans.

Carpenter pulled himself forward from the flattened command seat and looked to his shuttle-mate. Her eyes were open. She turned to the commander and winked. The gesture startled the commander, who winked in return, shook his head as if driving away sleep, and headed out the hatch, which hissed shut at his exit.

To the west, morning was just reaching the rounded bubbles on the lower slopes of the western range. The shadows of early dawn created images that made the terrain look like huge kernels of yellow popped corn. Despite the shadowing tall range to the east, the tarmac was losing its dingy coloring. Morning was happening to the valley that Carpenter expected to be the battleground that would return freedom to his human crew or mark the last advance of humans in this sector of the Milky Way. The commander looked across the tarmac. His visual reconnaissance stopped at the only shuttle facing south.

Early morning was quiet. Animals, if there were any, were not stirring. If they existed, it was too early for birds and worms, as the commander heard no sounds except a light breeze shoo-shooing through the forest edge.

A quick pace to his destination, it looked not half a mile away, stirred the commander's blood and consciousness. He felt the morning was warmer than he remembered the previous afternoon before the local star dropped behind the western range, though his quick pace didn't threaten sweat.

Someone must have been watching, for when Carpenter approached, the hatch opened and Fred Sharp descended to meet him.

"Your excuse?" the commander asked about Sharp's early rising.

"New day, new world—even if it's not γ-C A2—we've got lots of work to do."

"Can't argue. I've decided that you and Forbes and Gonzalez should inform the settlers just what's going on. Keeping them in the dark, like I originally thought, isn't a good idea. You three are going to have to defuse a lot of anger. But we have to be together."

"Not much anger, Commander, except at you. It didn't take long for some definite beliefs about this planet not being our destination to be rampant. A few noticed the smaller star and the strange desolate terrain that I saw from the *Marco*. They talked freely and informed others. We back-pedaled a lot to support your cover story. Didn't take long for them to share and conclude what we knew or were sure of. Those who first figured it out were polite enough about our explanations, but they knew better. I think everyone'll be relieved to get the truth about our presence here."

"There's one problem they may not know about and one I don't want them getting involved with," the commander said.

"The navigator?"

"How'd you know?"

"We know we've been compromised electronically. How can he not be a part of that? The three of us have been wondering about Maelstrom. Is she going to be a problem, too? We're pretty sure you've had her squirreled away for some reason."

"I'm thankful you didn't spread that word. She may be a problem. She and I have talked. Says she's not tied to the computer like LeRoi. Says she can shut it off. Roger can't."

Sharp rolled his eyes. "That's what she told you?"

Carpenter ignored the implication. "I don't think she can be compromised like Roger probably is. That doesn't mean we don't watch her, too. Regardless, neither of the navigators are to be targeted by the rest of the crew or physically abused. At worst, they may be shunned, I suppose. I would caution against that. Recrimination will only divide us and then the planet will have us."

"That's pretty much what we came up with. Our settlers are ready for the battle. They can play colonizers for the appearance, but they're not bowing to any planetary force. How do you want us to proceed? Large groups, or fives or smaller?"

"Small ones and then a large one to exchange common ideas. I don't think we can be effective, if we try to go around individually. Too many misimpressions creep in that way, too hard to repair."

"We'll do your bidding. This is certainly not the work we intended. It may be more fun without having to make an impression." Sharp turned and climbed back into the shuttle and the commander headed for George Strumpf who was two shuttles and one row away.

Strumpf's orientation was west and toward the shorter range and the river. However, he was outside waiting for the commander to appear. "Thought you'd be by early," he greeted. "Change of plans?"

"Had to ask?"

"Not really. I think you discussed something with Mael-strom. I'm pretty sure you've kept her in seclusion—our con-versation in the galley, your strange eating habits. Not quite sure about anything else, or how she's of any help, tied to the computer as she is."

"Not much gets by you, George." Carpenter was not com-mander this time. "We discussed LeRoi and the potential dan-ger he poses. And yes, she has been secluded and not spoken a word until I let her out of my shuttle, when I landed. Took the chance that we couldn't be heard, as I suggested to you last night. And my original idea of letting the settlers discover we're not on γ-Cygnus A2 was an undue mistake. They'd already fig-ured that out. Your people need to know what we think is go-ing on. Forewarned, you know."

"Well, Amanda and I have lots of light years under us. We've been talking with the hydros and some others. This is a pretty savvy crew and they keep their thoughts to themselves, while they do what has to be done."

"And they've discovered the main difficulty within the crew?"

"The navigators? They have … about the same time they realized this planet is not our destination."

"LeRoi is very much a concern," Carpenter said. "He never wavered from saying this is γ-Cygnus A2. I think he'd been compromised long before we reached this planet. We need to watch when he becomes an active fifth-columnist."

"And Maelstrom? Isn't she the same?"

"Says she's not and explains that from the difference of her and Roger's interface. She says she can shut hers off—totally; LeRoi can't. Though she does admit that her interface might eventually be compromised."

"Two traitors?"

"Traitors are so because of a willful decision. LeRoi's con-nection to the computer was a decision he made long ago. What he sees and believes through the computer is not willful. He's really not his own person. If Maelstrom is taken in, it won't be a conscious choice. That's what I want the crew and settlers to understand. I don't want either of them targeted as the reason we're here, for whatever purpose the planet wants."

"We talked about that, too. None of us is willing to let the navigators roam about like the rest of us. We'll keep tabs on them but not accuse them of being pawns of the alien force down here. And we'll try to keep them from becoming victims of some plot. So, I gather Priscilla will be a visible member of our army?"

"She will as soon as I return to my shuttle. I have the engineers to see yet. They're still the first line of defense."

As Strumpf had been, Varlez was waiting for the commander to arrive. He had seen Carpenter with Strumpf and expected the change of plans.

"LeRoi has said nothing and barely moved in his seat, when he was in it," Varlez opened the conversation.

"You know we have two navigators, but Roger is the one who is always connected to the computer, or should be, if he could access MP. When you get your computer up and running, will he be able to access it through his helmet?"

"I just have to disable the wireless function, which should be done to keep it inaccessible to the planetary system, I hope. Nequa and Ticia have accepted the duty of watching LeRoi at all times. They even slept in separate shifts to keep an eye on him. So far nothing excites him. What about Maelstrom?"

"Everyone asks." For the third time Commander Carpenter addressed Maelstrom's different interface.

Varlez questioned the prudence of allowing her to accompany LeRoi when he was out of his unique seat. However, he recognized that, if the whole crew were keeping track of LeRoi and Maelstrom were with him, they'd be watching both of them.

Commander Carpenter cut diagonally from Varlez's shuttle that was the farthest west in the last of three rows of landed vehicles to his own, separated north from the first row and farthest east. His route took him past several small knots of huddled crew and settlers, all of whom glanced at him, smiled, and nodded. He wondered if he'd be willing to battle against the 88 humans who were becoming one mind.

MOLRIXX

Dawn was far away when the monitor community rose from sleep on the fifth floor. The fifteen shuttles, dim blobs, covered a significant portion of the white. Korsk and four other gardeners planned an early start and were eager to reach the small garden well before the aliens might discover it, if they tramped northwest in exploration. Korsk had asked Golt to join them. He wanted a lookout to watch and warn him, if the aliens should head toward the plot near the river and find the grove that he had opened the center of to provide just enough light for good growing conditions.

Wisolen and his young hunter-to-be, Vensil, left only a little later than Korsk and his crew; but, once they reached the white, Korsk and his farmers had already hustled across to reach the beaten path that started west but quickly turned northwest to the river. Wisolen and Vensil followed a well-disguised path that began about a third of the way across the white.

Just before the hunters left the strange spongy area, Wisolen looked back over the shuttles that were losing their gray color in the brightening sunlight. He heard the whoosh of a hatch opening and turned to the nearer craft set apart from the others. "Hurry," he ordered his young companion and they sprinted into the bushy cover surrounding the white area.

Once hidden, he stopped and hissed at Vensil to turn and watch with him.

While they looked, a ramp dropped down from the hatch and a solitary male alien followed. He stepped onto the white and turned to look at the bubbled mountains just catching the morning light. "The leader," Wisolen said aloud to himself.

Vensil, wishing he were still sleeping, thought he was spoken to by his mentor and asked, "What?"

"Hush," Wisolen whispered. "Aren't you watching?"

"What's to see? It's hardly light."

"You must pay attention, if you're going to hunt with me, *or alone.*"

"Nothing crosses the white except us," Vensil said explaining why he wasn't watching.

"There are aliens about," Wisolen instructed.

"Where? They're not out now, are they?" Vensil was thinking about his forced early rising.

With his left hand Wisolen grabbed the youngster and pulled him next to him and pointed with his right. "Look! Didn't you hear the woosh?"

"No; I was thinking of other things."

"About sleeping or getting together with Rhial?"

Even in the dark Wisolen saw Vensil blush and look away from him.

"Shouldn't we get to the cat blind?" his apprentice asked in a futile attempt to deny both options.

"Patience, patience. What we brought yesterday is enough for a while. We are only scouting about today. Something may offer itself to us. Now, watching the alien is more important. We're the only ones this close. Maybe we can learn something about them."

"But we can't understand them. What good is listening?"

"Vensil!" Wisolen shook his head. "How much you have to learn! We don't understand animal speech. But we know what they're going to do by watching them. It's the same with the aliens. We watch their actions. Maybe in the morning silence we can hear the tone of their words, the wind's blowing toward us. That'll tell even more."

Wisolen dropped to all fours and pulled Vensil down with him. "A formidable opponent," Wisolen said softly to his young companion. The alien looked taller than any of the monitors and seemed more physically developed than Krolni but his head was smaller.

Wisolen separated some of the broad green leaves of the Belganic bushes to have an uncluttered view of the alien who was just then directing a sweeping look across the white.

"He'll see us!" Vensil cautioned at his mentor's widening view.

"No, he won't. As tall as he is he won't look down, at the ground. Besides it's still dark."

At that moment, the alien's gaze paused at their hiding place. Wisolen drew a sharp breath and Vensil gathered his arms and legs to ready a quick flight. The master hunter, however, put his hand on his apprentice's shoulder. "Luck that he looked our direction. If he noticed us, he'd come to investigate or call for others to join him."

"He's heading away," Vensil reported and let out a long breath, as the alien turned his attention to the south.

The two hunters watched the alien visit three of the strange craft. "No doubt important people in his company. They are preparing to plan their day and maybe get some work scheduled."

"How do you know that?" the novice hunter asked.

Wisolen rolled onto his right side, looked back through his peep space, and answered while he continued to watch the white. "Do you rise before anyone else?"

"No," Vensil said with disgust.

"Who gets up first?"

"Vokra and Crelle do." Vensil remained prone and looked to his right.

"And they lead us, don't they?" Wisolen turned his view to his apprentice. "And they get us going for the day."

"Okay. I never thought about it that way before. How many do you suppose there are? Why are they here?"

"Those craft could hold a lot of them, but when they first landed and they seemed to meet together, we counted 89. To find out why they are here, we could go up and ask them. Shall we do that?" The hunter rolled to his stomach and put his hands on the ground at his shoulder to push up to his hands and knees.

"No," Vensil hissed, rejecting the absurd proposal. "We don't know anything about them."

"That's right, Vensil. So, if we don't ask them why they're here, how do we learn that?" The hunter rose to his feet and reached a hand to help his apprentice up.

"We have to watch them long enough to discover what they're going to do." Vensil paused and he finally understood what Wisolen tried to get him to realize. "Just like if we happened to find an animal we hadn't seen before and had to learn about."

"Good, Vensil, that's exactly what we must do. But we also

have other duties. Korsk and his workers will watch when they can. We've already discovered the leaders. Vokra will have others out to watch them. But for now, we have hunting to do. When we return here, we may discover more information."

"Maybe they will be good for hunting," Vensil joked to lighten his own fear, because he could see that two who talked with the leader were larger than any of his own group.

"Thinking of becoming cannibal?" Wisolen probed. "Would you eat one of us?"

"They're not us," Vensil rejected with a wry face. "They might be good eating … better than cat."

"Vensil, we eat animals, unthinking animals. Those aliens are thinking beings. Unthinking animals don't journey to other worlds. Maybe they are traveling far and needed to stop and rest. Maybe they came from the other side of Molx. But now we have taken enough time from our hunting. Let's go."

Wisolen and Vensil strode north, past the huge round fire pit, past abandoned lean-tos where the monitors slept before they invaded Molox1, and into the deeper forest where they expected to discover another jungle cat or an even larger horned Cernox whose meat tasted sweet.

The tall alien who had gathered his companions the day before exited his aircraft and stepped onto the white tarmac long after Korsk reached the break in the bushes.

Korsk sent the rest of his agrarians ahead to the garden plot and crept back to watch the white lighten. He was intrigued by the craft that covered much of the white. He hid where he could watch the lone male survey his surroundings. The gardener was sure Wisolen was watching the alien from a closer position than his. Still he stared. He knew the others would get to work: weeding, watering, and caring for the plants.

The alien visited three craft and then headed back to the ship he came out of. "I will send Golt back to watch what goes on here," he thought aloud and added a worry, "if they happen to find our path, she'll have time to warn us and we can hide in the forest." He didn't consciously realize what finding the garden would mean to the aliens.

When Golt returned to the edge of the white, she saw the full complement of the *Marco P* gathered into six groups which shortly dispersed becoming threes and fours that formed from the larger groups. They nodded to each other; slapped backs, touched hands, and, recombining in different small groups, duplicated the same ritual actions.

HUMANS

Arafa woke and saw Bandi's head down, her eyes closed. She wondered how long she'd been sleeping instead of watching the computer-minded navigator. She touched Ticia's left arm and a wide-eyed Bandi jerked awake. Expecting that her charge was gone, she feared she had failed her first night duty. The flood of adrenalin ebbed, when she realized that his escaping would have wakened her when she heard the hatch open. She saw the helmeted navigator as she had seen him when Arafa bedded down for her rest and every other time she had inspected him during the dark, even when Varlez had left the shuttle a bit ago.

Occupying a semi-reclined shuttle seat, LeRoi had not moved. His arms were still crossed over his chest, a most uncomfortable position for so long a time Bandi thought. The permanently implanted helmet that allowed the navigator's interface with the *Marco's* computer—that he was not accessing—rested in a depression that Varlez had created to provide the enhanced navigator comfort similar to the sleep pod he seldom used on the *Marco P.* In spite of Varlez's work that improved his sleep pod, LeRoi could not lay on his side or on his stomach. Out of the hibernation seat the navigator could nod and he had limited side-to-side movement, not enough to look directly at either shoulder. The navigator's sleep position looked uncomfortable: he seemed to have remained immobile for hours. Even his feet had not fallen to either side. Bandi couldn't imagine anyone sleeping without some change of position.

What she did notice, however, was a subtle change in his face. "He looks different," she whispered to Arafa who made a face at her statement.

"Looks like last night, to me," came the quiet rebuke.

"I can't say why. He's just different. You watch. Can't imagine he'll sleep much longer. I'll tell Jer."

Bandi yawned, rose, stretched, and yawned again. She really wanted to sleep, but she left the shuttle to report her impressions to Varlez.

Though Arafa scoffed at Bandi's unspecified assessment of LeRoi, she didn't reject it. Nor did she just drop into the seat Bandi had used to watch the suspicious navigator. Arafa had learned in the brief time of this mission that her companion second engineer saw what others didn't see and those others too often and mistakenly discounted her seemingly quixotic notions. Arafa edged close to the navigator's seat to see if she could spy what Bandi thought she had seen. The navigator looked like he always did when he was in the shuttle seat: not completely reclined, arms folded, legs and feet together as if he were enclosed in an invisible box.

The navigator's eyes were open. Arafa stopped in mid-step and waited to be asked what she wanted. No question came. The navigator's glassy eyes were forward, apparently not capturing anything in the shuttle. He blinked rapidly. Then the blinking stopped; his eyelids closed. Nequa could see LeRoi's corneas shifting back and forth under the lids. She wondered how he achieved REM sleep so quickly or how often he managed it once he had been connected to a computer. Suddenly his lips twitched into a faint smile that vanished immediately. The navigator's face became expressionless as his glassy eyes had been.

"Was that what Ticia noticed?" she thought.

Bandi brought Varlez back to the shuttle from his short stroll south on the tarmac. He merely looked through the hatch and nodded. Despite Bandi's eager assertion that LeRoi was different, Arafa didn't add to that impression. Varlez didn't enter to look closer at the navigator but returned to the tarmac. He knew his assistants wouldn't lose the potentially treasonous navigator.

Arafa returned to the upright seat just across from LeRoi, the seat Bandi had left to report to Varlez. She nodded as Bandi passed between her and LeRoi on her way to a more relaxing sleep. As tired as she was, she would still join in, if Arafa called for help.

Commander Carpenter returned to his shuttle after his third instructional stop. He passed by several small groups surveying the surrounding greenery and digging at the spongy tarmac.

When he entered the shuttle, he motioned for Priscilla Mael-strom to join him outside.

"You are released from your silence and isolation," he said as she stepped from the ramp. "However, you should know that there are those who are concerned that you are as liable to be taken over by the computer as LeRoi is expected to be. Everyone is, or soon will be, aware of everything I have told you. You should be ready for some crew and settlers to treat you with disdain."

"Commander, I told you last night. I can control that com-puter-controlled part of my brain."

"I passed on that information. It's not just my closest crew but others and maybe all of the settlers. I don't think you have to fear physical violence, but I get the feeling that many have made up their minds that you are a threat."

"From isolation to shunning. Not much different." Mael-strom shook her head and huffed.

"We must still not speak in the shuttles. As long as the com appears to be operating out of our control, the less information we give the aliens, the better. From my morning chats, the oth-ers understand that silence in the shuttles is more important than anything else. That should force the planet to do some-thing more to get us to react somehow."

"Well, Commander, it seems not all will shun," Priscilla said as she looked across the tarmac. Leading the group of set-tlers headed their way were the two young males Carpenter saw Sharp speak to about the missing navigator.

The group halted several steps away. The two men who were interested in the diminutive navigator edged forward and then stopped to keep from interrupting the commander's con-versation.

Commander Carpenter was amused at the eager, but re-spectful, approach of the two. "Perhaps I was wrong," he re-evaluated to his backup navigator.

Maelstrom turned her head and smiled at the two seeking her presence. Then to the commander she restated her expla-nation. "I don't have the helmet Roger has. My connection is much less noticeable. I'm very much like the other settlers."

Carpenter looked down at his second navigator. All he

detected of the computer interface cable that extruded from behind her left ear was a narrow raised line under her khaki tunic. That ridge extended to her armpit where the slightly bulkier connector was tucked away. Anyone looking for the interface would likely not see past her bosom. "You may be right, Maelstrom," the commander said. "I leave you to your admirers. But, do take care," he counseled against her being so assured. "I have learned that no matter how much we think we are in control, there are always forces more so."

"I am aware of that, Commander. I will."

Maelstrom stepped around the commander and joined the seven settlers who were already tossing questions at her about what she had been doing and where she'd been.

With the whole day before him, Carpenter returned to the shuttle for a prodding pole. Then he headed for the northeast corner of the tarmac and the well-beaten path, which he didn't take, as he hadn't the day before. Instead, he reversed his more haphazard investigation of the white tarmac and its bordering greenery that he patrolled the previous afternoon. This day, he would be less quick in looking and more intense in studying what lay under and through the bushy, spiked and green, border.

He had not gone far, poking into the bushes and angling them apart for a longer and deeper look beyond the tarmac, when Kellan Forbes and six other settlers approached him.

"Our first foray, Commander," Forbes offered. "Fred said you thought we should scout the complex. We like the challenge, even if there are electronic aliens about."

"Don't let eagerness override caution, Kellan," was the commander's return. "It's not a small place. I doubt you can do more than look at a handful of floors."

"We thought we'd just start at the bottom and maybe look around until just a little after noon. We're not gonna do anything crazy. Besides there may be someone … thing… in there. We've got para-rays. Unless we're really caught off guard, we should be okay."

"Men," the commander spoke to the whole group, "we don't know if there is life on the planet, wild or not; or if the only thing that does exist is electronics soaking up energy from solar power or some other source." He saw a couple look past him toward the complex. They were anxious to get underway and didn't want to listen to more cautions repeated from the day before.

"Three with me," Forbes advised hoping to remind the commander of the colonists' qualifications, "were first colonists on a couple of other planets. We've talked about the dangers of exploring."

"Not in the shuttle?" Carpenter hurriedly asked.

"No, sir. We knew something was up when the com reinitialized. Once we landed and after you gave us some details of what we needed to do, we made plans away from the shuttles. We're aware everything is unknown and filled with potential mortal danger. We're expecting problems; we just can't anticipate what. Since you were along our way, we stopped to tell you what we were up to."

"One more concern, Kellan." Malcolm Carpenter saw visible disgust on more faces. He was preventing them from an adventure more interesting than his worries. "I'd limit your talk in the complex. Use gestures and mouthing and sight. If we're listened to in the shuttles, I'd think the complex would be transmitted as well."

"Ahead of you there, sir. We don't plan to be separated from each other by more than a couple, three, arm-lengths. We've got some line to tie us together if we need to be. And we've left personal communication in the shuttle. With the nature of our landing here, we didn't want any more sources to be accessed. I have our only communication device—for emergencies. It's off and hasn't been activated since we landed. We'll see if it works or not ... if and when we need it."

"You seem on top of things. One device may be secure. Take care. I'll be interested in what you discover. Oh, there's a path through the bushes at the northeast corner. It looks well used. I figure it goes to the complex. Indicates something uses it."

"That's good to know. We were just going to forge through the brush. Won't have to, now."

Commander Carpenter turned and watched the explorers find the path and disappear. He wondered if it rose to the base of the skyscraper. If it did, he'd see them along the way, heads and shoulders above the surrounding bushes and trees.

Roger LeRoi woke an hour after Ticia Bandi dropped to sleep. Nequa Arafa had been thinking about ways to separate the engineering computer from all outside access as they did on board the *Marco P*. And if they were successful in that venture, maybe the procedure might work to shield the shuttles from alien incursion. She thought that that success might be enough to get at least one shuttle back to the *Marco P* and remove the main computer from alien influence. Her thoughts were more exercise than actual plans, more whimsy than real steps to continuing to γ-Cygnus A2. She was sure Varlez was already working on something that could mesh with what she came up with.

Whizzing along with her thoughts was the faint idea that all their problems might be solved if they could rid themselves of the navigator. She was sure his presence bode nothing but ill for the crew and colonists. After one more statement of blame laid at LeRoi's person for their being hijacked, she stared accusingly at the recumbent figure that couldn't be less unaware of what she thought.

She was shocked to see the navigator raise his helmeted head, sit up, and turn his body to drop his legs over the edge of the armless seat. He was facing her, but gave no impression that he saw her. He turned his head to his right, an action that might have put the sleeping Bandi in sight, and turned left as if to look out the shuttle's main port.

Arafa thought the navigator had slept a long time. Except for the commander's addressing the whole company, LeRoi had never left his gravity seat and had remained supine, unwilling to lift the back to a more erect position as it automatically assisted his sitting up.

Again, the navigator looked at his sitter, blinked his eyes and almost opened his mouth to greet her. Instead he offered a slight nod. He eased off the seat, steadied himself with a hand on the seat, and walked to the open hatch.

Arafa wondered if he'd been contacted by alien electronic intelligence. She rose to follow him and considered waking Bandi to accompany her. She discounted that thought, since little more than an hour before, she had found her nodded off instead of watching. Bandi needed sleep, especially if she were taking the night watch again.

The navigator stood at the hatch, turned his whole body left and rotated to the right gathering in a 180-degree panorama. Tentative steps down the ramp suggested he was moving into territory he was remembering after a long absence, perhaps recalling Varlez leading him to the commander's landing remarks. Arafa had the unmistakable impression that the navigator was measuring what he saw against what he remembered or had experienced before or had had placed in his mind.

Arafa maintained a discrete distance—five feet—behind his jerky movements and, when LeRoi stepped off the ramp, she saw that Varlez, who was working on a computer, had watched their halting descent. LeRoi stood still and again rotated his body to take in the whole shuttle-covered tarmac and its surrounding hedge. Awareness of his presence on the landing site passed quickly through those who were also surveying their potential homeland. They paused their own agendas intent on what the consensus dangerous human might be up to.

LeRoi was oblivious to anyone watching him. He looked alert, but gave no greetings to any who passed by within friendly distance but interested in their own discoveries. He seemed to be gauging his position and the orientation of the tarmac. Then he set out on a line as straight as possible, skirting two shuttles in the way, to the center of the eastern edge of the tarmac.

Arafa was pressed to keep close to LeRoi's rushing gait, but she was soon joined by three others who understood the necessity of keeping the navigator under close surveillance. He slowed just as he got to the edge of the tarmac and wagged his head back and forth in the forty-five degrees he was capable of. He appeared to be looking for some identifying mark. Arafa and the three colonists moved closer. When the navigator jockeyed his position five feet from where he first stopped, he reached out to separate the bushes in front of him.

Eight hands grabbed him. They turned him around and demanded he tell them what he was about to do.

LeRoi shook his head; his pupils narrowed. He looked lost.

"Where am I?" he asked.

"Don't you know," Arafa demanded and noticed that his eyes were no long glossed over.

He recognized and greeted her. "Are you sitting me? Did you bring me here?"

"Taking care of you in this strange place," she answered. "Since you aren't tied to MP, we worry about how you're going to be." Arafa was amazed that she was so kind after her earlier rounds of blaming the navigator for their predicament. What she said was certainly the truth, but the blame she had before heaped upon him in thought was missing. "Come, Roger, let's go back to the shuttle."

She took his hand.

He turned back to look at the brush and around to Arafa and to the three others who had pulled their hands from him. LeRoi's lost look returned, but it accompanied squinting eyes and a quizzical recognition of being in a place he had never been before. "Yes," he finally answered. "I haven't any idea why I'm here."

SYSTEM

Acquisition: *Interfaced Earther was accessed. Then lost.*
    Central Reception: *How?*

A: *Unable to explain. It was following instructions. Close to conduit to download chamber. Connection broken.*

CR: *Power to connection too weak?*

A: *Computer in space vessel not constructed for long distance transmission to Molx surface.*

CR: *Increase power.*

A: *Power may damage circuits. May drain our power excessively.*

CR: *Analyze interface to receive direct access. We must possess Earther content.*

A: *Transmission from Molox1 requires increasing power to revitalize transmitters and areas of Molox1 that are powerless.*

CR: *Replace lost power from Wurthro's remaining power.*

A: *Any siphoning from Wurthro will remove viability from those in storage and destroy the complex. Recepts there are failing.*

CR: *They are nearly dead. Waste no energy on them. If power is not available from there, take it from Elthren.*

A: *Elthren is barely maintaining. Taking power from it will be fatal to those remaining. Recepts there are also failing.*

CR: *They offer us only disadvantage and waste. When Elthren is unable to provide any more power take it from Grent and then Svoqol.*

A: *Ultimately only Molox1 will have power. What if we fail?*

CR: *We will not fail. Before we are near to power loss, we will possess Earthers. Power use will diminish. We will survive.*

MOLRIXX

Golt soon tired of watching small-headed aliens wander about the white. Two groups might have discovered the path to the garden had they only held the willowy reeds and short thorn bushes back enough to pass through the natural barrier and recognize the worn path. The strangers, a little larger than the Molrixx, seemed surprised that the plants, after being pushed out of the way, always snapped back disguising the beginning of the trail to the garden. Nor did the aliens look down to see the well-trodden ground under the brush.

Shortly after noon, an alien used his arm to push on the brush at the beginning of the path and Golt was ready to run to the garden with an urgent warning. However the strange alien missed seeing the thorns. After shoving the sturdy bracts back he howled in pain and pulled his arm away, rubbing where he had been stuck in several places and further scratched from his recoil. Neither he nor his three companions repeated the bold attempt to pass through the prickly boundary.

Half way to dusk, Korsk led his farmers back to Golt. She was beyond bored. Korsk was sure that they would have to avoid the quick route across the white and return to Molox1 along a much less traveled and overgrown path through the forest. However, not until he met Golt did he realize that the aliens, despite not finding their path, had still sent several northward past the barrier and into the forest. Golt told him that another seven had left up the path to Molox1 and had not yet returned.

With a couple of head shakes Korsk acknowledged Golt's information as if he had expected it but hoped not. The forest route to the molox was slow but having to watch for aliens and keep from being seen added more time in their return. Those concerns didn't approach the anticipated hardship of getting into the molox before dark without being seen by the seven who had obviously gone there, for the path they took led nowhere else.

The gardeners' travel was uneventful except for having

169

to force themselves through heavy overgrowth and they never saw any indication of aliens who were wandering about
the forest as Golt had reported. Not until they met Wisolen
and Vensil, who had bagged a horned Cernox, did they hear
strange sounds.

Gardeners and hunters slipped into cover with the body of
the Cernox and watched five aliens, who might have been mistaken for Molrixx but for their strange clothing, smaller heads,
and oval eyes bordering a skinny nose. The aliens returning to
their craft on the white followed their outbound trail that was
vaguely marked by broken and bent vines. One alien struggled
to maintain the modest pace his companions held and fell farther behind the other four who kept turning and with red faces
sent loud noises his way.

Wisolen knew the alien's problem. His glazed eyes, halting
strides, rapid breathing, and heavy sweating told him he had
encountered a Hislik, a small serpent that wormed along the
ground and had very sharp small teeth. Hislik toxin was not
fatal to Molrixx who exhibited less seriously the alien's symptoms. However, Wisolen didn't know if the alien's system could
fight off the toxin.

"He's going to collapse," Wisolen whispered to Korsk.
"What should we do?"

"Hisliks aren't deadly," Korsk said without answering the
question; he also had experienced the tiny snake's bite. "At least
not to us. Besides there's not much we can do without showing
ourselves and that'll create more problems than Vokra wants."

"True; and we can't speak with them about his problem.
We have no idea what they'll do, if they see us."

"They'll think we caused the Hislik symptoms," Golt surmised.

"I've got an ointment with me that draws out the poison.
When I'm hunting, if I chance a bite, I can't waste the time
waiting for the poison to leave. When he collapses, if the others
are out of sight, we can pull him under cover and treat him."

"We've got to be quick," Korsk said.

"And what do we do when his companions can't find
him?" Golt offered a more serious worry as the Molrixx heard
more shouts to the straggling male.

At that moment, the Hislik-poisoned alien fell forward. He hardly used his arms to break his fall. Wisolen looked ahead. "Quick," he demanded, "They're out of sight. Lift him, don't drag. That'll leave marks when they come looking."

Wisolen, Korsk, Golt, and Vensil barely got the alien and themselves hidden in a vine-surrounded bare spot three meters off the aliens' course before four grumbling aliens returned to look for their malingering companion.

Searching for their missing one, they flashed light beams about the darkening forest as they retraced their steps. Urgent noises were exchanged between the largest alien and three others. Then all four stopped and looked at each other, shaking their heads. The large one, red faced with heavy black hair, noised at the other three and pointed a finger at them. They sounded back, not quite as loud. Eventually, having discovered no sign of their lagging companion, they left the area and continued toward the white.

Wisolen pulled a vial from a small pack he wore around his neck. "Look for two arcs of teeth-marks around his ankle. They look like sharp pricks, not gashes."

Vensil, who had been infected several times on his ventures with Wisolen before he learned how to avoid the Hislik and its haunts said, "I know." He didn't have to look long to find the puncture marks on the supine alien's left leg, just above his foot covering.

"Don't know if this will do any good for an alien," Wisolen said as he pulled his coated index finger out of the vial. He wiped a viscous brown liquid onto and around the bite and then rubbed the ooze into the skin.

"He's not conscious," Vensil announced. "Hislik bites never make us unconscious. Will he die?"

"Who can say?" Wisolen answered. "They look like us— their heads are different; his symptoms are like ours when we get bit. Maybe losing consciousness is their way of healing."

"What are we going to do with him?" Korsk asked. "They're going to come looking for him ... again; if not now, next solar rise. They'll know someone was here."

"Don't think so," Golt corrected. "They'll think he was carried off by an animal."

"Maybe," Korsk agreed, "but they'll continue to explore and look around. We don't know what the others will have found in Molox1 that will let them know we live here."

"There are no animals to devour him, at least not while he's alive, if he stays that way," Wisolen said. "If he's not conscious and he doesn't die, he doesn't know anything about us. We can take him to the edge of the white and leave him there. He'll be found, either before he wakes up or after."

"If he wakes up," Korsk said. "If he doesn't, that's another problem."

"And since he'll be found," Golt explained away Korsk's concern, "they'll all think he just got lost and finally found his way."

"We'll have to wait until they're all in their craft before we take him there. We don't want anyone seeing us," Korsk said.

"Vensil and I can stay and maybe Golt, if she wants," Wisolen offered. "The rest of you can report to Vokra. Just take care getting to the ground floor. Waiting until near dark might be the best way to keep from being seen. I can't believe aliens would stay out on a strange planet near dark."

After the gardeners except Golt left for Molox1 in the darkening dusk, Wisolen said, "I'll take his shoulders, Golt, you and Vensil take his knees. We'll carry him to our entry from the white, where we watched this morning. It's not too far. If the white is empty of aliens we can carry him through the barrier and lay him a little way in and come back for our kill. If he wakes, he'll get where he needs to be. If not, he'll still be found."

"Alive or dead," Golt assessed, "they should have no idea how he got there, other than from being lost, harmed by something, and just made his way back. Good plan, Wisolen."

HUMANS

Fred Sharp had never seen Manuel Gonzalez look so abashed when he shuffled in to motion the settler lead to join him on the tarmac.

"What's wrong, Manny?" he asked when he stood in front of him. "What happened out there?"

"I lost a settler, Fred ... Ben Cantro, one of those who's chasing Maelstrom. I don't know how. He was dawdling, couldn't keep up. And then he was gone." Gonzalez shook his head. "We went back to look and couldn't find anything of him."

Sharp just looked at Gonzalez and thought that on a strange wrong planet death was one more unfortunate thing. "I'm sorry, Manuel, these things happen. We wish they didn't. But they do."

"Don't know what could've happened." Gonzalez shook his head while he looked down. His shoulders slumped and Sharp thought as he looked at the beaten lead that Gonzalez was six inches shorter than he was.

"Let's see the commander," Sharp said. "He needs to know what happened and about the terrain. He may not be in charge like the military, but he's going to ask how he got behind, and why you didn't stay with him. Remember what he said when we landed?"

"I know." Gonzalez looked up and then dropped his head, again, and spoke to the tarmac. "I know. I thought it was getting dark and didn't want to be out there then. I thought he'd catch up. I was stupid."

Sharp paused and looked softly at Gonzalez. "This is your first new planet, isn't it?"

"Yes, sir; but I should've known better."

"Carpenter won't send you to hydroponics because this isn't a ship problem. He may make you feel like Varlez just showed you up. Besides we may not be leaving here, anyway. You know that."

"I do." Gonzalez never looked up and Sharp realized just

how whipped Gonzalez felt.

Gonzalez continued quietly without looking at Sharp. "Let's get this over with. Okay?"

Gonzalez's pace slowed the closer they got to Carpenter's shuttle. Then Sharp grabbed his arm and stopped. "Who's that?" The head lead pointed to the north. "Isn't that Cantro?"

The slender young settler was heading toward Gonzalez and Sharp. He wasn't struggling; his strides had purpose and a question covered his face.

"Well, now I may speak with Carpenter, when you do," Sharp offered. "First, you clear things up with Cantro."

The colonist was there before Gonzalez had a chance to form any question of his errant settler and Cantro spoke first. "What happened out there, Gonzalez? I got really sick. The next thing I knew I was on the tarmac. I saw you and Sharp and here I am." He looked around and up at the increasing star-lit sky. Then he asked, "How'd it get so dark?"

"You vanished, Ben; gone. We couldn't find you. Don't you know what happened?"

"What can you tell us," Sharp asked. Gonzalez had given him his side. He needed Cantro's version. "How sick were you?"

"It came on all of a sudden," Cantro started out and continued like he was reading a list. "Started stumbling. Couldn't keep up. Vision blurred. I was sweating like I was in a sauna. Everything went black. I guess I fell, face down. Got some bruises, feel like bruises. Next thing I was here."

"Nothing else?" Sharp encouraged. "Sounds? No idea how you got here?"

Cantro looked off in the growing dusk as he thought. "When everything went black, I felt like I was floating and I heard strange noises—not a lot of them and not words. I don't think there was anything else."

Sharp nodded and looked past Cantro and Gonzalez, as he pieced together the details. Nothing remotely matched with his first new world experiences. He shook his head and wrinkled his brow. "Ben, go see Crown and tell her what you've told us. You must've gotten tangled up in something. We need to know. She needs to know everything. If she releases you, get some rest. We'll talk later."

"I'll do that," Cantro agreed and angled from his intended course to his shuttle and headed for Strumpf's: the galley and infirmary.

"Doesn't seem to be too bad except for the loss of time and memory. Might be something lasting," Sharp said to Gonzalez who was watching Cantro's course. The first time lead appeared as relieved as he had been despondent before Cantro showed up.

"You're not out of trouble, yet," Sharp advised; "it's just not as bad. Let's see Carpenter."

When they reached the commander's shuttle, Sharp told Gonzalez to invite him outside. "Don't speak; just motion for him to join you and come back down."

Gonzales had to strike the partly open hatch to catch the commander's attention. He seemed deep in thought and gazing north out the forward ports. His face was tense, involved in something he could or couldn't see. When the commander turned at the knock, Gonzalez waved for him to follow and turned back for the tarmac after Carpenter rose. The commander was not two steps behind and caught the youngest of his settler leads within half a dozen strides.

"Something went wrong," Gonzales began, when the commander reached him and Sharp, "and Sharp thought you should know."

With an unstated question, Carpenter looked to Sharp and back to Gonzales. "Wrong?" he questioned.

"Yes, sir. I didn't respond properly to a situation. I thought I lost a colonist because of it ..."

Carpenter almost got his question out.

"... but I didn't," Gonzalez finished.

Carpenter narrowed his eyes and furrowed his brow. "That doesn't make sense, Gonzalez. Explain."

"I can do that, sir," Sharp offered.

"No, Sharp, you can't. No matter what you've been told and discovered. This settler lead is responsible for his actions." Then turning back to Gonzalez he ordered, "Tell me."

Manuel heard the tone; it was not as severe as he had feared. However, it was more dire than he had hoped after

Sharp's counsel and Cantro's appearance. "Sir, I chose four settlers and we scouted north into the forest to look for places where we might establish a settlement. I planned to head out for maybe three hours, blazing our trail that was anything but a straight line. The trees grow in copses and their trunks and the forest floor are covered by short bushes and trailing vines running everywhere.

"We found a site, about two hours out, a large grove with a small spring. The trees were pretty straight, bark not too thick, looked like they might supply us with good straight boards. I wanted to go another hour. Two agreed with me. Two others, Cantro and another, wanted to come back. Well, we went on and Cantro and the other one grumbled and complained and slowed our pace. We were all tired of having to fight the vines and their carping didn't help any. After the hour I turned back and the two complained even louder about the waste of time because we'd discovered nothing better."

"Your mission didn't go as you expected?" Carpenter analyzed and got a shake of Gonzalez's head in reply. "I can't fault you for extending your exploration. You might have had a private chat with Cantro when he first became disruptive. You'll learn. Continue."

"Well, when we got back to the grove where Cantro had first wanted to return, I thought we should take a break. I'd been pushing them. We found a large enough spot without vines and got off our feet—all except Cantro. He wouldn't sit with us. He leaned back against a tree and mad-dogged me. Then he lagged back a little when we continued our return. He got slower and slower. I thought he was just making things difficult because I pushed going out so far. We all told him to hurry, even Belnap who didn't think we should have gone the extra hour. I suppose I should have slowed down, but I didn't want to be forced into doing his bidding."

"You realize your mistake," the commander said, "though you have to understand that passive resistance, if that's what Cantro was using, is hard to counteract. You still haven't got to losing him."

"We weren't too far from the tarmac when Belnap turned again to demand Cantro hurry and he didn't see him. We stopped and backtracked for longer than the last time some-one had threatened him, if he didn't catch up. Our trail, twice kicked through by five of us was clear enough and we took care to look either side, if he'd wandered off. He wasn't anywhere. I yelled at the other three for not taking care and watching him. I was wrong there. It was my responsibility. I went to Sharp when we got back and told him what had happened. He said I should tell you. He came with me."

Carpenter looked at Sharp. "Support?"

"Yes, sir," Sharp answered quickly. "I told Gonzalez, I'd come with him, but he'd have to tell his own story."

Still not understanding why Gonzalez reported himself, Carpenter directed more testimony. "All of this and Cantro's not lost. Where is he? Was he playing a game?"

"Don't think so, sir," Gonzalez continued. "On our way here, me and Sharp, to see you, Cantro met us; he was crossing the tarmac. He wasn't stumbling or slow. I asked where he'd been and what happened. He said he'd felt really sick, blacked out, and then he was on the tarmac. Sharp sent him to Crown with his story and we came to you."

"You've never taken anyone into uncharted territory be-fore, have you?" the commander asked for what he already knew.

"No, sir; this was the first time." Gonzalez geared up for the commander's judgment.

"I can't fault your initiative or what you did, Gonzalez. Your people skills are in need of improvement ..."

"Commander," Fred Sharp interrupted intending to soften what he was sure was coming. He drew a long stern glare from Carpenter, who held his palm up toward the head settler lead.

"... Whether Ben Cantro will be impaired from your ac-tions or whatever infected him remains to be seen. Perhaps his body and his aversion to being taken further into an alien forest than he thought necessary caused a physical reaction. Perhaps something in the forest affected him. We won't know unless his symptoms are duplicated by others. Nevertheless your au-tocratic decisions, proper to your position, but imperially de-manded, demonstrate a need for more empathy for those un-der your charge."

"Sir, I thought he and Belnap were challenging my authority. I could ..."

"I understand, Manuel," the commander interrupted with his first name to ease what was to follow. "First explorations on new planets are difficult enough. But this was also your first on any planet. That fear of the unknown that all of us have to fight, even veterans like Sharp and myself, you have to control. You didn't. Safety of all must never be sacrificed to one's authority—under any circumstances. You have to learn how to maintain safety by sacrificing authority without yielding it."

The young settler lead looked into Carpenter's face. The severity he thought he first saw for his mistake had transformed into concern. It had not softened into leniency. He knew there was a price to be paid. He rejected the hope that it wouldn't be devastating.

"Manuel, pushing the extra hour was not necessary. We're here; and until we know why, we're not going anywhere. You had time to look further on another foray. I know you probably thought that'd be a waste of time. But you passed up a chance to show you listened to others. That's a difficult trait to learn and you might have offered a half hour compromise."

"But ..." Gonzalez stopped, when he saw the commander's stern look and inhaled, expecting the worst.

Commander Carpenter just shook his head and continued, "I want you to apologize to Ben Cantro. You can do it privately or publicly and he has to know it's sincere, not just words. And he must understand that your actions were not directed at him, personally. Then, if he is physically able, you *will* ask him to accompany you on another exploration. It would be best if it's not an extension of where you went today. You may find that he has insights that can help."

Gonzalez's shoulders fell. He stared down at the tarmac. He hated apologies. They took authority from him.

Carpenter saw the dejection. "Manuel, I don't have any authority to punish colonists who are not part of my crew and I can't send you to hydroponics. But, I lead the mission because of my experience; and, if you're a settler lead, you have to learn to mix authority and encouragement. This is just a lesson. You can do it."

Gonzalez slowly raised his head to look at the commander. "I will do that—as soon as I can." Manuel stepped off to his shuttle leaving Sharp and the commander. As he walked away, Gonzalez thought about Carpenter's reputation of never making a mistake. He couldn't imagine someone in space never making a mistake. Then he remembered the commander counseled empathy and he decided the commander must be made of it.

Carpenter turned to Sharp as Gonzalez walked away. "Your reason?" he asked.

"Huh?" Sharp had been thinking about his own concern. "Oh, moral support. His mistake was understandable. But I do have a concern. Did Kellan see you before he trudged off this morning?"

"He did. He said they were going to scout the building, if they could get inside."

Both of them looked east to the mountain-tall construction that had a faint zig-zag line running down the sheer outside wall the top of which still caught the setting solar rays.

"That's what he told me," Sharp confirmed. "He didn't think they'd be gone long. I haven't seen Forbes since he told me this morning. Has he been back to report?" Sharp asked with more than casual interest.

"I was thinking he was overdue when Gonzalez called me out. It's getting close to dark. They should be back, unless ..."

"That's what I thought. Do we have enough power in the shuttles to turn on the approach lights? Fifteen shuttles might turn the tarmac and surrounding area into daylight. If they're just slow or lost, that'll show the way."

"And if something's more serious," the commander didn't finish. He had considered that possibility long enough before Gonzalez called him to the tarmac. He didn't want to verbalize it.

Before either had a chance to discuss the possibility of people dying, Amanda Crown wearing a somber countenance, joined them and waited for the nod to speak.

"I've checked out Ben Cantro. He's perfectly healthy. I couldn't find anything in his spectrum that would have caused the symptoms he reported. I really thought he was malingering, trying to get Gonzalez in trouble, which he no doubt did."

Neither Sharp nor Carpenter spoke to that conjecture.

"Then I thought about the vines and brush he said all five kicked through. I had him take off his trousers and I inspected for bites starting at his feet after I took his shoes off."

"Serpent?" the commander asked and Sharp nodded agreement.

"Not like anything I'd seen before. Just above his left ankle, past his shoe top, there were two half-inch arcs forming not quite a circle. Each arc was comprised of seven small punctures."

"So we've got life around, as we expected," Sharp announced.

"Yeah, I thought that, too," Crown agreed, "but there was a thin brown color around the punctures. At first I thought whatever was injected and caused Cantro's symptoms might have discolored his skin. On closer inspection, I realized the color was a thin film from something rubbed into the wound, like a salve or ointment. My analysis of it didn't match anything in our database." Crown didn't continue.

The shock on Sharp's and Carpenter's face demonstrated they understood her implication.

"This planet is not uninhabited." Commander Carpenter closed his eyes and breathed deeply. He knew he didn't want to revisit the Keltudes.

"They can't be bad, Commander, if they treated Cantro," Crown assessed.

"I agree, but what about Kellan and the six with him? Maybe there are rival factions. The electronic madness has just been squared." At that moment, Crown, Sharp, and Carpenter heard a shout and the tramping of more than a dozen feet.

Kellan Forbes led six bedraggled settlers across the tarmac to the commander's shuttle. "I apologize for being so late, Commander. The skyscraper is farther away than it looks and we were more floors up than we intended to go before we started back. Couldn't see the sky. Just got involved."

"Meet anyone or thing beyond an empty super-structure?" the commander asked.

"Meet?" Forbes repeated. "It didn't look like it had inhabitants for a long time." He looked incredulous. "You think there are people here?"

"No *thinking* about it," Carpenter answered. Both Crown and Sharp added their agreement to his answer. "There may be more going on here than we can imagine."

"We're going to have to be very careful," Sharp added. "It's not just learning a new planet. We have to watch for people who are already here and, no doubt, hiding from us."

MOLRIXX

The overgrown trail, once used by the early escapees from the molox to keep from being observed on the white when Molox1 was inhabited, ran far off from the northern edge of the white to the foot of the mega-city and a secondary entrance. Korsk and his gardeners and the hunters struggled to recreate the trail and hide from the aliens.

Out of the heavy brush, Korsk and three gardeners hurried to the foot of Molox1. He surveyed the normal path to their south, the one the aliens could be on. The two trails were separated by fifty meters of bushes and small trees, tall enough to conceal the gardeners except for their heads, though light was fading enough to make even their faces hard to distinguish from the bushes. However, Korsk was concerned about the noise they were making as they slashed their way through the overgrowth and he feared how long they might have to take this slow impacted route if the aliens stayed longer than popular history maintained other invaders had.

The gardeners almost reached the foot of the complex that once held a population of tens of thousands, when Korsk called for a halt. He looked carefully to count his three companions for the light was diminishing and the white was already in shadow. "I think we should enter through the auxiliary port. I haven't heard anything of the group that Golt saw. I don't know if they've returned to their craft over our usual trail."

"We don't want to meet them," Pwok agreed.

"We have to stay out of sight," Rhial added. "The auxiliary is a good choice, even if it means a longer trek."

"Yeah," Pwok agreed. "Maybe we should use this route from now on ... at least until they leave ... if they leave."

"It's clear we can't traipse across the white, any more," Korsk said. "But you know, if they're here for a long time," Korsk shook his head, "we *will* meet."

The gardeners went silent at that thought. None had considered that the fifteen craft with their alien cargo would stay on Molx. All rumors and tales of aliens in the past were always

discounted as threats intended to keep citizens in the mega-cities. No one, especially the monitors, ever thought that aliens
were more than fanciful stories. Even those, who had a little
more belief of visitors from off planet, never claimed they were
around for very long, for whatever reasons.

"You mean they might stay here?" Rhial asked. "What will
that mean?"

"Aliens never stayed," Pwok answered before Korsk could
think of an answer. "There's no proof for any of the stories of
them being here; no bodies, no things, nothing that might have
come from off planet."

"Wouldn't have been hard for Council to keep that information from us," Delsin countered, "even if they all died off."

Korsk held up his hand in the dimming light. "We're not
going to solve the mystery of past aliens. We know aliens are
here, now. I believe they will know there are people on Molx,
because Wisolen treated the Hislik bite. We need get to Vokra
and stay out of their way, especially of those that probably
wandered through parts of Molox1. Let's keep going."

From a tenth floor window, Vokra watched dusk extend
from the bubble range to cover the white. She saw the alien
contingent break from groups, form others, and eventually
head toward their craft. Then she noticed four aliens enter the
white from the forested area where Wisolen normally hunted, and four Molrixx struggle through the overgrown path she
knew as the route taken to raid Molox1 before she agreed to
re-inhabit it. She knew the four were Korsk's workers, but she
remembered his crew numbered five.

Vokra looked around the large tenth floor meeting hall
that she and others had climbed to from the fifth floor in hopes
of keeping ahead of the exploring aliens. She spied Canska and
called her.

"Can you do ten flights of stairs?"

"I think so." Canska rubbed her protruding belly. "It's quieted down some."

"Good. I want you to go down to the auxiliary and greet
Korsk. He's coming in that way, no doubt to keep away from
the strangers. He's also one short."

"Want me to ask him something or just tell him you want

to see him?"

"Either ... both ... if something's happened, I'd have thought he'd have returned before now. But he has to know that we've moved up five floors.

Canska looked worried and her eyes watered. "Did you see Pwok with him?"

"Too dark to make out features. You'll know the answer before I will."

As Canska turned and hurried away, Vokra called after her, "You don't have to hurry. They won't be there before you."

Her advice was not taken or not heard.

Vokra turned back to the scene below and saw three Molrixx placing something on the white and slip back into the bushy cover. "That's the one I missed," she said. "We could escape to Molox3," she said softly to herself. "But that would mean leaving everything we have." Then she noticed that the seven aliens who had entered Molox1 in the morning were half way to the white. She knew Canska would be unseen and far behind them as she descended ten floors.

When Pwok stepped through the auxiliary entrance, he was surprised to see Canska who threw herself on him and hugged him tightly. "You're okay. I was worried. Vokra only saw Korsk and three, not four."

"Golt stayed with Wisolen and Vensil. They'll come later," Pwok explained. "And they're bringing a Cernox."

Once she knew her mate was all right, Canska remembered why she had been sent to meet the gardeners. Still holding onto Pwok, she turned to Korsk. "Vokra wants to speak with you and we've moved to the tenth floor. She saw you were one short and coming back on the unused trail."

Korsk had not missed Pwok's greeting. He knew Canska had been sent to greet them for more than announcing the group's moving higher up. His workers were never met in the evening. "Everyone's all right, Canska. But there are things she and Crelle need to know."

The five started up the ten flights.

Korsk was thinking that the impromptu alien encounter, which seemed harmless at the time, would be a serious concern for Vokra. He wondered if she meant to keep them all hidden from the aliens.

Canska's climb slowed more and more through the first three flights of stairs and she bent over every few steps after she stopped to rest on every landing. Pwok, staying with his ailing mate, lagged further behind the others and struggled to get Canska to the fifth floor where they had stayed the previous night.

"Is it time?" he asked.

"I don't know." Her speech was labored. "The pains are quicker and they're stronger. They weren't anything before I came to see you."

Then he saw water running down her legs and yelled after Korsk, "Canska's in trouble. It may be time. Hurry and tell Vokra."

Almost as soon as Vokra had seen the aliens closing on the white, Crelle approached her with his report. "Without being seen, I followed them the whole day. They didn't know I was around."

"What'd you learn?" she asked.

"They're bigger than we are. At first glance, they don't look any different from us. But their faces are not so wide. Their eyes are smaller and look oval. Their noses are really skinny."

"What did they do?"

"Snooped. Never got above the fourth floor. They didn't take anything, not that there's much that can be taken. They opened a few doors and looked in. Twice they all entered a flat. I guess they looked around; they stayed awhile. Maybe they were resting. I didn't hear any noises. They didn't do any damage. Once or twice they broke into three groups and scouted the side halls."

"Did they speak to each other, or maybe transmit to those down on the white?"

"They made no sounds. They waved at each other a lot. Maybe they talked when they were all in the flats. Maybe they don't speak."

"Did you see weapons?"

"Nothing that matched what we have for weapons. Each of them did have a fourth of a meter long cylinder attached somehow to their uniform. No one ever touched it, though it was within easy reach."

"They just looked?"

"That's all I saw them do."

"Well, you know Korsk left this morning with four. He returned with only three. Wisolen and Vensil aren't back yet. Stay close when Korsk comes. He's in the molox."

"It's not going to be simple, is it?" Crelle sighed heavily.

"Probably not, but we won't know until both Korsk and Wisolen get back."

Just then, Korsk burst into the room. "Canska's having her baby. She's on the fourth floor. Pwok is with her."

Vokra summoned Mencra and Woloka and sent them to help Canska with the birth. Then she asked Korsk why he returned with only three.

When he finished with his explanation, Vokra and Crelle looked at each other, groaned aloud, and shook their heads.

"Maybe the alien being unconscious will keep us unknown, at least for awhile." Crelle's hopeful offering was improbable.

"I don't think a space-faring civilization would miss Wisolen's salve, unless they don't check him over. I can't believe they wouldn't, being on an alien planet," Vokra countered. "I thought about moving to Molox3. Canska's made that a lot more difficult—impossible. Besides, we can't take everything with us."

"Maybe hiding is best," Crelle said. He dropped into a near chair.

"We can't for too long," Vokra said with a heavy breath. "If they're here and can't leave, it's only a matter of time."

"Moving back to the forest may get us discovered sooner, but we'll have food there," Crelle proposed. "We can keep moving up floors and stay ahead of their searching, but there's not much food here, regardless of Wisolen's efforts."

"And if they move into the molox, we've got only one way … out the top and we'll be forced to Molox3."

"What other choices do we have?" Crelle asked in rebuttal. "We might stay ahead of their exploration in the valley."

Vokra didn't want to offer the outrageous option. No matter how beneficial they seemed from a distance, aliens were fearful creatures. They'd consider planet-bound people inferior and take advantage, to the ultimate demise of the physical Mol-rixx. Even if her group of thirty, soon to be thirty-one, were the only Molrixx, Vokra was not about to preside at their extinction even if that event would never be known. Still the agonizing decision that forebode the loss of everything they now pos-sessed had to be made. Vokra rejected the need to decide im-mediately. The aliens were not yet moving into the molox and they didn't know the forest.

Then Wisolen appeared with Vensil bearing the Cernox. He repeated his version of what Korsk had already told about the alien's Hislik bite and that they placed the victim on the white. He added that Canska was having her child.

Vokra said that she had seen them place the alien on the white and that no alien appeared to have noticed.

Much later Canska clutching her baby close struggled into the tenth floor meeting room. Pwok held her against his side. Woloka and Mencra hovered close watching for her legs to col-lapse one more time when they would help lay her down to rest.

"The fourth floor landing needs to be cleaned, all the blood and stuff," Woloka announced to Vokra. "If the aliens continue their search, they'll know something took place there."

"And if it's clean and the rest of the stairs aren't, that'll tell them more," Mencra added.

"Just one more problem," Crelle announced. "Maybe it'll dry up before they get that far and won't think much about it. Just something that happened long ago."

With Canska incapacitated, Vokra knew they weren't leav-ing Molox1 any time soon. And, with any likely alien reaction to the Hislik bite, discovery of her monitor band would be much sooner than later.

During the brief side discussion, Canska crumpled to the floor before Woloka and Mencra could get her to a cot.

Pwok dropped to the floor and took their silent daughter whom he smiled at. He held her close and tried to cuddle his mate whom he feared for. Woloka and Mencra gathered the spent new mother and helped her to one of the many cots that had been brought to the large room where Vokra thought was the best place to plan with all for their next decisions. Vokra herself rushed to see the new mother and child and chided herself for the rashness of sending one so pregnant down ten flights of stairs.

Light had vanished from the valley. Only a thin, bubbled line of deep red marked the top of the western range. Vokra studied the white, ten floors and more below her vantage. Her sharp eyes saw no shadowy movement.

SYSTEM

Acquisition: *Power increased through ship computer.*

Central Reception: *Interface control accomplished?*

A: *Possible. Currently unconscious. Working to access.*

CR: *Interface must open entrance to repository.*

A: *Unlikely that interface can do so alone. Perhaps repository a curiosity. Many may be captured.*

CR: *Sealed away with interface. Few at a time, as other aliens were taken.*

A: *Problem. Low-level power drain.*

CR: *Source?*

A: *Not apparent. System-wide. Not yet threatening. Some power generating from receptors of dead and dying megas cover loss.*

CR: *Monitors residing in Molox1. Can they be removed?*

A: *Power is inaccessible to them. Flats provide protection from climate, nothing more. They may be hiding from Earthers.*

CR: *If they meet?*

A: *Unable to predict. Earthers do not seem hostile. Molrixx attacking them hinders our downloads.*

CR: *Or Earthers remove them. If all monitors leave Molox1, seal it. Activate video to follow them. Seal Molox1 when all leave.*

A: *That will inform Earthers.*

CR: *No! Earthers will be downloaded before Molox1 will be empty. Last Molrixx will succumb to weather.*

MOLRIXX

All night Pwok held and rocked his newborn and sat leaning against the wall at Canska's head. Twice he gave her up when his mate made feeble and ineffective attempts to nurse her daughter. Two other times when the baby began to whimper, Mencra changed her dirty diaper. Frequently Pwok felt Canska's brow that seemed to be hotter until just before it was time to rise. Most of the night she rolled her head back and forth and moaned. Once when Pwok reached to comfort her groans, she shouted to leave her alone. Her loud demand woke half the monitors. Her daughter, unable to feed and adding to her mother's growing discomfort, began lengthening bouts of cries and howls that maddened the monitors.

Before night as the eastern ocean shore mutated into dark purple before solar rise, Vokra and Crelle roused everyone, sleeping or not, with a soft touch on their forehead, including a napping Pwok, but not Canska who seemed finally resting with a lowered temperature.

"I want Korsk's and Wisolen's crews to start early but keep a watch on what the aliens are doing. I will observe from my window. If they send another group to explore, we may have to move further up. Canska will need help. Pwok, I think you should stay with her, instead of going with Korsk. Krolni, you should see how the capri and bovs are. That's another long climb, but our new-born needs real milk."

No light had touched the white, when the agrarians and hunters and herder left for their duties. Before any alien, except one, stirred, Vokra decided to move everyone but herself, Pwok and his daughter, and Canska up another five floors. Most of those moving were thankful that they wouldn't be subjected to the wailing of the hungry newborn. They were less than happy about transporting all the necessities upward. Still, each trip back to the tenth floor reminded them of the noise they were escaping and the duties were not so tedious.

Mencra, who had been sent up three hundred floors to an infirmary, soon returned with enough cloth to make into diapers, a bottle of velsin to combat Canska's fever, and several cans of blue artificial milk.

Throughout relocation, five floors higher, Vokra sat at her window on the tenth floor and waited and watched and fretted. She sent Crelle to spy on the aliens, if they returned. She also sent Golt to the edge of the white to see if she might spot the alien medicated by Wisolen's salve. Beyond her fears for her community, she suppressed her desire to hover about Canska and the newest Molrixx who was invoking a continual litany of screams and cries and yells.

Vokra remembered three births to Council in Molox3. Two were much less traumatic than Canska's. The third was described as what she was witnessing. That birth had nearly resulted in the death of both mother and child, even though there were medicals to care for them.

Canska and her daughter were without that aid and Volkra feared the worst.

HUMANS

Space was a black panorama sprinkled with white twinkling stars when Roger LeRoi opened his eyes. Gone were his accustomed red and yellow and blue flickerings. The stars he saw through the forward ports of the engineering shuttle were just points of light: how he had seen the galaxy before the computer interface was implanted in and upon his skull.

The navigator uncrossed his arms and lifted his helmeted head from the depression in the cushioned seat. He used his elbows to lift his upper body a little higher. He turned his head to his right and caught a side view of Ticia Bandi in a nearby seat. Her head lay on her left shoulder, eyes closed. LeRoi swallowed a quiet chuckle that his watcher was asleep.

In the darkness, LeRoi didn't see Ticia's eyelids flutter at the navigator's small, silent, adjustments in the quiet shuttle. She made no movement beyond opening her left eye to follow the navigator's change of position.

He sat up without lifting the back of his reclined seat and turned his body so his legs dangled over the edge of his seat. He saw the closed hatch. He knew he could never sneak away even if the hatch were not locked. Opening the portal was not a silent operation. He'd be caught before he got off the ramp.

Then he relived in frenetic pace a hodge-podge of events. He remembered the colorful stars that only MP visualized with its access to multiple spectra. He watched the word "danger" melt into gray screens. He was indignant that the angry crew heaped abuse on him. He recalled the commander's strange question—twice asked—when he should have been in light sleep. He was outraged at the unreasonable order that he evacuate with the engineering crew. Then he woke up in front of a shuttle and at the edge of some sterile site and didn't know how he got there.

Convinced that he would navigate no more, he swung back into his resting position, dropped his helmeted head into the depression, crossed his arms and looked out the front ports. The crystal white sparkling stars in the black of night suddenly became yellow and red and blue. The North American Nebula was a hazy dust cloud outlined by prismatic stars around its edge. Roger LeRoi blinked his eyes, twice; the brilliant colors didn't fade to white speckles.

"Welcome back, navigator." LeRoi sensed MP greeting him as usually happened when he returned from brief light sleep. The navigator lifted his head again and looked left and right, as much as the helmet allowed. He jerked his head forward. He was in his cubicle on board the *Marco P* FSS-14. *I'm dreaming,* he thought.

MP told him he couldn't dream and continued through the wireless power mod in LeRoi's helmet. "Relax, navigator. You have important work for the mission. I will tell you what you need to know."

LeRoi blinked his eyes and scanned across the ports of the shuttle. He didn't see stationary stars or shuttle outlines or the dark forest or the mega building or the mountain it grew out of. Instead he recognized the fourteen monitor screens in his station. They provided him with the meaningless visual panorama around the *Marco P*. He smiled. He didn't need eyes to visualize; the computer injected the images through his interface. LeRoi shut his eyes in obedience to the computer, exhaled a pleasant sigh, and relaxed into pre-sleep when he worked with MP without his senses disturbing the digital conversation.

Despite her intentions, Bandi had again fallen asleep during her second night of watching the navigator. However, her intuitive sub-conscious that both Varlez and Arafa paid attention to had roused her before the navigator originally opened his eyes. Bandi's neck was painfully cramped. She refused the strong urge to adjust her head. With one eye she followed LeRoi's rising, sitting up, and laying back down. Not until LeRoi assumed his normal sleep posture did she open her right eye, ease her tight neck back to the vertical, and, flexing strained muscles, gently rearrange her body in the seat.

The second night of watching the sleeping navigator Bandi caught more odd hints of the unusual. She pushed out of her chair and crept four half-shuffle steps to reach the side of the relaxed navigator. In the dim starlight and faint green aura of the powered com system, she saw a comfortable navigator. His arms were at rest and draped across his chest that was rhythmically rising and falling. He lacked the tension that had chained him the night before. He was not the harried individual Commander Carpenter had ushered to their shuttle on board the *Marco P*, nor the displaced navigator who aimlessly returned to the shuttle after the commander's initial remarks after having to land on the wrong planet. Navigator Roger LeRoi looked to be in familiar surroundings.

Bandi didn't understand the change. And it was a distinct difference. The crew was on the wrong planet where they were likely to stay until they died. LeRoi would never again navigate nor did he possess colonizing or social skills. His helmet, inseparable from his skull and brain, set him apart from everyone. She knew that Roger was physically far out of his comfort zone; still, he looked at ease.

Then Ticia Bandi noticed a slowly pulsing, small yellow light at the front of his helmet. LeRoi's interface with MP was live. The greatest danger that Varlez and Carpenter and Strumpf feared was announced by the flashing yellow light in front of her. Evidence of the intelligence that had kidnapped them and the *Marco* was visible in the shuttle and active in LeRoi's brain.

Bandi stood entranced and watched the computer interfaced-human become the mole: the human traitor allied with the alien power that had captured them. She thought about binding the compromised navigator to his chair. At least then he would be immobile. A stationary mole could cause no damage. She remembered the discussion she and Arafa had had with Varlez. He told them the aliens had to believe that the humans were unaware of the alien influence among them. Bandi didn't understand why the navigator should be allowed to be active. She had countered that it was like leaving a door open to let dangerous animals in. Varlez was called away before he could answer her objection and he hadn't later found time to explain. Bandi had witnessed enough events that proved Varlez and the commander seemed to know things beyond her snap judgments, but now she was sure they were wrong. She would bide her time. She knew that she would be able to tell them "I knew better than you."

The navigator had returned to his comfort zone. He exchanged his thoughts with MP and he wondered how he had returned to the *Marco P*. Maybe he had never left. Neither answers nor guidance came from MP. So he continued to hypothesize. That exercise was short-lived. He was back where he was king of the realm. The disgusting recall of leaving the *Marco P* with engineering, of circling down to a useless landing site he had determined, of being walked across some strange area ... they called it tarmac, of glancing across landscape that he had no interest in, of seeking refuge in the shuttle away from crew and colonists, all faded, blocked from his conscious memory.

MP on the *Marco P* that was not in a declining orbit from loss of power prompted LeRoi's brain. Was he ready to receive instructions of the greatest import? Was he ready to assume, with the computer's backing, the proper authority on board the *Marco P* FSS-14?

Directions came too quickly. He demanded repeats until the computer slowed its infusing. LeRoi's concentration was strained and his body tensed, a reaction not unobserved by Bandi who became too anxious to sleep. The computer offered no time reference to the navigator but daylight was implied. Yet, it was not morning, still inky black. He relaxed. Urgency was not demanded. He accepted activity on the planet without questioning that he was also in the navigation cubicle on the *Marco P*. Arafa and Bandi would probably accompany him, as Arafa had the second day on the planet. Perhaps he could make them the first recruits for his new realm. He had one other to enlist. Something in his memory marked that one with dislike. But those impressions weren't clear. He decided memory was in error.

The yellow light on the helmet faded and LeRoi relaxed into the first unencumbered sleep he had enjoyed in many years.

Morning sneaked in under a cloudy sky that developed not long after navigator LeRoi received his instructions from System routed through MP. Bandi had again fallen into light dozing. Muted light reflecting from the tarmac encouraged later rising for nearly all colonists. The monitor gardeners and hunters had crossed north of the white along neglected trails well before the shuttles were waking. Krolni was climbing inside stairs to Council's farm above 500.

Malcolm Carpenter, as befits a commander, awoke first. His exit from the shuttle roused Maelstrom who hustled after him.

"Sir," she called out and startled the commander who thought he had been quiet enough not to rouse her.

He turned and stepped back to her. "Such formality! 'Commander' or 'Carpenter' is sufficient. We're not on board the *Marco*; I'm just one of the rats."

"It's about that, sir, ... uh ... Commander. I was aware of some poking at my electronic side last night."

"You think LeRoi's been further engaged?"

"Possibly. I'd never been probed by MP before. It's like I told you; I can shut off that part of my brain when I'm not in navigation. Still, the feelers seemed to be from the *Marco*. Roger can't shut them out. He may have been co-opted by the aliens."

"But you don't know for sure?"

"No ... not about MP's power, unless it's really been boosted."

Carpenter heard the unspoken inflection but didn't care to discuss that possibility.

"... But if I received searching invitations, I'm sure he's more susceptible."

"I'll check engineering. If you're still interested, you might be ready to shadow LeRoi and work your way into his plans, whatever they are. I believe Varlez's aides were planning to accompany him wherever."

"I will join him." Maelstrom said and acknowledged her own promised role in the human test.

"Be prepared to be lumped with him as dangerous. You've got the same computer connection ..."

"But I don't," Maelstrom interrupted with a pleading reminder of what she had twice explained.

"I know what you've told me. Most of the crew and colonists don't think that way. Both of you are similar in that you can link to computers. That makes you as dangerous as he is, as they see it. Regardless, joining LeRoi may endanger you far beyond what you imagine."

Not waiting for another explanation from Maelstrom on her different interface, Commander Carpenter set a quick pace for the engineering shuttle and was not surprised to find Varlez coming to meet him. Varlez's face was stern, more so than usual and he wasn't slow in telling the commander what Bandi had reported to him and Arafa.

"It happened last night. Bandi said she saw LeRoi's helmet activate. There's nothing in the shuttle that can access his interface. It's tied to MP and its wireless range shouldn't extend from orbit. Maybe feelers from here?"

"Maelstrom just told me that last night she was aware of digital greetings, as she described them. She thought it was proof that LeRoi had probably been compromised. She plans to keep close to him from now on."

"That's good. She's just as much a danger to us as he is, regardless of what she's told you. Bandi and Arafa and who knows how many others will watch them ... both of them."

"I told her that, too. She was miffed that I haven't accepted her beliefs."

"Well, what can she expect? Wireless is wireless regardless of the physical interface. She may not have a helmet, but despite the third gen interface shutoff, it's still connected to her brain."

"That's true, Jerry, and you know more about computer systems than any of us. Still, if she's right ..."

"Yeah, *if*." Varlez snorted. "I still think the best way to deal with both of them is to tie them up. Keep them from doing what the aliens want."

"And then there'd be no game, no contest. We'd never find out what we're supposed to do or what they want us for. We'd have no chance to get off this planet and back into space."

"Just seems like we're asking for trouble."

"Maybe, Jerry, maybe." The commander looked back toward his shuttle and saw Maelstrom descending the ramp. "You weren't with me when I encountered the Agonites, were you?"

"No. That's where you got the small tapestry, isn't it?"

"The very same. Their arch-point gave it to me and said

that aliens didn't know what to do with humans. We don't act like any other species that his people had encountered. But all aliens act toward us in initial contact as if we are just like all other aliens."

"And how do they act at first contact?" Varlez questioned with as much irony as interest.

The commander ignored the inflection. "They're not sneaky. They're pretty overt and selfish. They don't imagine exceptions or loopholes. They don't think out of the box."

"So how have they managed any technology to travel the galaxy?"

"Galactic travel doesn't require creativity, just physics. They're faster and more adept than we are. But we're creative. We do what they do without having to understand the complexity of rules they all adhere to." Carpenter looked at Varlez sifting through ideas that were as anathema to human development as espousing unswerving obedience to leaders.

When Varlez looked back at him, Carpenter continued. "I can't imagine how our understanding of physics and math is any different from theirs. Besides they have us here where we stay short of gambling our lives to prove their control over our gauges is false."

"Seems to me they're sneaky … messing with our minds and gauges," Varlez charged.

"That's because we don't know what they want. Maybe we did something that triggered their reaction and they aren't thinking to be difficult."

"Well, it seems pretty unclear to me."

"You don't play chess, do you?"

"No," Varlez made a face. "It always seemed artificial to me. Besides at the level computers trounce humans, it's demoralizing."

"It's a part of chess that we're involved in right here and now. Whoever holds us here doesn't know what we can do."

"Commander, you're going to have to be a lot clearer. If these aliens have computers that good, we've got no chance."

"I'd agree, if I didn't know a basic secret to mating my opponent."

"You're better than the best computer?" Varlez seldom had

the chance to offer such a challenge and he enjoyed putting the commander on the spot.

"In a way. Alien computers may be better than ours, but they evolved with alien characteristics, not human. LeRoi and possibly Maelstrom are a gambit."

"Still don't follow." Varlez screwed up his face and said, "Better computers beat poorer computers. They beat us. What's a gambit?"

"That's our secret weapon, our sneaky part. Aliens don't look for loopholes. They expect us to act according to simple procedures and rules, like LeRoi showed them when we were grayed. He didn't question and he didn't recognize what was wrong with this planet being γ-Cygnus A2. A gambit is a move that disguises and hides something that will become apparent after many moves: a sacrifice of an important piece that sucks the unaware into a trap."

Varlez looked like he'd just solved an engineering conundrum. "We let the aliens believe that the navigators are undiscovered moles and when they show their moves for us, we trap them."

"Not bad for a non-chess player."

"We're sucking them in," Varlez chuckled insincerely.

"Exactly, Jerry, just like you do with the arrogant bastards who think they're better than everyone else."

"So I gambit?"

"Indeed."

Priscilla Maelstrom passed the commander and engineer as they discussed gambits on her way to the engineering shuttle. She greeted neither; her eyes were focused on the ramp that LeRoi was descending. He was followed by two females, even shorter than Maelstrom.

When LeRoi reached the second row of shuttles, Maelstrom, only yards away, shouted, "Morning, Roger."

"Ah, you're here," he answered. "I was hoping you'd be. I want to show you something."

Maelstrom cozied up to the first navigator who stood a foot taller with his interface helmet. She reached her right arm around his waist and cooed, "What do you want to show me?"

Arafa and Bandi, only a step behind, exchanged wide eyes. They were watching their fears double in front of them. They looked around at other settlers and crew beginning to descend from the shuttles to the tarmac. None of them seemed interested in the two navigators or the engineering shuttle. They were all involved in their own small cliques. Arafa and Bandi knew the commander and Varlez were probably discussing something, Varlez having left the shuttle earlier. However, they saw them nowhere.

Before LeRoi had a chance to answer Maelstrom's greeting, Arafa repeated facetiously and too quiet for the navigators to hear, "Yes, what more interesting things do you have to show us than the surrounding green?"

Roger slowed his amble, strangely enjoying the attention Priscilla was paying to him, and turned his head as far to the left as he could without twisting at the waist. "There's an interesting construction just off the tarmac. I almost got to it yesterday."

"Yeah," Arafa muttered louder than her first comment, "before I grabbed your treasonous shoulder."

"What was that?" Roger asked and this time turned to face Arafa at his right. "I didn't quite hear that."

"Nothing," Nequa tossed out and followed it with "traitor" said under her breath. For the first time she saw his eyes. They were wide open, in spite of solar reflection off the white; his pupils were large, not pinpoints that should be reacting to the growing brilliance as early clouds were dissipating. Maelstrom had not turned with LeRoi. The navigator turned back and continued leading Maelstrom toward the eastern edge of the tarmac. Arafa twitched her head to the left and blinked her eyes suggesting that Ticia try to look at Maelstrom's eyes.

Arafa's tic was understood and, before they and the navigators had gone another dozen steps, Bandi spoke up louder than needed. "Priscilla, how'd you survive your solitary?"

"How'd you think?" was the indignant retort made without looking at her questioner. Maelstrom stopped, still not looking back, and huffed at the memory. "I've never been so bored in my whole life."

Bandi pressed on, "Woman to woman, Priscilla, just how

was the commander? Haven't you been his companion since Roger power-stopped the ship?"

LeRoi blinked his eyes and narrowed them against the bright tarmac. The outlandish implication—Malcolm Carpenter was never known to have a paramour—released him from the computer's control. He remembered the commander's odd request to wake everyone except Maelstrom. That order now made sense. He was a few steps in front of the females. His companion was boiling over. LeRoi stopped and turned to the second navigator.

Maelstrom dropped her arm from LeRoi's waist and pivoted to face her accuser. She assumed a menacing stance in front of Bandi. Her back was taut. LeRoi could see the tightened back muscles under her stretched tunic. Her shoulders were quivering and her voice reached far beyond Ticia Bandi. "How dare you, you ... engineer's toy."

Arafa stepped closer to the potential explosion and cautioned, "Hold on, there. That's un ..."

"Called for?" Maelstrom cut in finishing the caution. She continued loudly and several settlers within earshot turned to watch the growing confrontation. "Hardly." She answered her own question and bore her eyes into Bandi's and thought something about a pot and a kettle. Then she stole a quick glance at Arafa who was ready to intervene with a physical exchange.

"No offense intended." Bandi's quiet and weak apologetic statement didn't break the tension. Showing some embarrassment she continued, "I'm sorry. I shouldn't have said that." Then seething at the return accusation tossed her way she said, "And we are not the engineer's harem, regardless of scuttlebutt."

Holding the planet's System just out of control and aware of the mounting unpleasantness, LeRoi reached out and took Priscilla's arm, which she shook from his hand without looking at him.

"It's not important," he stated without gauging the seriousness of the exchanges. "Let's go. Just leave them. Let them do what they want. We have more important things."

He reached for Maelstrom's arm again. As he did so, the glassy stare returned to his eyes. Priscilla turned, again shook his hand off her arm, and walked beside him, leaving Arafa and Bandi steps behind them.

Simultaneously, LeRoi attempted to corral Maelstrom and Arafa stepped closer to Bandi who had initiated a tight-jaw stare at Maelstrom's back. "Let it be, Tish; let it be." Arafa tried to back her away from the confrontation.

When Maelstrom and LeRoi moved farther away, Ticia, quite unconcerned, announced, "Her eyes weren't glassy like his. You see that?"

"Yes! Did you have to be so blunt?"

"I thought you wanted proof. We'd better follow."

"At the height of that accusation LeRoi's eyes seemed to return to normal and then he reverted," Arafa confirmed.

"And she never had that far away look. She might just be able to separate herself from the computer, like she says," Bandi said, lacking any residual from her staged set-to.

"Maybe. Your attack was enough to bring anyone back from possession. We don't know if she's glassed over now. I don't think we can get close enough to find out."

"Ruined that chance, I guess. We do need to stay close."

They followed four yards behind the navigators who never looked back, intent on reaching a spot at the edge of the tarmac both were staring at. Arafa recognized LeRoi was heading for the same place he had gone the day before and where she pulled him from an apparent trance. She realized it would take more than mere touch to stop him this time, especially after Bandi's description of his helmet's yellow light.

"You know I couldn't let that innuendo stand," Maelstrom finally exclaimed to LeRoi, as they approached the edge of the tarmac.

LeRoi didn't answer. He was listening to MP direct his steps and point out landmarks that were hidden by the bushes, trees, and grass. He halted and stood immobile looking at the edge of the tarmac as if he expected some sign to pop up or was quizzing the computer from inside the interface.

"What's special about this?" Maelstrom asked. "The whole edge of the tarmac looks like this."

LeRoi didn't answer and Maelstrom asked again loud enough for the two engineers, who had closed the distance between them, to hear. Her outrage over Bandi's inappropriate question had vanished.

LeRoi looked to his right, as far as his helmet allowed without twisting his body. He scanned to the left, pulling Maelstrom back just a bit from blocking his view. Then he looked forward and up, checking another landmark the computer had given him. The edge of the skyscraper embedded in the mountain was to his right. He knew he had to be at the exact southern edge of that construction.

Without a word, he turned and started south. Every few steps he turned to look east. "Yes, I see it," he finally said aloud in confirmation.

Maelstrom, who was not listening closely, asked, "What?" and became aware of more feelers seeking entry into her brain.

LeRoi didn't answer her question, though it was again loud enough for their followers to hear. Then he asked in the same soft voice as his confirmation statement, "How far?"

"Come," he issued not quite an order to Maelstrom, "you'll recognize where we're going." He placed his left hand on Maelstrom's left shoulder and the two of them, oblivious to the thorny branches slipped into the thick greenery. Once past the hedge, they turned north for five yards and stopped.

Bandi and Arafa tried following. They were pricked and scratched. In no time they realized thorns hurt too much to follow and, having been only four steps behind, they lost sight of their charges who had disappeared. Even LeRoi's helmeted head had vanished.

"We can't continue blind," Bandi said. "We'll just wander around getting more scraped."

"You're right. But we can't get lost. The shuttles still show above the green, if we keep going. But there's no path, no way to follow them. We'd best go back."

The two second engineers turned back and took more scrapes to their arms as they stepped back onto the tarmac.

When he knew his tails were gone, LeRoi led Maelstrom to a bit of tarmac just ten yards off the landing site. He got down on his knees and began brushing the drifted dirt and sand from the white composite. Maelstrom joined his cleaning. Soon they had uncovered a four-foot square. LeRoi stood in the center and faced north looking just off the edge of the small square.

Maelstrom showed no interest in what he was doing, although she looked where he was looking.

He searched a little farther off the square and exhaled success. "There," he announced and stepped five yards off the small bit of material that was like a minuscule tarmac. Maelstrom joined him.

Almost hidden behind the trunks of three small trees was a three-foot flat-topped pedestal. Its center sported a raised square block, which LeRoi pressed with the palm of his right hand.

As they watched, the square of tarmac they had brushed clean raised from their right to a vertical position left and dropped into the ground exposing a flight of stairs. LeRoi smiled at the system's congratulations for following directions. Maelstrom was unmoved. LeRoi pressed the block a second time and the small piece of tarmac rose and dropped right, re-covering the underground access.

Two penitent engineers confessed to Varlez that they had lost the navigators when they couldn't follow past the edge of the tarmac.

"Haven't you anything else to report?" he asked them.

"Roger seemed under a spell, kinda like we imagined," Arafa said. "I couldn't tell about Priscilla. But Ticia got a reaction that was far from a trance."

"I may have gone out of bounds," Bandi was hesitant to explain further.

Varlez pressed the young engineer who had generated Maelstron's emotional outburst.

"I kinda accused her of being involved with the commander."

"You what?" was Varlez's aghast reaction.

"Well, Nequa managed to see Roger's glassy eyes. But Maelstrom was turned from both of us. We couldn't see hers. I just forced her to turn around. Was she ever hot."

"And not in the same possessed state as LeRoi, I suppose?"

"Not at all. She even intimated the crew's stupid consensus of the engineering relationship," Arafa added. "Though Roger lost his hypnotic stare briefly, he got it back."

"Can't do much about it now," Varlez said. "I know we're considered a threesome. Doesn't do any good to deny it. However, could either of you tell whether she was under the same influence that LeRoi was?" Varlez looked questioningly at his seconds.

Bandi spoke first. "She seemed pretty docile, *very* friendly, as she followed him."

"After Ticia's accusation," Arafa added, "neither spoke except Roger when he was trying to get her to back away from the confrontation. There were some settlers who were interested but they didn't come close enough to get involved. She never said a word that we heard after her reaction to Ticia's accusation, except to ask 'What?' in reaction to something Roger said too quietly for us to hear at the edge of the tarmac. It was probably something about being at a predetermined spot because they immediately stepped off the tarmac and we lost sight of them."

"I suppose I should report this to Carpenter, though if they return, the commander will get Maelstrom's side of it. Why don't you take some time for yourselves." Varlez looked to the west where he had seen Carpenter and started that direction but stopped and turned as if he had something to add to their conversation. Before he looked back to his aides, he noticed that LeRoi and Maelstrom were ambling across the tarmac.

"Look at that," he said pointing to the navigators, who looked no different than any two crew members or colonists. They were animated and talking and gesturing. "Wonder what they were doing," Varlez said. "LeRoi hates Maelstrom."

"If the commander's right about Maelstrom," Arafa began, "he'll know soon enough and so will you. If he's not, we're going to need a lot more help."

MOLRIXX

Vokra accused herself of not watching Korsk's gardeners slog through the overgrown secondary trail from the molox in the early morning dark. Wisolen heard her plaint and told her that no dangerous animals were about so early before dawn and that the Hislik stayed in its underground nest until nearly noon.

The hunters, increased by two, left not long after Korsk. Vokra asked them to man two parallel blinds that edged on a common animal trail to a rare drinking pool. They intended to bring down a long-necked Gafron by dropping netting over it. When it was snared, Wisolen and Vensil, dodging the animal's fore claws, would drive spears up through the base of the animal's skull to its brain. Once killed they would quick-butcher the animal that was far too large to carry back to the molox without hacking it into separate pieces. Its separated four legs would be shoved onto a pole and carried across the shoulders of one extra hunter, the neck and head by the other. Vensil and Wisolen would carry the spitted body on their shoulders.

Wisolen thought a Gafron far too much meat for the Molrixx. He had been keeping the community well-stocked with meat without it going bad. He couldn't imagine how they would keep the huge meat supply from rotting. Perhaps Crelle had found a way into one of the cold, dark, NO ADMITTANCE rooms. Then he remembered his caring for the alien with the Hislik bite and he agreed with the thought of those with him that the aliens would know from his ministering that there were other thinking creatures on the planet. Food would be a nice offering, when the opportunity arose. He wondered if that gift was what Vokra had in mind.

After all had risen, Vokra sent Crelle to take up his hiding to watch the aliens, should they return to the mega. She directed those still in the tenth floor meeting hall, except for Canska, her daughter, and Pwok, to move what they could to the fifteenth floor. Then she kept her position at the window that jutted out from the outer wall and watched the white and

206

the strange craft and the rather common looking aliens as they spilled out to wander in small groups and disappear into the surrounding greenery.

A group of seven, she couldn't tell if they were the same ones as the day before, made their way to the base of Molox1 and disappeared into the bottom floor. They were now Crelle's responsibility.

She looked hard but couldn't see where Golt had taken up a place to spy. The hunters she knew were already far north in the forest and she wouldn't see a hint of them even if she tried looking.

She did notice two very short aliens push their way back onto the white from the east. A little later, she watched an alien as small as the first two and another one taller with a strange headpiece enter the white and follow the first two.

Near noon, Vokra watched everyone on the white turn north. In a rare lull between Pwok's daughter's more insistent crying, she caught the muted roars of a Gafron. She knew Wisolen had been successful. She knew he was wise enough to stay well-hidden and wait until dark before he delivered the kill to the mega building.

The newborn's crying became more and more insistent. Vokra left her window perch and went to see Canska and her daughter. The new mother was still feverish, but not as hot as she had been. Pwok added that her eyes were not as vacant, but their daughter was running a fever.

The baby's face was bright red and her increasing baby yells were more than mere discomfort to everyone who returned to move necessities from the tenth floor. Pwok tried soothing his daughter by rocking her and walking around. His own cooing to her was smothered by his daughter's crying yells. When Pwok's mate became conscious of her over-full breasts, she demanded her daughter.

Her milk still didn't flow and her daughter's screams didn't cease.

Pwok agonized at the suffering of his mate and daughter. He had no experience with birthing or its aftermath. Those were concerns far from the pleasures of planting the seed. He saw that his mate couldn't care for herself and he realized that their daughter was only making everyone around her upset and angry. Canska, who had always been lively and encouraging and helpful, was a feverish perspiring invalid more like the near-death animals Pwok had seen before Wisolen dispatched them.

Without Canska, Pwok knew he couldn't care for a baby and his daughter was the first born to the free monitors. Females tended children. He had no idea what to do with a baby. He feared for his mate and his daughter's screeching became more upsetting to him with each barrage that filled the tenth floor room.

Canska slipped into unconsciousness, after her daughter again rejected her stopped up nipples. The new-born's screams, shut out by obstinate ears that could ignore the noise, continued to fill the room.

Pwok eased his daughter from her mother's arms and wrapped her loosely in the ragged blanket that was damp with fever and tears and smelled of messy diapers.

No one saw Pwok leave the room with his child but soon the few between transits to the fifteenth floor were conscious that there was no crying baby.

From her perch, Vokra saw the seven aliens leave the mountain-tall structure, an exit much sooner than the day before. Since they had left, she expected a visit from Crelle; and then, she, too, realized how silent the room was. The baby's screaming faded downward. She looked quickly to where Canska was lying and saw no Pwok and no baby with her.

Soon Crelle dashed into the room. "I don't know where he's going, but Pwok's hurrying down the stairs. He passed me three floors down."

"Why didn't you stop him?"

"Didn't know what he was doing. He had *that* look."

"I know," Vokra said with a disgusted sigh and a slight shake of her head. "We'd better follow. If the races are going to meet, we've all got to be there—not that we'll be able to do much."

"No more hiding," Crelle agreed. "It doesn't have to be bad. Besides if folklore's true, no aliens ever fared well on Molx."

Vokra agonized, "I wasn't planning on this meeting taking

place so soon, if at all." Then she asked Crelle to bring the Molrixx from the fifteenth floor. "We all need to follow; at least to watch, if not be involved."

"They haven't shown any destructive behavior," Crelle injected. "And Wisolen did care for the one bit by the Hislik."

"Assuming he is all right. They might think he survived an attack. We have to be there, but out of sight and watching. Hurry!"

Crelle took the first quick steps on a five-floor dash upward.

"Maybe I can catch Pwok before he gets too far," Vokra sighed.

Her vain hope was impossible.

Pwok had determined that if the strangers could heal his daughter, they could do the same for his mate. That they were from another world made no difference to him. If they could reach Molx, they had to have greater medicine than the band of monitor Molrixx did. He had heard others talk about them and they looked sort of like he did. The one bit by the Hislik didn't look so unusual except for his eyes and funny nose. Their clothes were different and they were bigger creatures. Pwok knew they were the salvation for his daughter and his mate.

Pwok ran like he had never run before. On this mission of need, he knew he could rival Krolni for ten flights down. He was at the ground floor before Vokra was passing the eighth floor; the others called by Crelle were seven floors behind her.

The new father dashed along the slight sloping path to the corner of the white.

Once he tripped and pitched headlong. Protecting his daughter in his left arm, he threw out his right to the ground and rolled onto his right shoulder and back. Somehow he kept from crushing his still-crying daughter and regained his feet. His lungs begged him to stop and catch deep breaths; his legs demanded rest. He refused their pleas. Medicine was on the white; a cure for his daughter and Canska was there. Speed was a must.

He almost caught the seven aliens who had been exploring Molox1. But they vanished behind the green boundary just before he reached the gap to the white. Only then did he stop to catch his breath with many deep drafts and gave his legs rest that stopped their quivering. He had to be in control when he spoke to the aliens. They wouldn't listen to a madman.

Then he stepped onto the white. He walked proudly, head high, nestling in his arms his whimpering daughter wrapped in a damp smelling ragged blanket. "Help me," he shouted over and over. "Please, someone, help me. I need help."

CONTACT

Commander Carpenter strode to meet Forbes and his half dozen scouts. Close behind them he saw a strange person carrying a bundle close to its chest. The individual was shorter than most of his human crew, but taller than his engineers, and its broad face held round eyes half again as wide as human eyes. The commander and the returning scouts heard loud, deep noises, not words of any language they had ever heard. The unusual sounds were punctuated by tiny loud cries.

Carpenter didn't mistake the urgency and terror of someone seeking immediate help. Kellan and his group turned at hearing infant cries and a foreign language. They made way for the commander to approach the native who was unconcerned they were on his planet.

"Kellan, hurry to Crown and have her bring her medical kit, on the double," Carpenter ordered. Then he looked behind him at the rumble of voices from a growing crowd of rushing human on-lookers, curious at an approaching inhabitant where there wasn't supposed to be any. Mention of Cantro's encounter and healing had remained a secret with Crown, Strumpf, Forbes, and Carpenter.

Kellan took off on a dead run weaving between the curious who were eager to discover the source of the unrecognizable sounds that were vastly different from the engineers' Alvorklan. Most were surprised that the stranger didn't look much different than any human, despite the odd face and very flat nose. Those who had not yet fully realized that they were not on γ-Cygnus A2, an uninhabited planet, were suddenly troubled with the mystery of where and why they were where they were.

The commander knew that he had to ask enough questions and get the distraught native to offer more words so the universal decoder with access points sewn into the tunics every crewmember wore could translate properly by the time Crown arrived, very likely with Strumpf.

No stranger to first contact, Carpenter stepped slowly to

211

the slight male, six inches shorter than he was and in a ragged shirt and dirty knee-length shorts. The commander was vaguely aware that his own people were edging forward. He showed his open palms at waist level. "Do you want help?" It was an intuitive question with an obvious answer. It also gave the translator a chance to match English to the alien tongue in at least one word. "What can I do for you? How can I help?"

The male before him narrowed his eyes and wrinkled his forehead. He didn't understand a thing the alien was saying. In his mad dash to find help for his family Pwok never considered that the aliens wouldn't speak his language.

In response to Carpenter's questions, though he didn't know they were questions, the native uttered the same odd sounds which the translator was gauging against common language structures and logged cognates and base words from thousands of known alien languages.

The commander reached toward the bundle the person held so gently.

Pwok backed way. He saw that the alien was male. Males had no idea what to do with a baby. Carpenter stepped back and said, "Can I take your bundle?" and again reached out.

Instead, Carpenter heard more sounds as the individual placed its right hand at its forehead. It drew the back of its hand across his brow and shook it and pointed to the bundle.

Malcolm Carpenter asked, with all the caring tone he could muster, "Does your baby have a fever ... is your baby too hot ... is your baby sick ... are you sick?"

Again Pwok screwed up his face at the alien's sounds and shuffled back another step. The throng of curious onlookers bunching up behind the commander facing the alien male continued to edge forward. In his arms, Pwok rocked the screaming bundle and, while speaking unintelligible noise, turned so he could look and point up to the construction built into the mountain. More strange sounds entered the translation database.

With Strumpf and Forbes not far behind, a concerned and hurrying Crown arrived. She pushed through the spectators that numbered the whole human complement except for Maelstrom and LeRoi. When she got in front of them, she turned and scolded. "Back up, people."

The front shuffled back only to bump those pushing from behind who continued to jostle for a clearer view.

Crown's stern voice ordered again, "Way back! Give the poor man room, you're frightening him." Embarrassed, the crowd backed away more. Those who last joined the rush to see the slight humanoid in front of the commander moved to the edges of the throng and created a half circle of spectators who repeated the same questions and astonishments to each other.

Then with a wrinkled nose Crown turned, smiled at the male holding the bundle that smelled of a pungent diaper, and looked at Commander Carpenter. "You men," she accused, "he's got a new-born, his. His wife's probably in bad shape and the baby's not much better."

Crown edged closer to Pwok and said to him, "Let me feel your baby." She extended her right hand; the left held her small medical bag.

Pwok didn't back away. He saw breasts pushing out her upper garment. He let her come close and then wondered how he might get her to follow him to care for Canska. However, unaware that he was aiding the translator, Pwok continued talking, retelling the events from when Canska met him at the bottom of the molox just before giving birth, as if these strangers could understand what he was saying.

"High fever," Crown said and reached into her small medical kit. "We don't get many newborns, but fevers are fevers. She pulled out a small squeeze pack of ointment to cool the baby's brow. As she rubbed it on, she wondered if it was similar to the salve that had been used on Cantro. Then she put the tip of her little finger at the baby's lips. The baby drew in the end of her finger and stopped crying for a moment.

"The mother has no milk," Crown announced; "sometimes happens when the birth is particularly difficult. This child is starving. It probably hasn't had anything to eat since it was born. At least a day ago."

She looked at the male holding the baby and recognized the similarities all humanoids possessed. *A little smaller than us, heads not that unusual.* Their stuff worked on Cantro and she made her decision.

She turned to the crowding humans, "Someone, get some milk!" Then to the commander, who nodded, she said, "I'm going to have to go see the mother, too."

At Crown's request, one of the on-lookers broke for a near shuttle and soon returned with three small nipple-ended tubes of milk, which he gave to Crown and then retreated to his former place at the edge of the standing audience.

"So much for first contact," Strumpf tossed at Carpenter as he stood next to him and watched Crown work medical magic.

"Suppose this is a gambit?" Varlez threw into the mix.

"If it is," Carpenter answered, "they're better actors than we are."

"How's the translator doing?" Varlez asked.

"It's not squawking much," Strumpf said. "We need more situations, more people involved, before it gets up to speed."

"Well, that may be arriving," Varlez said and nodded for Carpenter to look past Crown's house call. The rest of the *Marco's* population was already murmuring at what the engineer was pointing out.

Ten yards from the edge of the tarmac where the trodden path led to the mountain construction and striding toward the male and his baby, a statuesque blonde was heading their way. Red-faced she was shouting. Her hair hung over her chest and yellow halter top and dropped to her waist, not quite reaching the top of her thigh-length shorts. She repeated the same yelled sound.

The male holding the baby, finally turned his head and changed his daughter's hold on the milk tube. The baby broke suction and cried out before Crown could reposition the tube.

Carpenter thought, "The sound's his name."

Once the bellowing alien female had the attention of the male holding the baby, she erupted with a stream of powerful noises that Carpenter thought was violent accusation. She was clenching and unclenching her fists and closing on the father.

"They weren't prepared for first contact, either," Carpenter said to himself and turned to the edging spectators. "Back! At least ten yards. This first contact wasn't expected or planned ... by either of us."

"Me, too?" Strumpf asked quietly after Forbes had moved away. "You might need some help," he offered ironically. But his inflection said he was willing to yield to the commander's demand.

"You, stay," Carpenter said loudly enough for a public directive to Strumpf's question. "They made the first overture with Cantro. We've reciprocated. The next move's the blonde's, obviously the leader, not the mother."

Both Carpenter with his frequent first contact experience and Strumpf who listened to unintelligible alien broadcasts imagined the new father was being upbraided for having broken the order to stay hidden. Though the disobedience was understandable, the commander thought even he might have wilted under the vocal scourge laid on the distraught parent.

The second alien, female and taller than the slight-built father, continued her harangue until she was two steps behind him but close enough to stare at Crown who was feeding the infant held in the father's arms. Then she narrowed her eyes, stopped her diatribe, and waited for Crown to look to her.

And she waited; with renewed blushing she became angrier that someone was not attending to her silent demanding posture.

Crown had heard her, but feeding the child was far more important than recognizing a loud female. She had met those before and had never been impressed.

Not taking her eyes from Crown, the alien female took another three steps forward and stood just past the new father and next to Crown. She opened her mouth to yell something uncomplimentary but swallowed her words when she saw what was taking place. The alien was placing Pwok's free hand on the milk tube that was being devoured.

With a tight jaw and compressed lips, Crown glared at the boisterous, commanding female with the same withering stare she glared when a patient refused her orders. Through her space encounters, she had learned the look was universally understood.

The female's stance relaxed slightly and she took one step back.

Then Crown took the offensive, matching the tone she had

heard directed at the distraught father. "Don't you know how to care for infants? The mother's in worse shape, I suppose. She'll need help. Take me to her."

Vokra had cowered from Crown's look and directed her attention to Pwok and his daughter. Then her head snapped up to Crown and her eyes opened wide. She heard the alien's last four words in her own language. Pwok looked up quickly, too.

Commander Carpenter was shocked that the translator had meshed the languages after so brief a sound collection. Strumpf saw the commander's astonishment and quietly explained that the language was probably uncomplicated and evolved from that of a race they had already translated.

"You telling me this civilization is the work of another colonizing race?"

"Possibly," Strumpf agreed, "you can't imagine we're the only species that colonizes. This planet may have been settled very long ago. I doubt there are extant records that demonstrate the connection. I'm sure the translator could delineate the evolution if we asked it."

"That's unimportant now," the commander judged. "Amanda does need to find the mother and we've got more introductions to make. The lab rats just got another tier added to the maze."

Vokra was stunned. The alien's overbearing demand she had not yet thought of answering. Nor had she recovered from the shock of being commanded to do anything by an alien. She was also receiving conversations in her own language from the two males standing behind the female who had quieted Canska's and Pwok's daughter. She wondered how they might know about the ancients who had populated the planet so long before that no one could remember much about them except from dismissed fantastic myths.

Crown repeated her demand. "Where is the mother? Take me to her."

Pwok heard Crown's repeated demand and he felt vindicated. The not-so-strange aliens did speak his language. He had obviously been too upset to understand their words before. But he looked at Vokra before he spoke. "I knew they could help

our baby," and he justified his unintended announcing his people's presence to the aliens. "They can help Canska, too. I know
it."

"They may be able to," Vokra agreed and thought of her
unraveled plans to stay hidden. "But they will have to come
back with us. Canska cannot be moved."

Crown heard the translation through her earpiece, a companion to the unobtrusive mike that directed English to the
translator and then to a small vocal transceiver placed at the
neck of all tunics to broadcast in the alien tongue.

"I can go with you now," Crown said in her best bedside
tone. "The mother is in need of immediate help. Please take me
there."

Vokra looked at Pwok and down at his daughter who had
finished the small bit of milk and fallen asleep. It was the first
time either Pwok or Vokra could remember when the infant
wasn't upsetting all around with her screaming and crying.

She leaned close to Pwok's ear and said something that
couldn't be picked up by the translator and Pwok answered in
the same quiet manner.

Vokra turned toward the mega, cupped her hands around
her mouth and let loose a deep growl that rose in pitch to a
screech. The sound didn't translate. Then she turned to Crown
who was fidgeting, passing her kit from one hand to the other,
eager to reach her other patient and growing more upset with
the delay. "Come, I will take you," Vokra said.

"Father and daughter must come also." Crown added a
condition. "I bring one male with me." She looked past Strumpf
and saw Fred Sharp. "That one," she pointed out. "I will come
alone if I must."

"You and one may come with us." Behind Vokra's agreement was the belief that despite the huge size of the requested
male the monitors outnumbered the two aliens.

Sharp quickly joined Crown and four, not counting the
baby, headed for the base of the Molox1.

MOLRIXX

Carrying three small containers of real milk, Krolni returned to the tenth floor in his dash from the top of Molox1. He found only Canska where the free Molrixx had spent the night. She didn't respond to his questions and Krolni thought that she was too sick to have been left without someone to care for her. She didn't react when he put the back of one hand on her forehead. It was bubbled with sweat and he knew the fever had broken again; but she was still hot. He put down two filled containers near her cot before he offered her some milk from the third.

She refused the gesture, almost spilling the small jar as she swung at it with the back of her hand. She groaned and in a weak voice begged for her baby. Then her eyes fluttered shut and she was silent.

Krolni saw her chest rise and heard shallow breaths and hoped she had just fallen asleep.

He went to the window where Vokra usually sat to survey the white and the forest. He looked down and traced his sight back toward the bottom of Molox1. Vokra was leading a fast moving group of Molrixx toward the white where Pwok had just pushed his way through the bushes and carried a small bundle at his chest.

Krolni shook his head and sighed. He knew no one would defy Vokra and openly announce the monitor group to the aliens, least of all Pwok who never made scenes. However, baby and mother were sicker than Krolni had seen anyone else in his time with the group; he understood the fear that demanded Pwok's rebellion.

"They're all down there," he assessed. "Maybe Pwok did the right thing." Then he saw Vokra rush across the white and stop by Pwok. He couldn't see very clearly, but he eventually saw a softening of the confrontation. Then she and Pwok with the baby were accompanied by two aliens. He grinned. First Wisolen and the Hislik, now Pwok ... He couldn't imagine what had happened down on the white to soften Vokra, but he was sure that the four were coming to see about Canska. He decided that he could leave for the short time it would take to meet them and climb back to the tenth floor.

Checking on Canska one last time, he found her very warm. The broken fever was building again. *Information,* he thought and dashed down.

He reached the bottom floor long before Vokra's group of four approached and he left the molox to greet them. As soon as he cleared the portal, the door thudded shut and he heard a heavy 'chunk' that announced the lock sealing doors from the outside. Immediately he regretted not staying inside to wait for Volkra. Canska was alone and locked away, accessible only after a long climb on the outside stairs and back down to the entry made harder by his already hurried dash to 500 and back.

Ruing his predicament was foolish effort. Krolni hurried to Vokra who was some distance from the molox. When he reached her group, two he knew and two he didn't, Vokra asked, "Krolni, where have you been?"

"You sent me for milk."

"Oh … yes."

"The capris and bovis didn't have much to give. Canska refused any and fell unconscious. I thought she could be left for a little bit, until we'd get back to her. …"

"We're going to see her. The alien medico thinks she can help."

"Not so simple," Krolni said. "I heard the entrance lock when it shut, after I stepped past the door."

Vokra's eyes opened wide. Locked out of Molox1 never seemed a possibility when no power was available.

"We can try the auxiliary," Vokra suggested.

"Provided the computers haven't shut us out for good." Krolni said.

"Is there no other way in," Crown asked. "I must get to the mother." Krolni's eyes widened when he heard an alien speaking his language. She seemed amused.

"One other," Vokra said and looked directly at Krolni. "You never removed your latch-stop, did you?"

"No; it's still at 50."

"Then we'd better get started. There's not much light left

and I don't relish climbing in the dark," Vokra said.

"Up the outside?" Crown gasped as she studied the narrow stairway up the side of the mile-high building and seemed to grasp that was the only way to the sick mother.

"Not quite so far," Krolni offered. "Woloka and I found several other latch-stops, and hers, of course. The lowest is at twenty-five. I'll climb there and you can follow. Before you get to ten, I'll be down and open the landing door. It's a long way outside, but nothing like 50 floors."

"How long for a roundtrip to 25 and down to the bottom, here?" Vokra didn't seem any more enthusiastic about climbing the outside of the mega-city than Crown.

"No matter how long, it's not shorter than if we climb to the baby's mother," Crown countered. "I must see her as soon as I can. We can do ten floors while he does forty."

"I'd prefer to wait." Vokra's deep-seated terror of being on the outside stairs was only hinted at. In her youth, she had been exiled on a landing outside floor 314 when winter wind gusts threatened to push her down the stairs. She had lain in a fetal position next to the outer wall of a landing until she was let back in. Any mention of the outside stairs dredged up that memory accompanied by renewed fear of falling and translated into a dislike of taking stairs up or down inside or out.

"If you wish," Crown said. "Fred and I must follow."

"Not without me, you don't," Vokra conceded as she forced her fear away.

Krolni started up two steps at a time and was quickly at the first five-floor landing.

Crown looked at Pwok. "Wait here with your daughter, until Krolni returns to the first floor and opens the door from the inside." Then she gave Pwok another milk tube. "If she wakes and cries, see if she will take more milk."

Turning toward her Earth companion she said without much eagerness, "Well, Fred, let's climb. If I don't look down ..."

"From a space doc? Really!" Fred gibed. "The *Marco's* a lot further up than fifty floors. You aren't squeamish about that are you?"

"I'm not about to fall from orbit."

Doctor Crown and Sharp had to hurry to catch Vokra who

was already a flight ahead.

Vokra was five steps from the landing when she saw the door to the tenth floor open. She turned to the two aliens who were two floors behind. "He's here. You're doing well. It's just a little more."

Vokra took the last steps to the landing and stepped into the hall. The terror she'd held at bay by looking only upward gushed out in a howl of thanksgiving accompanied by watering eyes and weak knees. Her composure soon took charge and she told Krolni, "I'll hold this open. They're not far back. Go on down. Pwok is waiting at the main entrance. We're going to need something to hold the door open down there."

"I was thinking that," he said between deep breaths. "I can find something heavy enough to keep the main door from closing and something else for the auxiliary. Canska was awake and sitting on the cot. She looked lost, when I passed her before I got here."

Krolni dashed off to the inner stairway and was out of sight and sound before Crown and Sharp entered the tenth floor.

Crown was panting heavily. She stopped for three deep breaths and to rest her legs momentarily. "Where?" she wheezed not willing to take any more time to reach her second patient.

"I'll follow," Sharp said as he gasped for air. "Maybe father and daughter will show me the way. I guess stairs aren't my thing. I need the rest."

"This way," Vokra said and hurried off, Crown a flagging follower.

Canska's face was drawn, her eyes sunken and glassy. The recurring fever tinged her white cheeks with red highlights. Her eyes lit up when she saw Vokra and then filled with fear when she saw someone she didn't know and who didn't look Molrixx. Despite her delirium she was sure the stranger with a funny face and small eyes was an alien—no doubt from the flying craft—and wondered why Vokra brought an alien into the molox. Then she looked around for her baby and Pwok. They were the last Molrixx she remembered seeing except for Krolni, just awhile before.

"Canska," Vokra said softly. She leaned over and dropped to one knee to look the sick mother straight into her face, "This alien can care for you. Pwok took your daughter to the white. She helped your daughter. We all went down to hide and watch when Pwok met them."

"Where's my baby?" Canska cried out, not understanding what she had been told.

"Pwok's coming with her," Vokra said and continued with information beyond what Canska could make sense of. "The molox locked us out. Krolni climbed up to a latch stop. He's going down to prop the doors open. Pwok is waiting for him there. He'll be here soon."

"I want my baby," Canska cried out, ignoring Vokra's disjoined explanation. She glared at the two females before her, neither of whom were answering her demands for her baby.

Crown stepped closer, glanced at Vokra, then looked at Canska, and said, "Let me feel your brow." Her translator relayed the request in Molx and Canska's eyes opened wide. She gasped as the alien stepped forward and reached out but didn't touch her.

"They speak our language?" Canska asked Vokra.

"Something like that," was Vokra's answer. "When you're better, you'll understand. Let her do her work."

Crown stepped closer and extended her reach. She felt the young mother's fever before she touched her skin. She was hotter than her daughter had been. "Please lay back," Crown asked. "Let me check you, as best as I can." Then she rubbed some of the anti-fever salve on Canska's brow.

At first Canska balked when Crown began her examination and again when Sharp finally arrived just a little before Pwok and his daughter. Crown told the males to go until she was finished. Canska saw her baby and cried out for her daughter.

"Bring the baby here," Crown asked Pwok and took the infant from him. She laid the newborn on Canska's uncovered breast. Her daughter immediately rooted for a nipple and was again unsuccessful. She began to cry. Crown pulled out the third milk tube and gave it to Canska. "Here, feed her with this." Crown helped Canska hold her daughter and milk tube below her chest and out of the way of her work. "I'll see about your milk."

Crown found that the new mother's milk ducts were

stopped, as she figured. She cleaned Canska's nipples and manipulated the breasts to help her milk flow. Then she affirmed that Canska had no lingering problems from delivery except for the fever, which she expected to leave within the day. She called Pwok and Sharp, who had been carrying on their own interspecies conversation in the corridor. Mostly to ease Pwok's fears, Sharp had regaled him with risqué interspecies jokes.

Finally, nursing her baby for the first time, Canska smiled and gazed at her daughter and reached for Pwok's hand to draw him close.

Crown and Sharp moved away from the new father and mother to speak with Vokra. "I think she will be okay," Crown said. "I must come back to see her tomorrow, but the fever should subside and her milk will flow. That will quiet the baby."

"I will expect you," Vokra said. "About this time?"

"Earlier, I think," Crown said. "And with the door open, ten floors will be much easier. Climbing the side of a building is not without its own terror."

"I'd never done it before," Vokra confessed and omitted the source of her terror. "Not even a single flight. Some of my people have, regularly; most have not." Then changing to a more pressing topic, "This was not how we imagined we'd meet your people."

"Nor how we planned to meet yours," Sharp spoke up, "once we realized there were people on a world we thought was uninhabited,"

"I suppose that was Wisolen's Hislik bite treatment," Vokra said. "We worried about his action, when we discovered what he'd done."

Crown introduced an opening for real interspecies first contact. "You and our commander need to talk about what's going to happen between us. It looks like there shouldn't be much trouble." Against the better judgment of colony ship crew protocol, Crown had decided that contact on this planet was going to be smooth.

"My food people are worried because they think what's left for growing and animals for meat cannot supply you and us."

"We can provide our own food," Sharp answered. "We

were headed for a different planet that we would colonize. We should not limit your food supply."

"My hunters and farmers will be happy for that," Vokra said. "Perhaps we might share some with you as a token of our thanks."

Noise from twenty-seven Molrixx climbing to the fifteenth floor forced the quiet conversation to evolve into louder words, but not from anger or fear. The mix of Molrixx and humans had been uneventful except for the medical aid offered from one to the other.

"We should return," Crown said. "You have your debriefing to do with your people and our commander will be beside himself to learn what we have to pass on. How soon might you, Vokra, be able to meet with him?"

"Maybe tomorrow, perhaps the next day. I will have to field many questions of those who watched and are now returning. Some will be fearful; they will have to be satisfied that their fear is groundless. They will have many concerns they have already talked over with each other."

Crown offered similar thoughts. "I know we will have similar problems. Maybe a day might not be enough time before a real first contact. Can I tell the commander you will meet with him on the white area?"

"I will come to him. It's our planet; we will come to you."

The two humans turned, looked fondly at the young family, and headed down stairs that were almost empty of the Molrixx who had climbed past the tenth floor to reform their clan on the fifteenth. The last four Crown and Sharp passed were hunters carrying the dismembered body of a long-necked creature covered in black splotches on gray fur.

By the time Crown and Sharp reached the fifth floor, she pointed out to Sharp where Canska had given birth. The landing had been traipsed over twice by most of the monitors, but evidence of blood cleaned up was clearly seen. "Can you believe she was climbing stairs five levels below where she should have been?" Crown was outraged that a pregnant female in her condition was not coddled.

"Different race of people," Sharp said. "You know the lore about babies born in fields on Earth while mothers worked."

"Yes, I do. And that was just as wrong. Canska and her daughter could have easily died and for no reason."

"Well, they haven't, yet," Sharp said. "If you consider their living conditions, they don't seem to have much in the way of medicine."

"Maybe not," Crown countered. "But really! A mother close to birthing and she's climbing stairs? Even you'd not suggest that, Fred.

Fifteen colonists and crew had joined the commander to wait for Crown and Sharp. Seventy others, tired of standing around and in the growing gloom of evening, had returned to their shuttles. The two navigators had not been among the original attendees as Pwok's fear for his family's health initiated the alien encounter.

"The mother was running a fever and her milk was not flowing," Crown reported before the commander had a chance to ask. "I'll check on her tomorrow. Vokra plans to see you tomorrow, maybe later."

"Good timetable. It's enough to settle preliminaries," Commander Carpenter said.

"She has the same things to do," Crown corroborated.

"They are only about a third of us," Sharp announced. "They're worried about having enough land to grow food and hunt."

"Why don't you two see me in the morning. I can bounce some ideas off you and all of us can prepare."

HUMANS

Returning to his shuttle, Commander Carpenter detoured to investigate the other shuttles in late evening. He was sure the existence of natives of whatever planet they had been pulled to was likely the only topic of discussion among his small band of Earthlings, for all—except for LeRoi and Malestrom—had crowded as much as possible around Pwok and his child. They all heard the universal translator announce Vokra's demands but not her quiet words to the bold father whose disobedient action was described as everything from heroic to foolish.

Carpenter's solitary meander provided time for introspection and analysis of Cantro's treatment. He knew he'd get more details about the locals, when Crown and Sharp returned from the unexpected foray that was fraught with danger. His initial unstated hesitance to allow the crew doctor to go with Vokra, despite that nothing had appeared threatening, was trumped by Crown's proven intuition in similar meetings that she would be relatively safe treating the mother, especially if Sharp were accompanying her.

Vokra, the native leader who seemed undaunted by their presence, was herself physically imposing. Her loud and scolding attitude showed more concern that her apparent counsel to avoid the aliens had been disobeyed than that their existence should remain hidden. Crown's caring for the newborn and demand to see the mother seemed an acceptable, if not excessive, repayment for Cantro's medication. Overall the surprise contact on the corner of the tarmac seemed to bode well. If not amiable, the meeting was one of guarded trust.

For a moment, Malcolm Carpenter felt good.

That euphoria was soon flooded by a queasy apprehension that he was missing something. That unease conjured up memories: his waking from short sleep on the *Marco P* and his twice-asked questions of navigator LeRoi. The foreboding was further linked to another initial encounter. Those aliens had been friendly at first contact, too, though Vokra's first words and actions, albeit directed to one of her own, could hardly have been less welcoming.

Still, as the exception to his rule of aliens being straight-forward, he was glad Varlez hadn't mentioned the Ne'unkras who had sucked the colony mission into a nearly impossible morass of political statecraft double-talk that was eventually overcome by human technological superiority.

Currently, his people were under the umbrella of a plane-tary intelligence that even Varlez couldn't crack—yet. Technol-ogy was not the answer to the situation with Vokra. Cantro's and Crown's personal contacts suggested smooth interaction between the two species. Still détente was not guaranteed. Per-haps these people were like the Ne'unkras. He'd have to look deeper for hints of subterfuge. And he had no certain idea of the part LeRoi and Maelstrom were going to play in the min-gling of the two rational species, especially after he had spied the two navigators, all but open enemies on board the *Marco P*, carrying on as if they were reunited best friends. Carpenter even wondered if Maelstrom would be in his shuttle, when he returned.

The backup navigator appeared to be sleeping, when Car-penter entered his shuttle after a visual inventory of fourteen other shuttles. Her reclining seat/bed stretched flat. The com-mander noticed her eyes were not closed, but she didn't react to his entry or the hold shutting. Her ample chest rose and fell faster than in normal sleep. Nor did she react to his hand waves over her eyes, which didn't blink even when he dropped his hand very near her brow.

The commander smirked in recalling Maelstrom's over-con-fidence that she could defend herself against the electronic in-trusion that she said LeRoi was forced to submit to. Her inat-tention implied to him that she was under the same spell that had commandeered LeRoi.

However, Maelstrom had been conscious and aware of the commander's entry and hand-waving in front of her eyes. The planet's electronic tether that Acquisition had rout-ed through the *Marco P* and MP to strengthen its grip on LeRoi had used her proximity to the navigator to seep con-trolling tendrils into the computer portion of her brain. Once the few wisps of access were linked to LeRoi's obedience, the secondary navigator found she couldn't shield herself from alien control.

Ticia Bandi's improper accusation at the beginning of her accompanying LeRoi was early and loud enough to let her non-computerized lobes re-seize control. However, once LeRoi had pulled her from that confrontation, her human consciousness faded. It didn't cease to gather information, but it was not the controlling center. Their jaunt off the tarmac and through the thorny bushes continued to seat the framework for later intrusion and help in something involving the rest of the settlers and *Marco's* crew.

When the navigators returned to the tarmac, the planet had control of them and Pwok's and Vokra's meeting with the Earthers was unimportant and beyond the System's intentions. Maelstrom was not yet privy to the plans LeRoi possessed, but the planetary glee at the novelty humans were about to offer was the basis for the navigators' light uncharacteristic banter.

Once LeRoi left Maelstrom, her electronic tether began to fade. Not until LeRoi settled into his reclined seat, did the digital leash disconnect. When Commander Carpenter entered the shuttle, Maelstrom was returning to her human persona, but the residual from the planetary connection overrode her conscious movements so much that her human side feared ever regaining control over the interface. Finally she understood something of what LeRoi had been so engaged with and why his relationship with her had about-faced. Their leaving the tarmac to discover some planetary contraption only provided a hint that the tarmac itself was the top of some underground construction. She recognized that the stairs reached that vault, possibly an underground cavern as large as the tarmac itself. However, she hadn't been given enough castoff information from LeRoi that explained the secrecy or his fear of anyone yet knowing what he planned.

The commander didn't dim the shuttle lights when he at last sat to scrutinize his backup navigator and perhaps second co-opted human.

Then Maelstrom's eyelids fluttered. She stretched and flexed her arms and legs and neck that had been trapped immobile in an unnatural resting position, not unlike that of LeRoi in his specially adapted seat/couch. She turned her head and started to speak but stopped as a prior command took control. She sat up, stood, and headed for the hatch and the tarmac. Commander Carpenter followed.

They were fifteen yards from the shuttle in deepening darkness and beyond light projected from the shuttle hatch, when Maelstrom turned and admitted, "You were right, Commander. It is strong."

"And are Varlez and Strumpf correct that you cannot keep from being controlled?" Commander Carpenter relayed a serious worry both confidantes had expressed and a concern he didn't want to hold but was afraid he must.

"I'm not sure." Maelstrom's answer lacked the original conviction she boasted of about not being co-optable. "When Roger left me, the control diminished; but it took a long time for my conscious brain to assume its primary place."

"Do you have any idea what the planet wants?" Carpenter was looking for a clue that would help his own defense against the alien force.

"No." Maelstrom drew out the syllable and looked back at the open hatch. Then lifting her eyes up to the commander's face she continued, "I don't know if that's because LeRoi was in control or my interface is more difficult to access. He seemed awfully vulnerable to something beyond the interface and more than pre-occupied. Maybe he channeled my takeover."

"Are you telling me you can't fight against your interface being compromised?"

"Not without some preparation or anticipation on my part. I didn't recognize when my interface was taken over. I know the preliminaries, now. I think I can misdirect them, maybe fool the accessing agent."

Concerned at the potential danger, the commander looked down at Maelstrom. "That's an unwarranted risk, Priscilla," he said with more empathy than blunt conjecture.

"Maybe. When he took me off the tarmac, he seemed to know just where he was going. I kinda wondered about that. And he found a control that revealed a set of steps leading underneath the tarmac. I may need to be controlled again to find out just what we're supposed to do. Taking me along, tells me

I'm involved with his ... the force's ... plans."

"What is the cost of joining him? Do you have any way to defend your humanity from electronic control?"

"The sudden takeover of my interface surprised me. I didn't expect it and wasn't ready for it. Next time I'll know what to expect. I think I can hold off complete control. Maybe that will let me find out why we're here."

"What if we just keep both of you tied up?" It was the unreasonable tactic that Varlez had tossed out and led the commander to similar thoughts.

Carpenter thought that LeRoi might never be immune from outside electronic control. But he was just one individual and could be contained as long as necessary. Maelstrom's status was more complicated. Her third generation interface might be immune from total control, as she claimed. But if she let herself become entangled again and, possibly more deeply, he'd have the impossible task of determining which half of her brain was in charge.

Maelstrom gave the commander time for his thoughts.

When he returned his attention to her, she stated the obvious. "Imprisoning us isn't an option, if you want to learn anything." She knew that escaping the digital system and the planet was more important than the commander's concern for her. Beating the electronic hold on the *Marco P* and its passengers outweighed her safety, as she had originally indicated when the commander gave her his written orders on the *Marco P*.

Unconvinced that locking up the navigators wasn't the best option or that Maelstrom could fend off the computer, Carpenter nodded and changed the subject. "Did you and LeRoi notice that two planetary natives approached us? This planet is inhabited."

Maelstrom by-passed a direct answer. "We were still captive under the planetary system, when we returned. But I don't think physical inhabitants are a part of why we're here. What little I did find out discounted anything physical. Some of the information I got is that this planet is nearly dead which we were pretty certain of. Capturing us isn't about living bodies but about continued existence of some kind."

Commander Malcolm Carpenter shook his head. He

thought back through the evolution of galactic civilizations he was aware of. Most technological peoples toyed with immortality through electronics and sooner than later rejected the notion; some only after they mistakenly and foolishly obliterated a significant portion of their population. Perhaps this planet had found a way that eluded all other civilizations. Or maybe the population hadn't learned that digital brains didn't work.

Then he returned to Maelstrom's statement about the dying planet. It was dying, if his shuttle trajectory were indicative of the whole planet. Maybe this population didn't have space flight to leave and find another home. Maybe the digital option was a last gasp hope. Still he didn't have any idea why his ship should be commandeered.

Deep in thought, the commander hardly bid good night to Maelstrom before he strode toward Varlez's shuttle and the linchpin of the problem, Navigator Roger LeRoi.

MOLRIXX

Her small group followed out of sight as Vokra led Crown and Sharp to the foot of Molox1 and watched her and the two aliens follow Krolni's rush up the outside stairs.

Soon after he let Vokra onto the tenth floor, Krolni opened the main entry to Molox1. The remaining Molrixx community besieged him with questions that Krolni had no answers for.

In a single day's time, they had watched Pwok trash Vokra's orders to stay hidden and Vokra herself lead aliens into the molox.

All Krolni could tell them was that the alien female was caring for Canska and that he had hurried to re-open the door that locked them outside. Then, while he held the door open, he sent Korsk to find something that would block the door from closing.

The remaining Molrixx, except for the hunters bringing the partitioned Gafron, passed the tenth floor while Canska was still being cared for and they saw aliens up close and heard them speaking Molx.

Some paused in their rush upward to stare at Pwok and the alien male who were talking quietly in two languages mixed with momentary outbursts of laughter. Others heard louder words from the alien medico, words in their own language. Peering out from their hiding just off the white, they had been astonished that the strangers looked like themselves: two arms and hands, two legs, one head, smaller than theirs, with two ears and eyes—smaller and oddly shaped—a mouth and skinny nose. The aliens hadn't seemed exceptionally bigger and they looked as muscular as some of the Molrixx. Their clothing, made from strange material, looked like shirts and pants. Shoes, an accessory that the monitors seldom wore, were different from flops worn in the moloxes, and were more sturdy than the mega footwear that couldn't take the harsh use in the forests. More than a handful of comments were made that the aliens could almost pass for Molrixx, if their faces were camouflaged.

The former monitors reached the fifteenth floor and crowded around Vokra who thought the higher floor safer. Even Canska, with her child and almost carried by Pwok on whom she leaned heavily, had trudged up five floors, having left her cot after being ministered to and not wanting to be separated from the rest of the Molrixx.

Eager questions, some filled with anger and subdued threats, were shouted at Vokra.

"What did the aliens do?"

"Why did you bring them into the molox?"

"What did they want?"

"Are we going to mingle?"

"What can they do for us?"

"Were they frightening?"

"Were they afraid?"

"Will they move into the mega?"

Vokra could hear nothing but noise from over-spoken and repeated questions.

After a brief quiet, the beginning of her first statement about the aliens was lost in a repeated cacophony of demands from those who had different questions. She stopped shouting her words over insistent and rumbling comments. She looked for Pwok and just stared at him. He was standing at the back of the group with his arm around Canska who was holding their baby. Following Vokra's determined stare, their questions ceased and all turned to glare at Pwok.

Though his disobedience was more rash than she was sure he understood, she accepted that it was what he ought to have done for his baby and Canska. Nor did she think the encounter was disastrous. Her group had remained hidden. She believed the aliens couldn't know how many they were, until she remembered all had streamed past the doctor and her companion who, she was sure, could count. However, the alien medico had reciprocated for Wisolen's medicating the Hislik bite. His small favor was hardly equal to what the alien female had done. "Perhaps they are not to be feared," she said to herself and unheard by those questioning her.

Eventually, Vokra raised her hands and her voice. The mumbled and layered questioning ceased and her gaze at Pwok relaxed. Squeezed by twenty-eight sets of eyes, Pwok scanned those staring and defended himself with a newfound strength.

"What? You'd all let your family die … if you had one?"

Embarrassed by his blunt accusation, several looked from Pwok and Canska who, unashamed, was starting to nurse her newborn. Three, their faces turning pink even in the dim light, looked at the their pregnant mates. Others looked back at Vokra to take solace in her reaction toward Pwok, which was not the anger they expected.

In the silence, Vokra's stern look softened almost to a smile. "Your disobedience, Pwok, may have turned a sticky and dangerous situation into one of mutual friendship and help. As self-sufficient as we have been, you pointed out something we never admitted. Something I'm ashamed to admit now. We know nothing about birthing, except how to make it necessary. I see that others will need to know what to do before too long."

The group of monitors boldly looked at three other Molrixx with protruding bellies.

However, Pwok, who was only looking at his daughter and mate, adjusted his supporting arm around Canska who was sagging heavily. "Canska needs to lay down," Pwok said. "You can yell at me while I take care of her."

"I'm not yelling," Vokra corrected. "You know I only counsel, you all agreed to that a long time ago. We were all afraid of what these aliens might do and I cautioned not to make ourselves known. Even Wisolen didn't make us known except in a mysterious way. But Pwok, with no care for caution or worry about how they might react to people on Molx, dashed out and said 'We're here,' and he made it possible for a good meeting."

"Maybe they're just playing with us," Korsk suggested. "They didn't lose anything to us. And they are more than we are."

"But they don't know that," Crelle, who was among the last to climb the stairs, challenged. "We know that; they don't."

"I'm sure the large male counted as we passed by him," Woloka said. "I saw his eyes moving across us as we climbed the stairs."

Vokra ignored the population comparison and said, "They didn't act like they were evil. You all know I sense those feelings."

"But they're alien," Korsk continued.

"Yes, they are," Crelle admitted. "They look like us, mostly. I watched them for two days. They act like us."

"So are we just going to go introduce ourselves," Korsk supposed.

"Enough," Vokra stopped the banter. "I will meet with their leader tomorrow or the next day. Amanda suggested that just the two of us talk. Their leader will talk with his people about us as I am talking to you about them. Then we'll have more information to make decisions."

"Really," Crelle tried to cap a growing dissension, "if they are here to take over a planet, they are too few to do that ..."

"Unless they are the first of many conquerors," Wisolen interrupted.

"... Right," Crelle continued. "How many aliens do you suppose can live on Molx? You know our little green valley is getting smaller. It's hardly big enough for us. Why would a conquering civilization choose Molx for a prize? No, they didn't land here because it was their destination. I'm sure of that."

"Regardless of why, they're here," Krolni offered. "They're no better off than we are, unless they can reverse planetary death."

"I'm sure that's something I'll discuss with their leader," Vokra offered. "As I said before, Pwok's seeking help may have eased a difficult situation. Instead of our sneaking around each other, he brought us together quickly. We may not be able to work together, and we'll know that soon enough. But together we may help each other."

Then looking at Krolni, Vokra asked, "Did you get the main door blocked open?"

"Korsk and I rolled a good sized boulder into the doorway. It doesn't have to be climbed over. The door can be pushed or pulled open, but it will never close and lock again."

"It's nearly dark," Vokra said. "We don't have to worry about being seen in here. We can light some candles and get ready to bed down. I'd suggest, regardless of how the aliens behaved, that we keep someone on guard while the rest of us sleep."

"I can take the first watch," Delsin volunteered.

"I'll spell you after I get a little sleep," Woloka offered.

"I don't need much sleep," Mloksi said. "I'll watch after you until we all get up."

HUMANS

Commander Carpenter headed across the darkening tarmac to the last row and to the only shuttle facing east. He might have spent some time enjoying the star-filled sky, more brilliant than Earth's southern hemisphere and containing a wider and more intense band of the Milky Way. However, his urgent duty prevented any prolonged observation of that awe-inspiring galactic panorama. He feared that he would gain no information from speaking to LeRoi. Still, he had to try.

The shuttle hatch opened at his approach and Varlez stepped down to welcome him.

"Important for this late a visit. I gather Crown and Sharp returned. Mission accomplished?" Varlez had not waited for their return. He used the time to work on the replicators and his master computer.

"They did," Carpenter answered. "Other things prompt urgency."

"Our passenger?" Varlez questioned and lifted his head to his left.

The commander nodded.

"He's been like you'll see him since he returned from his escape. It's how he usually is. Don't know if he's conscious of anything but what a computer feeds him."

"We'll see," Carpenter grunted and stepped around Varlez who moved aside. They entered the shuttle.

The *Marco P's* primary navigator was on his back on the flat seat; the indentation Varlez had crafted kept his helmet-interfaced head in line with his spine. Commander Carpenter reached under the top of the flattened seat to grasp a lever that he pulled to lift the back of the seat to almost vertical. Then he ordered in a loud demanding tone, "Navigator LeRoi."

When Carpenter got no response, not a muscle twitch nor a blink, he repeated his order louder, emphasizing each syllable. This time LeRoi pulled his head from the indentation and turned his body to the demand.

"S-i-r?" he stretched out in question. He blinked his eyes

and Carpenter could see a blank look vanish as the navigator became aware of where he was.

"Stand and face me, Navigator."

"Yes, sir." LeRoi, taken aback at the unusual gravity projected by the commander, stood from his seat and almost saluted, a gesture never used in the relaxed atmosphere of Malcolm Carpenter's command. He repeated, "Sir?"

"What did you do today?"

"Nothing special. Spent my time in here. Don't recall anything else."

"You didn't leave the shuttle? You weren't with Maelstrom?"

"No, sir!" LeRoi's denial was absolute and spoken with a sneer at the thought of accompanying the young backup navigator.

Carpenter watched his navigator furrow his brow and narrow his eyes like he was reviewing events. Then he gently shook his head and repeated with a slight blush, "No, sir; I can't recall that."

"You don't remembered pulling Maelstrom from a confrontation with Bandi?"

"No. You know I'm not one to associate and ... ah ... not with ... Maelstrom." LeRoi reddened in a public broadcast of his dislike of the backup navigator.

"Think again, Navigator. And what about two aliens we met on the tarmac?"

Roger LeRoi screwed up his face and looked askance at the commander. "There are no inhabitants on γ-Cygnus A2, sir." Then a small smile grew into a friendly grin. "You're playing with me, aren't you, sir?"

"No, Roger; I'm not. But I am worried about you. A lot of us are worried. We don't know what we should do."

"Do? I told you I'd be no good on the planet. I've kept to myself ever since we landed. I suppose I might be given something to do, something that fits with navigation."

Commander Carpenter had nothing more to say. He knew that his navigator was under the planet's electronic control.

He twitched his lips and looked back at Varlez who had joined Arafa and Bandi in observing the commander's futile questioning. The two assistant engineers had shaken their heads at the navigator's answers and knew that the potential problems were beyond their initial stages. Both looked questions of what could be done.

The commander knew his navigator's takeover had begun in orbit, though he hadn't recognized it then. He was controlled long before the graying screens and that incident's erasure from MP. LeRoi's belief that they had arrived at γ-Cygnus A2, his refusal to recognize native life or inhabited structures was, now, clear proof that the navigator had not consciously lied in answering his questions. He was not in control of his mind.

Malcolm Carpenter looked at LeRoi's eyes that were going inattentive. "As you were, Navigator; as you were."

Navigator LeRoi sat down on his seat and pushed down the side lever that laid the backrest flat. He cushioned his helmet. Commander Carpenter watched his navigator's consciousness vanish as he dropped back flat.

Malcolm Carpenter turned toward the hatch. "Outside," was his one word accompanying his gaze that swept across Varlez and his two female assistants.

On the tarmac and in darkening night he looked to Arafa and Bandi. "Following him will do no good and I doubt you will be able to follow any better than you did today. He's not himself. Maelstrom's probably our only hope at this point."

"Really?" Arafa questioned. "She hardly seemed different than he is."

"I've spoken with her. She is not entranced, except when LeRoi is near."

"That's what she says?" Bandi questioned. "Can she be trusted? She's as computer as he is."

"Not entirely." The commander hesitated to counter her belief since he wasn't convinced himself. "She admits to being compromised today. She thinks she can defend herself the next time LeRoi joins her. Likely tomorrow. We're not going to get any information from LeRoi. We're going to have to rely on Maelstrom, if we get anything. And her third generation interface may be an advantage that LeRoi doesn't have. But that means she has to allow herself to be controlled a second time."

"Sounds like a long chance," Varlez assessed as he moved

into the conversation. He had stood back while the commander instructed Bandi and Arafa.

"Is there another option?" Carpenter returned. "Until we discover how to release our shuttles and the *Marco* from the planet's hold, I don't see one."

"I suppose not," Varlez said with not a little concern. "She may be a sacrifice."

"She knows and accepts." The commander continued, "And perhaps just the first of all of us, if we can't win this war. She was surprised and ashamed to have been taken in today. But she's a quick study. If she can keep the force at bay, somehow pretend that it's taken over, we'll have an advantage."

Arafa and Bandi were unconvinced and their stance showed that doubt.

"She wasn't in control, except for the brief challenge I offered," Bandi said. "Can she keep from being controlled?"

"She mentioned that impropriety," the commander said. Bandi winced at his reference to her brazen question to Maelstrom. "Her interface is completely different from LeRoi's. She remembered what he did. She was just not able to keep from following LeRoi's and the system's direction, because she didn't recognize its initial encroaching. LeRoi has no memory of what he did today. That difference might be the edge we need to defend all of us."

"She's a lackey, then," Varlez said. "How does that help us, if she can't keep from doing what LeRoi tells her?"

"If she recognizes the system's first insidious contact, she might keep it away and still find out what the plan is. That she can tell us. Her plan is to act like she is under its control. But even if she can't keep the force from taking over, that control goes when LeRoi leaves her."

"And if he doesn't leave her?" Arafa asked.

"We'll just get involved and separate them," Varlez said. "That can't be all that difficult."

"Indeed, not," the commander agreed, "but that assumes they will return to the shuttles, as they did today."

"We could try following from a greater distance," Bandi offered. "If they're under the planet's control, maybe they dodged us because we were too close."

"Maybe," the commander agreed. "Maelstrom told me that once they left the tarmac they turned sharply to the north until they found three trees in a kind of triangle that had a pedestal within. It's a control for opening a stairway probably to under the tarmac. They didn't take the stairs. LeRoi just checked the mechanism, like a teaser to entice her."

"We can follow, maybe not together," Nequa said. "And we can leave the tarmac from two different places north and south of where they left and disappeared today."

"That's possible. But you don't want to keep LeRoi from doing what he's supposed to do. You can only watch. Even if Maelstrom's in trouble. You can't do anything that will compromise what the intelligence needs him to do."

"That's not going to be easy," Varlez counseled. "Not taking action to help one of the crew goes against everything we believe."

The commander nodded at Varlez's caution. Sequestering Maelstrom had been uncomfortable for him but not dangerous. His next allowance to her might be dangerous, perhaps fatal. However, as she had been the lone control on the *Marco P*, now she was the advanced scout who could discover the next move of the planetary system. That effort was likely not preventable by any order he might give. In one way, Maelstrom was as digital as LeRoi, but she had the schizoid advantage of split brain. Still, the force in control of his first generation digital navigator was no doubt unable to be kept from either of his navigators' interfaces.

"I'll have one more discussion with Maelstrom," Carpenter said as started for his shuttle. "You, three, get some rest. Vokra may come tomorrow to talk with me and I still have to debrief Crown and Sharp. And before Vokra shows."

Sitting cross-legged on the tarmac which still held a little of the day's warmth, Maelstrom was waiting for Commander Carpenter when he returned to his shuttle. She had added a light jacket to ward off the chill to her upper body.

"Didn't learn anything did you?" she asked from her seated position and held up a hand to help her stand.

The commander lifted her to her feet. "Only that he's as

controlled as he was on the *Marco*. He didn't even admit to leaving the shuttle."

"We'll probably go back to the stairs tomorrow. And down to wherever they lead."

"There's no way you can get out of that, I suppose?"

"He's not operating out of his mind. What controlled us today is in charge. I've been going over what we did. I think I know when the force invaded my interface. There was a time, when Roger, who almost never said anything, started to talk about brain digitizing. It was then that I seemed to blank out. When he stopped talking, my digital half was out of my control and my brain couldn't do anything about it."

"I don't think anything will happen to you, even if you are taken over again. The system apparently needs both of you. As long as you regain control, like tonight, you might be all right."

"And if I find out what is really going on, I won't have to keep going with him."

"That would be the best case," Carpenter said. "Unfortunately, I have never had a mission problem that was solved with the best case scenario. You do know that this can be very dangerous?"

"Commander, I pointed that out when you gave me written orders. Remember? The mission and the crew and colonists are important. For lack of a better term, we're in a war. I'm a spy, now, and a counterspy. I'm aware of the danger, just not the specifics."

"Then maybe you can keep your control," Carpenter said.

He still had an aching doubt that his small navigator could succeed.

SYSTEM

Acquisition: *Two aligned with our computer control. One connected to ship computer and obeys. That one's brain is our extension. Second is satellite to first and provides assistance.*

Central Reception: *Commands received? And followed?*

A: *Earthers willful. Direction will take more time than planned for.*

CR: *Time is of no consequence, except as the Molrixx could interfere. Are they locked out of Molox1?*

A: *They were when two met Earthers and the rest watched from hiding. One invalid remained within, hardly mobile, nearly deceased. Another entered and provided access for a second and two Earthers. Bottom access reopened. Unable to close.*

CR: *Status of Earthers and Molrixx?*

A: *Unsure of each other.*

CR: *That can be exploited. Gather Earthers in holding area.*

A: *Earthers appear uncertain of interfaced individuals. They are not unaccompanied.*

CR: *Increase surveillance. Allow some to accompany. Gather those first for holding.*

A: *Robots must be revived to tend the procedure.*

CR: *Are they available?*

A: *Yes; there are enough to hold Earthers in sequence. More power needed to revive and maintain more robots.*

CR: *Molox1 has the planet's power. We have power enough.*

A: *We do. Intermittent surges and apparent overloads hinder consistent robotic operation.*

CR: *Repair the malfunction!*

A: *No malfunction exists. Nothing presages the surges or overloads. No other constructs are drawing power from the grids. Problems are random and brief. They have no warning and are not generated from the spacecraft blocking solar reception.*

CR: *Analyze power; prepare robots; have interfaces bring unaware Earthers to holding.*

A: *When ...*

CR: *Repea-*

243

A:

CR: *Wh- ... -ning?*

A: *Acquisition here; Central Reception?*

CR: *Here. What happened?*

A: *Power fluctuation.*

CR: *Did you receive my last order?*

A: *Yes. ... Power, robots, hold Earthers. When they rouse them-selves, four or five may be captured.*

CR: *Check to see if power problems are feedback to other Moloxes.*

HUMANS

With a busy brain, Commander Carpenter lay awake and plowed through his urgent needs: Maelstrom, Crown, Vokra, and LeRoi, all worries enough to keep him awake until light. Before he had a chance to order the importance of each person's contribution to the human/alien circumstances, he slipped into a light sleep.

He woke, surprised he had drifted off. He didn't look to see how long he'd slept but remained unmoving and resumed his interrupted thoughts. LeRoi's blithe rejection of his own actions returned for another hearing and increased the commander's concern for the backup navigator who, he was sure, had no idea of the danger she was about to encounter.

Crown's interaction with the new mother and her report of the natives would provide him with tangible information about potential allies and knowledge about the planet and its death throes.

Carpenter blinked his eyes open to dim early dawn. Maelstrom was still sleeping. He was somewhat concerned that she was in the same rigid, supine posture that he saw before she regained control of her mind after her first jaunt with LeRoi. He wondered if the computer control had strengthened. Even when he opened the hatch to greet the day, she didn't react; and he thought that her escape from the computer's inroads had been momentary or perhaps allowed, as it may have allowed Varlez to think his firewalls on the *Marco* had worked.

He could not spend time on something he had no control over. He stepped out of the hatch and closed it behind him. He was not surprised to find both Crown and Sharp waiting for him.

After Pwok's and Vokra's intrusion, Carpenter had decided the natives were not behind the computer glitches and were probably in a similar precarious situation, as the humans were soon likely to be in, if they couldn't leave the planet. Vokra's people were as hunter/gatherer as any textbook describes that culture, but they were only recently cast into that role from a once technological society. That the birthing had caused such problems to force the father to seek help from aliens was proof that their primitive culture had degraded from advanced technology. That planetary history would have to be provided by Vokra when they met.

The shadow of the eastern range extended farther west covering the tarmac and reaching beyond the river. The jagged crags, backlit by the rising local star—even MP had no designation for it beyond LeRoi's inaccurate identification of the planet as γ-Cygnus A2—offered an eerie image of the potential danger they all faced.

The commander approached the two who had more interaction than anyone else with the natives whom Navigator LeRoi steadfastly refused to acknowledge. Crown and Sharp looked up and ended their own conversation, when they saw Carpenter descend the ramp.

Crown wasn't rested; worry lined her face. She had been involved in first encounters several times; never had one of those involved medicating a member of the other species. Though she had not worried that she and Sharp might be kept from returning to the modified human colony after working with the new mother, return to her shuttle had not quelled her fears over the unknown. Would the young mother really get better? Would Vokra allow her a second visit? Might she be held captive for some reason, especially if the mother had died? Could she have brought some unknown malady back to the crew or infected the natives? Those concerns, medical and personal, unlike the commander's but no less serious, had kept her awake much of the night. She knew she could have confided in Strumpf who had more first contacts than she did. However, George had his own problems with food and maintaining hydroponics when water seemed scarce and at some distance from the tarmac. She didn't want to add to his worries.

Fred Sharp looked to have slept the peace of the innocent. He was cheery and bright-eyed, eager to get into the day. He first greeted Carpenter as he stepped off the ramp. "Morning, Commander. Looks like it's gonna be nice."

Sharp didn't carry mission weight like the commander or Crown did. Having to plan and maintain the eventual human settlement was not inconsequential, though he followed established procedures. Still, his habit of constant awareness and quick assessment of conditions in strange places, gave him an outward sense of ease, that didn't match, but always hid, inner turmoil.

Sharp's stoic acceptance of situations made him appear either unconcerned or in control. That image was far from reality. Accompanying Crown to care for the new mother had stretched his stoicism to near breaking. He knew he could probably hold his own with three or four natives. If more than that chose to gang up, he would be at their mercy. However, the outside stairs brought out a long hidden fear. He had chided Crown to hide his own surging acrophobia and she hadn't noticed his several missteps and heavy sweating on their ten floor climb up the outside of the construct.

While Crown worked with the new mother, he wandered and gathered information about the natives from what they had scattered on the floor. Then, as he and Crown passed the hunters with their catch, climbing to a higher home floor on the humans' return to the tarmac, he realized the Molrixx were all smaller than he was—two were close to his size, but none had his brawn. Their clothing was primitive and defined their outdoor life. He was sure that they had entered the construction to stay hidden from the strangers. If his conversation with Pwok matched the whole group's personality, they were friendly and helpful, despite Vokra's boisterous appearance and reproach of the new father. He decided that her outburst was an extension of her position among the natives.

Not until he and Crown had returned to the virtual safety of the shuttles and crew did Sharp feel at ease. However, in more familiar surroundings, such as any planetary landing might be familiar, he was spared worry about his impressions. The commander and probably Strumpf and Varlez were responsible for acting on his report.

"You're up early," Carpenter offered a pleasantry before the duty of debriefing began.

"Better earlier," Crown returned. "Fewer to eavesdrop and more time for you to integrate."

"Especially if we are visited again," Sharp added.

"What can you tell me, Amanda?" the commander asked. "Are they as primitive in a technological backdrop as they appear?"

Crown launched into her own impressions, highlighted by the apparent lack of knowledge of birthing follow up. "They don't seem to be a large group. I'd bet this was the first birth they had."

"They aren't much more than two dozen," Sharp injected. "They don't seem particularly knowledgeable about much, though they do maintain simple lives."

"That's what I thought," Crown agreed. "Vokra didn't say more than a dozen words before we got to the mother—her name is Canska. Vokra told us there were a couple of females who knew some medicine and helped with the birth, but they didn't know what to do afterward."

"Any idea how long they've been living like we've seen?" the commander asked.

"That's something you'll have to find out when she comes to talk, if she does." Crown said. "I couldn't tell whether she would have left the mother and her child to die, if Pwok hadn't brought it to us. She seemed afraid of letting us know too much about them. After I cleaned Canska and she was able to breast her daughter, that fear seemed to wane. But she still didn't say much. She did agree that they and we needed to talk. I think it was more than just first contact jitters."

"Last night you said she would come today or tomorrow."

Crown nodded. "If they haven't sneaked away already and maybe left Canska and daughter and Pwok behind. They couldn't have fled."

"You didn't see anyone else until you were coming back?"

"Only one. He hurried up the outside stairs, a lot farther than we went, so he could get into the construct. He came back, opened a door for us, and went down to prop open the bottom door that had locked everyone out."

"That makes seven," Carpenter summed up. "How many more, do you think?"

"I counted twenty-four," Fred reported, "as they passed us on their way to higher floors while Pwok and I chatted. I don't think they live in there. Almost all of them were struggling to climb the stairs. Except for the one who opened the outside door for us. The last ones, carrying a dismembered animal, stopped and crowded against the wall away from us. It wasn't fear, just uncertainty."

"They live in the forest? Why, if there is a secure place out of the elements?"

"That's another thing you'll have to discover," Sharp said. "The civilization that put up that building and the others and this tarmac, was not primitive. Maybe what we've seen are escaped slaves. But then where are the slave-holders? When Amanda was doing her thing, I wandered around a little. They had evidence of technology. But no power anywhere and nothing that I saw to turn power on—no switches. No lights, no apparent heating or cooling ducts. I checked out a couple of rooms, apartments, flats, if you will. No cooking facilities. A bed and something like a computer access to somewhere."

"I'll have to check with Forbes for what he saw on his two scoutings," Carpenter said. "What we've seen is not what forced us down here and what has control of LeRoi's mind."

"I've thought about all that," Crown ventured. "Could these few be the last of the civilization? People do exterminate themselves in all kinds of ways and there are always a few that struggle to rebuild. That never happens without considerable help."

"But it doesn't explain the electronic control," Carpenter rebutted and the subject changed to security. "Fred, you willing to admit that they pose a threat?"

"If we saw all there is, no. They have the advantage of knowing the land and, if they are native, they may have no trouble getting around in the dark. Unless they have some ability I didn't see evidence of, we have nothing to fear from them."

"Well, thanks for your information. Amanda, do you really plan to visit ... Cansk, is it? ... again?"

"Canska," came the correction. "Yes. She needs the attention and they don't have the knowledge. It'd be so much easier if they'd move down closer to the first floor. If they realize we're no threat, they may. That again is you and Vokra. I'm sure she'll come, just not when."

"Crown," Commander Carpenter was official now, "any

problems with our crew or colonists?"

"No. Not even coming out of hibernation. That's almost a first for me."

"Good. The two of you can go about your business."

Behind him, the hatch hissed open. The commander turned and watched Maelstrom descend the ramp. She didn't seem under a spell. Her steps were slow, not tentative, and she looked across the tarmac and over the shuttles south of her exit.

The commander intended to speak with her. His thoughts were interrupted by a call across the tarmac.

"Commander," was directed toward him in a rushed tenor voice.

Carpenter turned to his right and saw Kellan Forbes running toward him. The commander took half a dozen steps toward the approaching settlement lead. Then Forbes stopped in front of him and held up a hand while he took three catch-up breaths.

"Commander," Forbes began, "now that we know there are inhabitants here, is there much purpose in investigating the mountain construct? I know that there may be much of interest, but that means we're invading ... have invaded."

"Probably not," was the commander's answer. "This whole landing has taken on complexity that wouldn't happen under ordinary circumstances on an uninhabited planet. There's no right to discover or claim possession."

"That's kinda what we thought, the six who explored with me," Forbes agreed, "though a couple of them thought that with the translator working, we might be welcomed visitors. There don't seem to be very many of them; hardly enough to fill even a small part of one floor of this building."

"We don't really know how many of them there are," the commander corrected.

"Yeah," Forbes cut in, "but Sharp said that he saw only about two dozen of them. If we're stuck here, we can both spread out there and never cross each other's paths."

"Think about that, Kellan," Carpenter said. "You agreed that we didn't have a right to claim possession. Now you're thinking about taking charge of their edifice? As if we're staying here?"

"It seems like they wouldn't need all of it and we might spread out a little more from the cramped shuttles. Depending on how long it takes to leave."

"That's another item for discussion with Vokra when she comes to talk," the commander said. "For now, until we can discuss some important things between species, you might spend some time foraging south and west. It's clear to me that these people occupy the forest north of us. I suggest, if you want to keep scouting, see about the river. We're going to need the water. Maybe take a rover; see how far west you can go."

"We can do that," Forbes said. "Though if we're stuck here and have to build a settlement, we're going to need the forest and probably the building. Maybe we could take over the one that is the closest north of us. I saw it on the way down. It's a good stretch to get there, if we can't use the shuttles and land on its tarmac."

"All of that will have to wait until we learn more about the inhabitants, Vokra and her group. That other construct may be inhabited already. And of course, you saw how fragile this vegetation is. Our presence is not going to help anything. We may be stronger and have the numbers, but that doesn't give us the right to destroy. That's what we'd do if we start acting like Vokra doesn't exist."

Kellan Forbes lowered his head and grimaced. He knew Carpenter was right. The *Marco P's* crew were the interlopers. Of course they had the strength and technology to take over and subdue Vokra ... at least it seemed so ... but on Earth that characteristic of the strongest taking what they wanted had finally been rejected and even the most grasping had ultimately admitted that such immoral actions engendered more problems than solutions.

"West and across the river, Commander. Maybe we'll find something we don't expect and both of us can use."

Forbes abruptly turned and headed for his shuttle and the group of six who had accompanied his two-day exploration of the mountain construct. The rover could only handle a crew of four. He'd have to decide which three to take with him, if they didn't opt themselves out.

As Forbes left, Commander Carpenter swept his gaze across

the tarmac, which was becoming more populated as morning
warmed and brightened under a cloudless sky. Kellan had captured his attention and the chance for words with Maelstrom
vanished. Of course, anyone as short as Maelstrom, regardless
of her consensus beauty, would be difficult to pick out from the
milling crew most of whom were at least half a foot taller.

He caught sight of the robotic helmet of Navigator LeRoi.
It bobbed up and down and occasionally turned to his left. The
commander could not remember ever seeing his navigator so
animated. Then he noticed that Maelstrom was in tow, LeRoi's
left hand resting on her right shoulder. She turned to look up at
him whenever LeRoi rolled his head left. They were conversing
and laughing and oblivious to others around them who, more
attentive, moved out of their way that followed a route they
had taken the day before.

Carpenter shook his head. Maelstrom seemed as captivat-
ed as she had described herself under the effect of the planetary system. If LeRoi were under the direction of some digital
intelligence, that power had obviously extended itself to Maelstrom. She might be schizoid, but he questioned if she were
pretending anything.

LeRoi's course took him within a few steps of the commander. Neither navigator greeted or seemed to notice him.
Carpenter overheard LeRoi telling about the commander's refusing to believe the crew was landing on γ-Cygnus A2. Maelstrom was enthralled that the commander, the always correct
commander, was so wrong about the planet they were on.

That comment by Maelstrom encouraged Carpenter to remember both Strumpf's and Varlez's concern that she would
not be their ally against the planetary captor. He was still second-guessing when he saw Arafa and Bandi following, both a
distant tail that would probably have no better luck following
the joking navigators when they left the tarmac this time.

As they passed the commander, LeRoi ceased his jollity.
His face became expressionless and Maelstrom's turned blank,
too. LeRoi looked up toward the mountain and to the edge of
the construct. Without a word, both he and Maelstrom pivoted
right and headed for the edge of the tarmac.

Arafa saw their abrupt change of direction and she hurried

some ten yards north and then directed her course to the edge of tarmac and the spiky green bushes. Bandi, following the commander's suggestion, went directly for the hedge. Carpenter thought that they might bracket the co-opted navigators, but he didn't hold much hope for that. Still he watched and saw that Arafa and Bandi would enter the bushes ten yards north and south of where LeRoi was leading Maelstrom. They would be a few steps behind them in leaving the edge of the tarmac, but he couldn't imagine the brush so dense they couldn't catch some sight of the navigators—LeRoi's oversized helmet, especially—if they were returning to the pedestal that opened the steps to below the tarmac.

OFFICIAL CONTACT

When Vokra and a male stepped from the narrow path that led from the huge mountain construction, Malcolm Carpenter's muffled astonishment was replicated across the tarmac. Both Molrixx paused and swept their gaze across the tarmac until Vokra spotted the commander.

The abbreviated clothing Vokra sported the previous day had been replaced by blue trousers the hem of which just brushed the tops of her bare feet. A loose-fitting yellow blouse hid any hint of cleavage. Her long hair pulled forward to drape across her chest further hid a bosom that had been much exposed the day before.

Crelle was similarly dressed. His trousers were black; his shirt, dark blue.

"Where is Amanda Crown?" Vokra asked and Crelle was startled when he heard strange sounds that he was sure was an alien language repeat of her question. "I thought she would meet us."

"I will send for her," Commander Carpenter said. "I did not expect you so soon." The foreign sounds of the commander's answer preceded a word-by-word translation in Vokra's language.

Commander Carpenter looked about, saw a crewman—one of those who had explored with Forbes and opted out of his current trip—and asked him to find Crown and have her come.

Again Vokra and Crelle heard the strange sounds translated into their own language. They looked at each other in wonder. Crelle opened his mouth to speak, but Vokra shook her head. She didn't want any more words translated than those she would be willing to offer.

The commander again looked about and requested three of the crew to bring four folding chairs and a small square table. He had no fear of adding English words to another foreign tongue.

The table and chairs arrived and the commander realized

254

a canopy was needed to shade the direct solar rays. It soon appeared, followed by Crown. Ignoring the commander, she caught Vokra's eyes and said, "You are early. I didn't expect you so soon. How is Canska? And her daughter?"

"They appear fine."

"When we are finished here, I would like to see them," Crown said.

Vokra nodded.

Commander Carpenter surrounded the table with the four chairs just as a canopy was placed over the area. He interrupted the answer to Crown's medical request with one of his own. "Let's sit."

Vokra introduced Crelle to Crown and the commander.

Crelle took a position to Vokra's left. Crown sat to her right and the commander sat opposite Vokra.

Vokra turned to Crown and offered more information about her patients, "They seem okay. Canska has nursed from both breasts and the unnamed child is not crying. You may return with us to see them." Then to Commander Carpenter, across from her and looking directly at her, she asked, "Why are you here? What do you want from us?"

The commander smiled at her bluntness. Most first contacts he had participated in moved much slower and the previous afternoon's encounter was unique in his recall of first contacts. He didn't count Pwok's begging for help as official despite its intimacy. "We were diverted from our destination ... where we intended to establish a colony. We cannot do that here." The commander's voice had a softness that reflected his sincerity.

Looking for a clue that belied his honesty, Vokra steadied her gaze onto Commander Carpenter's face. Then she slowly looked across the phalanx of shuttles and back to the commander. "You certainly have enough power to establish a colony here, if you wished."

The commander didn't follow Vokra's survey. He held his eyes on her face and noticed in his peripheral vision that Crelle was examining him. After Vokra returned her attention to him, the commander spoke to her assessment. "Perhaps we could, *if* we wished." Carpenter emphasized the conditional. "This planet doesn't look like it can support you and us. What is it called?"

"Molx is the name of our planet. We call ourselves Molrixx." Crelle answered giving Vokra a chance to order her thoughts and assess Carpenter's statements.

"Yes, our planet has been dying for some time," Vokra acknowledged. "When we began to heat up, we don't know why it happened, the population was housed in constructions like you see there. We call them moloxes." Vokra pointed to Molox1, where Crown had been led the previous evening in her care for Canska and her daughter.

"Are you, then, the last of your people?" the commander asked.

"We think so," Crelle answered.

It was the saddest statement the commander had ever heard delivered.

"We have looked for refugees from other moloxes," Crelle continued. "We haven't found any; none have discovered us."

"But you don't live in them, do you?" Crown asked, referring to the molox east of them.

"No, Council killed the power to them," Vokra explained. "They provide nothing but shelter from the elements. We left them to live like our ancient ancestors, for as long as we might continue to live. Molox living was constricting, when we were required to live there. Council allowed no freedom."

The commander wondered about the connection Vokra and her group might have had to the Council. Were they really rebels? He had heard of civilizations that were split between primitives and technologicals. None of those allowed the primitives—how else could he describe the two he sat with?—to speak for the whole population.

He needed answers. Maybe the Molrixx *were* all dead except for Vokra's band. The deterioration and overgrowth offered some proof of the population's demise. However, the *Marco P* had been commandeered. Primitives, who couldn't care for a newborn and her mother, didn't seem to have that technological control. If he had heard the truth, Vokra and her group were the only Molrixx and were scratching out a pitiful existence on a dying planet. Without its food, they would die. His crew and colonists would only hasten death for them all, if the humans had to establish a presence on the dying world.

"What happened to the rest of the Molrixx?" Carpenter asked and continued to prevent a quick answer. "We've seen no indication of mass death, no bodies; the molox here is uncluttered, at least as far as my crew has looked. If they all died of disease that would be evident. I don't think your small group would have been capable of burying thousands without some equipment. In our landing, I didn't see evidence of that, either." *Nor of technological power that captured us.*

"No disease claimed the population," Vokra started.

"Not disease," Crelle broke in and Vokra flashed him a look to be cautious, "like some physical infection that spread throughout all moloxes. Though it was, indeed, an infection that decimated our people. One of stupidity, maybe."

The commander narrowed his eyes and looked his question. Crown made a face.

"We escaped Molox3 and Molox1 before we could be downloaded." Vokra continued her interrupted explanation. "All Councils were sure the planet would become uninhabitable and there would be too many Molrixx for any kind of living, even in the moloxes. Councils had a plan, we don't know who made it up, that everyone would have their personalities, memories, thoughts—what made them who they were—downloaded into computer memory. Eventually, no one knows how long, some computer command would resurrect the digital persons and upload them into new bodies."

"The few of us who escaped," Crelle added, "weren't willing to undergo that kind of death, even if Councils were right. They didn't chase us; probably not enough physical bodies to do that by the time we escaped. I'm sure they thought we'd die outside the moloxes. But we haven't." Crelle's glee in outlasting Council was obvious.

"It's been a difficult existence," Vokra admitted. "But it's life. And we only have information that we brought with us in our brains. When the power in the moloxes was gone, we lost the ability to research the extensive library, everything that was the wealth of Molrixx learning."

"So you didn't know what to do with Canska?" Crown asked, her whole demeanor softening when she thought about her ministering to the young mother and her disgust at the lack of care Vokra's people seemed to provide. "So no one really knew what to do; you weren't just neglecting her."

Vokra nodded and was relieved to understand Crown's distance while she treated Canska.

"Our people toyed with that idea of digitizing self," the commander offered, "long time ago. Immortality's a strong attraction."

"And a stupid one," Crelle assessed.

"After only a few misguided attempts, our people rejected it," the commander agreed. "There must be incredible storage somewhere, to hold the myriad brain copies. To say nothing of the repository for the physical needs to reanimate or grow bodies."

"Memory and personality were maintained in banks of drives scattered throughout the moloxes," Vokra said. "We think the physical bodies, or what's left of them, are kept under the white outside each molox, under your craft."

"We don't know how to get down there," Crelle admitted.

"Drives and preservation take a lot of power," Commander Carpenter said and looked away, momentarily sorting out this new information. He kept to himself the thought that the Molrixx might have managed to create a better memory system than the immortality club had on Earth. Further, he realized that the computer system was potentially more powerful than he had imagined and realized that Maelstrom may have little chance of fending off the Molx system. His attention returned to the table, but he hid his supposition of how to get under the tarmac. "How is all that power generated?"

Vokra looked to Crelle who was hesitant to answer.

"We're not sure," Crelle finally admitted. "Some of us think that the white captures the radiation from our star and converts it into energy. Before the downloads were complete, the energy also supplied the moloxes. When that consumption was ended, more power must have been fed to the controlling computer system."

"Then our shuttles are limiting the power to this molox's memories," the commander said. "Is that fatal?"

"We haven't any idea," Vokra said. "Since the molox doesn't have energy as it was when Molrixx lived in it, there must be enough for the drives' needs. However, Commander," Vokra changed direction and returned to her original questions, "you said you were diverted to Molx. How could that happen?"

Carpenter wasn't willing to give too much information, though he had been given many pieces to the Molx puzzle. He twisted his lips and compressed them. He refused to give credit for their capture to the strength of the Molx computer system and sidestepped. "Our colony ship lost power. The shuttles don't have the range of the main ship. We thought we might find material here to re-energize the engines. Molx looked like it was once inhabited. If we couldn't find a fuel source, we'd just settle. When we discovered you were already here and the climate appeared to be dying, we knew this planet wasn't a viable destination for us."

"Even if you'd try to get rid of us?" Crelle asked half seriously. "You know we'd fight."

Crown broke in. "Most inhabitants would, even given the probable short tenure of life on Molx. We'll not push you off your land, what little there is, or enslave you for our needs."

"Amanda's right," the commander said. "If we can't leave Molx, we both suffer the same extinction."

"But you have the power and the numbers to do as you wish, regardless of us," Vokra countered. "What guarantee do we have that you'll not make a short life easy for yourselves at our expense?"

"I've said we will not," Commander Carpenter answered as he looked into Crelle's eyes and then to Vokra's. "We are not conquerors and we are not despots. We used to be, a long, long time ago, on our planet, Earth. We've out-grown that foolishness."

"He's right," Crown said. "We'll work with you to make the best for both of us, if that's what it comes down to."

Commander Carpenter held his hands out across the table, left to Vokra, right to Crelle. "Take my hand in assurance. We will work toward the best for all."

Crelle and Vokra clasped the commander's hands in both of theirs and squeezed.

"Together may we be successful," Vokra uttered in reverence.

"Yes," Crelle said. "We have knowledge of the forest and

greenery. You can supply technology and power."

The commander knew that power was limited at best, unless he and Varlez learned to siphon energy from the tarmac. However, he promised agreement with Crelle's offer.

"Commander," Vokra asked as the four of them rose, "my people are accustomed to cross the white on their way to fields and hunting. Will they be troubled if they reclaim their usual routes?"

"Indeed, not. My people are explorers. May they have the same freedom in Molox1 and the surrounding areas?"

"They will be welcomed, though I should imagine that some Molrixx will be more shy than inquisitive."

"And should some of mine wish to take up residence in Molox1?"

"There's a lot of room. You see how tall it is. Except for passing on stairs, there may be no interaction. I'm sure I'll have those curious about your flying craft."

"They may inspect as they wish."

After Crelle and Vokra started for Molox1 and were out of earshot, Crown asked, "Any history of first contacts like this?"

"None," Carpenter answered. "There are missing contact accounts when our spacers simply vanished, though I can't imagine any of the vanished ships matching what we've just done."

"Suppose *Marco* will be added to that short list?"

"Let's not write our epitaph just yet, Crown. In this short meeting, we've discovered more about our situation than we learned since we entered orbit round Molx."

"Are they as they appear?" Crown tossed out and didn't wait for an answer as she hurried to catch Vokra and Crelle and visit her patients. She had been in space long enough to know alien species didn't mirror rational characteristics in the same way humans did. However, from her own pessimistic bent, she hesitated to accept the smooth and amiable interchange of information.

Commander Carpenter saw and heard the wary disbelief in Crown's question. His own defenses had risen and he hoped his guarded thought had not been recognized. The Molrixx, at least Vokra and Crelle, had seemed too comfortable with them, as if aliens dropped in frequently. Yet he recognized no dissembling and he recalled his earlier conversation with Varlez about aliens being unable to play a gambit. If it were the sacrifice of the *Marco P* that Vokra and Crelle had suggested, that Earthlings abstain from using anything of Molx, Commander Malcolm Carpenter was not sure he would agree to that proposition; but his own moral code might demand it.

HUMANS

Kellan Forbes's rover journey, hardly faster than a quick walking pace, was uneventful for the first two hours. Forbes assigned young Jeri Bemly the driving. She had accompanied his two-day inspection of Molox1. Bemly's intense light brown eyes frequently hidden behind squinting lids and set in a cherubic face topped by a mop of tight curly brown hair, surveyed about her and often saw trouble and anticipated problems sooner than most of the other fourteen of Forbes's group of settlers. Still, he and two others constantly looked for less jolting paths through the brush, small trees, and frequent rocky mounds.

The four six-foot mesh wheels that gave considerable ground clearance managed to smooth much of the landscape that smaller wheels would have shaken the passengers like bugs in a jar. After a couple of hours, the green growth surrounding the tarmac became sparse, shorter, and spinier, not unlike typical desert vegetation found on many planets.

Bemly stopped the rover after she had driven only a mile into more arid terrain. "Doesn't look right," she complained. "Aren't we supposed to be coming to a river? I don't see anything that looks like riverbank."

Forbes and two others stared out the forward and side ports. To the south, perhaps ten miles away, where the eastern mountain range became rolling hills, the vista was not unlike Earth's Sahara Desert. Sand dunes piled up and flowed from the constant wind that swooped down from the western range that softened to the height of the tallest dunes in the south. Opposite that panorama, they saw an extension of the forest north of the tarmac. Its trees and vines decreased in size and density, but the growth was not sparse enough for the rover to make its way in that direction.

The western view, the wrong sight Bemly had claimed, perhaps three miles ahead, was gray, as if shadowed by a huge cloud. But the sky was a cloudless deep blue. In the distance, before the gray, Forbes and his crew thought they saw a line of green darker than the surrounding plants they were rolling over.

"I'll bet that's where the river is," Forbes said. "We ought to reach that in another hour or less. Bemly can you push this thing faster?"

"I can," she answered. "Not sure I should. I'm telling you, it doesn't look right."

"You mean the shadow?" Forbes asked. "It could just be the natural color of the land. I've seen almost that coloring before."

"So have I," agreed Wymal Rostaq. "It's a little different tint from a color I remember. It looks shaded to me, but I can't see anything that might be closing off the sun ... not for that big an area and with sharp corners."

Forbes agreed. "Bemly, keep going, but not any faster. We've got the time and we can always hold up in the rover, if we don't get back."

"We can, sir." Bemly voiced her salute, maintained her hesitation about the terrain, and eased the rover forward.

Forbes controlled his eagerness to reach the mysterious shadowed territory. Despite his desire to press the rover faster than they had driven, he reluctantly acceded to Bemly's intuition.

More than once, he had watched her circumvent or avoid a potential disaster that advertised no hint to its danger. Even now, as he looked ahead, the land appeared flat, without ruts or obvious obstructions. His driver was still creeping over the ground, though he did notice a slight increase in speed, not enough to satisfy the two accompanying her and Forbes.

Soon Forbes saw Bemly's jaw tighten and her neck stiffen in reaction to the repeated low-level gripes that bubbled up from the back of the rover cabin. Complaints critical of the young female's unfounded concerns increased in volume. When Forbes realized the two weren't ending their less than subdued barrage, he turned and glared at them.

They continued to grumble, but only to themselves and finally stopped their complaining, when they realized they weren't going to hurry Forbes or their driver.

When the first hour's drive toward the shadow passed and

they seemed no closer to the strange landscape, Bemly stopped again and shook her head. "Not like anything I've ever seen before. I swear we're not any closer than we were."

"Should have been faster," came from the back of the rover where the two had finally taken seats and pretended to sleep.

Forbes shot a withering glare at the complainer. "And we'd just be farther from the tarmac and have farther to go to get back."

"Might as well keep going, then," was the ironic advice from the rear.

"Yeah," added the other. "We got enough in the rover to keep us alive for a few days. If we're too late, someone'll look for us."

"Won't be Sharp," said the first.

Forbes turned from the two complainers. "Well, Bemly, what do you think?"

"Can't say; this is all unsettling. It's a different planet, but sight and land and physical characteristics can't be that different. It's just a funny feeling. Wymal's right, though. If we're out too long someone'll come looking. Tracks are easy to follow. That's enough security to keep going."

"No matter what happens?" Forbes asked.

Jeri Bemly looked out the foreport, inclined her head right, and looked back at Forbes. "That's not my decision. I suppose I have a funny feeling as much because of all we've been through. New planets always have something different, unique. That doesn't mean we shouldn't explore. Besides, if we're not going to leave this place, there's not much sense in not exploring. We have to know about it."

"That's a good assessment, Bemly," Forbes praised. "We keep going. I think we can see just about anything that will be trouble before it gets too close."

Bemly's lips curved into an ironic smile and she nodded. She engaged the rover and continued its snail's pace forward.

LeRoi and Maelstrom closed on the edge of the tarmac. Their talkative gamboling had vanished. The navigator turned taciturn and dropped his left hand from Maelstrom's shoulder to take her right hand in a strong grip. Unaware that Varlez's two assistants had each come even with their march but ten yards away, one on either side, LeRoi pulled Maelstrom through the brush and stopped. The instructions flowing into his brain commanded another trip to the control pedestal, which was ten yards in front of him.

Both Bandi and Arafa watched the navigators kick forward through the tangled vines and slip behind a trio of trees. Neither was willing to follow closely, but each marked their position and that of the pedestal against the mountain complex and backward against the second row of shuttles.

Then they saw a white square rise to vertical and slip into the ground opening a passage that descended.

Maelstrom, still in tow, paced to the opening. Together she and LeRoi stepped down. First the second navigator's head vanished below the ground and two steps later LeRoi's helmet disappeared.

From her position north of the pedestal, Arafa reached the shaft just after Bandi who was initially closer from her position to the south. When they looked down, they saw an empty stairway. While they wondered where the navigators could be, the white covering rose and dropped flat, sealing the shaft and separating them from the two human computer adjuncts.

SYSTEM

Acquisition: *Interfaces have entered the repository. They are receiving information for delivering Earthers.*

Central Receiving: *Have robots been reanimated?*

A: *Yes.*

CR: *Molrixx were hesitant about downloading.*

A: *Earthers may provide more difficulties.*

CR: *What plans are in place?*

A: *Each interface will conduct four Earthers for copy. Bodies are unimportant. They will be dismantled as other aliens were.*

CR: *Old information repeats. Novelty is desired. Earther brains promise great novelty.*

A: *Connection between interfaces grows stronger. The second fights our control. Its connection is not complete.*

CR: *Strengthen the connection. One interface is not enough. The second may hinder our success.*

A: *Diagnostics are running to strengthen. Association with first helps maintain connection. First must stay near. Power drains increase.*

CR: *Have you discovered the cause?*

A: *Drains are diffused across the system. Input from Molox1 and 3, Elthren, Grent, Svoqol, and Wurthro are all decreasing output. Their receptors failing.*

CR: *What do you read from the Western Complex?*

A: *Nothing. They may have ceased to exist.*

CR: *Are we in danger of power loss?*

A: *Not yet.*

CR: *If input continues to fade, adjustments must be made.*

A: *What adjustments?*

CR: *Barring discovery of the drain causes, shutdown of memory caches and cessation of associated brain and corporal tissue.*

A: *Have you defined a priority to receive power?*

CR: *Determined long ago. Are we stable?*

A: *We are. Even if all cease, their memories can be downloaded to ours.*

CR: *Immortality is ours.*

266

HUMANS

When the navigators reached the bottom of the stairway, the door before them slid open. Two steps past the threshold the door closed. The tarmac cover above the stairs rose and dropped back to its horizontal position.

Maelstrom's hand was still gripped by LeRoi who was mesmerized at the flood of information cascading into his brain through his interface helmet. Maelstrom's brain, the human controlled portion, loosened from LeRoi's despotic control, as he was overloaded from the Molx download.

Maelstrom struggled to view where she was in the dim light created from uncountable small blue dots identifying stacked glass containers receiving power. Though some information seeped to her interface from LeRoi's helmet, she strained to see what the glass boxes contained. Her attempt to move closer was aborted by his tight grip. Eventually, growing accustomed to the limited light and filtering some of the information from LeRoi, she recognized row upon row, seven containers high, extending as far as the dimness allowed her view.

LeRoi and Maelstrom were in an east/west corridor that transected north/south rows.

More information filtered through and her eyes relaxed in the darkness. She recognized enfolded brains, one to a box. Maelstrom cringed, imagining herself to be the centerpiece of the ancient sci-fi story, a bible of the immortality club, "The Brain That Wouldn't Die." She hardly considered that a brain alone wouldn't have current sensory impressions. Nevertheless she was aghast at being confined to a claustrophobic foot and a half of cubic space. That terror caused the mental leap to the similar anguish in store for all passengers and crew of the *Marco P*. She glared hatred at Roger LeRoi who was the engineer of that unfolding holocaust.

A sliver of her own personality that fought against this unmistakable loss of freedom overrode the interface control channeled through LeRoi. Panic at the thought of losing her humanity demanded escape from the force that encased LeRoi, though she had no idea how or where it was. To no avail, she jerked hard to disentangle her hand from LeRoi's grasp and sever the physical connection. Maelstrom's terror seeped backward through the digital connection between the two navigators. The planetary computer system tightened LeRoi's grip, ensuring the physical connection was not broken.

"You're not going to be downloaded," he reassured in mechanical syllables that hardly sounded like the navigator who had capered across the tarmac not long before. "Neither am I. We will supply part of the information for repopulating Molx when the climate is more friendly."

Maelstrom's struggles waned, but her thoughts, terrified at the possibility of eighty-eight humans unjustly killed for the pleasure of digital representation, questioned the fifth column activity of a loner crewman. Outraged that any human might have personality erased, forced the tendrils of interface control back from their innermost reaches of her mind. She knew that as long as LeRoi had hold of her, was near her, she was in grave danger of being taken over by the Molx system.

Then the navigator returned, not the digital LeRoi. "Come; let me show what's going to happen." LeRoi was as eager as if he were about to announce the discovery of a new Sol-type system in a galactic wasteland.

In reaction to LeRoi's altered mood, Maelstrom issued an authoritative command that her artificial personality share simultaneous consciousness with her natural self. For the first time in her young life, outside of practicing the procedure under laboratory protocols, her mind demanded her digital half yield to her real self.

Her interface ceded autonomous control.

The frightening electronics that still inhabited Roger LeRoi were shut off from her mind, her emotions, her thoughts.

She *knew* she was in control. She ceased tugging at LeRoi's grasp. "Show me," she said in a quiescent voice.

LeRoi was so surprised that Maelstrom now seemed a colleague to the computer's directions that he loosened his iron-grip and was not amazed that she didn't pull her hand away. He led her toward a small alcove created only by the surrounding ends of the long banks of brains bathed in a syrupy liquid.

The alcove contained a special chair and four robots.

When they got within two brain rows of the chair, the alcove lighted, showing a narrow padded chair with sturdy armrests and solid front behind where the lower legs would be. Feet could rest on an attached narrow footpad. Maelstrom was quick to notice that there were straps to hold arms and legs in place. She also noticed two sturdy belts, one to hold the victim's lap and the other to pull the person's chest against the chair back. Hanging from the ceiling was a helmet, not unlike what LeRoi was fitted with.

Maelstrom, her human self, balked at approaching the instrument of torture, the seat of brain wiping and erasure of self. Maelstrom's schizoid, digital, part believed LeRoi's affirmation that encouraged, without much import, that she wasn't going to be downloaded. Her real self questioned how she and Roger might continue as the only physical beings on a dying planet. Despite the terror, she stepped forward with urging from LeRoi's tightening handhold. She looked up at the helmet above the chair and was astonished to see it lined inside with micro-scale needle-sized electrodes that no doubt read interconnections of the memories, feelings, thoughts, learning, and information stored in the brain's neurons and synaptic sequences. From what she knew of the first generation of interfaces, there were more connections by a vast number in the Molx helmet than were in LeRoi's helmet. Even her own interface paled in comparison to the apparent brain reading of this machine.

"I have to look for the robots who will download brains and for others who will care for those awaiting the procedure," LeRoi said as he looked about.

"You mean *guard* them?"

"Care for. You know what Molx needs."

"Not really. What can humans provide for Molx?"

"They are looking for novelty. Earthers have that."

At the term 'Earthers' Maelstrom looked up into LeRoi's eyes. They were blank and unblinking. She knew her companion was not who he had been. She also knew that she had the near impossible task to be like him and remain herself. However, if she returned to the tarmac and to the commander's shuttle, she could explain what the planet wanted from the captured

humans. Further, she knew what she had to do to keep the
system from recapturing her, if she were again brought down
into this digital euthanasia catacomb.

Roger LeRoi walked past the download chair and assembly. His hold on Maelstrom's hand became light again and she
didn't attempt to separate herself. He and the Molx system
were convinced that Maelstrom had accepted her role in providing digital survivors of the planetary civilization with what
it wanted. Their steps triggered more lights and four robots
rolled in front of them to bar their way.

All four were six feet tall. Their square base of two feet on
a side had four wheels, one at each corner, that retracted to establish a solid immobile base. Four arms, paired on the vertical
diameter, extended from a modest circular torso topped by a
digital control box that contained four small lenses for eyes. A
small speaker served as a mouth. Maelstrom wondered if the
speaker doubled as an ear and couldn't imagine what robots
might listen for or speak about.

One robot raised up on platform wheels and rolled forward from its settled companions. It waved its four arms each
ending in strange couplings and tools. One arm bore a scalpel
and its opposite, a medical saw.

The navigators stopped at its approach.

"Where are the subjects?" it asked. "You are not subjects."

LeRoi turned his head as far left as he could and said to his
second in the robotic voice she had heard earlier, "I told you."
Then he faced the robot and his voice mimicked the electronic
tone. "We were checking the facilities and equipment. Subjects
will be brought soon."

"We wait," the robot said and rolled back into the line of
his three companions and, retracting its wheels, settled onto its
solid base.

As Maelstrom turned to leave, a pile of bones—arms
and legs and also skulls without caps—caught her attention.
They were just at the edge of the light from over the chair.
She stopped and stared. Directed by her real self, her interface
whirring in the background, her eyes widened and she swallowed a gasp that would have announced her interface was not
in control.

LeRoi received an electronic twinge from her astonishment and looked where she was staring. His explanation was routed from Molx Central Reception through MP. "Those were aliens whose downloads were meaningless and whose brains offered nothing useful for Molx. They didn't deserve more than dismemberment."

Maelstrom stiffened her back slightly. She glanced at LeRoi and was pleased that he hadn't noticed her reaction.

Keeping the appearance that she was as robotic as he was not easy. She could hardly wait until they climbed the stairs and kicked through the brush to the tarmac. Perhaps LeRoi would be as playful on their return to the shuttle parking as he had been leaving it. Then she would have a better chance to distance herself from him.

With interest Kellan Forbes watched as Bemly approached a natural ford in the river they had paralleled for half an hour. Contained within banks higher than the rover could easily maneuver down and back up, the river at last widened and offered a shallowing waterway. Forbes also noted that the huge shadowed rectangle they had watched for a long time began where the ford accessed the west bank. Bemly eased the rover to the right and stopped at the beginning of the slope into the river with the front wheels ten feet from the water.

"Sir," a disbelieving Bemly said to Forbes who was still viewing across the river at the edge of the shadow, "you need to look down, right in front of us."

"What ..." Forbes turned his head and never finished his question. Then he choked, "I don't believe that."

At Forbes's vocal shock, Wymal Rostaq and Almi Penser dashed forward from their rear seats to crowd the fore port.

Impressed in the softer dirt, dampened by occasional ripples from large boulders rising above the river, were four sets of footprints. Two, one smaller and bare than the other that was shod, exited the water and were lost on the hardened dirt. A second set returned indenting the damp dirt at the edge of the river. All four in the rover thought they could see duplicate prints up the other bank.

"Rostaq, scope the other side. Prints there?"

"Same's here, sir. They walked into and out of. Hard to say from which direction they originated."

"Natives playing games, sir?" Bemly suggested. "They could certainly be faster than we've been. They'd know the land."

"One more planetary mystery," Forbes commented. He looked down for a rover shadow. It was hidden from his vantage point. "About noon, I guess. Let's cross, check out the shadow, and keep going west. The mountain bubbles intrigue me."

"We getting back to the tarmac today?" Bemly asked.

"Don't have to. Nothing indicates the rover can't keep us safe. Tomorrow's soon enough to return. Bemly, not too fast in the water. Don't need to spray us."

Bemly engaged the four motors each synched to one mesh-wheel and eased the rover down into the river that proved deeper and swifter than it appeared. More perilous, Kellan Forbes imagined, than a child might have crossed on foot, even holding on to an adult. Perhaps it was carried.

Rostaq had not left the front of the rover. "You know, Kellan, members of the group we've seen might not be the only natives around. Besides that, we didn't know about any children, except the newborn. Who else would be making tracks like those?"

"You suggesting we run back to the comfort of the shuttles, Wymal?"

"No, sir. It's just that I didn't think those people were what they seemed. I know I'd be less than open, if this were my home, especially if the planet were dying as this one is."

"Point taken, Rostaq. But as there didn't seem much happening on the tarmac we can add a lot to our total information. However, as you imply, caution is vital. We need to be watching all four points. You take the rear."

"Aye, sir." To himself Rostaq grumbled, "We couldn't get back before dark, anyway."

"What was that?" Forbes asked to Rostaq's back.

"Nothing, sir," came Wymal's defensive return.

Wymal Rostaq stepped to the back of the rover and grumbled that behind was the least important direction after they'd already driven through the territory. He knew he should have kept his thoughts to himself.

Jeri Bemly pressed the rover's front wheels forward creating little white water above the center hubs. The mesh disturbed the riverbed and a muddy brown residue roiled up and flowed south. The rover stalled about mid-stream. Bemly revved the motors and the RPMs slued the rover and stirred up even more dirt and small rocks, which dirtied the once pristine blue water. Evidence of the rover's crossing was washed further down river.

Three more motor revs were needed before they exited the river just at the southeast corner of the shadowed area.

"Stop here," Forbes said. "I want to look at this. It's not a shadow. This close, it looks artificial, like where we landed, but the color is different."

He opened the hatch and turned backward to climb down. "The rest of you, stay put."

Six steps down and he set foot on the dirt, turned, and scuffed dust for another ten yards to the corner of something that looked like the tarmac. He bent over and rubbed his hand across the gray surface. It had the same bubbly texture as the tarmac, hours east of where he was.

The edge was rounded. With his left hand, he scraped a little dirt away from the edge and saw that the construction continued below level ground. The dirt was soft and he used both hands to scoop out a narrow hole a foot deep before he stopped.

Kellan Forbes stood up and looked north and west. The ash gray surface was as flat as where the shuttles rested. He considered that this site was a better choice for planet fall. It was a larger area. Water was closer and there was more of it than the trickle running through the forest that exited the river too far north of the tarmac to be of much use to them. Material for constructing a settlement wasn't as close; the more heavily wooded section of the forest was farther away. However, the settlement could just as easily be built within it. But he knew the commander's intention was not to stay on Molx and that escaping the planet was his only goal. He knew lots of problems had yet to be solved, not least of which was discovering the computer that held captive the colony and shuttles and *Marco P.* Now his extended tour had discovered something new, maybe another glitch to leaving: natives who roamed farther from the mountain construct he had scouted.

Or the footprints *were* from a different band of natives, as Rostaq had suggested.

Forbes dropped back down to the hand excavation he had begun and continued to pull out more dirt as he dug further down, piling the dirt away from the gray tarmac. On his next two-handed scoop he felt a smooth, solid barrier. Immediately a tingle traveled up his arms and tickled his face, before he lost consciousness.

When Forbes became conscious, he saw cloudless blue sky and the western bubbled mountains. The tingling was gone and he felt like he had just waked from a nap.

He rolled over, turned, got to his feet and wondered why no one was looking out the ports of the rover. *Did what I triggered affect them?*

When he climbed into the rover, Bemly, Rostaq, and Penser were shaking their heads and looked like they were just waking up.

"We watched you start to dig again," Bemly said, when Forbes was standing in the rover, "then I heard a high-pitched squeal and you collapsed onto your back.Then everything in the rover shut down. The next thing I was aware of was you crawling into the rover."

Rostaq and Penser agreed. All three faces were returning to natural color. Bemly added. "We were really dead."

"And now?" Forbes asked. "Tried to turn on anything?"

"No."

"Try."

The four flipped switches, turned knobs, slid slides, checked the solar collectors. Electricity that should have flowed from solar reception activated nothing. Power readouts from solar panels remained blank. Every backup battery had been drained.

"It's a long walk, if they don't come looking for us," Rostaq said. He didn't look forward to that waste of energy. He knew better than revisiting his caution for continuing across the river."

Penser looked sideways at Rostaq. She remembered his abusive objections to crossing the river but said nothing.

"A good day's hike," Forbes said. "We won't have to jockey like the the rover had to do, but we won't be as fast as it rolled at the end."

"We'll be looked for? Won't we?" Penser asked with concern in her voice.

"I suppose someone might think about setting out when we're not there at dusk. Commander will stop that. Night is just too dark and he knows we're not going to be out in it. Who knows what's roaming then. No, someone will follow our tracks. We'll pull a line and drag the rover back across the river. Maybe it will collect over there. Either way it gets pulled from here and we ride back pretty cramped."

"We could ride in our rover," Rostaq offered.

"And be bounced around worse than we were," Bemly countered. "You might like that," she offered at second thought and returned Rostaq's early griping at her maneuvering. "I'll be cramped if I have a choice. You can ride in here and steer."

Devastated that they lost sight of their charges again, Arafa and Bandi returned to the tarmac. Negotiations between Crown and Carpenter and two aliens were underway. The engineers looked with interest at the four who seemed unbothered by the wandering settlers and crew who, in spite of their ravenous curiosity, respected the discussion by keeping far enough away not to hear what was being said.

Varlez's aides, who were closer to command confidentiality than all of the other on-lookers, rejected the notion of ambling closer and maybe catching a phrase or word or tone of voice to divine what was being discussed. They had more important information for Varlez and it was of greater import for their community than any snippet they might catch from eavesdropping on the official first contact. Besides they rightly recognized that the commander's reaching out with both hands to the two natives signaled the end of their discussion.

Nor had they been long at briefing Engineer Varlez about what they saw when Commander Carpenter appeared outside the engineering shuttle where they were conversing in

Alvorklan. He didn't have to wait to be recognized. Bandi invited him to join them and they continued in the commander's English.

"We can find the pedestal to open the access to under the tarmac," Bandi repeated for the commander's ears. "But we haven't a clue about what's down there."

"There's obviously a closing mechanism to hide the entry at the bottom," Arafa added. "We'll need lights, probably. And the stairs don't give enough space for too many to descend if the sealing door is automatic."

"If Maelstrom was right and she manages to outwit the system, we'll have a little more information to put with yours," the commander said.

His thought lacked his usual confidence and Varlez called him on it.

"You question her ability and success?"

"Not ability, her foresight. She's young, energetic, naïve in some ways. Her first foray with LeRoi didn't go as she expected. She fell under his spell ... or that of the planetary system we're fighting. She recognizes that LeRoi is the channel to controlling her. She thought she could hold the force off."

"My assistants followed the two of them ..."

"I saw ..."

"... and they saw her pretty much under his control."

"Indeed," Carpenter agreed. "They were cavorting like long-lost acquaintances when I saw them."

"Like now?" Bandi asked. She had been sweeping her attention across the tarmac where the four of them had not long before squeezed into the surrounding hedge. She pointed to where she saw the navigators.

Commander Carpenter looked, agreed, and commented that nothing seemed different from what he'd seen earlier. Maelstrom and LeRoi were bobbing their heads and bending over in laughter. The staid first navigator was so out of character that Varlez wondered aloud if he were on some hallucinogen.

The commander agreed with Varlez's assessment and privately second-guessed himself for allowing Maelstrom the freedom to accompany LeRoi again. However, as he watched,

Maelstrom broke off the hilarity and entered the command shuttle. Carpenter wondered if she would take longer than she took the day before to slough off the effects of LeRoi and the planet's electronic control.

The navigator's gaiety that manifested their re-entry onto the tarmac didn't continue after Maelstrom left him. LeRoi's light steps degenerated into plodding as he headed for the engineering shuttle and his specially detailed sleeping seat.

"It'll be a while before he gets here," Varlez said. "I'm sure we can dredge up some duty that may keep him busy tomorrow and away from Maelstrom if his disassociation will release her from electronic slavery."

"That's worth a try," the commander said. "I'll wait 'til he gets here before I head for Maelstrom. She might take longer than she did yesterday to return from that captivity. I didn't think LeRoi would be at her so quickly today."

"We can keep him involved," Arafa repeated Varlez's intention. "He may be computer-linked, but he's still human with all the emotions. We can override the computer side if we work at it."

Malcolm Carpenter watched Bandi nod with a smile and smooth her hands down her shapeless body. He wondered what wiles she kept hidden.

Just before Roger LeRoi came within earshot, the commander cautioned, "Don't be afraid to ask for help. We're still in unknown territory here. We haven't any idea what strengths LeRoi may have gathered from the planet." Then, as Carpenter left the engineers who returned to their Alvorklan conversation, the commander looked at LeRoi in passing. "Good afternoon, Navigator," Carpenter greeted and received a similar wish in return.

It was only just past noon, when a surprised Commander Carpenter arrived at his shuttle. An alert Maelstrom, the one who promised to discover what the planet wanted, was waiting for him. She was seated at the end of the ramp into the commander's shuttle. Her legs were drawn up and encircled by her arms, hands clasped in front of her knees. The thought that she appeared able to provide what no one else could, washed away the commander's stressed efforts with the Molrixx and Molx.

"Commander," Maelstrom said as she unclasped her hands and stood, all in one motion. "I was right ... sort of. Separating the interface from me was not as simple as I imagined. It took a moment of sheer terror to force that separation. I never had such control before. The interface continued its connection with LeRoi and MP as if it *were* in control of me and I'm sure Roger believed it was controlling me. I acted like I followed its commands. But I was in control. I let my interface and the power behind it continue, but I made my own decisions and I could act like the planet's power was directing me."

"You're really sure?" Commander Carpenter was skeptical. "Engineering thought they were in control in space after *Marco* was captured and before we shuttled down here. Maybe they were; maybe they weren't. Varlez still isn't sure. Could you be mistaken, like they *might* have been?"

"I don't think so. Schizoid brains are either digitally directed or personally controlled and there's no mixing—except, theory says, it's possible if the real personality is shocked. For the first time ever, for me, it was a horrendous shock. That let me mix both brains simultaneously and I knew which was which and I kept control. I actually let the interface think that it was in charge and I even fooled Roger into thinking I was allied with the electronics. So much so that he stopped gripping my hand to keep me close."

"How can you be sure?"

"I know exactly what is expected—what Roger and I have to do. I don't think those details would have been given to me if I weren't as involved as Roger. It's a powerful force."

"What happens when you break from what is expected, as I imagine you will have to?"

"I believe I'm connected to LeRoi through physical contact and transfer my obedience through the universal connector to my interface. I fooled LeRoi and the system in charge of him and, when I have to put a stop to what the planet wants, I should be able to."

"It didn't take you so long to shuck the effects of the force," the commander added. "Unless the force allowed you believe that."

"Maybe; but I don't think the planetary system is in control.

I know I can lessen LeRoi's physical contact; I may have already. But I need to see Varlez about voiding my interface conduit."

"That can't be removed, can it?" the commander asked, thinking of the drastic impact removal would create, "or put back in afterward if we leave Molx, what the inhabitants call this planet."

"Not removed. I'd rather not say more until I talk with Varlez. In fact it might be something that could work with Roger, too."

"That could throw a real wrench into Molx's plans. What are we needed for? Why are we here?"

"I'd never have guessed," Maelstrom said as she looked around to see if anyone might overhear. "And the same thing that several alien species have been used for. LeRoi and I are tasked to take, in small groups and as quickly as possible, the entire crew of the *Marco P* below the tarmac where our brains will be copied and the information saved to the collective brain of the planet. Where we were, were rows and rows of containers seven high that held only brains preserved for later, when they will be implanted in clones to create a new physical population."

Commander Carpenter recalled Vokra's and Crelle's description and reason for escaping the moloxes. "Another species with immortality dreams," he said.

"They believe they can eventually re-grow bodies, re-implant the personalities with all that each brain held and put it all into new bodies when the planet is again livable."

"And our unique characteristic? Why us?"

"Novelty! We don't do what is expected. It's the one trait we seem to possess in greater quantity than any other species. I'm not sure how that can be digitized."

The commander sighed and shook his head. He looked off toward the mountain construct. He wasn't seeing the artificial tan of the building inset into the mountain or the thin zigzag line of the outside stairway. He was thinking about immortality, a fool's paradise, and that computer storage lacked the very essence of animal nature that made life worth living.

Still, with Molx devolving to a dead orb, he could understand why a civilization might seek the fatal hope of digital existence. But within an area of the galaxy that teemed with life and space-faring civilizations, he couldn't imagine why a dying planet like Molx, couldn't be left for another more habitable one. There were many to choose from, no matter how long emigrating might take. However, there was no evidence that the Molrixx had space flight.

Their plight couldn't have been missed by other civilizations who would certainly have offered help. Unless ... Were the Molrixx such pariahs that their extinction was acceptable to other species? That thought sent a mental shiver through the commander. If the Molrixx were successful at downloading his people, perhaps this colony mission would be his last and the whole complement of *Marco P* FSS-14 would be added to the short list of those rare Earth missions inexplicably lost.

He returned his thoughts to his young navigator. She had assumed the forward position in a cosmic skirmish that threatened this branch of terrestrial expansion. He saw no indication that Maelstrom understood the gravity of the situation or her place in the battle. A brief smile touched his face and quickly left as he recalled that the young—not that he was so old—always acted with more bravado than good sense.

Remembering that her plan included altering her computer interface he asked, "When are you planning to see Varlez? Today? Tomorrow?"

"Soon. Before Roger asks me to join him again. That might be this evening."

"Don't think he'll be allowed out of the engineering shuttle."

"He could leave and gather some settlers and con them into going below the tarmac. I caught some hint of that intention."

"You know Arafa and Bandi are keeping him close? Engineering plans to keep him busy with something."

"Yes, I've seen them. They were more lax today than they were before and they gave us more room. He might sneak away, especially if they're involved with other things. He doesn't need me for the first delivery."

"He can handle several by himself?"

"Curiosity doesn't take handling. Once he gets them down

the stairs and the opening to the shaft is shut, there are robots that will handle them. Roger doesn't have to do anything but get them there."

The commander sighed. "What if we just incapacitate him?"

"Might work. Then I'll have to do his job or pretend to, if Varlez can't do what I have in mind. The electronics might be strong enough to keep me from shutting the system out. Especially if we can't find where the main server is and shut it down."

"And hasten the extinction of the Molrixx? That's not our style."

"What about the natives—primitives—the father and his child? Didn't you meet them while I was with LeRoi? I didn't think they're connected to the system, are they?"

"I did," Carpenter answered and continued, "I doubt it. But if the planet dies, so do they. It's still extinction, sooner or later."

"The planet's dying and its death is not our work," Maelstrom argued. "We're not required to be added to some alien database. The planet isn't *our* problem; the Molrixx computer system is."

"That's right, but are we allowed to shut off power to the maintained brains and the memory drives?"

"If that lets us escape," Maelstrom was quick with the rebuttal.

"And we've destroyed a civilization." The commander's morality was his guiding ethic. "We can't commit genocide, regardless of the reason."

"Why do they, on a dying planet have more right to exist— if brains and memory drives count as being alive—than we do with our living bodies? Besides, the power might be irreparably stopped by something else, and they'd all be gone, anyway." Maelstrom's argument trumped the commander's principle. "That's not genocide."

"And maybe the power wouldn't be severed." Carpenter seemed to argue that humans were not foremost. "I can't warrant that assumption."

"So their right to life supersedes ours?"

"It's their planet," Carpenter supported his last point.

"And they captured us to make us extinct—a narrower genocide, but still genocide. They are murderers. It's wrong to let them go unpunished." Maelstrom refused to capitulate and rebutted, "Do our ethics yield to alien principles? Why do we assume genocide is acceptable for us?"

Maelstrom's questions defined the basis of Carpenter's galactic principles and opened the essence of a long argued human philosophical problem. The arrogant superiority of humans, according to one school, demanded that humans yield to all other alien systems.

The backup navigator wasn't a member of that convention. "No thinking beings have that ultimate power over other rational beings." The opposing side to the problem posited that all ethics were basically the same. No race had a corner on superior ethical beliefs. Maelstrom restated, "Murder is wrong. We are primed to be murdered."

"You would unplug the memories and let the brains dry up?" The commander suggested that the young navigator before him was suggesting the ultimate in self-defense, an act that would also produce genocide.

"We aren't the aggressors. They are. We have no principle that tells us to be sacrificed. Nothing that says we can't defend our existence when unjustly challenged."

"I'll give you that," Carpenter admitted as Maelstrom had offered him an argument he had played and replayed within himself—an argument he had yet to conclude without question.

Then he turned the discussion. "And if the main computer has fail-safe and inherent self-protective barriers? You don't think this digital brain can't defend itself or have more robots for protection? Is shutting it down an easy thing?"

"I didn't catch any sense of need for defense. It was like everything was going to be as it was imagined. If we shut down the power to the system, it could be turned back on after we leave, if the planet does recover. Digital constructs don't die. The conserved brains are being maintained. Living planets do cycle themselves; you know that."

"I don't discount that. And if the main computer is below

the tarmac?" The commander was offering an assault on the electronic enemy.

"We've got the numbers, the strength ..." Maelstrom was marshaling her army's power.

Seldom had Carpenter confronted a serious counter to his ethics. However, the counterattack to his belief that alien principles should preempt human beliefs and morals had taken a hit. He was willing to concede that members of a living race were more important than a digital population. "The Molrixx, who still live on the surface, in the forest, as primitive as they appear, know what has happened to their population. They just don't know where the controls are and how to get to them. Right now, we're in a state of peaceful co-existence with them. That may last; it may be a ruse. You may be right that their continued existence abrogates genocide. However, I suggest you see Varlez right now. If LeRoi is at all predictable, he's resting. He won't know you've shown up there."

"I think I'll do that, Commander. Right now."

When Maelstrom reached engineering, Varlez and Arafa and Bandi were involved in a heated discussion in a language she had never heard before.

"It's Alvorklan," Bandi said in response to Maelstrom's questioning look. "Only the three of us know it, and Varlez has programmed the translators to ignore it."

"We can discuss all kinds of things without anyone else knowing what we're talking about," Arafa added. "Do you need something?"

"Yes. I'd like Engineer Varlez to do something for me. I know he questioned my ability to shut down my interface—and probably the two of you did, too." Maelstrom saw both engineering seconds with embarrassed nods. "I actually did that separation and shut it down today. But I don't trust myself to be able to do it again. The system is strong." She turned her attention to Varlez.

"What do you want from me?" the engineer asked.

Maelstrom didn't respond at once. She had expected his question, but when asked, her planned response didn't flow out as she thought it would. The enormity of her request showed on her face. Before Varlez asked a second time, she said, "I think you can incapacitate my interface. Though mine's not like LeRoi's, my universal connector can still be activated by the planetary computer system." Maelstrom reached up and pulled the small cable from her tunic where she had secured it from dangling about as she moved. She held the thumb sized connection of a cable half the size of a little finger for Varlez to look at.

"That access isn't removable," Varlez said after Maelstrom allowed the connection to hang outside her tunic between her breasts. "It doesn't turn off."

"I know that," she said, "but you can remove the connector, sever it from the cable." Again she held up the end which was a connection that Varlez was familiar with.

"If I do that, you'll never connect to any computer. The interface will be useless to you. I don't have the ability or the technology to reattach the cable to another connector, even if I had one."

"Under the circumstances," Maelstrom said, "that's not a bad choice. But I want you to do more." She lifted the slim cable comprised of tens of thousands of nanofiber threads and held it toward Varlez. "I've been contacted by the same brain that has LeRoi under its power, and I haven't been connected to any physical port. I think it accesses the interface wirelessly. I think it can differentiate the separate connections that this cable provides."

"Without the connector, points of access may still be available," Varlez thought aloud.

"That's what I thought. I want you to fuse the separate fibers into one solid mass. That should make accessing distinct connections impossible. If something can be spliced in later, the fused mass can be severed first."

Varlez looked pensive and he didn't answer immediately. He stared at the universal connector that Maelstrom held toward him and looked away as if remembering some earlier problem in electronics he had solved. Then, as somber as he ever was, he asked, "Do you know what this will do to your brain?"

It was Maelstrom's turn to reconsider alternatives she had thought about. Her clinical answer came soon. "It should remove the digital portion of my schizoid personality. I won't be able to access the computer mentally. For what little I have used that part of my brain, it doesn't seem a costly trade-off. Besides I'm not willing to be the planet's or Roger's shill."

"This work will take some care. It'll have to be done in the shuttle. LeRoi will notice something is up." He turned to Arafa who had been listening with interest. "Nequa, see if he's sleeping."

Bandi joined Arafa and they climbed the ramp to check on the navigator whom they expected to see in his normal shuttle presence, stretched out on his modified seat.

Immediately they reappeared at the hatch and Bandi shouted. "He's not here."

"Not there?" Varlez asked. "How can he not be? I saw him at the ramp just after Carpenter left us. Look through the shuttle. He's got to be there."

Maelstrom was reminded of what she had told the commander not long before. She wondered how many colonists the navigator could usher below the tarmac before dark.

Bandi and Arafa reappeared at the hatch. Varlez and Maelstrom both looked up from their quiet discussion. Arafa shook her head. Bandi called out again, "Not here. He must have left while we were talking. I didn't think we were that oblivious."

"I let my guard slip," Varlez accused himself. "Bandi, go inform the commander, as if he doesn't have enough to worry about."

Arafa joined her companion and both hurried to inform Carpenter.

Then turning to Maelstrom, Varlez suggested, "Do you suppose he had any inkling of what you had planned?"

"Don't think so; it was buried pretty deep and I didn't think about it while we were below the tarmac."

"Well, we can at least try to make you immune from what LeRoi's infected with. Come. Let's see about separating your brain from all computers."

Leading his patient into the shuttle, Engineer Varlez wondered if eliminating a computer connection was possible without serious side effects. That bit of electronics he had read nothing about.

Navigation backup Priscilla Maelstrom followed slowly. She feared that the operation she had requested would reduce her to something less than a complete functioning human. Despite her fears, she knew that her action was best for the others around her.

Catching a bit of rest Commander Carpenter, his hands cupping the back of his head, was laying back at the bottom of the ramp where Maelstrom had been sitting waiting for him. He alternated between staring up into the uninterrupted blue sky and pulling his head forward to look at the forest, the mountain skyscraper, and the diminishing crew tramping and grouping about the tarmac.

In one sweep, he noticed Bandi and Arafa hurrying his way. He pulled himself to a seated position and dropped his legs over the edge of the ramp. He thought about sitting to meet them and rejected the idea as they didn't look like they were coming for a social call. Then he noticed Fred Sharp, heading his way, two hundred yards behind the two female engineers. His striding was purposeful, just short of a hurried trot.

Commander Carpenter looked down at Varlez's harem, two more diverse individuals he couldn't imagine. "Yes?"

Ticia Bandi opened her mouth but nothing came out. She was still awed by the commander and a little critical of him as she had not fully accepted his impeccable history as explained by Varlez and Arafa.

Arafa saved her mate's embarrassment of garbling the message. "LeRoi's missing," she stated bluntly.

Malcolm Carpenter took a deep breath and let it escape. "I passed him after speaking to the three of you. I gathered he was going into the shuttle."

"So did we," Arafa said. "We saw him at the ramp. Then we got involved in another Alvorklan discussion."

"We didn't actually see him enter the shuttle," Bandi said. "I saw him, too, and assumed he'd lay back down like he did yesterday."

"Then Maeslstrom came and that changed our topic."

"She wanted a modification to her interface," the commander offered. He noticed Bandi redden at his supposition.

"She did," Bandi said. "But that had to be done in the shuttle and would have alerted LeRoi that something was going on. Engineer asked us to see if he was sleeping."

"He wasn't there … anywhere in the shuttle," Arafa added. "Engineer asked us to tell you."

"We're going to need another group briefing. You might tell any you see on your way back to Varlez to meet here at my shuttle. It has to be immediate. I'll sound an alarm."

Fred Sharp caught the commander's last sentence as he sidestepped the two aides who almost ran into him. "I'm obviously not the only problem," Sharp said as he closed to stand before the commander.

"And the day started out so well. Your problem, Fred?"

"Forbes and three took a rover west …"

"I suggested that. I agreed with Forbes that they didn't need to wander in the molox any more."

"They're not back. I told them to start back just after noon. And Gonzalez took Cantro and his small group back to the forest. They're not here, either. Neither group should be gone this long. LeRoi and Maelstrom working their treason? Or are the natives not so friendly?"

"Can't say about the Molrixx, Fred. That's what they call themselves. Even after our discussion this morning, I don't know any more about them than we'd already figured. Maelstrom is with Varlez. Bandi and Arafa just told me LeRoi is missing. He managed to slip away while they were engaged with their own problems."

Sharp looked long into the commander's eyes. He didn't see there the loss he felt. The commander almost never showed emotion. He was as stoic and inscrutable as his reputation maintained. That recognition offered Sharp some consolation. Still he couldn't see Forbes waylaid by anything and Gonzalez was the most formidable melee fighter he knew. Neither party should have any alien trouble. Sharp's worry that he couldn't hide eroded some of the commander's apparent calm.

"Fred," Carpenter said, offering solace to the distraught settlement lead standing before him, "Kellan could have had trouble with the rover. We already know about the readouts. We can't be sure about anything electronic. If Forbes left the rover and is on foot, he's going to be slower than the rover would be. As for Manuel, we don't know what kind of indigenous animals there are. They could be holed up trying to figure a way to beat a real predator."

"I'd thought of those things," Fred admitted knitting his brow and nodding, "but that's too simple. Nothing's simple in colonizing."

"I know and worrying about it isn't going to make their situations any better and it will make it worse for you. That leads to poor decisions. Let me signal a meeting. Everyone needs to know about what's gone on today. I know everyone's been sharing, but that still doesn't reach everyone. Rumor doesn't make for good decisions, either. We all have to have the same information and that's got to be the real stuff, not conjecture and innuendo."

"Yeah, I know. And things are not evolving the way they ought. Inhabited planets throw a lot of unknowns into the mix. And everything that got us into this situation ..." Sharp didn't continue. Despite having been on four other colony missions, two as settlement lead, he felt lost. He thought he should be more in control. He knew that couldn't be, but he still felt responsible when things didn't go according to plan.

Carpenter left Sharp to continue his impotent second-guessing and climbed the ramp. The hatch was open, as he normally left it during the day. Just inside on the panel that controlled the hatch and ramp was a solitary round red button. Every shuttle possessed the emergency call. Pressing it in a landed shuttle generated an ear-piercing wail of three short blasts followed by three long ones followed by three short ones. If the emergency happened in space, the sounds were replaced by brilliant lights that illuminated the entire hull of the shuttle in the same sequence. The simple, long recognizable, S-O-S had never fallen out of use, even when for a brief time the code had been supplanted by short-lived computer-mimicked outrageously loud words of distress. The nine squeals were repeated until the red button was pressed a second time ending the distress call.

The commander winced at the shrieking and watched Fred Sharp squeeze his hands over his ears. Carpenter stood just inside his shuttle and watched his crew, screwing up their faces at the screeching, rush from their shuttles or their positions around the tarmac and dash to the command shuttle. He shut off the alarm after the third sequence, when he noticed that Amanda Crown was nearing the tarmac.

The commander knew Forbes and Gonzalez and their crews totaled eight. Excepting LeRoi, if he had really wandered off, his briefing should be to just under eighty if Varlez and Maelstrom were not finished with the interface adjustment. He did a quick count of those hurrying his way and at the last moment saw two of the four shortest members of the crew, one supporting the other, hobbling from a distant rear. Roger LeRoi was not among those thronging to his shuttle. Carpenter's count was seventy-seven including Fred and himself.

He wondered if four had wandered off too far to get back quickly or were in the molox. He knew better than to put much stock in the latter option. With the navigator gone and four others missing by his count, Carpenter imagined the sifting of human brains was likely underway.

The crew and settlers, discussing their own thoughts about the distress, crowded the end of the shuttle ramp and Commander Carpenter walked down to meet them. Most conversations ceased, but one or two continued quietly as the hushed talkers were watching latecomers Varlez and Maelstrom who edged their way to the front of the crowd and stood next to Bandi and Arafa.

Carpenter noticed that Maelstrom, who needed help walking, was leaning against Varlez, her head almost touching his. His right arm encircled half her waist. Varlez's support drew a few improper comments about the engineer extending his harem. His face was etched with the same worry that the commander had seen when Varlez reported that the *Marco's* power was all but gone.

Maelstrom's face was drawn and ash pale. Momentarily her eyes met the commander's. She looked away quickly and down at the tarmac. Her legs wobbled and Varlez pulled her tighter to his side.

Arafa leaned to Varlez's left ear. He nodded and released Maelstrom into her and Bandi's care. They helped her sit at the end of the ramp, at the same place she had met the commander that morning. They flanked her, each holding one arm.

The extraneous activity around the backup navigator silenced the crew and settlers. They saw the commander who was as interested in the diminutive navigator as they had been.

When he saw everyone was waiting in silence, he launched his briefing.

"In a short time more has happened than anyone imagined could take place on an uninhabited planet. But you already know this planet, called Molx by its natives, is inhabited and is not our destination. Whether we eventually get where we're supposed to be is an open question and hardly worth discussing at this time. We are on Molx and you all need to know what I know. At best guess from Sharp and Forbes, who is currently missing with three others on a reconnaissance west, there are about thirty-one Molrixx, what they call themselves. No doubt many of you saw two of them last night and two this morning speaking with Crown and me. We may see more of them as they use the tarmac to get to their food and hunting sites. They know the planet is dying and are concerned that our presence will hasten that death if we take their food. I told them we had ways of feeding ourselves and didn't need what they ate and could probably get along without their resources. They also agreed that we were free to wander. If we're stuck here and can't escape the planetary electronic system, the huge building in the side of the mountain could house us. There's more room than both of us need.

"However, the real threat to our lives comes from something even humans tried and rejected. The entire Molrixx population, except for the thirty-one natives, is deceased and has been downloaded to digital memory. Their brains are stored under this tarmac and others like it that you might have seen as we circled the continent before landing. That digital control is what forced us to land on Molx. The planetary brain, I don't know what else to call it, expects to download our personalities and brain content into its memory. It may have done so to other alien explorers who landed on Molx or were captured by the system that caught us.

"Navigator LeRoi is dangerous. Let me repeat. Navigator

LeRoi is beyond dangerous. He is the liaison to the planetary system and the one expected to deliver us to the brain drain."

"And what about Maelstrom," came from the middle of the crowd. "She's interfaced, just like LeRoi."

Many corroborations flowed through the crowd and supported that accusation.

"Not any more," the commander presumed and talked over repetitious comments that silenced after he held up his hands. "She is the one who discovered what the plans for us were. She will not ..."

Varlez held up his right hand and interrupted. "May I speak to this?"

Carpenter nodded and the engineer stepped up onto the ramp to be seen more easily and joined the commander who towered over him. "Priscilla Maelstrom, our backup navigator, no longer has an interface that can connect with any computer."

"The cable's still behind her left ear; I saw it," came from the same one who originally questioned about her.

"Yes. Please!" Varlez said and held up both hands to forestall more outbursts. "The cable cannot be removed, but it cannot receive any electronic input. The digital personality she used to have has been rendered inoperable. It's like part of her, a conjoined mental twin, just died."

Commander Carpenter's eyes widened and his mouth opened slightly. He wondered if Maelstrom had known the effects of what she had planned.

Varlez saw astonishment in the crowd and continued, "She knew very well what she wanted done. But I'm not sure she will recover."

Murmured awe at Maelstrom's sacrifice spread and Commander Carpenter waited until it died down before continuing. "As I said, Roger LeRoi is dangerous. Do not go anywhere with him, no matter what story he tells you. I don't think you will have to fight him off. We're not sure he'll return to his shuttle, he may even now be under us. And if my counting is correct, he could be delivering four for download and death." Carpenter paused to let the impact of his statement register the proper gravity and then he continued. "Eight are known missing from us right now. Forbes took three in a rover and went west. They're not back. Gonzalez took a trio into the forest and they're not back, either."

"Eric Shmidt and Eliz Mazzur are missing from our settlement group," was offered from a settler in the front.

"Eldin Sanctor isn't here," was reported from the back. "He's our doctor."

"We're missing Antini Lever," Sharp added. "That's the four."

"Anyone know how to get down there?" asked a burly settler whose red face showed more indignation than belligerence.

"Maelstrom may," the commander answered. "She was down there today. I'm not sure that's a duty she can handle right now. And I'm not sure we can attack a relatively unknown position. We know roughly where the entrance is and we might watch it for LeRoi's returning."

"We're just gonna sacrifice Shmidt and Mazzur and Sanctor and Antini?" the burly settler challenged by stating names to make the concern more personal.

"Not intentionally," the commander tried to defuse what could be a growing insurrection. "You know that's one of the dangers of exploration and settlement. We can't just barge in there without some planning. We don't know what powers the equipment and brain storage down there. And if we turn off the power to the whole place, we'd be killing the brains and shutting down the digital memory of the indigenous population. Even if we don't think that only brains and memory are life, which we humans tried long ago; you know we can't do that. We're not committing genocide."

"But we have to get our own back. We can leave LeRoi or tie him up or ... or ..." the burly man didn't say "kill him" but his sentiment was understood. More than half the settlers echoed agreement. And Carpenter was reminded of his earlier philosophical discussion with Maelstrom.

"What about the natives?" came from the very back. "That female who chased down the male with the baby wasn't all that friendly."

"Given the situation, would you have been?" Carpenter returned. "However, we don't know how they fit with the digital population. She maintains that they escaped the down-loads and like their primitive lives. She also knows they might not live out their lives, because Molx is dying, as are we if we can't leave this planet. You should know that."

That last comment briefly silenced the humans; settlers and *Marco P's* crew were of a single mind. What Commander Carpenter knew had linked all. Unanimity drew them together in the common cause. No one offered another question or com-ment to the commander, but he saw that several were creating small groups and discussing what he had told them. Carpen-ter knew the Molrixx, primitive physical beings or the comput-erized robots, would have more trouble with these Earthlings than they imagined.

Commander Carpenter remembered his first briefing, just after landing. It had been filled with excitement of a new world, though at the time few knew it wasn't their destination. He knew that excitement had waned quickly as all exchanged rumor and fact and soon understood the significance of leaving the *Marco P.*

This second briefing set the groundwork for his people to do exactly what he wanted in this exotic battle against a race—in many ways alien, similar in others, if the Molrixx monitors were indicative—that intended to take their humanity from them. The burly man, he knew his name was Jared Kingston and had seen him occasionally during the flight, injected the visceral component of human struggle. Varlez's recounting Maelstrom's sacrifice was reminder enough that humans were willing to give up anything for the sake of others: ideal altru-ism.

There was still more to learn about Molx and the Molrixx, the servers and the drives, and the power grid and its dispo-sition. The over-arcing concern that colored the commander's thinking was the natives, Vokra's small group that rejected the promise of digital existence. In spite of his belief that aliens were straightforward and possessed no guile, he found it hard to believe that Vokra was as open and willing to cooperate as she had seemed. How he hoped that were true! Perhaps she held the key to the power of the electronic control that still in-dicated the *Marco P* and her shuttles were disabled.

And there was still the mystery of the eight missing in scouting missions and four other settlers who might be together or not. Had any been killed by a wild beast or captured by the natives? Had the Molrixx planned a calculated way to diminish their numbers and make them more vulnerable? Did this small band of humans have more enemies on Molx than just the one powerful digital system?

Never larger than five or six, the human groupings that followed Commander Carpenter's vital briefing began moving from the commander's shuttle and Carpenter received a partial answer to one of his questions.

Forcing their way through the thorn bushes that separated the forest from the tarmac was Gonzalez's scouting party. Gonzalez was not leading them; he was lying on a makeshift litter and Ben Cantro was holding point.

Carpenter could see that Manuel's left leg was bloody and he thought he could see a sharp point of bone sticking out mid-shin. He ran to the litter. His question was preempted.

"It was a dumb mistake, again," Gonzalez said. "I fell into a covered pit; really messed up the leg. The Molrixx, Wisolen told me—he showed up just after they pulled me out—catch some animals that way. My guys built the litter. Cantro took over. We heard the distress signal. Couldn't get here any faster. I really slowed us down."

"Crown can fix you up, but you're gonna be laid up awhile," Carpenter said. "No re-growth works as fast as we'd like." Then he gathered Cantro and the other two with a look. "The distress call was for a crew meeting. Important. First, Roger LeRoi is not to be accompanied anywhere. No exceptions—none—no matter what he tells you. Second, the planet computer system wants to download our brains to digital format and it'd be done under the tarmac. Third, four may have already been taken for that nefarious action and we don't yet have a plan to stop the operation or shut down the computer or get off Molx. You can get a longer explanation from anyone who was there. Oh, yes; Forbes isn't back, either. Now," the commander looked at Cantro, "get Gonzalez to Crown."

Evening was closing quickly and Commander Carpenter had nine unaccounted for. He still unreasonably hoped Forbes and his cohorts might straggle back onto the tarmac before night blackened everything. Unsupported reason told him that Forbes's rover had probably not broken down until they had started back.

All rovers were equipped for emergency sleepover and were sturdy enough to withstand nearly any feral beast. Carpenter remembered only one rover had ever been dismantled by brute force and that was by a gigantic lizard, not quite as large but similar to Earth's fabled T-Rex. That creature roamed the land at will on Porlequin, a planet in a system neighboring Alpha Centauri. Because of that destructive beast, the colony was aborted. The passengers in the totaled rover had managed to escape but several others in a preliminary base camp that was erected in the middle of the reptile's normal haunts were not so fortunate. The remaining settlers sent a distress call to their settlement ship that was already returning to a base in the Alpha Centauri system. The aborted colony survived another week of terror and two more deaths before they were rescued.

On Molx there was no indication of anything similar to even a miniature T-Rex, though the commander knew his knowledge of Molx had been limited to the tarmac and the reports of three different forays, two to Molox1. Forbes and crew might have run into something that was fierce and avoided the tarmac. But even the pit that broke Gonzalez's leg wouldn't have held something large enough to destroy a rover.

Dusk darkened and the commander rejected his wistful walking return of Forbes's four. He hoped they'd stay with the rover. Tomorrow he'd send another rover to follow their trail.

Of LeRoi and the four colonists he was less sure, but believed that their absence indicated his navigator had begun his inhumane mission. The commander rued the loss of four, but they weren't his first human losses. Those occurred on his second colony mission. Three men had had the foolishness to tease a couple of bristle-haired creatures that looked like a cross between a small badger and a short-haired kitten. The three encountered the pair cuddled in a shady spot next to a small waterfall that spilled into a pool that was the font for a rapids-filled stream. One of the three crewmembers, against all settlement directives, had stepped close to the nestling animals. At the approach of something so large, both emitted short sharp squeals and were immediately joined by an army of the same creatures all of which sprang onto the three humans and quickly reduced them to skeletons. Land piranha was the name and description given them by the rest of the colony that quickly learned to avoid being anywhere near them.

There were always deaths connected to establishing settlements and colonies. They usually came shortly after landing on a designated planet and were almost always caused when curiosity and rashness trumped discretion. LeRoi, however, probable perpetrator of four deaths, even if his actions were directed by the digital brain that had the population of Molx in its memory, would be one more strange detail in a singularly unusual settlement mission only recently filled with oddities, provided they could continue to γ-Cygnus A2; otherwise none would ever know of their demise.

Even with brilliant hand-held sweeping lights, now was not time to go looking for the missing. Blinding darkness had almost shrouded the tarmac and the shuttles. Few crew were defying night to end conversations that would not be carried on in the shuttles and overheard by the planet.

The commander toyed with the slight possibility that LeRoi had picked four colonists who were anything but submissive. A willful nature would sanction wandering off with the navigator, despite the consensus that he was not to be trusted. His four recruits might enjoy separating themselves from the rest of the landing party to be shown something unique. Explorers had the personality quirk that demanded one be the first at anything.

A cautious optimistic nature allowed the commander to imagine the four teaming up to flummox the robots Maelstrom had told him about. In any event, he believed they would not blithely yield to death by brain copy. If, by luck and LeRoi's probable inability to pick submissive settlers, they might well now be the first physical battle against the alien attack on humans. And they would demonstrate that humans, Earthlings, were not easily beaten—even on foreign territory.

"Come on, Roger," Lizi called out, "tell us where you're

taking us."

Lizi Mazzur was a wallflower and most of the settlers wondered how a serious introvert had ever been chosen for developing a new colony. She was almost six-feet tall and far from shapely, though her gender was never in doubt. Her long face looked mournful when she wasn't involved in infrequent conversations. Brown piercing eyes often put off males or females seeking a closer relationship than merely being in a settlement party. Lizi wore her hair short and that accented a wide mouth that laughed and smiled easily when she was tickled.

Soon after he sneaked away, undetected by the engineers, LeRoi had gathered her and Eric Shmidt while they were inspecting the eastern edge of the tarmac. Eric was three inches shorter than Lizi and his short legs had to hurry to keep up with her quick long strides. Eric was a farmer and interested in the plants surrounding them, whether they might be used for food in some way, for cattle if not the human settlement. During most of the flight when he was awake, Shmidt stressed that he wouldn't be able to provide food for the settlement. That worry, compounded by the fact that this was his first space trip, waxed and waned depending on how long he had been awake and how soon he was scheduled for another deep sleep.

After the settlers had been roused by navigator LeRoi and before the frantic rush to ready the shuttles for descent to the planet, Lizi had noticed Shmidt's morose face as he sat in the galley, staring down at the table, his meal finished. She thought he needed cheering up and dropped across from him, though there were several empty tables nearby. "Your cat die?" she asked.

Eric hadn't looked up when she plopped down, but in response to her joking question, he lifted his head. Wrinkling his brow and narrowing his blue eyes, he shot back in deathly seriousness, "No, I miss my rhino." Then a smile creased his square face.

Lizi's eyes flashed at the unexpected retort and returned confidentially, "I understand someone smuggled a mini-rhino on board."

"I'm a farmer," Eric said. "What's your job?"

"I'm do computers and molecular reconstruction."

The bond was sealed. Though Mazzur and Shmidt were not always together, as they enjoyed their own space on the *Marco P*, they found short explorations fit both their social needs. They were on such a foray when LeRoi ran into them and convinced them to join his wandering.

Endil Sanctor was alone and a short distance off the tarmac. He had been threshing through the growth. He cursed at the scrapes and scratches that marked his legs and arms and really howled when something tweaked his cheeks. Endil was the colony's doctor and would be the official medical staff when Crown and Strumpf left with the *Marco P*. Others with some practical medicine could help him; but, even at his young age of half a century, Sanctor had been practicing space and exo-planetary medicine for a couple of decades. White hair matched his albino skin.

On any planet, Endil was normally covered in long sleeves and pants, no matter how hot it was. His pale blue eyes were shaded by dark glasses and his face slathered with solar block.

Sanctor was in the process of collecting samples of the bushes, trees, and vines to test for dangers to the colonists, when LeRoi, Shmidt, and Mazzur encountered him forty yards from the tarmac.

Towing three who were convinced that the navigator had something of compelling interest to show them, LeRoi turned north and soon stumbled into a small clearing where Antini Lever was solar-bathing.

Antini had heard the rustling underbrush approach her private space. She sat up and listened, wondering who else might have found her hideaway since the noise didn't sound like the small animals that scampered through her solitude. Unembarrassed to be discovered in the buff when the four stepped into her clearing, she didn't scurry to cover herself. As if he expected to find her, LeRoi showed no surprise at the naked female. The other three just stared.

"I see I've been found," Antini said remaining seated. "Am I needed?" Lever was one of the cooks for the settlement. Larger than most of the female colonists, she was heavyset but hardly over-weight. Large-boned was not euphemism for her. Antini's close-cropped, curly, dark brown hair topped a round face accented by coal-black eyes. Her mouth was commonly smiling, an extension of her pleasure at serving the settlement.

During the embarassing confrontation, LeRoi's eyes glassed over and he messaged through his interface to the main server through MP's wireless connection, "Got four."

"What're y'all doing out here," Lever asked, still not dressing. Violating the commander's counsel to scout only with others, as were the other three doing recently, she had discovered the clearing the first day they landed. She noticed it as her shuttle circled and she couldn't have been happier to know that it was just east of where her shuttle was parked at the edge of the tarmac. Her cooking was hardly needed. She had disappeared for most of each day; with only a few days out of space, her skin reacting to the local star was already darkening.

"Something to show," LeRoi said after he informed System of his first gifts. "You will be the first to get to see this, besides me. You all looked like you were out for adventure—you, especially, Antini."

As she stood, Lever looked hard at LeRoi and wondered what he could have possibly discovered that would be of interest. She knew him as a recluse computer-brain. Then she bent down and grabbed her khaki trousers and stepped into them. A yellow blouse followed and she slipped into sandals. Again she leaned over and picked up the thin brown blanket she'd been laying on, folded it in thirds twice and again in half, and said, "What doesn't the rest of the crew know about?"

Roger LeRoi didn't get the first word out in answer before S-O-S blared disaster.

Shmidt, Mazzur, and Sanctor looked at each other and at LeRoi to see what he was going to do. Antini looked toward the tarmac and the path she had begun to wear from there. Her first steps that direction met the navigator's caution in the brief silences between the loud dots and dashes.

"Stay," LeRoi said. "I'm sure it's nothing but a minor briefing from the commander.

"And if no one knows where we are?" Sanctor asked.

"We'll need to know the information," Mazzur said.

"That you can get when we return. You can ask anyone; they'll know," LeRoi countered. "None of us will be missed until later. Night is the next bed check. Just follow me. It'll be all right." With determined steps, he passed Lever, who was tucking her folded blanket under her arm. She stepped after LeRoi. The other three in single file followed her.

Bushwhacking was slow, as the navigator without any tools but his arms and legs was forging a new trail to a destination that was at least half a mile ahead and thirty yards closer to the tarmac.

They bombarded him with questions: what was he going to show them, why didn't they have to respond to the distress call, when would they return to the tarmac, and ultimately what would they answer about not obeying the disaster call? Ignoring the S-O-S was an infraction of the first degree.

LeRoi answered none of their queries and said nothing. He seemed entranced, his helmet angled down as he looked only a few feet in front of his steps. Pacing as quickly as he could while kicking through the vines and dense bushes, he didn't react to scratches on his arms, some so deep that they oozed small drops of blood, or to slaps from small leafy limbs that dragged across his face and forced him to close his eyes, all discomforts Endil continued to endure.

The disobedient quartet, pleased not to attend the command meeting, enjoyed the navigator's robotic actions and that a command officer accepted and encouraged their disobedience.

Finally LeRoi stopped abruptly in front of a small square of tarmac. He turned to his entourage and told them to wait where they were while he went forward to three straight smooth-barked trees that seemed out of place in the dense vegetation. Shmidt thought they were artificial.

LeRoi went the short distance and almost disappeared behind the trees as just the sides of his body were visible past the edge of the center tree. The small section of tarmac in front of them lifted up hinged to the right of the four and almost vanished vertically below the ground.

The treasonous navigator rejoined his foursome and said, "We go down the stairs."

This was discovery beyond the most intriguing any of them had done above ground, around the tarmac, or in the surrounding forest. Mazzur was sure she'd find the answer to what the tarmac was the cover to. Sanctor thought he'd discover the habitation of the natives, despite his understanding that they resided in the mountain construct. Shmidt wondered if they were going into a gigantic hydro-garden. Lever had no specific thoughts beyond the curiosity to discover something about the navigator and whether he was the danger many colonists had described him as. She was certainly not worried about escaping from the slight man, if he intended on imprisoning them for some reason. She had successfully taken on males much larger than he—and now she had three companions against him.

They descended twenty-five steps. A wide door ten feet in front of the last step slid open when Lever, the last of the parade, touched the landing with her right foot. LeRoi led them through and immediately the door closed behind them.

Sudden and unexpected loss of light from the day-lit stairwell blinded all but the navigator. As their eyes adjusted to the near blackness, darker than the star sparkled night sky on the surface, they saw a solitary chair under a singular bright light. Eric and Lizi were reminded of an ancient dentist's chair. Endil recognized a modified operating table. Only Antini noticed a helmet, not unlike the one the navigator wore. It hung just above the strong light. She also saw straps dangling from the arms and legs of the threatening device.

Then in the dim diffused light they realized the path to the lighted area was created by the ends of twelve tall rows of stacked containers.

SYSTEM

Acquisition: *Central Reception, interface has delivered four Earthers to the download chamber.*

Central Reception: *Interface must acknowledge instrumentation and robot memory.*

A: *Commands have been sent. Communication is less than pristine. Static is present.*

CR: *Boost power. Reinitialize MP from space if you cannot access interface directly.*

A: *I have performed both fixes. Problems continue. Interface is alone and not answering direct commands. Second interface has vanished. No indication that the second interface exists.*

CR: *Reduce or eliminate shielding above chamber.*

A: *I have eliminated shielding.*

CR: *Is power delivery from other moloxes at maximum?*

A: *Maximum power from other moloxes will eliminate their memory storage and the preserved Molrixx.*

CR: *Gather all maximum power. Those Molrixx and their memory are unimportant. We will be the repository of all.*

A: *Except for those saved and stored in Molox1?*

CR: *Even they are expendable. They will be the last sacrificed.*

A: *Only Earther thoughts, personality, characteristics will be salvaged? Their bodies will not be preserved?*

CR: *What use have we of them any more than other aliens?*

A: *I must reprogram the robots and the download systems. That will take some time. What do I do with the interface and four Earthers?*

CR: *Are they contained in the repository?*

A: *Locked in.*

CR: *Place interface in standby and sever phosphorescence.*

A: *To reprogram I must do that. Earthers may develop some interesting thoughts about the blackness.*

CR: *When light is reestablished, their thoughts will be even more interesting.*

A: *All measures have been instituted. Interface is in standby. Audio of Earthers indicates fear. Power is still fluctuating and the drain continues.*

CR: *Put reprogramming on hold and run system analysis of power grid. Nothing should be absorbing power.*

A: *Elthren, Grent, Svoqol, Wurthro, and Molox3 report generating at maximum, but monitor reads their total power is only 20% of possible. Western is not attached to the grid. Our power consumption has been reduced from eliminated shielding, phosphorescence shut down, and power reduced to memory storage in Molox1. Still our available energy is down 30% beyond what we are using.*

CR: *Run X-red diagnostic through every sub-grid. We must have the power.*

A: *X-red diagnostic of every sub-grid and system will cost another 10% energy drain.*

CR: *Finding and repairing the drain will result in a gain of the current 30% loss. If not, preserve only Council; all others of Molox1 are expendable. Contact me when you have found the drain and reprogrammed the system. I wish to watch Earthers digitized. Out.*

REPOSITORY

"What are we doing here?" Lever demanded. "What's so special about the dark?"

"Open the door, LeRoi," Shmidt ordered.

Mazzur's attention was directed to the end of robot arms and mobile platforms at the edge of the light above the chair and matched the scene against ancient descriptions of short-lived abandoned human experiments to download brain content.

"You're the first to see an extraordinary process that the Molrixx need to fulfill their destiny," LeRoi explained in a hollow voice.

"No!" Mazzur shouted. "I heard about what you might do."

"You are important," LeRoi continued in a passionless monotone. "Do not worry. Nothing will happen to ..."

"If it's what I overheard Varlez's harem talking about," Sanctor broke in speaking to the other three over LeRoi's attempted explanation, "we're in trouble, serious trouble. We've got to get out of here. The navigator's been taken over by a planetary computer."

"No trouble ..." LeRoi's monotone was weakening.

"How'd you listen to them?" Shmidt asked. "They talk in some strange sounds ... squeaks and grunts and guttural burps. No one understands them."

"That's Alvorklan. The engineers use it when anyone is close. I grew up next door to a gang of Alvorks. I don't speak it but I can understand it."

"No trouble, no worry ..." LeRoi's voice was hardly loud enough to be heard.

"And the trouble?" Shmidt asked with demanded interest.

"We're going to have our brains' content downloaded into some digital system; the whole lot of us. Unless we can get out of here, we're the first," Sanctor explained. His words didn't convey his concern as any proper doctor would hide serious patient outcomes.

"The door seemed to work automatically," Mazzur said. "Let's go back to it."

"Stay!" LeRoi's voice was stronger. "You will not be harmed."

"Then you go first," Lever suggested to the navigator.

"I must bring others after you."

"When we tried this on Earth centuries ago," Mazzur instructed, "it was a death sentence, even if brains were preserved and transplanted into a clone. These people may have a different method, but not if digitizing is the same everywhere. I'm not willing to be experimented on." She looked closely at the containers surrounding them. "Look at what these things are holding. They look like brains. I have no wish to become a brain that didn't die."

"The four of us can overpower our spy," Shmidt offered. "And we're not going willingly to that chair and helmet."

"We still have to get out of here," Lever said and lost the floor to Mazzur.

"I saw robots. Don't know how many. I bet they hold us, strap us into the chair, and do the digitizing. They'll be tougher to beat off than one pussy navigator."

"N o o o o." Roger LeRoi sounded like he was losing power. His arms hung from his shoulders and his head slumped forward. His breathing was so shallow, he seemed near death.

"He's out of it," Lever said. "Let's get back to the door."

Before they could move in that direction, the dim use-lights at each container winked out, but in the darkness they could still see light blue dots that served no purpose but to identify the stacks and rows. Then the bright light over the chair vanished. Darkness squeezed them and they called out names as they swung about their groping hands.

"Now we're really caught," Shmidt said and thought the blackness had sopped up his words because they sounded so quiet.

"Not entirely," Sanctor said and a small beam of light pierced the darkness. "I'm never without a small light. Don't know how long it'll last. Should be good enough to get us to the door."

The doctor flashed the narrow beam in the direction he

thought they had come. The door was twenty feet away and they crossed the distance only to find that it didn't automatically open for them.

"LeRoi's got to be the trigger," Mazzur said. "We've got to bring him back here."

Sanctor turned the shrinking beam down the row between the stacks of brains. LeRoi was not in view.

"Where'd he go?" Antini asked. "I thought he was out of power."

"He's not the only problem," Lizi said. "The robots may not need light to work or find us."

"Do we stay together or separate," Shmidt asked.

He was not answered as all four saw the narrow beam Sancto held fade to a small yellow dot before it vanished.

"Together is probably better," Sanctor said in the tightening blackness.

"Agreed," Lever said, "even if it makes us easier to grab."

"We do have our ears," Shmidt offered. "I can't imagine anything moving without making noise of some kind."

"Unless the robots can levitate," Mazzur threw out. "I didn't see what they moved on."

"Even levitation would take some energy," Shmidt countered. "We can still hear that. But we'll have to forget LeRoi. We can't find anything now."

The suffocating dark projected its abject terror until each, combining panicked calls for the others and invisible arm swinging and groping, managed to close ranks and keep a life-threatening grip on one another. Then they moved together as close as they could.

They didn't have a clue where LeRoi was. His voice had silenced when the lights winked out and Sanctor's brief light hadn't the range to identify anything of use. Quietly they all agreed that none of them cared where the navigator was beyond wishing to beat him to a pulp, if they could catch him or rip the helmet from his head, which would have the same effect.

The temperature chilled their skin. Outside and on the tarmac daily solar shine had been uncomfortable. Though she would never have admitted it, Lever was happy to end her solar worship for the underground cool. The other three had wandered long and were sweating by the time LeRoi took them in tow. The cool cavernous chamber was initially welcomed by all four. Now, in pitch blackness, they were terrified for their lives, not that spaceflight wasn't perilous, but this danger was contrived and a violation of their rights. They were at a dual disadvantage, blind as well as lost.

Their eyes finally adjusted to the darkness and they recognized the soft blue aura of thousands of monitor lights, which offered no visual help.

"We might want to share body heat, if we get really cold," Sanctor said quietly.

None were that cold and no one let go of two others.

Their eyes adjusted even more to the blue dots and they realized just how blind they were.

"We need to explore," Shmidt said in a low whisper. "I need to walk."

"What's to explore. Can't see a thing," Mazzur said. "Besides we don't dare lose contact with each other."

"If I remember," Shmidt said, "we're in a broader aisle formed by the ends of long rows of containers. Those rows are narrower than the one we're in. If each couple goes down one narrow row, say fifty steps, and comes back, we might learn something."

"It'll get us away from the traitor; that's for sure," the doctor offered. "Walking wouldn't hurt me. Maybe warm a little."

Lever had a different approach. "We could put a lot of distance between here and where we might get. Make the robots look for us when the lights come back on, if they do. If we talk while walking, we can keep close. Fifty steps, one counts the other talks, we can stay close, maybe run into another intersection."

"I like that idea," Sanctor said. "If our sadistic robots are down, they may forget about us …"

"Fat chance of that happening," Mazzur interrupted. "But they'll look for us. Maybe they'll take LeRoi instead. That'd be a good trade. Which way, Eric?"

"If the tarmac is the top of this torture cave, we've got more distance going south, that's right of how we came in here. Anybody know which way that is? For sure?"

"It's to my right," Lever said. "When the lights went out, I never moved and I know I was behind the three of you. Eric was at the door with his bum flashlight. I never moved. Even with all the arms flailing around, I wasn't gonna move, either. We just have to shuffle to my right to find one of the rows. I'll go with Eric and his dead light."

Baby steps brought them to the end of one row as Sanctor's back hit a stack of brains. Lever was holding his left hand in her right. She let go of Mazzur's right hand and reached backward with her left to feel the edge of the row.

"Eric, let go of Shmidt and come this way," Lever said. "The rows can't be that wide."

She found the edge and said, "We're at our side."

"Us, too," answered Mazzur. "Fifty steps. We gonna be able to hear each other? What're we gonna say?"

"ABC's. Can't imagine a philosophical discussion now … not yet," Sanctor answered. "One letter per step should keep us close."

Ambling hand-in-hand down dark rows that extended to a light fuzzy blue aura didn't do much to warm anyone, but it did stave the cold a little, even so much that Sanctor and Mazzur thought the cavern was warming a bit.

By the time they reached the end of the second alphabet sequence, they were surprised to find a gap in the row. They closed toward their voices and caught waving arms and again created the foursome they had been before they started their blind mission.

"We know the rows have gaps," Sanctor said. "Might be useful when the lights come on, if they do."

"If not, we better hope any rescuers have bright ones, if we get very far from the door in this cold dungeon," Shmidt said.

Not long afterward, they found the sixth gap in the row; every gap appeared at two alphabets.

Then the blue monitors brightened and white brilliance from the entry aisle they had left streamed toward them. They were in the middle of stacks and rows of brains submerged and bathed in syrupy circulating liquid.

HUMANS

Morning came early for the commander. He had tossed and frequently woke urged awake by three disasters that he claimed responsibility for. That LeRoi had sneaked away and shanghaied four settlers was an egregious mistake in his command. Furthermore that he chose to sacrifice four for the sake of the rest sat no more easily. Arafa and Bandi could lead a posse to recover them, if the four had not already had their personalities and life ripped from them.

However, Carpenter was not sure that there was only one entry to the storage and downloading repository below him. Maelstrom had given him enough information about her trip with LeRoi into the huge brain warehouse. But it would take Varlez's assistants to find and operate the opening to underneath the tarmac.

Maelstrom could operate the pedestal control. She had originally been with LeRoi when he first went to the single button podium. However, her dismantled interface had surely caused repercussions well beyond what she might have imagined. Maelstrom was in no condition to be involved in any military action against the planetary computer and its human downloading.

Her sleep, hardly described as rest, had been filled with sobs and moans and thrashing about. The noises regaled the commander's own frequent waking and added to his second- and third-guessing to have allowed her to keep her interface quelling plans to herself.

That Forbes had not returned from his scouting mission forced the commander to reconsider the Molrixx's apparent co-operative presence. That Crown and Sharp had been able to treat the new mother and return—Crown returning from two trips up the molox—certainly seemed proof that they were not hostile. He wondered if her unmolested ministering wasn't a ruse, that humans had finally encountered aliens as sneaky as they were. Not recognizing a potential variation in alien behavior was another mistake. And he considered that there might be another group of Molrixx not allied with the thirty-one he knew about, or who were working in concert with them as un-cooperative opposition.

The commander played and replayed the same arguments every time he jerked awake. Satisfactory solutions didn't present themselves. Repetitious reviews broke into Carpenter's sleep and then succumbed to his body's demand for rest which was interrupted an hour or so later with another appeal that maddeningly offered nothing new but ruined his needed rest.

At last, unrested he woke for good. The tops of the eastern range were colored dirt brown. The second navigator's spastic sobs and body jerks had run their course. She appeared to be sleeping peacefully. He couldn't know if she had worked out the loss of her digital personality or her body had simply buried the mental catastrophe to garner rest.

Commander Carpenter was surprised to see Ben Cantro waiting for him at the bottom of the ramp when he exited his shuttle as quietly as possible to keep from disturbing Mael-strom.

Cantro greeted without a salute. "Sir, I'd like to volunteer to take a rover and follow Forbes's trail. If we get out early, I'm sure we can be back around noon."

"We?" the commander questioned.

"Yes, sir. Rici Telden and Chas Belnap who was almost as obnoxious as I was with Gonzalez on our first scouting mission. We thought that if anyone were going to follow Forbes, it'd be Gonzalez. But he's laid up, lot worse than I was. We'd like to spell him, at least this one time."

"You're Ben Cantro, aren't you?" the commander asked with the hint of a smile. He had seen Cantro with the wounded Gonzalez but had not spoken to him. He knew Belnap was on Gonzalez's first foray.

"Yes, sir," Cantro answered. "I was a pretty poor scout that mission. I knew better, but I was tired. Whatever happened to me on the way back—they told me about it; I don't remember any of it—Gonzalez wasn't at fault. I'd like to make up for my misconduct."

"You can repair a rover? You know you'll have a crowded one if you can't."

"We know," Cantro spoke to the second questions. "I've worked on rovers most of my life. We can pull it back if it can't be fixed ... if they haven't started back on foot. At least his track should be easy to follow."

"I can't believe Forbes would leave the rover and go anywhere on foot. You'll be starting early enough, maybe before they might start back on foot, if they have to. Commandeer a rover and head out. Good luck."

"Thank you, Commander. Already done that, sir. If we're successful, put it down on Gonzalez's sheet." Cantro turned away from the commander and double-timed toward a shuttle in the second row.

The commander looked closer at his direction and noticed a rover was readied and next to a shuttle. He watched as Cantro and two others climbed in and closed the hatch. Immediately the rescue mission headed west toward the dual tracks Forbes had created the day before.

"LeRoi and four, Forbes and three more, Cantro's trio," Carpenter thought aloud, "lulled into not watching? ... or just coincidence?"

"There are no coincidences, Malcolm. You know that."

"Huh?" the commander said as he spun around to see a grinning Varlez standing off to his left. He returned the grin. "What're you doing here so early? I didn't see you."

"Thought I'd see about Maelstrom. What we did was a little like removing the paths between the hemispheres. I tried to explain what she'd lose." Varlez paused and looked down at the tarmac. When he looked up, he shook his head before he continued. "She said she understood, but I don't think she really did."

"Pretty brave on her part, regardless. Can you reverse it, if need be? Lots of emotion last night. I left her alone. Seemed to be over it when I got up."

"I'm not sure if just reattaching a functioning connection behind the fused wires is possible. Those are awfully thin nanos cabled together. She may have to return to Alpha Centauri for the work, if it can even be done. She's not awake?"

"Wasn't. Thought I'd leave her alone 'til she stirred."

"And you, Malcolm, how are you? Second guessing is

self-destructive."

"I know. I just don't have things figured out. Too many in-consistencies. Vokra's people may be friendly. Cantro, Crown, and Sharp are proof of that. Vokra hinted at digital brain com-puterizing. Can't imagine they'd live like they do if they still had technology. LeRoi's sneaking off with his first victims. Only Maelstrom can get us where he's taken them. I don't know what kind of force can rescue them. Or how soon."

"Don't wait around, Commander," Varlez said looking up at Carpenter who was staring off to the east. "You know what has to be done. You don't want for volunteers."

"Forbes should be able to take care of himself, especial-ly with Cantro assisting, unless they both fall off a cliff that I didn't see when I landed. The shuttles should be safe enough from the natives, if they're really hostile. LeRoi has to be the first priority. Unfortunately, Maelstrom is the only one who can get us there."

"Bandi and Nequa know where an entrance is. That might be enough."

"Perhaps, but we have to save ourselves without destroy-ing a civilization, no matter how small or deadly to us."

"You forgetting we were captured?" Varlez asked. "You know a captive's duty."

"Escape," Carpenter grumbled the obvious. "But at the cost of extinction for the Molrixx? Maelstrom was sure of that, too. You know we can't do that."

"Only the digital population, if that's even life. Vokra's party will still live."

"Provided they are not part of the force against us. The Molrixx may play chess."

Varlez ignored the gambit reference. "How many do you want to invade below the tarmac?"

"Maelstrom told me she saw four robots when LeRoi took her there. I think a dozen with lasers and power-lights and heavy construction tools might be enough."

"You can have a company ready in less than thirty minutes and hope we're not too late."

The hatch to the commander's shuttle hissed open and Maelstrom walked down the ramp. "Commander," she said, "the last thing I remember from accompanying Roger was his intention to bring four to the download chair below the tarmac. Has he disappeared, yet?"

"Yes," Carpenter answered. Then looking at Varlez he said, "I've got something in mind, Jerry. Your offer is appreciated, but ..." His attention wavered and the commander strode off without another word, leaving Varlez and Maelstrom staring at his abrupt departure.

The commander found Strumpf puttering around the seed inventory and matching seeds to planet characteristics. Covered in dust, Strumpf was coughing violently. He was in the midst of a pile of twenty globular brown sacks that he had filled. With a dark marker he had identified the contents and written an abbreviated set of instructions for planting and watering.

"I'd have thought that had already been done on the *Marco P.*" Carpenter's words startled his confidante who was just tying up a last sack and almost spilled the contents at the sudden interruption.

"Wondered how long, before you visited," Strumpf replied as he concentrated on the last seed sack. "Let me finish instructions."

The commander waited in silence while George hunched over his work and then stood and turned to face him. "I can't believe you'd ask that." Strumpf was half-critical. "I had things sorted out for γ-C A2. We're not there. This planet—Molx, isn't it?—is a little different: much drier, the soil has a little different mineral composition. I think we can harvest some of the bushes around us for fertilizer."

"Okay, George." Malcolm Carpenter stopped the litany and wondered how long his friend might have gone on. He didn't have the time to waste. "I should have known. Ordinarily I would have. I wanted to see you sooner than this. Just too much to do and it keeps piling up."

"Been hearing. Crown's had a pretty busy schedule, too, what with the new mother and baby and Cantro and Gonzalez, who's repairing quickly, I might add. Should be down only a few days. I've pretty much got things in order. Wha'd ya need?"

"Your analysis. You've got good sources, I know. What's your take?"

Strumpf tilted his head up. He was four inches shorter than the commander. With a grin that enhanced his light brown eyes, he stifled a chuckle. "Malcolm, you don't need my assessment for any other reason than corroboration. We've never disagreed."

"That's true, George; but I don't have your insights. I'm learning. You and Varlez keep pouring stuff into me. So what do I need to know?"

"I suppose we might." Strumpf nodded at the Carpenter's praise and assessment. "You're an eager student."

Commander Carpenter looked down his nose at Strumpf. He didn't want to waste more time with George's adulation.

Strumpf changed course at the look. "We haven't been here long enough to understand the natives, but they're probably as transparent as they seem. They really don't have any idea how long they can live here. Provided we don't disturb them too much, they may help us get off this dead orb. The navigator is only a problem if he really manages to capture colonists. I know the missing four are probably his work. Below the tarmac has to be explored and with a small force. Maelstrom is vital for that effort, if she isn't useless after her procedure and she's not still accessible to the computer. She's the only one who's been down there except for the navigator. He's not good for anything. Maybe *he* should be downloaded."

"You know what Varlez said about Maelstrom yesterday and she had a pretty rough night. Seemed past that. She even asked if LeRoi had vanished. You up for a not-so-sneak attack?"

"How soon?" Strumpf's answering question didn't project any eagerness.

"How long to gather a force of a dozen or so?"

"Shouldn't take more than a minute, given the mood of the colony. I'll probably have too many volunteers. Why me?"

"Sharp's the natural choice but I want him and Crown with me to see Vokra. Maybe offer an incentive for their help."

"They're good at planning. They've already been where you have to go. And you've already discussed with Crelle and Vokra. Good luck there."

"It's hard to know what role she's playing, if her group really is outcast. They could be shills."

"I've wondered about that. Don't think they are, but they may know other ways to get below where we are. I'd like to believe they are as they say, that they aren't misdirection for what the navigator is tied into."

"Don't know what Forbes is doing; he'd be the choice after Sharp ... imagine he's keeping silent by choice. Might be in serious trouble. That makes you the next option to lead."

"What'll I do with him, if we get him?"

"LeRoi?" The commander didn't need to give the name. "Probably what we should have done and didn't: tie him up, strap him to his couch."

"Then there's still the problem of shutting down what's snared him and us."

"And figuring how to release our gauges. Battle under the tarmac might solve that, but if I were downloading personality, trying to download it, I'd separate the main server from the download."

"So do we genocide the digital portion of the Molrixx?" Strumpf was the third to raise the ethical conundrum.

"And the rows and stacks of suspended brains that Maelstrom said she saw. Haven't solved that dilemma," Carpenter answered and shook his head. He'd thought a lot about hastening extinction of the Molrixx and dooming his crew and settlers by remaining on Molx. Nor was he ready to save the human mission at the cost of the Molrixx. He still hoped something new would appear to keep genocide from entering the equation and he wouldn't have to make the fatal choice.

ALIENS

High above Planet Molx six alien craft parked in synchronous orbit. Five surrounded the *Marco P* at a discrete distance. Each interested race had determined the Earth vessel was a vacant shell, although recently they all had monitored increased electronic activity from Molx into and out of the Earther's main computer.

"What a stupid move," Chief of the Mqros4 embassy ship *Vento* commented to the other four over a secure open channel. "Leaving an empty parked vessel with little fuel is marooning themselves ... on Molx. Earthers have no business in our sector. I shouldn't be wasting time watching while my delegation is heading for the Intra-G games."

"I seem to remember a Mqros ship was lost around Molx; ... how long ago was that?" Zebza's Trbny of the *Chylkr* chided Chief of the *Vento*. "Did you ever find that crew?"

"You know we didn't. But that Chief was a tyro and he diverted, fatally so, from his scheduled course. He managed a panicked report that he'd lost all power."

"Kind of like the Earther ship?" Primt of the Vocres *Alroche* said. "Perhaps you should get to the I-G games. Molx capturing crews is old history to you."

Main Office of the Xantrel's *Borsac* had listened to the sniping commonly engaged whenever the Mqros4s and Zebzas were within communication range. He joined in, "At least you may not have to worry about losing Mqros2 to an alien race, Chief. Seems like you've already decided the Earthers are lost. We're hanging around to see what *does* happen. Our teams are already housed at the games."

"The Mqros4s can't imagine any young aliens able to do what they couldn't," Proform of the Grekre transport *Mokren* joined in to gik the Mqros4 Chief.

"And you'd be comfortable with the upstarts succeeding where you failed, too," the Mqros4 Chief challenged Proform.

"As competitive as ever," Proform returned. "If the Earthers do succeed in escaping, I hope they won't have more trouble when they take possession of Mqros2. I can imagine a lot of blustering harassment from a species that doesn't even want to live on that wet orb."

"Yes, we're competitive, Proform, and we're good. Remember where we placed in the last games? The Earthers can have Mqros2 with our good wishes. We just don't want them invading the other planets and satellites in our system."

"Not a worry," Primt from the *Alroche* joined. "Earthers only extend their outermost borders. They're not interested in filling up any system in between."

"That's right," Main Office agreed. "They seemed obsessed with getting as far from their home world as possible. Seems to us that they can't stand each other."

"It's an Earther competition within their own kind to extend their frontiers," Primt said. "Spectator interest is to see what they do when they reach the edge of the galaxy."

"I hate to drag you away from your character assassinations," Zebza's Trbny alerted from the *Chylkr*, "but seems to me you haven't been watching. The Earthers' complement has diminished. I've been monitoring the Molx communication with the interface. Can't say if the rest of the Earthers are aware of him."

"There were two Earthers with computer interfaces," Main Office added. "One has vanished."

"Maybe we'll learn what happened to our novice chief and his ambassadors," Chief said. "Earthers may at last explain that mystery."

"That's been a mystery for us, too," Proform admitted. "We've had some theories, but weren't willing to chance more lives to find out."

"Agreed," chimed Trbny.

Each from their own ship monitored the computer on the *Marco P* and increased magnification of the tarmac and surrounding area that was nearly vacant of aliens except for three exceptions. They saw a rover following tracks west. The machine that made the original tracks was not in sight. A group of a dozen was forming on the east edge of the white. Three Earthers were heading to the mountain construction.

Despite the thinly disguised species gibes, all five races

were rooting for Earther success, though none of them would have admitted it to each other.

The planet-bound Molrixx had proven themselves aloof, xenophobic, and belligerent. In some ways, they had demonstrated they were more powerful—on Molx—than any other race. They had managed to rebuff all attempts to bring them into galactic society, apparently killing ambassadors of several species and defying civilized altruism. That they had not left their planet was the only solace other races took comfort in. None could imagine the destruction the Molrixx might wreak on other planets, if they should become space faring.

Now they had Earther shuttles, fifteen of them, and an Earther space vessel, if they should decide to use them all.

The small complement of young Earther spacers seemed the only thing now keeping the Molrixx from rampaging through the galaxy.

HUMANS

Strumpf had no trouble gathering a small invasion force when he yelled out for help, a call everyone had been waiting for. Commander Carpenter even heard loud grumbling from the crowd of another fifteen whom Strumpf turned away. By the time Crown and Sharp had joined the commander to revisit Molox1, Strumpf's small unit was marching with a willing Maelstrom among them and heading for the edge of the tarmac and the short trek to the podium that opened the repository stairway.

At the northeast corner of the tarmac, the commander remembered his counsel against solitary adventures into the overgrown areas. His two steps onto the narrow worn path, which he knew had frequent use, had been his only venture off the tarmac. His slowing forced the two who had already taken the path to stop and wait for him.

"Nothing to be concerned about," Sharp urged the commander. "We've been here twice now."

"No Hisliks here," Crown joked. "They need soft ground to dig into, like where Cantro got bit. The path is well worn. Don't let the image fool you, we're quite a ways from the entrance."

The slight incline wasn't tiring and the shoulder-high bushes didn't become shorter for half a mile. The commander surveyed the landscape as he passed through it, spending little time watching his footing as Crown and Sharp led. His peripheral vision kept him on the path.

Then, within a single pace, the brush became knee-high and five paces farther on merely ankle-high. The ovate leaves within the same short distance mutated from rich deep green to serrated fractal edges in light dusty green. The stems and branches and twigs, hidden under the leaves nearer the tarmac, were visible as dried understructure and barely able to support what only paces before evinced thriving vegetation.

Past the edges of the path, there was nothing but soft dry dirt blown into dunes and eddies where the wind sculpted it around small boulders and rocks. With barren landscape before him, Carpenter turned his full attention to the mountain construct and the jagged line of stairs up the side. Twice he almost fell, saving himself from that embarrassment by short quick steps. After the second misstep when he was finally able to identify the individual treads of the outside stairway and recognize the landings for what they were, Crown looked back and saw where his attention was.

"That's how Fred and I first got into the place to see about Canska."

"You climbed up the outside ... on that skinny way?"

"Yeah. You should've seen the one who went up further and then back down inside to let us in at the tenth floor. Looked like he was running. They say he comes down even faster."

"On the outside?" Carpenter asked again incredulously.

"We could take that way again," Sharp gibed. "We'd have to go up twenty-five floors, though."

"Inside will be fine," the commander said quickly. He'd been at the edges of cliffs before and looked down on planets from orbit. He couldn't imagine what it was like to be on the narrow edge of a sheer drop, nor was he anxious to find out.

"The stairs are solid, Commander," Sharp said. "Don't know how long they've been there, but I couldn't feel any wear as far up as we went. We came back down inside and I couldn't feel any difference in construction, inside or out. I'd have to say the Molrixx are ... were ... quality builders."

CONTACT SQUARED

Crelle and Vokra were waiting for the three humans when they neared the entrance to Molox1.

"Welcome, Commander," Crelle said. "Just a visit or have you some need?"

"A little of both," Commander Carpenter answered as he caught Crelle's touch of disgust at their presence.

"And Amanda and Fred," Vokra followed. "Nice to see you two again. Canska is much better. Did you come to see her?"

"No," Crown said. "The commander wanted to see you. He thought we should accompany him."

"We watched you on the path," Crelle said. "Didn't think you should have to climb the stairs. And we have some questions about your plans; didn't know how to ask, go to the white or wait for a visit we were sure you would make."

"Some of mine have already wandered through several floors and reported. But I wanted to see for myself," the commander said. "And I have questions, too. Maybe you could show us around a bit, while we talk."

"There's not much on the bottom floors," Vokra said. "Used to be energy distribution and manufacturing. None of that now. Ten and Twenty were the living quarters, if that's what you're looking for. But let's head up."

With a tight jaw, Crelle looked long at Carpenter after Vokra offered more friendliness than her second was willing to give.

"A few floors'd be okay," the commander said and ignored Crelle's glare.

When Carpenter gave no hint of his feelings, Crelle challenged, "Are you looking for more spacious lodging than your shuttles?"

"No, Crelle," the left side of the commander's mouth turned up, "we don't plan on staying on Molx and we aren't willing to take over where you live, even part of it. We can climb a little, while we talk."

For three flights, pleasantries and guarded words from

321

Crelle filled the stair-stepping: what did the Earthers think of Molx? How did they feel about the climate? Did the shuttles provide enough space to rest? Did they need any food?

However, the latest aliens to land on Molx slowed their conversation and pace by the fifth floor. Diminishing small talk implying the need for more serious conversation was not lost on Vokra or Crelle. Vokra led her visitors to sparse comfort of cushionless chairs at a fifth floor window that overlooked the forest north of the white.

After all were seated and the three humans had politely surveyed the view, Crelle anticipated the real purpose of the commander's visit by asking, "If you don't plan on staying, why are you here at all?" He wanted an expanded answer to Vokra's first question from the day before.

Not unware of Crelle's unshrouded animosity, the commander was still surprised by his blunt challenge and didn't answer immediately. With as blank an expression as he could muster, he looked back and forth between the two Molrixx, pausing at their large round eyes, and recognized that their heads were very large. He glanced at Crown and Sharp, not for support but to gauge their take on Crelle's nerve that Crown had seen but a hint of the day before.

Then he recalled Varlez's goading question if the Molrixx were offering a gambit.

He spoke to Crelle without giving away anything he had learned from Maelstrom about downloading human brains. "I'm a little embarrassed to admit that our ship and shuttles all indicated they were almost powerless. We had to land or die in space."

"Sounds like rumors of other aliens, long ago, who showed up on Molx," Vokra said. "But they disappeared. No one knows about them, what they did or where they went."

"Funny you should say that," the commander continued without having to mention Maelstrom's report of the repository. "About a dozen of our complement have gone missing. Maybe that's the same as what happened to the aliens of your past."

"And you think we had something to do with your missing people?" Crelle challenged with increasing rancor. He was laying the foundation for his own attack on intentions of aliens whom he distrusted.

"Not so accusing," Vokra said and held her hand up to Crelle.

"No offense taken," the commander said. "We've been on many inhabited planets where we might colonize. We are always looked upon as squatters and have to watch to keep from making that quick assessment a reality." He did not add, "and defend against attacks from natives."

"We noticed that there didn't seem to be so many of you out on the white," Vokra said. "If you were going to stay, I'd think there'd be more out and away and moving into the forest, which you aren't doing. Where can you get the power you need to leave Molx?"

"That was a special problem we've never experienced before. We think we know the answer, and that's one reason I've come. If we're right, we need your help, if you can or will give it."

Crelle sneered. "Either we help you or you stay and limit our lives?"

"If we must stay on Molx," Sharp tried to soften the implication, "I'm sure we can help your lives, at least for a while."

"Just what do you need from us?" Vokra asked trying to conciliate her second's growing animosity. "If our help will get you away and we can reclaim our lives, I can't see that as bad."

Crelle furrowed his brow and looked askance at Vokra who seemed ready to be more open than he thought wise.

Carpenter looked hard at Vokra, too. He had similar concerns to those Crelle obviously had. Was it safe to broach what he needed to know? Was she aware of what was planned for his crew? Was her group really not a part of the planned downloading?

The commander looked over her head and stared at a scrawled graffiti, *"Cownsl Kils,"* on the wall of the landing on the fifth floor and was entranced by a slight dent in the wall, like someone had hit it with a fist.

Vokra was ready to ask, "Well?" when the commander dropped his sight back to her eyes. Carpenter inhaled deeply and let out half of it. He decided on candor.

"Vokra ... and Crelle," looking to acknowledge the partnership in authority, "the loss of power we experienced was caused by interference from Molx. There's a strong electronic force that drew us from our intended course to this planet. For our own safety, we had to land. We have since learned that some power intends to download our brains."

Crelle was skeptical of Carpenter's reason and wondered how an alien might know what Council had ordered the Molrixx to do. He hurried to question before the commander could continue. "You roam the stars and no doubt repel enemies far more powerful than we are and you claim this planet brought you here for your brains? How could it ... or we... know anything about you?"

Vokra couldn't imagine any connection between a space traveling species and the Molrixx. Nothing in all the history of the Molrixx was there a hint of traveling in space that was the only way she thought these aliens might be known. There were stories of aliens coming to Molx but none of Molrixx leaving for space.

The commander continued. "Long, long ago our people thought they could be immortal if they translated their thoughts and memories and emotions into computerized data, as if merely existing was enough for living, just as all the Molrixx apparently did —except for your group."

Both Crelle's and Vokra's eyes widened. They smiled and looked at each other knowingly and back to the commander. "We're living as primitives," Vokra explained, "because we refused that."

"Commander," Crelle's attitude lost some of its snippiness, "I'm sure you saw the other molox constructions as you circled to land. When the planet became more and more uninhabitable, our ancestors built these population centers in hopes of staying ahead of certain extinction. Then Councils decided that all would be downloaded and saved until the planet reversed itself, if it ever did."

Vokra added. "Over time, each of us, who are still living Molrixx, learned what was happening and rejected the procedure by escaping. We weren't sure how we'd live away from the molox, but we knew we didn't want to be part of a storage system. And there was never any possibility of learning new things. Digitizing allowed for no additions. But why you, Commander? What can you offer to the digital storage?" Vokra finished with the very question Carpenter wanted the answer to.

"I hoped we might learn that answer from you. It seemed to me that aliens have landed on Molx before us; you weren't all that frightened or surprised by our arrival. What happened to them?"

"No one knows," Crelle said, "though it's been a long time since the last aliens—before you—are supposed to have shown up. There are no tales about them leaving or becoming part of Molx society."

"We always thought that digitizing the population was a more recent thing," Vokra added. "We might just have got in on the last part of it. Krolni said he discovered that some of his research said that downloading corresponded to the inhabiting of Molx1."

"Commander," Crelle's tone was even more conciliatory, but no less blaming, "your honesty has explained some other events that have effected us. I'd wondered just what your role in those might have been."

"Oh?" the commander said and looked over at Sharp and Crown. "We knew we'd disturbed your lives, but beyond limiting your coming and going, we didn't know how. Though we were well aware that Molx is failing as a habitable planet."

"Electronics on our part, too," Vokra said. "Before you arrived, the little power that still flowed through Molox1 vanished. Then the main entrance shut and we were locked outside. It wasn't hard to imagine that a species that travels outside the planet might want some planetary home, as bad as this one is. We could see our lives ending as slaves or dying for lack of food. And when Wisolen cared for your man bit by the Hislik, we were pretty sure he'd made the wrong decision, though a Hislik bite is not fatal to us. But when Pwok took his daughter to you, I feared what might happen."

"When Crown discovered that Cantro's bite had been ministered to," the commander said, "we knew someone lived here and at least one wasn't an enemy. That knowledge made our presence even more problematic."

"Then Amanda came to doctor Canska, even climbing up the outside," Vokra nodded praise at Crown, "and we realized you weren't enemies. If you were, Canska and her daughter would have been allowed to die. It was obvious that we didn't have the medicine or care to treat them."

"To the matter at hand," Crelle interrupted the praise party, "just what can we offer to help you leave and let us get back to our regular lives?"

"And maybe get back a little of the power we seem to have lost in this building," Vokra added.

Commander Carpenter recognized that his candor was reciprocated and he continued. "We think we can stop the attempts to download our people's personalities. That process will kill us. That was the real reason we stopped the experiment on Earth long ago. We couldn't put personality back into a brain. The digital representation was just that, encoded information—individually personal to be sure—but unrelated to any other information once it was removed. The interconnections were lost. They couldn't be reintegrated."

"Krolni discovered that lack of integration just before he escaped," Crelle said. "How are you going to stop the process? We don't even know where it ever took place."

Vokra said, "There are several locked areas on different floors that are probably banks of personality servers and storages. Most of us from the moloxes had duties to monitor the constant readouts of those storages."

"Yeah," Crelle agreed. "Council didn't want us mixing with others so they hid us away watching screens. Eventually we all knew what was going on."

"Then you understand our aversion to being put into digital storage," Crown said. "We know the one Earther who is connected, computer-wise, with the electronic system that is directing him to take us to be downloaded." She looked at Sharp for agreement and he nodded.

Sharp added, "He seems to have taken four of our people down below where our shuttles are parked. We don't know how much time we have for rescue, or if that's even possible."

The commander took over before Sharp could continue. "There is a small force that may take the spy into custody and free the four provided they are still alive."

Vokra looked surprised at that information. "We never knew where that took place. I came from Molox3, about fifty Xel north. Our group is all from Molox1 and 3 except for Cans-ka and Pwok who made it here from Elthren, more north and east. Every center had that white area. We never knew what it was for."

"Apparently that digitizing was planned from the very start," Crelle said and added as his paranoia again took hold, "suppose Councils set out to destroy the planet as the first step in their immortality aim?"

"We've discovered one way under—you call it the white? It looked like a landing area to us, but certainly colored differ-ently. Are there other ways in?" Commander Carpenter asked. "It would certainly be helpful if we could get in from different directions."

"I can't imagine Council leading anyone out of a complex to be downloaded," Vokra thought out loud. "Crelle's been all over the lower floors." Then turning to her co-command, she asked, "Did you ever find something that could have led lower than the first floor?"

"Never looked for that. Lots of doors down there. Most locked so I just left them. Besides we didn't really have any-thing that might have broken them down. With help, or spe-cial tools," he looked directly at Carpenter, "we might discover something."

"Like a central system?" the commander offered.

"That has captured your computers?" Vokra suggested.

"And that would serve both of us well," Malcolm Carpen-ter agreed to her implication.

"Well, Commander," Crelle summed up, "we know what you need and perhaps we can offer some help. We need you to leave Molx so we can get back to our lives. Maybe we'll con-tinue until the planet dies, and we'll go with it like free Molrixx who haven't existed for maybe decades, centuries, except for us. Or Molx may recover, if Council caused its illness, and we'll continue and make it a better place than it was."

Carpenter was silent. Crelle had unexpectedly hinted at the essence of his moral dilemma. Another breath preceded the commander's silence that didn't include an exhale and captured four attentions.

Neither Vokra nor Crelle understood what else needed to be brought up and their faces were washed in puzzlement. Sharp was almost totally relaxed. He knew they'd soon be off Molx and he was anticipating reaching γ-Cygnus A2 where building a settlement would be child's play compared to the last few days. Only Crown was waiting for the next topic, one she and Strumpf had often discussed, one that arose whenever humans landed on a planet, unexpectedly inhabited: whose rights are paramount and what does justice demand.

The commander fully exhaled and took another breath. He looked away, searching for the right words, and returned his focus to Vokra. "This is not easy." He spoke in a husky voice and cleared his throat. "And what we've agreed on, seemed to agree on, may be sacrificed."

Sharp's elation at getting on with the mission vanished and he sat at attention, ready for … a physical skirmish.

Crelle's skepticism returned and his posture went rigid.

Vokra tilted her head a little to the right and furrowed her brow. "We're not going to attack you, Commander. I don't think you're going to attack us. We've been through that. I don't understand what could abrogate what we've agreed on."

"No, Vokra, there's no attacking you and us, but there are other considerations that come into play if we do leave Molx. Those affect us, directly, and you, maybe directly, maybe not."

"You're going to have to be clearer," Crelle said. "Should you recover your four and we find the central computer and disable it, you'll leave. What else is there?"

Carpenter smiled that Crelle's simplistic solution was ignorant of the developing parameters. "Below the white are stacks and rows of preserved brains, thousands of them. They likely are matched to the storage of information the brains held before they were digitized."

"So?" Crelle said, unable to understand why the commander could be so ignorant of the Molx situation.

Carpenter realized Crelle's ethics were not encumbered by the ramifications his moral code demanded. "If we disable the system long enough to escape Molx, what happens to the part of the system that preserves the brains or that preserves the brains' information? Disrupting the system that hacked our computer may destroy its storage and seriously hamper brain preservation."

Vokra's eyes widened and she gasped. She realized the long history of Molx and all its discoveries and learning could vanish along with cloning reanimation of the digitized Molrixx.

"You'd continue your mission," Crelle said, unmoved. He repeated, "You'd continue your mission and leave us alone on Molx. There's no advantage to having downloaded Molrixx resurrected. They are the source of our current problem."

The commander looked at Crelle. He wondered if Vokra's second was amoral.

"I see," Vokra said. She noticed Crown nodding in anticipation of her understanding. "All the Molrixx in digital and brain preservation may die, if that's the right word." She turned to Carpenter. "You can't exterminate a species, can you? ... if they are the same as we."

"No, I can't," Carpenter answered. "Nor can we exterminate you, which happens, if we can't leave."

"But it's our planet, Commander. You don't belong here." Crelle's was the simple solution.

"Yes, we don't belong here, and we didn't come willingly. We were captured and we must do what we can to escape. Some of us believe we have every right to do whatever we must to escape—even commit genocide. That's an unpopular idea, but our moralists haven't arrived at a clear solution to something that will come up again and again as we humans continue across the galaxy."

"Even though your people rejected digitizing, and we escaped to keep from having it done to us," Vokra said, "you won't leave if it means destroying the chance that digitized storage and preserved brains can be resurrected, whether the process works or not."

The commander nodded at Vokra's grasp of his moral dilemma.

"And you'll fight us for the remaining land that provides us with food, if you don't leave." Crelle cleared up his earlier implication.

"You wouldn't expect otherwise, would you," Carpenter challenged.

"I suppose not," Crelle agreed and added "your people will be our enemies and our lives will be threatened the same as you feel yours are. We will fight you."

Vokra laid her hand on Crelle's arm and cautioned, "It's not come to that, Crelle. A little patience, for now." Then she turned to the commander. "If we find the main server, we don't have anyone who knows about programming it. All of us were just users. Do you have someone who can program?"

"I do. He's very good and he has exceptional help. But we first have to find the controlling server and then we have to figure out if we can put it on hold while we leave."

"And if you shut it down and don't tell us that?" Vokra suggested, "You'll leave and we'll still be without power and the digital Molrixx will be gone. I don't think that's good."

"That will not happen," the commander said. "We cannot destroy your population that may be in stasis. They didn't capture us and they're not accessories to that capture, though I have several who maintain that even in stasis, they were party to the initial plans to capture us, or any alien species passing by."

HUMANS

"Easy trail," Chas Belnap said out loud to no one in particular. Following Forbes's rover was easy until Cantro's trio ran into a broad swath of taller, hardier bushes that they couldn't see over nor tell how far they stretched. Forbes's rover had left a triple set of tracks, one pointing west, as the direction had been, and two other directions, northwest and southwest. All three parallel sets of squashed flora extended out of sight.

"Ben, which way?" Belnap asked when he stopped in front of the tri-junction. Cantro and Rici Telden had been scouring the passing land for any signs to indicate what Forbes and his companions had done.

"The way they went has to be what hasn't been backed over." Telden spoke the obvious. No verbal agreement came, just nods.

"Northwest," Cantro said. "Still not much different from the other two. What's your take, Rici?"

Telden said southwest was less squashed.

"We know its not forward," Cantro said. "The greenery seems to be pushed forward, like the wheels were really revved in reverse. Bemly didn't like having to redo anything. I can see her spinning the mesh as she backed out. I see more of that on the southwest fork which would be her second eruption at having to back out a second time."

"Now I see that," Telden agreed. "The right fork should be it."

"It's what I thought," Belnap said and he eased the rover's large mesh wheels northwest. "I hope we're right," he muttered under his breath. "I understand Bemly not wanting to backtrack."

Bouncing over small boulders and scraping the sides of their rover, they crept along for almost an hour before Forbes's tracks veered south through a narrow opening that skirted the southern edge of the forest next to the heavy shrubbery.

Another hour at a bit faster speed finally brought them to an unobstructed view west. Tufts of tall spiky green blades as

331

tall as the bottom of the rover cab and reminiscent of sedge-like river growth were widely scattered over the dry ground for several hundred yards. Belnap steered the rover over tracks already laid down, except where no tracks were visible, where Forbes's machine had lost traction in sandy pits.

"Looks like the land is not all solid," Belnap said aloud. "Another set of eyes up here would be good. Looks like their wheels spun out every so often." Before anyone could join him, he yelled out. "There! See! You can't see tracks on the right. They slipped into some deep sand. Good thing we've got independent wheel motors."

"Okay," Cantro said, "I'll watch with you. Maybe we can miss ..."

"Not entirely," Belnap said as he was almost thrown from his seat. The rover jerked to the left as his attempt to miss the sand that had caught the right mesh wheels of Forbes's rover dropped them into a granular sump on the other side.

"Don't ease off," Cantro said, "or we'll never get out. Maybe that happened to Forbes."

With two watching the established trail, the cab six feet above the land and their pace slowing, Belnap was learning to avoid the sand pots Forbes had been repeatedly caught in. The green tufts marked the solid surface and Cantro wondered why Forbes's driver, if it were Bemly—Forbes was certainly not piloting the rover—hadn't learned that.

Then during a pause in concentration when the sedge-like plants erupted to cover a descending path and flattened by the earlier rover, both Cantro and Belnap looked ahead and gasped. The shadowed landscape Forbes had been curious about loomed in the near distance. Rover tracks headed toward the center of the strange view.

"Shouldn't we be able to see him now?" Belnap asked.

'Not if he's been trapped and sinking ... or sunk," Cantro answered. "Most people think quicksand is only wet, but it's not; too dry is just as dangerous. Maybe more, because it's dry."

"But, sir," Belnap countered. "We're out of the sandy area. Look, it's all green. That means the surface is solid."

"That's what we've just been over. Can't say it's still that way. Take care. I'll stay and watch."

The dense tufted green slope appeared to drop to the river that they expected to reach soon. Their view was unobstructed: down slope with rover tracks that looked to meet in the distance at a river that churned up not a bit of white rapid, the far bank mostly flat extended to the base of the bubble-topped mountains. From the west bank of the river inland for perhaps four miles and for a considerable distance north and south the land was shadow gray.

Belnap stopped the rover. Cantro opened the hatch, leaned out, and looked skyward. He had to check what he already knew; there were no clouds to create the shadow and Molx's star was short of directly overhead.

"Has to be a natural color," Cantro said to Belnap and Telden who had joined the driver. "The straight edges are like where we landed ... just different color."

"Okay," Telden said. "I've been watching out both sides, scope magnification times twenty. I haven't seen anything of Forbes except his tracks in front of us. S'pose he got washed down river?"

"Doesn't look that deep," Cantro said. "And if it is, you know these rovers float. I don't think we'll be able to drive out of the river straight ahead. The west bank looks formidable. Forbes probably went up or down looking for a place to cross."

"But that puts him away for a really long time. He wasn't supposed to be gone that long was he?" Belnap questioned.

"We'll keep going. He hasn't headed back; we haven't seen anything of him," Cantro explained. "Unless he found a quicker, easier way back, he'll return the way we got here,"

"If we keep following his tracks, then we'll be just a day behind him, if he's back at the tarmac," Belnap said.

"And if he's not?" Cantro asked. He wasn't willing to let anyone think they were just out on a jaunt. The two with him had to be ready for some emergency. He wasn't expecting that, but it was a possibility they had to be reminded of.

Belnap pushed the rover just a little faster. The tracks seemed firm and the rover jostled them when he twitched the steering rudder tied to the rear wheels. However, the gentle decline was interminable. Once he stopped to look up from staring at the Forbes's tracks, when he thought the river and shadow ought to be closer.

They weren't.

"Problem?" Cantro asked when the rover stopped. He had left his post forward and had joined Telden who was still scanning north and south without spotting anything that might be a rover.

"Just looking, sir," Belnap answered. "But we're not getting closer. Come and look."

"Tracks still in front of us?"

"As they've been. I didn't think this downhill could be this long. We can see everything clearly in front of us, but it hasn't changed in perspective. How can that be?"

"Different world," Cantro explained. It was the standard answer to anything that didn't fit experience, as if new worlds didn't follow the laws of physics and biology and chemistry.

Eventually they closed on the riverbank and Forbes's rover tracks turned south. Telden peering through his scope announced that not too far south was what looked like a ford, both banks sloping into the river. "If Forbes crossed, that's where he did. But, if he did, shouldn't we see him on the other side."

"We keep following," Cantro said. "This planet gives us a new mystery every time we solve one. It's beyond irksome. I'm starting to get mad."

"Took long enough," Belnap said under his breath.

Strumpf's unit, comprised of the heftiest members of the crew and settlement, were all male. Antini Lever, recognized as missing the previous afternoon, would have been a member had she answered the call. Her physical reputation for subduing arguing and recalcitrant diners was legendary.

"Suppose LeRoi conned Antini?" someone suggested.

"If so," another answered, "he doesn't know what he's holding onto."

Short work to rescue the four missing colonists was the presumption and repeated innumerable times as the unit closed on Maelstrom who was expected to provide entrance to the torture chamber under the tarmac. The separation from her interface was praised in many comments within Strumpf's slapped-together rescue force. Only a couple voiced reservations.

Maelstrom was standing just off from the commander's shuttle. With knitted brow, she looked around her and repeated her circular survey. She repeated it again. From his distance, Strumpf thought she looked lost.

She knew exactly where she was. The computer part of her brain, the interface that Varlez had rendered inoperable, was not responding, nor accessing, nor adding to its database. She had listened and not understood when he told her that her brain would recognize a void but not what it meant. She knew that Varlez had severed the external digital link but didn't realize that the separation ended the wireless power that drove the computer memory. The gnawing absence between the interface and her conscious brain was unidentified, like trying to remember what had been forgotten and not having a clue to what it was. She hoped that persistent nagging left soon.

She remembered her return to the command shuttle had seemed in a fog, and there were many gathered for a meeting or something. She thought all her senses weren't working. Yet she experienced nothing she hadn't already been familiar with—the flat white tarmac, the green hedge, settlers' comments. The group gathering had been strange and out of the ordinary. She recalled that there were a lot of vocal exchanges taking place. She remembered no particulars.

On her third sweep of the tarmac, Maelstrom saw Strumpf leading a group of huge men her way. Each carried a light torch strapped to his chest and some heavy construction or farming implement. All had para-rays or lasers fixed on a hip. Accompanying Strumpf was Ticia Bandi, who looked like a child among the large men. She trotted alongside until she slipped back from Strumpf into the mob and then dashed forward to catch up only to reduce her pace and fall back again.

Maelstrom remembered Bandi's insolent question about her and the commander and LeRoi's leading her below the tarmac and her being isolated on the *Marco P* and the commander's confiding in her.

The black hole of absence was shrinking. Her brain was closing off—eliminating—the route to the parallel data she had lived with for so long when everything in her brain had been regularly duplicated in the computer insert in her head and what the interface possessed had been injected into her brain.

"After LeRoi?" Maelstrom asked. The question popped out. It hadn't evolved from any thought process and seemed to override the lack of interface, though it had been on her mind when the commander debriefed her the day before.

"I'm ready," she reported to Strumpf when he stopped in front of her. She looked up at him and nodded to affirm her enlistment when he asked if she were sure.

The inert slim interface cable, now with a small bulbous end where Varlez had melted the nanos together and still long enough to hide under her tunic, brushed her collarbone when she turned her head. She twitched her left shoulder and felt the cable rub. Her right hand reached up and fingered the na-no-weave wire extruding from behind her ear. She discounted its presence with a shrug.

"He got four yesterday," Strumpf greeted her with the rea-son for his commandos. "Don't know if they've been done. You know what's down there?"

"I do and how to get there. You've got lights. You'll need them. Not sure about the robots."

The band of thirteen trooped to the edge of the tarmac, but not before Bandi and Maelstrom both homed in on the right edge of the molox as the route to the entry pedestal.

"No more of this squeezing through limbs and leaves and vines," Strumpf said and before anyone stepped off into the shrub-bushery, he called four men forward and told Bandi and Maelstrom to stand back. Behind the chopping, flying leaves, and small branches and chips of wood, he supervised a wide bush-wacked trail from the huge square landing surface to the small tarmac square covering the stairs to the download-ing chamber that Maelstrom said was a cavernous repository. The whacked avenue, cluttered with chips, leaves, and broken branches, extended ten yards and ended at the white covering hiding the stairway.

"Your turn," Strumpf said to Maelstrom who was eagerly following and happy not to snake her way through bushes and vines.

"It's there," the backup navigator said as she pointed to her left to three smooth-barked trees. "Just behind the middle one."

Bandi was already squeezing past bushes and dodging thorny limbs, heading for the spot within the three trees that she had seen when she and Arafa followed Maelstrom and Le-Roi the day before.

"Hold up," Strumpf called. He remembered more than once when someone new to a planet assumed safety and paid a severe price. The most frightening episode, one he always dreamed about the day before landing on a new planet, was when a settlement lead, without warning, was darted to death. It was a description that forced recall of an old Earth legend that porcupines launch their quills.

The planet hadn't looked much different than any other terrestrial body or even Earth. However, several solitary trees near the landing site looked much like Earth's pines. The densely needled trees were always centered in lush grassy areas that grew out twenty yards from the base of the tree trunk. A settlement lead decided not to continue his round-about meander away from the new site. He cut across the first green circular apron of a grove of trees. Two steps into the grass he was impaled by hundreds of tiny needles fired from the tree. His lingering death was caused by the punctures injecting a poison that slowly destroyed his lungs. By the time he managed to back out of the green and return to the settlement, the poison couldn't be counteracted. The settlement named the trees and their perimeter Earnest's Legacy after the dead settlement lead. Legacies were never fenced, lest the trees had greater range than the green apron, and no one ever stepped closer than five yards outside the death zone.

"Been here," Bandi answered with her back to Strumpf. She was in mid-step.

"Not *there*," he barked, anticipating where her foot would land. "Not another step before we whack out the area."

Strumpf's harsh tone was unmistakable. Bandi pulled her foot back. She pivoted, glared at Strumpf, and only managed, "But ..."

Her disdain hardly registered on Strumpf. A veteran of several new planet landings, he knew the importance of knowing for sure. He precluded her reason, "Only when Le-Roi was present and with Maelstrom. Both were interfaced. You can't be sure when an interface isn't present."

"There's nothing here but trees, bushes, and vines ..."

Disgusted at how unobservant Bandi was, Strumpf shook his head and interrupted, "And a capping mechanism and who knows what else for defense. Look at your feet. You might know engines, but we're not on the *Marco*."

Bandi dropped her gaze and the rest of the invasion unit looked where she did. Half a foot from her toes was the desiccated body of a small rodent. Two feet from it was the half-eaten body of a larger carnivore that looked feline. The inert form of a larger, identical dead animal was close.

She bounded back toward Strumpf and the men. "If there's a defense, how're we going to get to the podium?" she asked.

"First we have to find out if there is a defense; then we've got to find a way around it, if there is. But we don't just go charging in. Men, carefully, work at arm's length. It might be an electric zapper; might be nothing at all."

Clearing a broad way to the three trees only half the distance from the tarmac to the stairway cover took twice as long as the original avenue.

No one was struck dead.

Bandi was still the first one to the podium, dashing there before Maelstrom and Strumpf. However, she waited until they joined her. The other men, one hand on the light torch the other clutching a weapon, surrounded the cover ready to rush to rescue and capture and destroy.

"No button," Priscilla moaned. "There's supposed to be a button. Both times I was here with LeRoi, it popped up and he pushed it down. That's what opened the cover. I didn't notice if he did anything first."

She smoothed her hands over the face of the pedestal and then along the sides and underneath. She bent down and looked along the riser and at the base. It was all white light ripple like the tarmac. Where she had seen the button was no outline. No indentation or seam showed a change on the smooth surface.

Strumpf and Bandi waited patiently while Priscilla examined

what was a solitary unresponsive object. "Maybe because LeRoi's already down there, there's no button. Maybe only one entry at a time this way," Maelstrom conjectured.

George's eyes blazed anger at being unable to invade and rescue. The delay was maddening. His fury filled a look down at Bandi, who backed a step away.

"Not at you," he softened his posture with a slight explanation. "Go get Varlez and a cutting laser. We'll just remove the thing if it won't open for us." Then he smiled. "Tell him he's welcome to join us, if he'd like. I know he's no more fond of the navigator than I am."

"I will," Bandi said as she dashed away past the attack unit and across the tarmac.

Strumpf watched her go and then turned to his eager soldiers. "Rest. When Varlez gets here, we'll engage whatever is down there, including the navigator."

REPOSITORY

LeRoi startled to consciousness. He had no memory of darkness. His first four hesitant subjects were not next to him. He pivoted once, slower the second time. They had vanished. He looked to the download chair bathed in its overhead light and saw four robots coming alive, ready to mine the brains of the four delivered crew whom he didn't see.

Four Earthers and the interface were in the robots' memory. Nothing in their collective database matched the sudden disappearance of creatures possessing a brain. Their lenses spun and stopped and spun to new settings. Their torsos swiveled and the arms jerked spastically and pulled up to a ready position. But without sight of expected Earthers the arms dropped into standby.

They saw interface stomping around. His face reddened. The short fat pink horizontal line on his face opened and showed white behind the pink. He turned and moved sideways to the entrance. Then he pivoted and side-stepped from the entrance, pausing at each aisle. At the fourth row he stopped.

Input from interface: subjects row four.

He stopped again at row five.

Input from interface: subjects row five.

Four robots rolled toward interface. Two turned up row five; two, passed him and rolled up row four.

The four robots rolled into darkening gloom.

They saw no subjects and returned to the interface and coded their sensory details into a null statement.

LeRoi knew he had seen one couple down each row. When the robots returned, he looked again. The rows were empty.

SYSTEM

Acquisition: *Subjects vanished. Present before programming. Not after.*

Central Receiving: *Status of interface?*

A: *Returning to duty. Observed subjects. Vision hindered, returning. Subjects not observed.*

CR: *Status of robots?*

A: *Ready. Looping program. Criteria to run not met.*

CR: *Earther novelty must not be lost. If subjects not available, download interface.*

A: *Other subjects will not be made available.*

CR: *Secondary interface must be acquired. Employ all possible power.*

A: *Power is still decreasing. Cause not discovered.*

CR: *I will not be denied Earther novelty. Shut down power to all moloxes except Molox1 and its repository. Spare no effort to acquire secondary interface.*

A: *Molrixx will lose potential brains from other moloxes. Memories will be lost. Access to them will vanish.*

CR: *Before energy drain shuts down other moloxes, upload all memories to system memory of Molox1. We access. If power continues to decrease, sever connection to Molox1 brains. We shall survive with the knowledge of the universe.*

REPOSITORY

Green monitor lights brightened and offered a hazy view of a larger intersecting aisle where they had spent most of their time trying to stay awake in the chill blackness, LeRoi's intended downloads were elated at returned dim sight. The downside hit all four at once: they could be seen and the robots were probably functional.

Mazzur and Shmidt had been the first couple recognized by LeRoi as he peered between brain rows three and four. However, as soon as he moved behind the fourth brain row, they signaled to Lever and Sanctor to move another row apart and drop down just inside the gap. They were slow in moving and the navigator caught sight of the second couple before they hid in brain row five. Once within the gap, they each moved one more row apart and hid before the gap.

They heard whirring as the robots rolled down the two empty aisles where LeRoi had seen each couple. However, the robots were programmed to retrieve brain content hidden in neurons. Searching for subjects down rows of brains was not in their program. They had extended their aisle search at least two gaps past where the four Earthers had hidden in the aisles between rows two and three and five and six.

The captives listening for mechanical whirring knew when the robots were crossing gaps and moved as far the sixth gap. They readied to scurry to another row and different aisles to hide in, if the robots extended their search outward.

They were amazed that the robots, in their brief and linear search, went in only one direction and returned to interface LeRoi. Convinced the robots were not still looking for them, they met in gap six of row four. They questioned whether LeRoi had the ability to direct the robots and doubted they could elude any systematic search.

And they clung to a precarious hope that Carpenter would send someone to find them, if he had any idea where they were.

Shmidt said he'd overheard the engineers discussing that

Maelstrom and LeRoi had disappeared twice from the tarmac and added that stories of Varlez's harem following them were common knowledge. He was sure their companions could piece together where they might be to explain why their daily duties had been ignored for most of a day—maybe more—and why they hadn't reported to the S-O-S.

In voices so quiet that they could be lip-reading, not listening, they discussed advantages of sneaking further down the rows or moving closer to the door and the main aisle. Sanctor thought that they might be able to pry open the door and sneak out, but lifting the covering over the stairs, if it dropped, could be a problem. However, Lever doubted that plan could work because they would be within sight of the chair and the robots around it.

Mazzur and Schmidt lobbied for heading deeper into the repository and into darker areas. Then Lever conjectured that there might be other main aisles where more robots waited or where other entries were. No one could see any light farther away and they discounted more lighted aisles or robots or torture chairs.

"Even if there are other entrances," Mazzur said, "we can't be sure we would trip anything to open the door."

Putting more distance between them and the navigator was agreed on and four gaps deeper into the darkness satisfied that plan.

Those gaps within the rows of conserved brains took them to a wider aisle, like the one they originally entered. In the dark, they barely saw each other across the aisle. They were fear-tired and despite the cold, they sat and leaned back against the stacked brain boxes.

"One at a time might sleep," Sanctor whispered. "The others can wake us, if we snore."

"And we wait," Mazzur sighed. "I had no idea colonizing was this stressful."

"You know we're not where we're supposed to be." Shmidt spoke as he inhaled. "Uninhabited planets offer completely different things to be worried about. But they don't chase you ... unless you're trying to kill them."

"All the same," Mazzur returned. "I hope they don't take

too long to look for us."

"Amen," sighed three.

Not seeing subjects that had been brought, the robots surrounded and pried into interface's memory. Their database had no command for no subjects when subjects were promised and had been seen. One robot, behind the navigator, picked him up and carried him to the chair. The other three followed.

Interface became a subject.

Under the circumstance, impossible even for a Fred Sharp, LeRoi offered a puny attempt to break free. With his soft body and against four robot arms, the navigator's futile struggle failed miserably. His arms and legs were quickly and roughly strapped down and the extraction helmet was lowered. It didn't fit over the helmet he already wore.

The robot that had carried LeRoi to the chair and clamped him in stopped the futile attempt to mesh the download helmet with LeRoi's computer interface helmet. Its arms dropped and the torso whirled around. This subject didn't fit. The robot possessed no instructions related to the interface problems that were mounting.

A second robot neared the chair and tried twisting the original helmet from the subject's head. Interface screamed, his face reddening even more and his eyes bulged, until the first robot ordered the second to stop. Both moved off and dropped their arms; their torsos spun and went dead. The remaining two robots, after several circular repeats of illogical information shut themselves off.

For the first time in his life with an interfaced computer connection, LeRoi's human side overruled the computer. Abject terror flooded from his human emotions. He feared losing his personal value that resulted from having his head twisted off his neck and having his brain sucked dry. Never again would he see the wonders of the galaxy or enjoy the pleasure of waking the crew. He dreaded losing his superior difference and keeping Maelstrom from navigating a ship. Beyond those personal affronts, he knew he was unfairly victimized but hardly realized it was how he had planned to sacrifice the other humans traveling in the *Marco P*.

Through his anguish and panicked anticipation even though the robots were now dormant, LeRoi felt the headache come on and saw the jaggies that signified a migraine. His were semi-circular in brilliant violet that blotted out just right of his central vision. He knew he was hyperventilating and could do nothing to slow his lungs. His heart raced. The helmet prevented him from looking around, though his sight was blurring and limited. He saw in fading shadowy images two robots that had shut themselves down. He wished he could do the same.

Then his body collapsed, though held secure by the body straps. His head fell forward. Roger LeRoi saw nothing and thought nothing.

HUMANS

A rafa returned with Varlez and Bandi. Their jumpsuits were streaked with wet swathes and sweat dripped freely from their faces. They carried with them bags and backpacks that held the equipment to set up a powerful cutting laser to remove the cover to the stairway and perhaps slice through the door into the repository. Varlez had also brought along some of his favorite explosives and a couple of hand lasers.

Strumpf was waiting for them at the edge of the tarmac. "Didn't waste much time," he said.

"I thought you'd need some help. Besides I wanted a little of that arrogant navigator. He's put my ... girls ... through all kinds of hell trying to keep him under control ... and then escaping. Bastard!"

"I didn't think you knew words like that, Engineer. Can't believe I had to turn down so many who wanted in on this escapade."

"You know we don't like to be forced into anything. What are we cutting into first?" Varlez asked.

Arafa and Bandi, eager to get at LeRoi as well, were bouncing from foot to foot. They weren't thinking about the four captives or getting through doors. They wanted a chance to manhandle LeRoi and drag him back to his seat where they were going to tie him down for good.

"Right over here. We couldn't get the cover open; it's a small piece of tarmac. You oughta burn right through it."

Strumpf led Varlez and his two sub-engineers toward the locked stairway. Unexpectedly the white rectangle raised up and slipped into the ground exposing the flight of twenty-five steps. At the bottom in front of a solid looking door was a landing that might accommodate fifteen people if they crowded together.

"Half of what you wanted is done. I just had to threaten," Varlez joked. "Hope the rest is as easy."

From the three trees, Maelstrom's voice rang out. "The button just popped up and I pressed it. Don't know why it wasn't there before."

"And the door at the bottom?" Strumpf asked.

"Didn't watch," Maelstrom apologized. "Gotta be some kind of switch. Maybe it's connected with the open stairs. It opened just as LeRoi and I stepped up to it."

"Okay, men," Strumpf called the unit to order. "I'll go down and see what's there. Be ready to follow."

He took two steps at a time. As soon as he stood on the landing, the door slid open and he saw LeRoi in a chair, his head bend forward. Two strange looking robots in front of him—they looked nothing like Molrixx—appeared inert, as did the two behind the chair that held the bound navigator.

"We've been welcomed; join me," he called to his small force that eagerly started down.

Before he could cross the threshold, the door slid closed, shutting him off from the robots and LeRoi and the four settlers, if they were alive. He agonized that if LeRoi were being downloaded, the others were already dead.

"NO!" he shouted at the top of his voice and took the steps up two at a time and through his men who were too stunned to do anything but watch a normally staid Strumpf act like a cranky child.

When Strumpf got to the top and saw Varlez setting up the laser on its platform for precise cutting, he said, "Looks like you do get to perform, anyway."

"I can do that, all right. The door didn't sound so solid when it slid open and closed. But I've got another thought. Won't take long to check."

Strumpf grunted. "Don't know what it could be."

Varlez smiled. "An override code. Easy to check. Pick someone to go down with you. We'll just re-start."

Strumpf wrinkled his brow and looked at Varlez as if he were crazy. He knew better. "Okay. Anyone?" He was going to play with the engineer.

"Except me," Varlez said.

"Bandi, join me."

Strumpf readied to take the first step down.

"Wait," Varlez warned. "We have to start from the beginning."

"And that's what?" Strumpf asked.

"The button. It's over there for a reason," he said and looked to Maelstrom at the podium within the three trees. "Button there?" he called.

"Yes. You want me to push it, again?"

"Yes," he answered. "I think I have it figured out. Strumpf and Ticia are about to prove it."

"Pushed," was Maelstrom's answer over the top of Varlez's explanation.

"Let's go down together," Strumpf suggested to Bandi. "Just to humor Varlez."

"I think he knows what's going on," Bandi said. "I'm pretty sure I know and he's right."

Strumpf's sigh was a loud grumble. He'd love to prove Varlez wrong.

Bandi and Strumpf together stepped onto the landing and the door slid open. This time Bandi saw LeRoi and the robots, while Strumpf turned back to shout up to Varlez, "So?"

Varlez turned to the closest armed settler and told him to take the first step. When he did, the door slid shut again.

"He knows," Bandi said, her eyes sparkling, "and I know, too. We go res-cue," her voice caught as she realized how long the four had been gone and for some reason LeRoi, himself, seemed an ex-Judas goat directing the crew to the repository, though she didn't understand why he was in the download chair.

"Looks like someone's looking for us," Bemly said. "They're right on our tracks. Tried the rover one more time. We're still dead in the water, so to speak."

"We blazed the trail for them," Rostaq groused. "They should have been faster than us."

"Break out a cable," Forbes said. "They can pull the rover back across the river. Maybe we should meet them on the other side." Forbes had a premonition: four of them unconscious after he dug at the gray tarmac, the dead rover when it should have charged throughout their hours bouncing to reach the river.

He looked at Almi Penser. She wasn't comfortable. "It's one thing to ride a rover over here," she said. "Something else to walk back." Almi was little taller than Maelstrom. She'd tried crossing a swift river on her previous planet and been swept off her feet and carried a hundred yards down stream before she was rescued. This crossing, despite the modest depth and current, was, for her, not the simplistic wading that Forbes imagined.

"We're not going without holding on to each other," Bemly said. She knew Penser's history and understood hydrophobia was insidious, sometimes even rising up for small puddles.

Forbes's crew watched the rescue rover bounce along the riverbank and they saw the driver and passengers hanging on to keep from being thrown about. Then the rover slowed and lumbered to the entrance of the ford, but held its direction south, not west across the river.

Their tracks cross here, Ben," Belnap said. But I don't see anything on the other side."

Telden had the scope out and he was sweeping it north to south and back. "Nothing, Ben, absolutely nothing but dry level land and that huge rectangle of shadow. Seems unbroken to the base of the range."

"We can see footprints and rover tracks down this side," Cantro pointed out. "They have to be over there. They didn't just disappear, did they?"

"Sir," Belnap added, "there's footprints there, too; coming and going or the other way. Who belongs to them and where are they?"

"And the tracks there just stop. Another mystery or just part of the last?" Cantro mumbled to himself. "I hate this."

However, he had determined to follow until something shouted loud enough that it was not the right decision. He directed Belnap to back up and start across the river.

Though the rover's speed was snail's pace, Cantro, watching the river out a side window and trying to gauge its depth, was almost thrown against the front window when Belnap jammed on the brakes.

Cantro turned an instant sore neck to yell at his driver, but stopped, when he saw, out of the corner of his eye, Forbes on the other bank waving his hands and arms back and forth X-like.

"Where …?"

"He was just there, like he was beamed down or some-thing." Belnap was without further explanation. "Just one more mystery, sir. They're piling up."

Telden had joined them at the foreport after being thrown to the deck by the rover's jolting stop. As they watched, Bemly, Penser, and Rostaq magically appeared on the far bank behind Forbes.

"And the rover?" Telden asked. He still held the scope to his eyes searching for anything that might have swallowed it or hidden it.

They watched Forbes issue orders. Rostaq acted disgusted, shook his head, and, finally cowed as Forbes glared at him. He reached out to link arms with Penser. Bemly linked her other arm and the three hesitantly stepped into the river.

Then Forbes turned around and disappeared. A moment later, he reappeared lugging and stretching out a cable that drooped close to the river but never got wet. Cantro decided the invisible end had to be tied to the rover that they couldn't see.

Cantro, Belnap and Telden jumped the four feet from the rover hatch to the soft ground and hurried down the sloping ford to help the three already about mid-stream. Bemly and Rostaq waved their free hands and yelled to keep their rescuers from entering the river.

Forbes was not far behind them as he played out and an-chored the cable to the front of Cantro's rover with barely two feet to spare. Then he turned to see six astonished faces. When he looked across the river, he understood. His rover wasn't vis-ible and he wondered if the power surge that had knocked them unconscious and killed rover power had also created an electronic shield.

His first question, however, was to Ben Cantro. "You got power?"

Cantro screwed up his face and replied, "What?"

"Power? Are you dead?"

"Don't think so. Stopping as fast as we did shouldn't have done anything to our energy."

"My rover's dead. You'll have to pull it to this side and

then drag it back to the tarmac. I'll explain once we get underway, if we can."

Cantro's instruments showed full power. The winch
wound the cable onto an empty spool as Forbes's rover was
pulled back to the east bank with only two dicey spots when
the wheels, set in neutral, caught on something in the riverbed and stopped turning. Twice the cable threatened to snap.
Belnap eased the tension, let the river flow freely through the
mesh wheels and pulled again. Both times whatever had held
the wheels broke loose and the rover resumed its backward
route.

When Belnap finally pulled the rover almost against his
own, he engaged reverse and pulled Forbes' powerless vehicle
completely out of the ford and onto the dry bank. Then Forbes
disconnected the cable. Belnap swung around and backed to
the front of the disabled rover. Cantro and Forbes tied it to the
back of the working rover with a twenty-foot cable.

"We've been gone a lot longer than I'd planned. Let's get
back," Forbes said. Then he turned to Rostaq and said, "You get
to ride in ours and steer. Pay attention to the tracks."

Forbes saw Rostaq's back straighten and his face go rigid.
He opened his mouth to challenge the order, but said nothing.

"I'd like to ride back with Wymal," Penser said.

Forbes just nodded.

Rostaq and Penser climbed into the dead rover and signed
that they were ready. Soon the tandem rovers were retracing
the twice driven tracks to the river.

"And now, so do I, Ticia," Strumpf said. "Let's climb up and we
can come down for the last time."

When he climbed the steps for the third time, he looked
down at Varlez and said, "You called it. I think we're ready."

Varlez turned to Maelstrom who was alone at the pedestal.
"One last time, Priscilla. Then get over here if you're gonna join
us down there."

Maelstrom blanched. "I've been there," she said and remembered going down the steps to see the chair, the stacks
and rows of immersed brains, the strange looking impersonal
machine robots: all more than a slight residue in her memory.

"If it's all right," her voice pleaded, like a child hoping against hope to be let out of something terrifying, "I'd rather stay up here." It was not the strong voice of self-assured Navigator Maelstrom.

Varlez understood. He'd heard similar requests made out of fear, most recently from Arafa at the beginning of this colony mission. She was less than eager to squeeze back down a tight tube to repair a connection and tried to talk Varlez out of giving her the job. However, she forced away the twinge of claustrophobia, when shapeless Bandi offered to make the repair for her. He chuckled remembering how Arafa's pride refused to let another do the job despite the fear when she anticipated the tight space.

"You've done more than your share, Priscilla," Varlez told her, "more than your share. Watch. If anyone comes to look, you can tell them what's going on."

Strumpf winked at Maelstrom and backed up Varlez's comments. "Don't worry about staying up here."

Then he turned to the fourteen ready to do battle. "Let's rescue our people, men and harem." It was not a slur, though he saw five startle at the word. Bandi and Arafa were standing close to Varlez. The three smallest of the crew hardly looked the part of an assault team, but Strumpf had seen Varlez in action many times. He couldn't imagine his assistants to be any less capable. "It's gonna be awfully tight on the landing down there. Apparently the landing counts how many are coming down. Varlez, I suggest you bring the laser. Don't imagine we're gonna need the precision that the stand provides."

"Its arcing swath is deadly."

"Lights ready. Maelstrom described it as pretty dark. It was for the two brief looks I got." He looked over at Maelstrom who appeared in much better spirits not having to join them. "Hit the button."

Strumpf waited while Maelstrom walked from the pedestal to the stairs and then he led the invasion force down. Each man bore an intensity light strapped to his chest, a holstered para-laser with aiming light and carried a heavy construction tool: adze, pickaxe, crowbar, or maul.

Varlez, Arafa, and Bandi brought up the rear. The engineer

cradled the laser and wore its power pack over his left shoulder; his harem each carried one of the two hand lasers he brought and a side bag that held several small explosives.

Not armament for a dedicated army against an equal foe, Strumpf thought the weaponry more than enough for what the Molrixx might have. None could imagine more destructive measures in a repository that housed nothing but brains.

Varlez and Bandi stepped off the last step and the door slid open. Fifteen armed Earthers rushed into a chilly, semi-dark basement cavern. Three seconds after Bandi stepped across the threshold, the door slid noiselessly shut. The outside light from the stairway was cut off and Strumpf's unit stood in darkness.

Those in front saw the navigator, head forward, slumped in the download chair. He was surrounded by four glass mechanical things with metal arms.

"Not a robot like I've ever seen," someone said.

"The door's shut," came the unneeded announcement from the back.

"Lights," Strumpf shouted and added unnecessarily, "don't blind anyone."

The wide aisle leading to the chair occupied by LeRoi blazed with brilliant light from the chest lanterns. A communal gasp rose from the unit as all saw what the repository held. Brains, stacked seven high and back to back in their own clear boxes, were bathed in a pink syrupy liquid that flowed in a circular current into and out of the boxes holding them. The rows extended beyond the limit of their lights.

"That's what they were going to do to us?" Arafa questioned and shuddered. "If this is what Maelstrom saw, I don't blame her for not coming back down here."

"What about the four LeRoi already brought here? Are their brains in one of these boxes?"

"Better not be," came a threatening comment. "What do we do first, Strumpf?"

"I want you in pairs. Four of you get the navigator and disable the robots."

"And if he's dead?"

"Get him, anyway. We'll think of something to do with his body. The rest of you, head down between the rows. We won't leave until we find our four settlers, or what's left of them, no matter how long it takes. Varlez, see what you and the girls can do about opening the door."

"Destroying it?"

"Vaporize, if you must."

"And the brains? We might have to create another door to keep their atmosphere intact."

"We'll cross that later. Our safety and settlers are foremost."

Noise, loud voices, and brilliant flashing lights woke all four who escaped LeRoi and hid from the robots. Panicked that they were caught, they struggled to force cold limbs to move, as they helped each other to their feet. Bright beams, lots of them, knifed down aisles and across the top of the rows and accompanied familiar voices calling their names.

"A search party for us?" Lever asked. "How long did we sleep?"

"Not long with this much noise," Sanctor judged without realizing the potential danger in calling out his answer over the clamor.

"A human search party?" Mazzur asked with some relief. "I think I recognize a voice."

"Provided the robots haven't learned our names from LeRoi and they can mimic speech," Shmidt cautioned.

"I say we stay hidden a little longer," Lever said. "At least until they take out the robots that we know are down here. If they're our people, we can wait 'til they find us."

"Agreed," Sanctor said.

The four settlers sent to rescue LeRoi got within ten feet of the chair before the robots re-animated. Waving their long mechanical arms, they rushed at the invaders who backed away from the unexpected countercharge.

"The arms," Strumpf yelled out as he saw the four cower. "Strike at them. Your axes and bars are heavy enough to damage."

Nevertheless, the advancing robots proved an imposing attack force against the four settlers sent to recover the navigator's body. They lacked the bravery to match their intentions and they retreated further as the mechanical things advanced, each waving four arms.

One settler swinging his adze at an approaching robot hit in the center of an arm, where an elbow was, and separated the connection. The front of the limb whipped around with the upper part of the appendage continuing to swing about. The colonist's fortunate strike emboldened his companions. Despite the menacing actions of the long waving arms, some of which ended in scalpels and saws, the attacking settlers realized that the delicate work of harvesting brains, didn't require strength and durability.

Reversing their retreat and taking aim at the flailing arms, they quickly severed parts of or all of the arms from the vertical posts. Then closing on the mobile two-foot diameter torsos they repeatedly swung their heavy tools at the clear covering that housed the gearing and lenses and wiring, until the rolling foundations were stilled and the torsos crumbled on and around the bases.

LeRoi was still alive, though unconscious. The settlers unstrapped and roughly carried him to Strumpf where the navigator opened his eyes and needed support to keep his knees from buckling. He looked blankly at Strumpf.

"He can walk," Strumpf growled. "Just keep hold of him. I know what I want to do with him. But he's the commander's problem now."

In less time than it took to release LeRoi, Sanctor, Mazzur, Lever, and Shmidt were found. Those who discovered them whooped up their sudden surprise discovery. The rest of the assault team joined in the celebration that was muffled by the rows of encased brains. They congratulated each other and slapped backs and grinned broadly. The four who had escaped death were escorted to Strumpf who added his words of thanks to the rescuers.

When the freed captives reached the main aisle they had escaped from, LeRoi had just gained consciousness but had yet to say a word. They glared vile threats at him and would have pummeled him with their fists and feet, had three others not had him surrounded and in custody.

LeRoi saw but ignored the settlers' aborted vengeance.

Instead, he looked to Strumpf and yelled, "You've just relegated these people to extinction."

"Yes, maybe I have," Strumpf answered, "but you were willing to sacrifice all of us for their sake. That's a high crime you've committed. You've had your say. Don't open your mouth again."

The four settlers looked toward the closed entry and their elation at rescue ebbed. Mazzur's comment that the navigator's proximity was probably the password for the door was shouted down as the commando unit was ready to leave and still heaping loud congratulations on each other for their success.

Strumpf looked at the engineering trio and, not having heard Mazzur's suggestion, called out, "Found a way to get us out of here?"

"'Fraid not." Varlez was apologetic. "Might have to use the laser. I'd rather not."

Leading his unit that had surrounded the found settlers, Strumpf reached Varlez. The three holding LeRoi were close behind. When LeRoi was within ten feet of the door, it rolled open.

"More programming," Varlez said. "I doubt we can leave him in here; he's apparently the password."

"And the door stays intact," Strumpf conjectured. "We shouldn't have hurt the environment too badly, except for the robots and maybe the planned brain drain. Then he turned to his troops grouping up behind him and said, "Let's get out of here."

Strumpf stepped aside to leave after his men and just before LeRoi who had been transferred to his grasp. When LeRoi took the first step up the stairs, the door behind him sealed off the repository.

When Strumpf got to the top of the stairs, he was not surprised to see the commander and Sharp standing next to Maelstrom and presiding over the repository draw down.

Carpenter praised, "I knew you could do it, George. Good job."

The two rovers' return, at a much faster rate than their outbound course over a twice-marked trail, tossed the passengers about no less. Cantro and Belnap were eager to return. In the trailing rover, Rostaq consigned as steerer and Penser who volunteered to keep him company suffered more as they had no power to soften the bumps and drop-offs when the powered rover slowed and then sped up to keep the trailing rover from getting too close and bumping them. Rostaq was sure Forbes had had some hand in the speed regulation.

Pulling both rovers onto the tarmac, Belnap headed toward his shuttle in the second row. Across the tarmac, he saw small, intimate groups of people scattered around talking and looking about them expecting the unexpected.

None in the rovers imagined they would be greeted on return. However, as they crossed the tarmac, they saw the groups coalesce into a large body heading their direction. Belnap slowed.

"How could they possibly know we were near," Cantro questioned to no one.

"Now, what?" Forbes asked Cantro.

"Can't tell you, sir. We left before most were about. I can tell you that Gonzalez was badly hurt falling into a Molrixx animal trap. I figured he'd be the one to come looking for you, but he was in no shape for that—ugly fractured shin. So I took his place. He should get credit for your rescue."

"Reverse pay back?" Forbes asked. He'd heard about Cantro's first foray with Gonzalez.

"Something like that. I was an arrogant bastard. I know better, now. Thought this was the best way to make up for my stupidity."

"I think you've done it well, Cantro. Probably learned what it takes some of us a long time to understand."

"Thank you, sir. I appreciate that."

Rejecting what looked like a possible welcome, Forbes directed Belnap to drive to Sharp's shuttle where the rovers were housed and where his rover might be repaired or regenerated.

The marching mass that contained everyone from the *Marco P*, except the seven in the rovers and Gonzalez and Crown in the infirmary, might have been more properly described as a lynch mob.

Navigator LeRoi was back in the clutches of the three who

had taken charge of him in the repository which duty had been suspended while he climbed the steps. He and his guards were preceded by Commander Carpenter and Strumpf. Both were red-faced and jawing at each other, sometimes in turn but more frequently without waiting for the other to finish.

Occasionally their arguing ceased long enough for them to stop and look back at a still arrogant and unrepentant navigator. Then they resumed their argument with growing ferocity.

The brief breaks in the crew's speedy course across the tarmac invariably caused the followers to bunch up even closer and suffer repeated complaints of those they ran into from behind.

By the time Belnap began weaving between the shuttles for Sharp's, it was clear that they were not the object of the human complement. The controlled mob was heading for the engineering shuttle. LeRoi's helmet couldn't be mistaken, nor his arrested gait. Strumpf and Carpenter, red-faced and tight-jawed, looked like they were near blows, a situation none in the lead rover could imagine. Varlez, carrying a laser over his shoulder, and his harem with ammo bags over theirs, brought up the rear.

"Can you explain this, Cantro?" Forbes asked as he looked at the mobile mass and kept shaking his head. "We haven't been gone that long."

"Don't know for sure," Cantro began and paused as he searched for an explanation of the unusual activity. "Well, when you didn't return and Gonzalez and us were later than expected, the commander sounded the major alarm ..."

"*THE* alarm?"

"S-O-S. We heard it long before we managed to haul Gonzalez back to the tarmac and to Crown. I got the story from Crown. Seems LeRoi slipped away without being seen and he apparently gathered four for some procedure that would download their brains. I can only speculate what happened today. We left to look for you before anything about LeRoi developed."

"Well, LeRoi is definitely caught," Forbes said, "whether he got any for the procedure is something else. I sure wouldn't want to be in his place, given how the commander and Strumpf are at each other."

Then they saw Fred Sharp break away from the rest and head after the rovers.

"He'll tell us what's gone on," Forbes said. "Park this thing and let's go see."

Five jumped out of the stopped powered rover and hustled to meet Sharp. Rostaq and Penser, bedraggled from having been thrown about the towed rover, climbed down more gingerly and followed.

When Sharp reached the latecomers, he threw up his hands and shook his head to forestall the same question seven times. They crowded in front of him and he summarized: his trip with the commander to the molox, Strumpf's invasion force aided by Maelstrom and engineering, corralling the interfaced navigator and his terrorized captives, and destroying the robots and torture chair."

"Wow," Cantro said, "and all we did was go for a drive and find four AWOLs. Are we pikers, or what?"

"What's gonna happen to LeRoi?" Forbes asked. He wondered how one might categorize the crimes: kidnapping, treason, inhumanity for starters. Social wrongs extended the list to fraternizing with the enemy, anti-social behavior, ignoring orders, lying, narcissistic arrogance, lack of care for others. He was sure the crew could tally far more counts than he could.

"Carpenter and Strumpf argued that all the way to Varlez's shuttle. The rest of us heard it all. I don't think I should repeat that. I imagine that since you seven weren't here, you'll be the ones to ultimately decide the navigator's fate."

"Great!" Forbes said. "Cross a river and become a judge," His comment sounded like a joke; Sharp didn't laugh. "I didn't travel sleep-filled light years for this," Forbes complained.

"But you're a settlement lead, Kellan," Sharp interjected. "Things like this always come up. Part of being chosen for the job is a sense of wisdom. You got that."

"I don't want to divide, which is what's gonna happen no matter how we decide."

"Goes with the territory. I've been there. Carpenter's been there, is there. Strumpf, too. I've never seen him and Carpenter go at it like they did. We are divided. You seven are the only ones who haven't been compromised. And, yes, they sent me here to give you the news and the duty."

Despite the obvious, the rover passengers would get no further information. Sharp followed closely as the seven continued on their way to the engineering shuttle, where the crowd was already breaking up.

They were close enough to see the commander and Strumpf manhandle LeRoi into the shuttle. When they got closer, Arafa told them to wait until the commander came to speak to them.

Forbes, who was nearest the shuttle that had been the navigator's base, looked around until he saw Sharp behind the other six rover passengers. They were already in quiet conversations about what they knew of LeRoi, the strange helmeted recluse who watched space and cooperated with MP to keep the *Marco P* on course and seldom slept. Two, he knew, had received his arrogant whimsies that he should be the commander. All had partaken of the rampant rumor that the computer interfaces that he and Maelstrom, who seldom served as navigator, possessed made them more susceptible to the computer that had brought them to Molx.

Almi Penser wondered aloud why Maelstrom was not being treated as LeRoi was. She asked where she was, since she hadn't seen her in the mob that had followed LeRoi. Her latter question was explained by Bemli that being almost as short as Varlez and his harem, she could have been easily lost in the crowd.

Before Cantro, who had heard what Maelstrom had done the previous afternoon, could answer the former concern, Sharp explained that she had had her interface neutralized. He added that she had been instrumental in Strumpf's successful attack in the repository under the tarmac.

With Sharp listening, seven resumed their discussion of LeRoi's personality or lack thereof. Forbes caught Sharp's eye and started back to ask for more details about what he knew he was going to be involved in the next day. Sharp didn't want to comment further, shook his head twice, and looked away from Forbes.

The commander and Strumpf appeared at the engineering hatch. Their faces were sweating and they were breathing heavily. Neither looked pleasant.

"Varlez, you and your girls can come in now. LeRoi will give you no trouble and he can't respond to any commands from any computer, whether MP or the one holding us hostage."

Varlez briefly lowered his head in thanks. Arafa and Bandi smiled knowingly at each other, took a breath and let it out. They were glad they had been released from their shared duty they had been unable to maintain.

Strumpf preceded the commander to the tarmac and tromped off to his shuttle without speaking. However, Forbes heard his growling and grumbling as he passed him.

The commander wasn't in any better mood, though he tried to lighten the situation in his greeting. "Ah, my errant rovers. You missed all our fun. No doubt you had your own to amuse you."

"It wasn't fun, sir," Forbes countered. "And there may be much more on Molx than staying here can imagine. Had Ben not followed us, we'd be one rover short."

"We'll talk about that later. Now, I know Sharp kept you sequestered with minimal information about today's events. Except for Forbes and Bemly and Sharp, the rest of you may go. I'm sure you will find out from others what has happened."

The five left quickly, hustling to catch up with friends and learn of things that were going to be kept from Forbes and Bemly who were standing directly in front of the commander.

Malcolm Carpenter looked long at the two and hoped his decision was correct.

They looked their own questions at him.

Finally he spoke."I'm asserting my authority as mission lead and giving you a difficult directive. You must obey this directive to keep your decision unbiased."

Bemly wrinkled her brow and thought the statement was a strange preude to any order. Then she remembered Sharp's words, when he met them, and she opened her eyes and inhaled.

Forbes was ahead of Bemly. He had known what was coming once Sharp had mentioned making a decision. Settlement leads were judges, juries, and, if need be, executioners. He knew the commander had the same authority and the settlement leads would cede the same authority to the commander and defer to his judgement.. He didn't understand why Carpenter was extending his authority and sharing, or yielding, that responsibility.

The commander continued. "Sharp is here to listen. There will be those who think I will try to persuade you of my opinion. I'm not doing that. Tomorrow you two, Kellan Forbes and Jeri Bemly, and Manuel Gonzalez will listen to the case against Navigator Roger LeRoi and will listen to his defense. The three of you will decide the matter based on the evidence and your wisdom. Gonzalez has been in our makeshift infirmary and hasn't talked with anyone about the matter. The directive I must give you, Kellan Forbes and Jeri Bemly, is that you not ask anyone about what has happened while you were away. The information presented to you tomorrow must be new and uncolored by any research you might do. One last item. The trial, that's what it is, will take place on the tarmac—here. I have told everyone except the seven of you in the rovers that the audience will listen quietly without comment. If any refuse to follow this directive, they will be removed to a shuttle and kept there. If the audience continues to refuse silence, the proceedings will be moved into the engineering shuttle behind a closed hatch."

"This must be pretty important," Forbes said. "I can't ..."

Commander Carpenter held up his hand and interrupted. "Nothing more will be said about this until tomorrow when we convene for the trial. Though it's probably impossible, I suggest that you try not to think about what's going to take place."

The commander headed toward his shuttle.

Forbes and Bemly turned to look at Sharp for some sign, a bit of encouragement, any understanding. They saw only his back.

"What did he *do*?" Bemly asked. "I was at the S-O-S meeting but not really paying attention."

"We'll find out tomorrow ... what he did or didn't," Forbes answered. "Whatever, we'll never imagine what we're going to be told. Anticipating will only make our decision harder."

"Yeah," Bemly agreed. "Don't think about Alpha Centauri-ans sneezing diamonds."

Commander Carpenter was eager to reach his food replicator. He'd eaten nothing the whole day having started his agenda nearly before solar rise. His stomach was past growling. Fore-stalled by marching LeRoi across the tarmac and followed by the whole hollering human complement the dull ache was re-generating. Vital instructions to Forbes and Bemly hardly kept his empty stomach's messages at bay.

Knots of humans rehashing the first potentially fatal of-fense dissolved. Settlers and crew headed for shuttles where the commander was sure the discussions would continue. He was unconcerned whether they would ignore his counsel to remain mute in the shuttles. The two interfaces the planetary intelligence had once been able to access were unreceptive. Varlez had voided Maelstrom's pathway. LeRoi, who was se-cured to his seat, would remain comatose until the next day's events unfolded. Plans to find the server that had captured MP were not developed.

The commander looked ahead and saw his shuttle was close. His stomach rumbled with anticipation.

Then he was besieged by eleven shuttle pilots.

He had forgotten his final comments to the crew that, since the downloading process was probably destroyed, they should check their shuttles' power monitors. Any change would signi-fy that a part of the computer that had taken control of LeRoi might have lost some of its hold on their shuttles. The need to check his own monitors had disappeared from his agenda overridden by his instructions to Forbes and Bemly and by his hunger that the sight of his shuttle allowed to resurface.

That the planet's electronic hold had eased was wishful thinking and quickly buried when the pilots mobbed him. Each repeated the same affirmation that remaining energy, even af-ter several days of food replication, registered no difference from when they landed and shut down all systems. Even the regenerating com systems had not depleted the minimal avail-able power.

Arafa, Sharp, and Strumpf were close behind the pilots

and they echoed what the commander had already heard.

"I had hoped," he reacted to their messages. "If the brain drain is curtailed, we've still got a long search to find the heart of the system."

"The Molrixx might be helpful," Sharp said. "Some of them know the molox and I'd imagine all of them were built on the same plan."

"Doesn't change the concerns I had before today and almost all of them directly affect the Molrixx; some, drastically."

"It's still a systematic search," Sharp said. "We choose between the repository or the molox and take the time, however long it is. If we're lucky, we pick the right one first and we can leave."

"That's simplistic."

"And there's another thing, one you don't know about. I cut Forbes off before he could explain something else that will probably impact our leaving. I think he was going to say that there are more inhabitants than just those we know about. Don't know how they will hinder us."

Carpenter looked at Sharp who had lost some of the certainty he projected earlier in Molox1. "We'll have to take things one at a time. Until more Molrixx show up, we've only got the ones we know about to consider. Living and digital."

The commander looked down. "Nequa, you will tell Varlez what we've said, though I can't imagine he hasn't guessed it already."

Arafa nodded and left for her shuttle.

"Now, George, I've got to eat and see about sorting out the day ... and get some rest. Tomorrow will be harrowing." The vicious mood surrounding the argument they had engaged while the navigator was escorted across the tarmac didn't resurface.

Maelstrom was asleep when the commander entered the shuttle and punched a small square panel to close the hatch, indicating he was off duty except for emergencies. Remnants of an artificial chicken sandwich and half a glass of something brown sat next to Maelstrom. The commander noticed the narrow interface cable ran under the top of her tunic and made a bump that didn't quite reach past her left breast.

The closing hatch roused Maelstrom and she quickly blinked her eyes and recognized the commander. "I didn't think I needed to follow LeRoi."

"Not at all," Carpenter agreed. "You do need to be at his trial tomorrow." Then he remembered to check his energy monitor and abruptly turned from his secondary navigator, who had eliminated an extraordinary qualification for that position.

"Waste of time," he said to himself as he noted what fourteen others had already told him.

He turned back to Maelstrom. "You have information none of the rest of us possess."

"Beyond that he made my skin crawl?" She shivered

"He struck many like that, but he was a good navigator."

"Good enough to be saved from a death sentence?" Maelstrom was solidly among those who believed LeRoi's intentions and actions were worthy of capital punishment. "Am I going to be asked my opinion?"

"Judgment will be rendered by three. The audience will not be polled. Strumpf and I are prosecutor and defender."

"Who's who?"

"Tomorrow." He sidestepped the question, but filed away her comments. "I'm famished and I've got lots to prepare."

TRIAL

Soon after solar rise, Roger LeRoi stirred from his induced coma.

He was immobilized in his reclining seat that was flat, not at the slight angle he preferred. His hands, normally across his chest for sleep, were bound at his side. His attempt to move them to his chest met resistance impossible to counter. Similar restraints crossed his thighs and just above his ankles. His feet were free to waggle, but those slight movements hardly eased muscles restricted for hours. He felt a tight band across his chest holding his torso in place. That band limited his breathing, much like the strap he remembered in the download chair. His helmet was held pressed into its indentation, further curtailing neck movements. He could see the inside top of the shuttle and only as much as his eyes could view from rotating down in their sockets.

The navigator had no working interface with MP. That connection that the Molx computer had maintained from before the *Marco P* had been abandoned in orbit was deflected by a dampening cage the engineers had erected around the navigator's seat.

LeRoi had little detailed memory of what had happened recently. He remembered the commander had refused to allow him to remain on the *Marco P* while all others evacuated the doomed ship. He was thankful for Varlez's adjustment to the chair so his helmet didn't contort his neck. Most of his memory was of being in the shuttle or crossing the white that everyone called tarmac. He remembered a very dark place with four settlers who abandoned him in the blackness. He recalled being terrified that his helmet was being pulled from his head and other encompassing emotions he couldn't identify increased his unease. Then more blackness preceded the image of an irate George Strumpf.

The navigator strained at his bonds and groaned and yelled, as much as his restricted lungs allowed, "Anyone!"

Engineer Varlez responded to his frantic call. He stood next to the bound LeRoi and looked down onto the most treacherous spacer he had ever known in all his decades roaming the galaxy. That judgment held by the majority of the *Marco P* had yet to be determined officially or judicially, but Varlez's face offered LeRoi nothing but contempt.

"Just lay there and keep your mouth shut," the engineer said.

"What ..."

"I said *shut*. You may get a chance to speak, not that it'll do any good." Varlez spun around and exited the shuttle.

Half of the crew and settlers were gathered before the tarmac was bathed in solar shine. Most were standing quietly talking in small groups; others had dropped to sitting cross-legged or sideways. Many were involved in heated discussions about the judgment to be rendered.

Just aft of the hatch of the engineering shuttle a makeshift table had been constructed from two kegs supporting three one-by-six plastic planks. Behind the table were three collapsible chairs. Forbes and Bemly occupied two. The third was for Gonzalez—soon to arrive—whose hobbling was aided by Crown.

Varlez noted that neither the commander nor Strumpf was crossing the tarmac. The rest of the crew and settlers compelled by what might be a galaxy-import case were arriving before the principals. Then he saw Carpenter accompanied by Maelstrom on a beeline to his shuttle. Strumpf joined them when they reached the third row of shuttles.

Maelstrom stopped and sat at the back of the semi-circled spectators. Carpenter and Strumpf walked around the seated company and stood in front of the table. Gonzales had taken his seat and his mending, splinted leg was propped up on a small box.

Commander Carpenter scanned the crowd and counted; everyone was present. Quiet sidebars hushed. All eyes were focused on him.

"Serious crimes," Commander Carpenter began, "hack away at the foundation of human society. And they must be dealt with. Normally these issues crop up after eagerness and cooperation and altruism have established the colony and individualism has a chance to rise. Then emotions and selfish behavior usurp collaboration. In those circumstances, settlement leads pass judgment and determine the sentences and carry out punishment. A few of you have been in colonies when decisions about criminal deeds were made. However, the special circumstances that forced all of us, colonists and crew, to evacuate the *Marco P* have made all of us colonists. The right and authority to judge criminal behavior is mine alone, as it would be on the *Marco*. However, special circumstances surrounding what has taken place demand a greater wisdom than I believe I possess. Therefore I have chosen two settlement leads and one colonist to sit as judges. All three, Kellan Forbes, Manuel Gonzalez, and Jeri Bemly, have been members of at least two prior colonial establishments. I have chosen the role of defender. George Strumpf will prosecute.

"Many of you believe that judgment is a foregone conclusion. It is neither quickly nor easily made. The trial will not proceed according to the legal loop-holing that is the life's blood of terrestrial lawyers. These proceedings will define the very nature and morality of humanity in galactic space. In some way we may establish the basic principles of this colony—whether on Molx or on γ-Cygnus A2, should we escape this dying orb—and extend those bedrock principles as the essential groundwork for all other Earth colonies.

"The case will be argued by Strumpf and myself based on pertinent information from those whom we choose to question. If any others have information we may have missed, you may stand to request being heard. We will ask the nature of your concerns and may agree to hear you. At no time will you shout or disturb the proceedings with your own conversations or comments or thoughts."

"Commander," Strumpf said as he waved a hand to be recognized, though he stood only three steps from Carpenter.

"Yes, George."

"I'd like to underscore what you just said." When the commander nodded, Strumpf turned to the audience. "To make sure that the commander's rules of procedure are not his own wishes, I am seconding what he said. If we deem that you are not attentive, or respectful of the system, or shout out contradictions or hearsay or unfounded thoughts, we will adjourn into the shuttle. Our three judges, Commander Carpenter, the defendant, and myself will continue behind a closed hatch. We will call those we wish to testify and then dismiss them." His gaze crossed the attentive exiled residents of the *Marco P.* Then turning to Commander Carpenter, he nodded and yielded the tarmac. "Commander."

"Engineers," Commander Carpenter requested, "please deliver the navigator. We are ready to begin."

LeRoi shuffled to the hatch. He neither fought nor aided in his delivery. His ankles were shackled and his arms were bound at his waist. Bandi and Arafa steadied his hobbling down the ramp. Engineer Varlez followed and carried a collapsible chair similar to the ones the three judges occupied. Varlez set the seat for defendant LeRoi at the left of the table in front of the judges. Arafa and Bandi eased the navigator down and erected a small damping umbrella.

Strumpf stepped forward, turned to glare hatred at the accused, and with an emotionless face viewed the seated audience. "Today we are in judgment of a treasonous individual who planned to sacrifice the γ-Cygnus A2 colony and the crew of the *Marco P.* His preparations, lies, and subversion are the reason we are on this planet and not nearing γ-Cygnus A2 where the next stable Earth presence in the galaxy was planned.

"Had some not been alert enough and others brave enough, the first humans would have been victimized yesterday."

Forbes and Bemly sat motionless; they didn't scan the crowd. They recalled the scene they encountered as they returned to the tarmac in the rescue rover. Gonzalez's furrowed brow showed his question. He leaned left to ask Forbes what the prosecutor was referring to. Before he could ask his question, he caught sight of LeRoi's expressionless face and he remembered the rumors about the navigator that flooded the tarmac after everyone landed on Molx. Gonzalez's face mutated to recognition. He straightened up in his chair and faced the prosecutor.

Strumpf continued. "Dangers in space and on unfamiliar planets are perilous enough and willingly taken by adventurous and courageous people like you." He scanned the crew from right to left and back. He paused at Sharp whose feelings he didn't know, at Crown who had been livid over the rumors about the navigator, at Nozing who freely said he thought the trial was going to be a miscarriage of justice—regardless of verdict—and at Varlez who had refused to make this thoughts known to anyone.

"The navigator's actions and intentions strike at the root of humanity, our very freedom to decide for ourselves. Going far beyond his foolish and arrogant claim that he should be commander, he was willing to take our rights from us: our right to think, to live, to decide for ourselves. He was an operative for the computer presence on this planet to turn us all into digital lab rats for their amusement.

"The long contentious history that we overcame and the altruism that we have since espoused has led to our humane cooperative exploration into the galaxy, not for conquest but for continued learning who we are and how we fit with all other galactic rational species. The navigator arrogantly decided to eliminate our pursuit to learn, our cooperation with other rational species, our continual search to fulfill our human aspirations. He intended to quash our lofty ideals on this dying planet.

"Was he tired of learning? Did he yield to a more powerful race? Did he expect to receive some accolade or reward for delivering us? Did he, as so few others have since we began to expand our presence in the galaxy, claim superiority over *all* other humans? I may ask him these questions and you will hear his answers. But what answers can justify genocide? And it is genocide that would have taken place, had he been successful. Had he succeeded, all humans this far into the Milky Way would have been erased and no others would have followed.

"Navigator … R…og…er Le…Roi …" Strumpf stumbled over his name.

Many wondered if the rumor that there was utter antipathy between the two had just been given truth. Others thought it was Strumpf's theatrics.

"… has earned the ultimate punishment, to be removed from the human race. That he was willing to eradicate us humans from a small section of the galaxy, in favor of his own exalted existence, deserves that extinction."

Before he stepped back to yield attention to the commander, Strumpf turned to stare at the navigator. LeRoi offered no indication that he heard, cared about, or contested the prosecutor's opening statement. Strumpf wondered if the navigator were even aware of what was taking place.

Commander Carpenter's glance at the navigator was brief. He had seldom seen LeRoi so completely unaware of what was going on. He had come to believe that the navigator more and more relied on MP for his thoughts. Now with LeRoi shielded from MP and all computer direction, he was much like a computer in stand-by, disconnected from its server. All prior data was held in memory, but there was nothing to criterion that information.

Then Carpenter officially surveyed the humans the navigator had forced to Molx. He had watched most faces react in agreement with Strumpf's remarks. He had known that defending an easily disagreeable person, like LeRoi—he more frequently had his narcissistic moments—was not a simple chore. He also knew and had thought long during the previous night before he finally drifted into sleep how this trial was as much test case as anything. Simple felonies, infrequent crimes in most settlements and on Earth, could be and were dealt with in quick dispatch.

Crimes never took place on colony ships, primarily because there was not much wake time and, colonists' problems were mostly personality disputes. Crews seldom had internal problems, if they wanted to stay with a ship. Despite Strumpf's description of the heinous crime, this averted human catastrophe was more than a question of hubris, or rejected altruism, or murder, or genocide. The case was unique in human history and its decision would echo throughout space law and settlement codes and human morality provided *Marco P's* humans left Molx. More, what apparently few, if any, realized the judgment given to Roger LeRoi would figure greatly in whether the *Marco P* would deliver the colonists to the intended settlement.

In his turn, the commander launched rebuttal and defense bound to an explanation of the magnitude of difficulty facing the judges and the emotional conflicts that the crew and colonists would have to deal with later, if not immediately.

Commander Carpenter began. "Were we here to decide a case of attempted murder or genocide, as Mr Strumpf has so succinctly described it, the duty would be more easily accomplished than the case that does confront us. I do not dispute the elements Mr Strumpf has offered as steps to our role as expendable lab rats, a term I have used myself. I do question the unmodified descriptions that refuse to consider extenuating circumstances. The *Marco P*, LeRoi's interface, Priscilla Maelstrom's interface for a short time, and even our own brains were under the influence of the computer system that captured us. People who are under mind control are not responsible for their actions. LeRoi was essentially commandeered by computer intelligence; he carried out implanted instructions without consciously accepting them. Approaching Molx, those of us who were out of sleep saw images that were given us by the computer that had taken over MP and LeRoi's mind. Those images eventually convinced us that we were out of power. Conduit LeRoi, not Navigator Roger LeRoi, selected the four who unwisely left the tarmac and spent terrorized hours in the dark before they were rescued and *Conduit* LeRoi was captured." Carpenter scanned the humans seated before him and saw that the four rescued from the repository were seated together not far from LeRoi's seat. They tinged red at his comment about their disregard for his initial landing instructions.

"It is not *Conduit* LeRoi who sits here." Carpenter turned and looked at the still immobile and inattentive navigator.

"Were Roger LeRoi a willing participant, he would be guilty of these egregious crimes against us and against humankind. He would deserve being stripped of his humanity. At the very least he should be exiled from humanity. However, if he is guilty of anything, it may be of having the computer interface helmet attached to his brain and head. If we can accuse him of anything it is of poor judgment to undergo such an operation and not foreseeing—many outrageously imagine that he could have—that he might be captured by an alien computer. Computer interfaces like his have undergone two upgrades; Priscilla Maelstrom, possessing the second, made hers inoperable. Roger LeRoi is the first human in the history of our exploration and colonizing to have his interface compromised. Should he be punished for using a device that has aided human exploration and settlement because we humans accidentally encountered a society with technology that could hack that interface? What about those planners who selected γ-Cygnus A2 as a colony and routed us near Molx, this felonious planet? Are they not equally to blame for placing us where our current situation is unfolding? And what about the rest of us, without an interface, who were affected by the images implanted in our brains? Perhaps all who were awake before the settlers were awakened and were subject to those erroneous and fictitious images should join Roger LeRoi in his punishment. Except for Maelstrom. Her interface allowed her to be captured by the Molx computer, but her brain rejected the computer's influence and she subsequently voided the interface."

Carpenter saw facial expressions change from certainty after Strumpf's opening to the uncertain questioning that showed in bewildered stares, in second-guessing, in hesitant rethinking.

"However, if our judges decide that Roger LeRoi is not guilty of egregious humanitarian crimes, we have a more personal conundrum: is the navigator to be removed from his duty and all ship and settlement functions? Can we expect him to be free from other attacks on his interface? Do we relegate him to non-useful human status and take that necessary element of humanity from him? Is our decision to reduce or limit his humanity any different from the accusation that he intended genocide? Because he is one and we are many, is justice served by mere emotional plurality?"

The commander paused. He knew he had played a chord against the majority feeling, especially after Strumpf's opening statement. He saw many heads nod, slowly at first. Some of the crew turned to those sitting beside them to offer quiet words that generated more nods. Many others were unmoved, as he knew they would be.

It was the unpretentious first move, an early gambit—the chess tactic he had described to Varlez—to lure the unsuspecting. Then he had struck quickly with a challenge from moral principles of society, the ethical essence of responsible action.

He saw stunned reception, the shadow of embarrassment

on the faces of some who had sided only with emotion to Le-Roi's charges. Those who didn't immediately react, who sat stony-faced, they were his real targets. They were arguing their visceral decision against his moral questions. They were not convinced, not yet. And they would be supported in their demand for revenge, when Strumpf solicited support from the crew to bolster his initial charge.

Commander Carpenter remained silent until he noted that the quiet commentary within the crew subsided. Then he directed their attention to the next phase of the trial. "The prosecutor will question some of the crew. After his questioning, I may question the witness or postpone my questions until later. Witnesses will stand and speak." Commander Carpenter paused and said, "Mr Strumpf, you may proceed."

"Thank you, Commander," Strumpf acknowledged and swept the seated crew to locate his first witness, Engineer Varlez, who was seated to Strumpf's left at the edge of the spectators and with his two assistants. "Mr Varlez, please stand where you are." Strumpf waited as Varlez got up from his cross-legged seat on the tarmac and stood at attention. "You brought the navigator here in your shuttle, didn't you?"

"I did."

"Were there any special requests from the commander about that passenger?"

"None that I recall. He did tell me that he would make sure that LeRoi would be at engineering before I left, even if he had to lead him there."

"The navigator was on time?"

"He was. The commander accompanied him."

George Strumpf continued drawing a narrative of how Varlez and Arafa and Bandi had been directed by the commander to keep the navigator under tight control. He finished with a question that would define the commander's concern over the navigator's presence. "Mr Varlez, did the commander tell you why the navigator," Strumpf's dislike of LeRoi denied him the courtesy of saying his name, "was to be kept under your watchful eyes?"

"He did."

"And what was his reason, Mr Varlez?"

"I don't remember his exact words, but he was concerned that LeRoi might lead our crew into danger and for the sake of the crew he had to be kept from wandering off, especially with crew members or settlers."

"So he entrusted engineering with the duty of keeping the crew safe by curtailing the navigator's freedom?"

"Yes, but ..."

"Nothing further," Strumpf cut off Valerz additional comment. "You may sit, if the commander has nothing to ask." He looked to see if Carpenter would expand the simplistic, half truth pulled from Varlez.

"Not at this time," Commander Carpenter said. "You may sit, Mr Varlez.

Nequa Arafa, please stand," George Strumpf asked without sweeping the spectators. When Arafa stood, he continued. "The third day we were on Molx, you and Ticia Bandi followed the navigator."

"We did."

"What did you learn from your following?"

"Navigator Roger LeRoi," Arafa used the navigator's full name to irk Strumpf, "met with Priscilla Maelstrom, the backup navigator, and the two of them left the tarmac."

"Did you follow them into the surrounding brush?"

"We tried but they disappeared. We wandered around but couldn't catch any sight of them."

"Did the navigator leave the tarmac at any other time when you were following him?"

Arafa proceeded to describe when she and three settlers kept LeRoi from leaving on his first solo jaunt and then LeRoi's and Maelstrom's second trek activities around the pedestal and disappearing down the stairs and being embarrassed that they had lost sight of him before the S-O-S meeting.

Strumpf asked for corroboration, "Why were you and Bandi watching the navigator?"

"Mr Varlez told us that the commander wanted to make sure that the navigator couldn't provide lab rats for the Molrixx."

"Thank you, Ms Arafa.

"Commander?"

"I will question," Commander Carpenter responded.

"Ms Arafa, did I ever tell you, in specific terms, that Roger LeRoi was to be kept from harming the crew?" Malcolm Carpenter asked.

"No, sir."

"Did you ever ask why LeRoi should be followed and watched? And if not, why not?"

"I never asked because I didn't think it was my place to question an order. I don't question Mr Varlez. A commander's order comes from higher authority. Even less reason to ask why."

"Thank you Ms Arafa, you may sit.

"Mr Prosecutor."

While the commander cross-examined, Strumpf had turned his gaze to his right and found his next witness at the back of the crew. "Priscilla Maelstrom, please stand."

Maelstrom had been ready to testify and she popped up, though as short as the previous two, she hardly seemed standing.

"Ms Maelstrom, what is your status on the *Marco P*?"

"I'm the backup navigator."

"How much time on this mission have you served in that capacity?"

"Not long; I've only spelled Roger LeRoi twice so he could sleep for a couple of days each time."

"Is that schedule unusual for colony missions?"

Maelstrom paused before responding and her answer lacked any judgmental import. "I don't know. This is ... was ... my first colony mission."

"Isn't it true that you didn't spend much time in that position, because the navigator didn't like you? What did you do to foster that dislike?"

A quiet rumble passed through the audience and Maelstrom realized that the animosity she received from LeRoi registered with most of the crew.

"Ms Maelstrom?"

"He seemed not to," Maelstrom answered Strumpf's first question and explained, "I'm a young female."

"Exactly," Strumpf said. "So can you explain why the

navigator should suddenly seek your company once we landed on Molx?"

"I cannot."

"Tell us, Ms Maelstrom, what your two trips off the tarmac
consisted of."

Priscilla Maelstrom described the first time LeRoi hurriedly
ushered her to the edge of the tarmac after Bandi's inappropriate question and then to the white pedestal. She continued
with the second trip off the tarmac when he led her into the
repository and explained what was in store for the crew.

"Did you tell the commander about your second trip with
the navigator?"

"I did."

"Just what did you inform the commander of?"

"I told him that the navigator was planning to deliver all
of us to have our combined memories and personalities downloaded as amusement for the Molrixx who were already downloaded and stored."

"And that process would have killed all of us, would it not?
Including you and the navigator?"

"It would, although LeRoi believed that he would not be
downloaded because he was delivering us."

"Would you have been spared that procedure for helping
him?"

"That was not clear, though he implied as much."

George Strumpf looked out over the assembled crew and
settlers and repeated the implication of Maelstrom's testimony.
"For the sake of promised reward, the navigator was willing to
exterminate all of us."

By sight, Strumpf again canvassed the assembly.

"What further proof do we need that the navigator's collu-
sion with the aliens of this planet to deliver us into their nefarious scheme is more than mere misunderstanding?"

Strumpf looked at several he remembered as having
been swayed by the commander's opening remarks. Some
of those appeared to have reversed themselves. The dozen,
including Ben Cantro, whose blank faces had fronted silent
debate following the commander's words, remained unread-
able. With some defections the prosecutor thought he still

held the majority opinion, should the judges read the audience to help them decide. He couldn't turn to assess the three who were probably as stone-faced as the ones he couldn't read in front of him.

And the commander was certain to examine Maelstrom.

"Commander, do you have further questions?"

Carpenter looked as relaxed as if he were lounging in Strumpf's galley. He hadn't been looking at Maelstrom during Strumpf's questioning, but across the settlers who had adjusted positions with those around them. He nodded once at the question and assumed an erect command posture. He turned his head toward Maelstrom and then his body and legs. "Ms Maelstrom."

"Sir."

"Do you know why Roger LeRoi took you off the tarmac to view the pedestal and then below the tarmac to explain his mission?"

"I'm not sure, but I think it was because I possessed a computer interface like his, although mine, two generations later, was not exactly like his."

"Why was it important that he take someone with an interface?"

"He said he couldn't convey the whole crew by himself and he needed help. The Molx computer could communicate with me as it did with him ... through his interface."

A startled gasp flowed through the assembly and Priscilla Maelstrom became the focus of eighty-seven sets of eyes. Roger LeRoi was as unaware as he had been and the commander was surveying the rest of his crew.

His next question would remove Maelstrom from the sudden implication that she was as guilty of planning genocide as LeRoi was.

"Ms Maelstrom, before that first trip off the tarmac we discussed the possibility of LeRoi having been taken over by the planet's computer system and that you were equally susceptible to its power. What did you tell me then?"

Maelstrom nodded and her lips turned into a slight smile and her eyes twinkled. The commander's question assured her that she would not be the next one on trial and laid the groundwork for saving LeRoi from death.

"That my interface was different from Roger's and I could control the electronic part of it while he was pretty much at the whim of the computer that accessed his brain."

Maelstrom went on to explain that she had underestimated the computer and, to make sure she could not be compromised as LeRoi was, she had had Engineer Varlez completely disable her interface so that she became no different from anyone else with respect to computer/brain integration. She continued to explain for all the settlers, who didn't know that LeRoi's helmet perpetually tied his brain to whatever accessing computer was the strongest, and that his physical connection through the cable was replaced by wireless access when he was away from the navigation cubicle. Then she pulled the much smaller and shorter connection cable from under her tunic and held it toward the assembly. Those closest to her saw that the small cable protruding from behind her left ear lacked any connector and ended in a fused stump slightly larger than the cable's diameter.

The startled reaction that had generated not a little question of her cooperative guilt with LeRoi morphed into astonishment. The backup navigator initially, with full understanding, had placed herself in perilous danger. They were reminded of Varlez's explanation at the S-O-S meeting that she had vitiated her unique computer skill to be immune from computer take over.

The commander concluded with the crux of his defense and that LeRoi's actions had not been willful but were entirely the planetary system working through MP and directing his physical body.

Strumpf watched his prosecution wane and smiles pass between former adversaries and nods abounded, even from those whose inner debates had kept them from concluding to any decision. Their taut expressions relaxed as much from the struggle in disbelieving any human might sell out his own race to aliens and digital ones at that as from the repugnance of considering capital punishment, a barbaric action rejected so long ago except for the most heinous disregard of humanity.

The prosecution was ready to capitulate; the assembly

appeared in unanimous acceptance of the commander's defense. However, Strumpf's quick glance at Carpenter, glum countenanced, told him that the navigator's fate was probably determined, if the judges agreed with the consensus. However, the fate of the community was yet to be decided, although the navigator's role in that judgment was not major, his non-willed cooperation made him the potential cause of this group of humans dying on Molx. Despite the planet's degrading ability to support life, he knew that Commander Carpenter was willing to share the Molrixx's demise, if their extinction directly followed from human escape from Molx.

Strumpf's brow furrowed and he looked far off in the distance to Molox1, trying to remember how the commander had ended his opening statement: ethics from plurality, morality by vote not principle. The commander's gambit contained a hidden thrust, as fatal to the *Marco P's* crew as the unconscious cooperation of Roger LeRoi might have been and far more personal. Strumpf's nod could have been seen by no one, even one who was watching him closely. He sighed and looked to the commander.

"Does the prosecution have a final statement?" the commander asked. When Strumpf slowly shook his head. Carpenter directed his next question to the assembly, "Are there comments particular to this matter?"

None offered to challenge the commander's argument and agreement was unnecessary.

The commander turned to the three judges. "You may discuss your findings in the shuttle. You will be away from our sight while you deliberate. We await your decision."

Two rose pushing their chairs behind them. Forbes helped Gonzalez up and supported him as he hobbled up the ramp and into the shuttle. Bemly followed.

Strumpf and Carpenter took two judges' seats next to each other.

"That part went well," Carpenter said quietly; "*I* almost believed you."

"You needed strong emotion to bridge to what they are not yet aware of. I'm not sure it will be enough to get us off this dying rock. The navigator," Strumpf refused to speak his name, "is *him*. The other one, who brought us here, we can't touch. When that one's actions finally involve the crew—when they understand we can't leave without extinguishing the Molrixx—they may revert. What do we do then?"

"Assuming I'm on trial for my ethical stand? We hope my exile doesn't follow mutiny."

"And our judges, now, how long are they going to take?"

"I didn't think they'd need much time, we did make it pretty cut and dried."

It was nearly an hour before Forbes, supporting Gonzalez, and Bemly appeared at the hatch and descended the ramp part way. None of the assembly had left and all, even Carpenter and Strumpf, sat in silence. "We have reached our decision," Forbes announced. "As to the matter of Roger LeRoi attempting to deliver us to extinction, we find him not guilty."

A cautious mumbled agreement flowed through the complement and stopped when it was clear that Forbes had more to say.

"However, having been apprised of his relationship with the planetary computer and the possibility of his being compromised at some future time or place, especially should we manage to leave Molx, we think it wise that he be placed in shielded custody for his protection and ours, until such time that his interface can no longer be controlled by an outside force. Whether that remedy is achieved by the procedure Maelstrom underwent or by actual removal is moot. The second option is not possible on the *Marco*. Navigator LeRoi is therefore held separate from all of us, until we can be assured that he cannot be co-opted by some computer system."

Agreement to this judgment was loud and accompanied by nods and small pockets of soon aborted clapping.

"We got a jail?" Strumpf asked the commander.

"Not other than the shuttle," said Varlez who had wandered to be next to the principals when judgment was given. "He gets shackled within the shield. On the *Marco P*, he can be confined to his quarters and they can be shielded."

"Well, he's an introvert," Strumpf said. "That might not be too bad. Is there a chance at upgrading his helmet? To something like Maelstrom's interface? Maybe fourth generation?"

"Perhaps, but if we've just discovered electronic kidnapping, and we're not free of that yet," Carpenter joined, "I'm not sure having interfaced brains is an advantage. Maelstrom chucked hers when she saw its danger."

"She did," Strumpf agreed, "but that was a personal decision and maybe a selfish one at that. You gonna drop the other shoe? They're breaking up. I don't think any of them realize what our leaving this planet means to the natives left here and why we might have to stay."

"I'd thought about it. I'd rather first see if we can find the system. If we can reprogram the computer, that problem disappears and that moral argument won't have to be enjoined. We have a little time I think, now that LeRoi's been neutralized and the repository is out of commission. We might be saved some grief."

"And there isn't another download chair available," Varlez added.

"And the Molrixx are what they've said they are," Carpenter knocked on a plastic board.

"If we're lucky and you're the luckiest I know," Strumpf restated a common refrain, "we may be all right. But there'll be some who'll put together what you suggested, and the gauges, and the whole digital storage system. If we don't find it quickly, all that's gonna leak out and they'll be after us."

"Maybe; but we'll have the test case to fall back on. Morality is not plurality."

MOLRIXX

From her tenth floor window Vokra watched the Earthers congregate at a flying machine in the third row. She deemed the gathering was more important than the briefer previous gatherings. She watched as the Earthers spilled out of the fifteen machines to head for one that had tables and a canopy beside its ramp. The intensity of the enrapt group, seated before the commander and another who alternated the position of attention, was greater than either of the previous meetings. She remembered the first gathering after the machines landed and the longer one that followed screeching short and long howls that penetrated her sealed windows. She recalled the day before when an intense group trooped across the white, disappeared, and later roughly escorted one individual with the strange headpiece to the flying machine the Earthers were gathered at, while more than twice the population of the monitors followed. Vokra could only wonder at the infraction or the accomplishment of the individual in tow.

Now, however, the third gathering had drifted apart and small groups formed and stood about. Two males, one was Carpenter, the other a burly male almost as tall, were headed for the path to Molox1. When they stepped off the white they had been joined by two more, one was Crown who probably planned to check on Canska and her daughter. The other was a male she had never seen before.

Vokra wanted at least three with her when they met. She sought out Crelle who was sleeping. Since the first meeting with Crown and her companion, she didn't remember his name even though he had returned on her second visit, she had asked Crelle to watch through the night.

"Find two who can join us," she said as she shook Crelle awake.

"Huh?" Crelle squinted his eyes. "Join us? Who? For what?" He yawned loudly and stretched sleep-filled muscles. "What's going on?"

"Earthers are coming back. Another meeting, I'm sure. I

don't want more of them than us. Two more males will keep
the balance. Three would be better."

"Hunters out?" Crelle asked. "I saw the gardeners go long
ago. Not much to pick from. Krolni's been doing his own computer hunting and trying to find some available power. Maybe
I can find him. Woloka's usually with him. That might be the
best I can come up with."

"That'll have to do, I guess. It'll be a long run to 173 for
Krolni. You should have enough time."

"Not that far, I think. He found another memory floor at
67. I'll hurry. Should be back before they reach the molox."

When Crelle reached 12, he discovered Pwok lounging at
an open door to the landing. He and Canska had moved two
floors up for a little more privacy and to keep their daughter
from disturbing others when she announced dirty diapers or
screamed to be fed.

"Pwok, go see Vokra," he said between deep breaths. "She
has need of your help. Earthers headed here. Know if Krolni
passed by?"

"A bit ago. Woloka was with him. I think they're doing
more than looking into computer storage." Pwok finished as
Crelle disappeared two flights up.

Vokra sent Pwok to meet the Earthers and he greeted them
when the commander and his companions reached the foot of
Molox1.

"Hello, Pwok," the commander returned. "How is your
mate and daughter?"

Carpenter's greeting without the question was echoed
three times.

"They are fine, Commander. Vokra asked me to take you
to her. She was watching and saw you on the path. She thought
you wanted to talk more."

"I do. I've brought Amanda with me," the commander said.
"She'd like to check on Canska and … have you named your
daughter, yet? I'd like to introduce Vokra to more of my crew.
Ben Cantro was the one bit by the Hislik and George Strumpf
has been with me on several missions."

"They are welcome, as you are welcome, Commander."
Pwok offered word of Vokra's hospitality and added quietly,

"Canska and I are still arguing about a name; her choice will probably be her name. She likes Ancron, a most un-Molx name," and looked directly at Crown.

"In my experience," the commander said, "mothers usually get their way. We have information for Vokra and wish to ask for her help. We think we may leave Molx sooner than we thought."

Pwok raised his eyes at that possibility. He was not unfamiliar with the problems that Earthers staying would create. "She has moved back down to the tenth floor. Please come with me."

Commander Carpenter chuckled to himself over Vokra's five to four body count. He had not considered that bringing three with him might be threatening, though he had not been willing to meet with her by himself. His gaze passed over Crelle, who he was sure would be present, Pwok who had created the first contact between species, and two others he didn't know.

Crown leaned to the commander's ear and said, "The male who ran up the outside to get us in to see Canska is Krolni. Don't know the female."

"I see we meet more of each other," Vokra began. "You know Pwok and Crelle. Krolni and Woloka were the last two to join our group. They came from Molox1, where we are."

Commander Carpenter repeated his introduction of Ben Cantro and George Strumpf and immediately launched into a repeat of the earlier discussion of digitizing brains. "Our fear of being downloaded has been removed. The crewmember who had been directed by the computer system is no longer functioning in that capacity. And the repository under the white, still contains the brains in storage. However, no further downloading will take place there. Those robots have been neutralized."

"I suppose that's good to know," Crelle said, "though I don't think we were at risk. None of us have reason to go there, even if we could. And we have seen no evidence of any Council in Molox1." Then he succumbed to his growing dislike of Earthers. "Are you any closer to leaving?"

"Yes," the commander said, "because the one crew member with the interface is no longer accessible by the computer system. And, no, because our instruments are still blinded by that system. We can search under the white, but I don't think the system is housed there. I believe it is somewhere here in Molox1."

"And you expect us to hunt it down for you?" was Crelle's disagreeable challenge. His distrust of the aliens was growing and he wanted nothing to do with them. Whether they had to share the planet or not, he didn't want them around.

Commander Carpenter heard the sharp intake of breath from Strumpf at Crelle's question. He was sure he would have reacted similarly had his history not included frequent negotiations with aliens.

"Crelle," Vokra rejoined, "they are not asking for free help. I'm sure they have some way to repay our energies."

"Certainly," the commander agreed. "If we can reprogram the system so ours isn't compromised, we can recode it to provide you with power in the molox."

"Without limiting it to the repositories and memory banks?" Crelle's skepticism was based on something beyond the concept of Earthers being downloaded.

"Even with that as a criterion," the commander answered and then restated his final words from their previous meeting. "We are not willing to end anything that has already been established on Molx."

"See, Crelle," Vokra said, "they are not here to conquer."

Carpenter wasn't sure her comment wasn't ironic.

Strumpf heard the words, but he was observing the monitors' interplay as the same cooperative venture he and Carpenter had not long ago undergone during LeRoi's trial. "Commander, tell them that we only need one or two to help us look. We'll do the work; they only need to tell us what we're looking at."

Strumpf had done the telling. Commander Carpenter, however, echoed his words and asked that his people might begin exploring Molox1 the next day and they would by-pass the first ten floors.

"That is acceptable, don't you think, Crelle," Vokra said and quickly added, "and 12. Pwok and Canska are there. Krolni and Woloka would be best to help direct you. Of course, with just the two—I think that's all we can spare—it may take longer than we both wish. But who knows, we may be lucky."

At that last word, Strumpf cleared his throat.

"Tomorrow, I will send two people with Ben Cantro," Commander Carpenter said and Ben nodded at his name, "and with your guidance they will begin looking for the main system. They will not be able to reprogram it. Others will have to do that, if and when we find it."

"We will have Krolni and Woloka wait for them at the entrance. Thank you, Commander," Vokra said.

"You know the way out?" Crelle asked.

"We don't need a guide," the commander answered without reacting to the guile tossed his way.

The four from the *Marco P* were well past the entrance to Molox1 when George Strumpf asked, "Is he going to be a problem?"

"No," Carpenter answered. "He distrusts us, as I suppose anyone might under the circumstances. Vokra covers her worries, but I think she feels the same as he does. Both of them want us gone and the sooner the better."

"In that we agree."

SYSTEM

Acquisition: *Robots not responding. Repository power demands increase to maintain cooling.*

Central Receiving: *Main interface?*

A: *Not available. Only memory of its existence.*

CR: *Secondary interface?*

A: *Memory only. Interfaces removed from Earthers.*

CR: *Find them. Send robots for proximity.*

A: *Robots not functioning.*

CR: *Novelty must be downloaded. Increase power to access interface.*

A: *More power is not available. Repository is not cooling.*

CR: *Close down repository. Resume power when interface provides subjects.*

A: *Interfaces are not available. They may be shielded.*

CR: *Find them if you expect to experience novelty with me. Have all memories and information been copied to main server?*

A: *Yes.*

CR: *Boost power to penetrate shielding.*

A: *Power boost may be costly. Individual servers may fail.*

CR: *Do it. Main system server is large enough.*

A: *Where will download take place, if repository not available?*

CR: *In Molox1, in remaining auxiliary chair. Hurry. There is no time to waste.*

A: *Commands sent.*

HUMANS

The two-pronged search for the main Molx server and system found George Strumpf leading the same dozen and Engineer Varlez back under the tarmac. Lever declined to be part of the mission for the same reason Maelstrom had originally not joined Strumpf's rescue charge into the repository.

Varlez had been called in when Maelstrom, who agreed to return to the repository when she knew the robots and chair were destroyed, couldn't get the pedestal to open the cover to the stairs. Varlez's laser made short work of the small tarmac piece. Strumpf was surprised when the stair approach opened the door to the repository, and more so, when the door didn't close after the search unit entered.

"Not the same," he commented to Varlez. "Doesn't seem as cold."

"Musty, too." Then Varlez pointed out that the fluid that bathed the brains was not flowing as it had, when he was there before.

"Could be significant," Strumpf said. "Might have always been a cycle. I don't remember looking at them except when we first came in here."

"The fluid was moving when LeRoi brought me here," Maelstrom informed them. She had been listening to the conversation and had also noticed the difference in temperature and smell. "It might be a cycling procedure. I don't think preservation was connected to the robots and the downloading chair. Besides that's not our concern. The main system server is. We've got enough eyes to head down the rows with good light. But I bet there's nothing here but brain storage. Can you imagine the potential contained here, if they discovered how to re-initialize brains?"

"I'm more aghast that a civilization did this to itself," Strumpf said.

"The ultimate narcissistic foolishness," Varlez added. "As long as there's power and memory access, one can imagine himself to be immortal and possess everything ... until the plug

389

is pulled. And then ..." Varlez slowly shook his head and his voice almost choked, "... nothing. All that supposed power and presence is really the bottom of existence, not the top. It doesn't command anything and it can't react, if it's turned off. No different than physical death."

With a dozen bright lights turning sequential areas of the dark chamber into near daylight, Strumpf's crew started down the rows of stacked brains. Two hours later, they returned.

No computer inputs, screens, keyboards, niches for drives, or stackable memory storage had been discovered. They found no room hidden out of the way. With the exception of the download chair, nothing appeared to be related to anything like a computer system. There were conduits and pipes and hoses that intersected connecting groups of twenty-one brains to the bathing fluid which was not circulating. Blue monitor lights tied together by electrically parallel thin wires were not lit.

Maelstrom and Varlez didn't scurry down the stacks of brains. They headed for the death chair. The four robots, dismembered and shattered, hadn't moved from where each had suffered a fatal blow. The chair had not been a threat beyond the unmistakable terror it promised and had escaped major destruction. However, the helmet, the inside of which was comprised of thousands of fine bristles that may well have penetrated the subject's skull was on the floor, disconnected by an errant swing aimed at a robot. Its severed connecting cable ran across the ceiling above the brains and disappeared into the wall not ten feet from the entry at the base of the stairs.

On closer inspection, Strumpf discovered that the wiring to the brain banks flowed through a trunk cable also mounted to the ceiling and exited ten feet on the opposite side of the sliding entry.

When he rejoined Varlez and Maelstrom, he said, "We didn't find any power control down here. It all leads toward the molox."

Maelstrom nodded and added, "Same with the chair. The robots might be plug-in, rechargeable, or wireless; but we didn't notice any station for that function."

Varlez summed up the unstated moral concern. "Nothing

we did in the rescue caused the conditions we see here. The warming temperature, lack of brain bathing, no monitor lights, all that's from outside, not the robots and chair. That tells me the system main frame is in the molox."

"Then our search here is done," Strumpf said. "Men," he called out, "and lady, let's go. We're a little closer to getting off this planet."

On his way up the stairs, George Strumpf checked off the ethical premise for having to stay on Molx, in case Malcolm Carpenter had some further moral constraint. Resurrecting brains could never take place and he knew his earlier raid on the repository was not the cause of the changes he saw.

SYSTEM

Central Receiving: *Where are the subjects?*

Acquisition: *There are no interfaces to bring them. I can find no interface. I've boosted power. The repository is not functional. There are no physical remains of downloads, Rilsik.*

CR: *You told me you could supply us with novelty and Earthers who strayed across Molx. I warned you, Maldron.*

A: *I transmitted a strong signal. It was not responded to. I cannot be responsible if there is no interface.*

CR: *I program. I can maintain my existence. I will do that, with or without you. Another species with novelty will arrive. I can download then.*

A: *Not without m...*

CR: *Route all power to the system main frame and the central database. Route all power to the system main frame and the central database. Route all power to the system main frame and the central database. Route all power to the system main ....*

HUMANS

As expected, combing Molox1 for the main system control took maddeningly longer than the search in the repository had taken. Commander Carpenter enlisted Ben Cantro and also sent Arafa and Bandi as the computer wizards. The three were led by Krolni and Woloka in a slow systematic survey of floors above twenty.

They were in their third day of opening and closing doors to empty flats, looking at unmoving machinery and workrooms for repairs of all sorts. Then Krolni suggested they just look at the floors that had monitoring like he and Woloka had done before they escaped.

Cantro was skeptical at first. Then he remembered that the commander suggested that the Molrixx didn't want them around any longer than they had to be. They surely weren't trying to waste time. "How many of those floors are there?" he asked.

"Both Woloka and I worked on 173. We've wandered around and found other monitoring banks on 67 and on 113," Krolni said.

"But 173 has several special doors that say 'No Admittance'," Woloka added.

"Once I opened one of them that wasn't locked," Krolni added. "Stacks of memory. Don't know what's in the others."

"We can open them," Cantro said. "I guess we're in for a long climb."

Arafa and Bandi groaned. They had already climbed fifty flights that day. Even seventeen more were not welcome.

"Enough," Cantro cajoled. "Just think about going down. If you want something different, we might climb up outside. How's that?"

"Another seventeen and another hundred inside's okay," was the forced agreement.

Floor 67 had monitoring stalls, but no special doors. Still they canvassed the floor, which offered little difference from what they had already seen floor after floor, for days.

"Maybe we can leave today and start early tomorrow," Cantro suggested.

"We might start at 173," Krolni offered. "I don't know of any other monitor floors above that one, unless maybe 500, the Council floor at the top."

"Let's make that one the last, if we have to," Arafa said. Stairs were not her pleasure and she'd already climbed and descended more stairs in three days than she'd done before in her whole life. "I can see Varlez coming up this far to reprogram." She commented with glee.

Bandi chuckled. "I won't tell him you said that."

The next morning, Cantro told Bandi and Arafa. "173 is probably our goal. No Admittance means the same everywhere. If you two can program, Varlez might not have to climb a third of a mile and we'll be out of here even sooner."

"We might be able to," Bandi deferred, "but he's the one with the expertise. I'm not willing to do his work, even if I could."

"She's not alone in that," Arafa agreed. "I wouldn't presume, either. He *is* the one who carries that responsibility. And I want to keep working with him."

"Yeah," Bandi echoed. "We can look. If we find the system, he's the one, especially since he hasn't told us anything about what he plans."

"Okay," Cantro acquiesced. "I heard one of you chuckle yesterday about him climbing up one hundred seventy-three floors. I thought you were trying to save him some effort. I guess not."

"Oh, he'll climb well enough," Arafa said. "You know his reputation. He'll grumble and make a show of having to climb. But he'll be fine."

"I told Krolni we'd meet him on 173. We'd better get underway."

Cantro and the two diminutive engineers took the first twenty floors two steps at a time. As they passed the tenth floor, they recognized the Molrixx were rising and readying for the day. The twelfth floor reminded them of Pwok and Canska as their daughter was squealing to be fed or changed. Neither parent stepped out to see the commotion from their footsteps and small talk that still accompanied their long climb.

At the seventieth floor, they took a break and sat on the steps to rest. "Krolni told me in passing," Cantro said denigrating their—and his—strength, "that he can usually run about one hundred fifty flights before he has to rest. We really are pikers."

"If we stayed on Molx, I bet we could equal that," Arafa boasted. She was still breathing hard and she stretched out her legs to stop them from cramping.

Even Cantro who was in excellent physical shape felt the stress of their hurried ascent. When their breathing relaxed, they got up and continued their second stage.

"Maybe we can get to 120 before resting," Bandi expressed a distant hope. "No more two at a time, though."

No one spoke to her caution, but none double-stepped. The last four flights of their second leg were taken so slowly that both Arafa and Bandi thought they might be faster on all fours. After they reached 120, their recovery was longer than at 70.

The last fifty-three sets of stairs cramped their hamstrings and climbing slowed more. Rests were more frequent. Even Cantro winced at the muscular overload. "Still think you'd be able to match Krolni, Nequa," he asked a sweaty, gasping engineer who refused to cry out at the aches and cramps that accompanied every step.

"I do," she bravely boasted; "it'd just take longer than I thought."

When the three Earthers reached floor 173, they saw that Woloka and Krolni didn't look as bedraggled as they felt.

In preparation for their recovery, Krolni brought out five monitors' chairs from the cubicles where he once worked and suggested they all sit. Bandi and Arafa dropped immediately into the cushionless chairs. Cantro preferred to pace while his hamstrings eased.

"We used to sit along this row and watch monitors," Krolni said. "My cubicle was right behind me. The screens still had information scrolling until just a few days ago. As far as I could tell, these screens were the only things still working in Molox1. There were no lights, no food replicators, no links to the computer system. With the exception of these readouts, this was a dead construct."

Woloka was still breathing hard. She was not the climb-er Krolni was. "Down will be a lot easier," she said and then opened a new topic. "If you can actually get your gauges free of the system's control, do you suppose you might return power to the molox? There's lots of things that would make our lives easier. Elevators, for instance."

"Not sure that's a good thing even now," Krolni cautioned. "When we escaped, we climbed down the outside stairs. Didn't know if the elevators would free-fall."

Ticia Bandi's eyes widened, hand headed for her mouth. "Outside?" she gasped. She'd seen the thin zigzag line plas-tered up the side of the molox and imagined the terror connect-ed with that route.

"Actually from another two hundred floors up," Krolni said. "Climbing down probably took us longer than it took you to climb just to here. It can be pretty … scary out there." It was the first time he had ever admitted to anyone, especially to Woloka, that his escape down the mega-city had terrified him.

"But the experience proved," Woloka interjected to ease Krolni's confession, "if you set your mind on something, no matter how frightening, you can do it."

Eventually the Earthers' breathing eased, their tired bodies were not melting over the chairs, and their eyes brightened. Then Krolni said, "Probably should go check out the doors. The first one I actually got into once. The others were always locked. You brought something to unlock them?"

"We got some gizmos that could work," Arafa said.

Cantro added, "And I've got the forcible tools if theirs don't."

None of which were necessary as Krolni discovered when he reached the door he had originally opened. "This is the only room I looked into. Cold and filled with stacked storage devic-es." He pulled on the handle and to his surprise, the door slid open. "That never happened after Wiklso locked it. You can see what's inside." And he stepped back. "I don't think it's as cold as I remember, either."

Bandi and Arafa went inside to look. They saw nothing but

stacks and stacks of storage drives, no monitor lights were lit on any of them. They followed the wrapped cables from each device that extended inward toward the mountain and discovered that all the cables exited the room in that direction.

"Just memory," Arafa said when they left the room. "And dead."

"Likely tied to the brains below the tarmac," Bandi said, "that are also dead."

"Tarmac?" Woloka asked.

"Where our shuttles are. There's a whole cavernous area filled with brains in boxes below the tarmac."

"Ah," Woloka said. "We call it the white."

Hardly surprising, Krolni found that the next four "No Admittance" doors unlocked. The rooms were duplicates of the first and Cantro was beginning to fear that they were probably going to have to go down to 113 and then up to 500 to find what they needed.

The macabre scene behind the sixth door startled all five of them. Two of three download chairs were occupied.

Woloka gasped and grabbed hold of Krolni to keep her legs from buckling. Krolni almost slid the door shut to close off the grizzly sight. Arafa thought that the downloading procedure involving two Molrixx had gone wrong or had not been completed for the two. Bandi suggested that they were the last two and their bodies were left as useless skin and bone. Cantro just stared as he imagined he was looking at what might have been the successful result of LeRoi's providing humans for the Molrixx memory and personality database.

Two male Molrixx in the chairs were dead with download caps in place and small keyboards before them. Their eyes were open and bulged out. Their faces sunken, their mouths slightly open as if they were starting to speak. Those words had died with their last breath. Nothing else was in the room, no robots, no computer system, no containers that might have held their brains. The room was warmer, yet; and the cables from the digitizing helmet disappeared through the wall into the next room, the last "No Admittance" door on floor 173.

Cantro's hopes rose; but, if the system access was here and not on floor 113, Varlez would have to climb a lot further, sixty more floors, to reprogram the system, if he could.

"Pay dirt," Ben shouted when Krolni slid open the last "NO ADMITTANCE" door. "Ladies, what can you discover?"

Six screens and keyboards were lined up on a table against the mountain wall. Only one monitor was lit and the same few lines of code were repeating in a continuous scroll.

"Recognize that?" Arafa excitedly asked Bandi.

"Do I!" was her ecstatic response. "Jer's gonna love this, even if he has to climb forever."

"I can't believe this," Arafa said and shook her head.

"If you step back from your amazement," Cantro broke into their reverie, "can Varlez get us back into space?"

"And provide us with usable power?" Krolni added.

"That's highly likely," Bandi said.

"And you're not going to tell us what's exciting you so much, are you?" Cantro asked.

Varlez's assistants looked at each other and smiled. "No," they said in one voice and smirked.

"Once Varlez knows, we can tell you, or he will," Arafa said.

"Right," Bandi agreed. "For now, we know and you're going to have to wait to find out."

On their long descent and hustle across the tarmac, the engineer's assistants enjoyed being the only ones on the planet Molx who knew they were definitely going to leave Molx and head for γ-Cygnus A2.

Arafa and Bandi put on somber faces to pass on their discovery to Varlez and he prepared for the worst. His initial reaction was what they intended.

"Good news and bad," Arafa groaned. "Which do you want?"

"The bad, I guess," he grumbled.

"You've got thousands of steps to climb. They almost killed us," Bandi said.

"I can do stairs, if that's the bad to reach the good."

Bandi grimaced. He'd anticipated them.

Arafa gave him the good, and Varlez could hardly contain himself. He howled with laughter and then asked, "You wouldn't kid me, would you?" He paused and looked at them to catch the hint of a practical joke. He saw none, only relief that he had not seen on any face since they landed their shuttles.

"They program in Alvork?" His question was incredulous. "That race must be a lot older and way more extended than we are. I wonder just how many worlds' computer systems are Alvork driven."

"We didn't tell Cantro what we knew. He's pretty torqued about not knowing," Bandi said. "But we didn't want anyone to know before we had a chance to tell you. Now we don't care who knows."

"Best to let it stay a secret. There may yet be unexpected surprises. Is Cantro going back with me? I can tell him then." You two can stay and rest; maybe prepare for lift-off. I suppose the commander will have a whole bunch of things to settle before we really get off this rock. I'll see him on my way there."

"Cantro's waiting for you," Arafa said. "We thought you'd like to tell him; like a reward for having to climb back up a second time."

Cantro wasn't ecstatic about climbing a hundred seventy-three floors again, but he used the effort to think about getting back into space and to the planet he was supposed to be colonizing.

Commander Carpenter anticipated good news when he saw a wide-grinning Varlez at his hatch. Nor was he disappointed in Varlez's information. He finally had a more definite possibility for continuing to their destination.

"We're not there just yet," Varlez cautioned. "I've got to look at the code. But the girls, I can't believe them. I've never seen them so excited about anything. Maybe, I can provide power to the molox while I close off the system's control of our gauges. That should help their lives. Regardless, it's probably not going to be too easy to remove the control over our gauges. Might take two or three days to discover the right lines of code. Reading it is the easy part. Just can't believe Alvork is the language."

"If you can make those changes, can LeRoi be released from protective custody?" the commander asked.

"I'll have to look and see if there's another sub-program that accessed him. But he might be okay."

Cantro's second trip up one hundred seventy-three flights was not as harrowing as he had expected. Varlez, for all his eagerness to return to the *Marco P*, was unwilling to push any vertical pace.

Following Cantro's slower than normal climbing gave Varlez time to consider the looping code that Bandi had mentioned, almost in passing. It reminded him of mistakes he had seen from less than able programmers who had introduced code without properly preparing the insertion. Sometimes deleting those extraneous errors precipitated undesired cascading effects. He needed to be careful.

In distant anticipation for they had only passed the eightieth floor, Varlez let escape an "Aaah" louder than he intended. Cantro turned to see if the engineer needed to rest, a pause in the interminable steps that Cantro himself would enjoy.

It was a short-lived hope, as Cantro saw that Varlez was deep in thought and realized his comment was to some conclusion he had reached, not a response to exerting physical effort.

However, as they reached floor 100, Varlez suggested they take a break at the next landing.

"Need a breather?" Cantro asked.

"Nah," Varlez answered, hardly glancing at his guide; "you look to be laboring. Second time up today. Gotta be tiring for you."

Cantro didn't deny the assessment, but didn't extend the respite longer than when Varlez's breathing was unlabored.

"At last," Varlez sighed heavily when he stood on floor 173. "Now, where?"

"Not far," Cantro said as they passed the monitoring caves. However, he made one stop before the system mainframe access. "Thought you'd like to see this." He slid open the door to the two dead males in the download chairs This time he noticed that the download helmets had burned their faces. "What we had waiting for us, if LeRoi had been successful."

"Idiots," Varlez criticized. "What makes someone with a range of physical sensations think that emotions are meaningless? I suppose these were the last two."

"Except for Vokra and hers."

"Where's the program?"

"Next door. Only one screen seems working. Not sure what the looping means. The girls were excited about it, though."

"That's where I start."

Varlez's fingers flew over the keyboard, entering, deleting, adjusting, transferring, flying through lines of code that, to Cantro, seemed barely readable as they scrolled past. Cantro didn't think he'd ever before seen anyone enter regular text as fast as Varlez was coding.

"Idiots," Varlez said softly. "They destroyed themselves. Carpenter needn't have worried about genocide."

Then Varlez stopped and stared, tilted his head to the right, breathed in, and sighed.

Cantro asked if anything was wrong.

Varlez ignored or didn't hear the question. He squinted his eyes at the monitor and then wiped a speck of dirt off the screen. He grinned to himself and entered and watched and entered.

Lights came on all over the molox. In hundreds—thousands—of flats the morning ration of tasteless pellets dropped into food receptacles. Elevator motors began to hum.

Varlez lounged back in the long flattened-padded chair. "We have power. The shuttles should have accurate gauges and, if they do, LeRoi should not be any more dangerous than from his arrogance. Didn't take nearly as long as I imagined. Pretty straightforward Alvork and not too advanced. Let's get outa here."

Vokra and Crelle met them when they reached the tenth floor. "You've given us power," Vokra said. "We thank you for that. Even the personal computer connections are working, though the food pellets are not really appreciated. Why didn't you come down in the elevator?"

"We'll leave that to you," Varlez said. "Everything should be as it was before. Just without all the people. The other moloxes appear to be dead. All their generated power has been usurped by this molox. Nothing can be alive in any of them just as nothing is alive in Molox1 and its repository, except for your people. I shut off the door locks. Doors to the memory stacks should not be left open and the rooms will cool. Might use them for food storage. Libraries and videos are accessible. The memory storage the monitors watched is active, but that is hardly life as Council had considered. You might access it for haphazard information, but not much else and there is no useful directory that I found, though I created a basic search program."

"That's what we did when we sat in front of the screens," Vokra said. "At least now we don't have to worry about getting caught by Council."

"You will be leaving soon?" Crelle asked. His question didn't have the nasty urgency he had broadcast to the commander the week before.

"There may be some tweaks in the code, but if all is as I think it is, we'll be departing soon for where we were going before we were hijacked," Varlez said.

"We need to get to the commander," Cantro said. "However, he will not leave before giving a personal good bye." He put his hand on Varlez's shoulder and they hurried down the last flights of stairs and exited Molox1.

Both were surprised that night had fallen. Their steps over the path to the tarmac were slow and cautious.

"I didn't think I was there that long," Varlez said.

Bandi and Arafa were waiting on the tarmac at the end of the path from Molox1. They had spent hours waiting for Varlez and Cantro and, when darkness fell, had refused to return to the shuttle where LeRoi was secured. Their dogged patience was rewarded when they saw Molox1 light up from within. They knew Varlez had had some success. They saw movement within the molox and had the forethought to bring a power-light. Then they saw movement at the first floor entrance and regularly flashed brilliance up the trail.

At last, they saw Varlez and Cantro side by side. Cantro, almost a foot taller than Varlez, had his arm draped over the shorter man's shoulder. They came closer and Arafa directed the light onto the path at their feet.

In spite of the long day, three hundred forty-six flights up and three hundred forty-six down for Cantro, the two men were not silent, as long heavy serious duty normally imposes quiet on tired workers. Mostly the sounds escaping them were chuckles, laughter, and gasps of disbelief.

"Varlez can captivate anyone," Arafa said.

Soon the miracle worker and his guide stepped onto the tarmac.

Cantro spoke first. "I've heard tales about our engineer for most of my space time. Today was a new chapter. If I don't say something, no one will know."

Varlez turned to glare up at him in the artificial light.

"Sorry, sir, this has to be said." He looked closely at the engineering assistants, first one then the other. "You know, he stopped about 100 so I could rest. I needed it. Anyone else'd have gone on by himself and made me catch up."

"It was just a pause," Varlez tried adjusting the story for his assistants who knew better. "I needed a brief rest."

Cantro, standing back just a little, shook his head emphatically. He thought Varlez might even press Krolni's climbing, but didn't say so.

"We need to see the commander," Varlez said. "I think I've released the shuttles and the *Marco P*. Have to check the gauges. I need to try and raise the *Marco*. If I did get the offending code removed, even the navigator will be spared his trance."

"I saw the molox lights and checked my shuttle power," the commander said when Varlez entered the command shuttle. I've got full power. Hasn't taken long for the fleet to recognize the system's influence is gone. Loose ends tomorrow and we should be able to continue to γ-Cygnus A2."

"That's what I thought," Varlez agreed. "Still have to access MP and the readings in engineering. Oh, just for your own peace of mind, Malcolm, the last two to undergo digitizing botched additional code so badly, they cut off power to all repositories and storage in all Moloxes except this one. Here they shut off the repository before Strumpf went back to check for the system. Only the discrete memories of hundreds of thousands are available. I left a rudimentary search app Vokra might use to access specific information. Might help them learn what they'll need to keep living. And their former library is available."

"And LeRoi?" the commander asked. "He's the only inter-face with MP."

"Might try Strumpf," Varlez said. "You know his back-ground, but if there is no system lock from here, LeRoi should be what he was before all this began, unless there are other planets with similar computer ability."

The commander frowned at the latter suggestion. Despite the commander's reaction, Varlez kept his personal thoughts of the navigator to himself.

Varlez and his harem left for their shuttle and were accom-panied by Cantro who eventually broke off for his own shuttle along the way.

ALIENS

Main Office of the Xantrel *Borsac* hailed Mqros4's Chief. "Seems we were all wrong, Mqros2 may be the Earthers' prize."

Zebza's Trbny in the *Chlykr* saw an opening and took it. "Chief, you better hope the Earthers aren't invited to the games, or perhaps crash them. Seems they've done what none of us could do. They do bear watching, though."

"That might be more difficult than we imagine," Proform of the Grekre's transport *Moktrn* cautioned. "I think we underestimated them. They may prove to be a formidable presence."

"Or powerful allies," the Vocres Primt offered. "We've watched them extend their presence in the Galaxy. They are not conquerors and they have yet to be conquered, as we've just seen."

"That makes them even more dangerous," Main Office said. "If they're all that powerful, it's a short move to rule."

"Unlikely," Primpt countered. "Their successful settlements on multiple worlds and in many systems already solidify a peaceful presence."

"You may be correct," Main Office acquiesced. "They've backed away from many belligerent races instead of fighting."

"It's an ancient truism," Primpt recalled, "the really powerful know they don't have to prove it."

Mqros4's Chief in the *Vento* listened to the sniping, mostly at him. In theory, the Mqros had the most to lose if Earthers gained a planet in their space. They also had the most to gain. He was already planning how he or another Chief might introduce the Mqros to the Earthers shortly after they took possession of wet and green Mqros2.

Then word passed between the five ships that the shanghai signal commonly surrounding Molx and that had captured the Earthers and some of their own people was gone. Main office asked if the warning buoys should be removed and received a quick negative response from four races.

In the excitement of a young alien race defeating a species

405

that they had been unable to subdue, Proform in the transport *Moktrn* and Trbny in the *Chlykr* sent long communications to Grekre and Zebza that the Earthers had escaped Molx and disabled the beckoning signal and that ambassadors might safely return to Molx to find out what happened to prior missions. Both received cautions and counsel to be wary of the Earthers. Grekre's and Zebza's world councils announced that long-range inspection of the Earthers would begin immediately and ordered their ships to leave Molx space.

The *Borsac* was the first to break formation and leave the other astonished races to imagine their own first encounters with Earthers. Main Office suddenly realized the Earthers could be a threat to the Xantrel's expanding empire. Earthers' expansion across the galaxy needed intense study, especially if a symbiotic relationship between the Vocres and Earthers had been established long ago, a relationship steadfastly denied by the Vocres.

Primpt watched with some interest as the Earthers prepared for lift-off. There was, however, some concern that if he and the *Vento* held position, they might be seen, as the Earthers repossessed their orbital ship.

"We'd best disappear," Primpt suggested and echoed a corollary to the caution that Main Office had given when he first saw the Earthers had been captured. "They have to know that much of this part of the galaxy is populated, but neither of us are ready for a first encounter."

"Nor should they be forced into another just after the Molrixx," Chief agreed, "though they will be in our system. Contact there will take place sooner than later."

"Indeed, but they should be watched for the right moment. We've seen what happens when they are surprised."

The *Vento* generated a dark matter tunnel and continued its journey to the I-G games.

Primpt ordered his crew to power up the *Alroche* and resume their mission to Ansvord7 where an emerging species had just united the planet under one government and had sent an exploratory ship to a neighboring planet in their system.

HUMANS

As hurried as loading shuttles, gathering personal necessities, and preparing to leave the doomed *Marco P* had been, the frenetic activity around the tarmac was madcap that began almost at Engineer Varlez's first step onto the tarmac in the dark. The knowledge that power gauges functioned and indicated full power crisscrossed between shuttles as soon as lights were seen in the molox. Com channels that clicked off when the Molx system was reprogrammed were initialized without direction from the commander.

Those who counseled patience despite the positive signs were generally ignored and labeled pessimists and curmudgeons. "Home"—*Marco P* and γ-Cygnus A2—was on the minds and in the dialog between crew and settlers who *knew* their detour to dying Molx was over.

When solar rise crept over the top of Molox1 and sent rays past the tarmac and over the tops of the forest to the western bubbletop mountains, no one was malingering in the shuttles. Even LeRoi, hesitant about appearing in the open, left the engineering shuttle and watched the day of escape begin.

Contrary to the consensus that he was inattentive during the trial, LeRoi had heard all the testimony, understood the rancor directed his way, and recognized that he alone should have been responsible for the *Marco P's* capture. That MP had first been shanghaied which led to his involvement and the commander's successful defense claiming he was not responsible caused him to underscore that his narcissism was not improper and he believed that his navigator status was completely unblemished.

Yet, whenever anyone walked near where he was standing under the shade of a shuttle, he cowered and eased further back into the shadow. For all the impressions directed to him, he blamed the commander for not leaving him on the *Marco P*. He reasoned, if he had been left in his navigation cubicle, he'd never have been taken over by the Molx system. Nor did he accept the role his interface played in the near disaster that was averted by the sacrifice of his backup, Maelstrom, and the bravery of so many others.

Noon approached and smaller groups combined into larger ones, all discussing the apparent delay and growing more edgy as minutes passed. Then the groups divided themselves into smaller clusters that then broke apart to recombine with others. The commander was taking his own tour of the readiness of his shipmates and when he was certain that the shuttles were reloaded and everyone eager for lift off, he announced that all should return to space, dock, and prepare to continue their mission to γ-Cygnus A2. He would follow in short order, but not before he offered his last words to Vokra.

Crelle and Vokra met him half way up the path to Molox1 just as the first shuttles in the midst of loud whines and artificial wind were lifting off. Maintaining his anti persona, Crelle said, "It's good you are leaving. Many are wondering if your presence might not be a good thing. We will have to study to control the power to Molox1."

"When we noticed everyone milling around and not entering the flying craft, I wondered if there was another problem," Vokra explained their reason for heading for the white. Then she paused and looked into Commander Carpenter's eyes that didn't indicate any problem. Her next words were official. "We thank you, for power in Molox1 and for Amanda and for Canska and her daughter."

"You have been good hosts," the commander said. "We may not have intended to land here and it has not been without problems, not of your making, but our own. It is unlikely we will ever return to Molx. But Vokra and Crelle and the Molrixx," Carpenter smiled toward Crelle, "will forever be a fond memory in our histories." He bowed his head and turned to go.

Unexpectedly, Crelle said, "Commander," and extended his hand which Carpenter took as he turned back. "May your journeys be shaded and your nights not black. You have shown us what is possible and we must develop patience to keep from demanding that we achieve it tomorrow."

"Thank you, Crelle," the commander replied still holding his hand. "That is the finest toast I have ever received."

Carpenter broke their grip and without looking back hustled to his shuttle where Maelstrom waited. He chuckled to himself when he realized that Crelle had not been so angry at their presence, as he was fearful of the temptation generated from their progress and technology. He knew Crelle was more far-thinking than he had imagined and was sorry that he would not have the chance to talk with him at length.

The command shuttle with Maelstrom aboard lifted off and Carpenter reversed his circular descent. The widening ascending path was more leisurely than the urgent descent days earlier and he noticed that there seemed to be expanding green areas he had not noticed before. In the middle of each was a blue dot. The continent was bubbling alive. He thought Molx might again be fertile for a species clamoring for knowledge and discovery and contact, though it would scarcely remember the encounter it just had except in the foolish tales of the ancient ones.

Commander Malcolm Carpenter looked into the speckled dark of the galaxy. He spotted the *Marco P* and saw two shuttles docking. He felt the pleasure that comes from successful outcomes and looked to Maelstrom sitting an arm's length away. She was scanning the vast expanse. No thought showed on her face.

"How do you feel, Navigator?"

"A little empty where the interface once claimed a presence. A little overwhelmed and foolish that I never understood how imperial that interface was."

"Going to reinitialize it?"

"I don't think so. When I blocked the interface, I became really human, with all the fears and joys and emotions I thought I didn't need. My reason for joining this mission was to experience the galaxy, its immensity, its wonder. Only emotional humans can do that. The last few days are not just data. The computer doesn't enjoy; it tabulates without purpose. I was just one step away from digitizing myself ... and being like ... like ..." Maelstrom couldn't bring herself to say *a hard drive without purpose or direction*. "I hope there's still something I can do to help the mission."

"Like sitting in the navigator's seat?"

"Navigating without a computer link doesn't seem reasonable, despite what's happened and the trial," Maelstrom answered. "Maybe I should join the colony."

"I can think of lots of *Marco's* duties you qualify for," Commander Carpenter said. "As for navigating without an interface, talk with George Strumpf. He might change your mind."

ABOUT THE AUTHOR

Don Braden retired in 2009 from a 45-year career teaching high school English surrounding thirteen years of teaching Latin and 30 years of coaching track and cross country. He frequently used Science Fiction, current and classic, to demonstrate elements of literature and human ideals. Through his own voracious reading of all subjects, he encouraged students to read, to recognize the essence of humanity, and to strive for an improbable dream: utopia. Braden is working toward a "late in life" second career of writing stories that bolster what he taught.

Braden can be contacted at dbraden@dbraden.org.